# Praise for *The Defector*:

'An absolutely thrilling read based on deep research which brings this MI5 asset's importance to life'
**Gordon Corera, co-host of The Rest is Classified**

'A truly gripping, untold story of how a Russian defector helped British intelligence defeat the Soviet spies. Richard Kerbaj's painstaking research, including interviews with key players, upends much of the orthodoxy about what happened in the Cold War. *The Defector* reads like le Carré but uncovers important truths that are being played out in Putin's Russia today'
**Robert Verkaik, *Sunday Times* bestselling author of *The Traitor of Colditz***

'A lucidly written account of a significant setback for Soviet intelligence. Dynamic and vivid, reads like a spy thriller. Kerbaj skillfully makes major figures of the Cold War cloak-and-dagger operations come to life: defectors Oleg Lyalin and Anatoly Golitsyn, CIA counterintelligence chief James Angleton, MI5 director Martin Furnival Jones, KGB chairman Yuri Andropov, and many others'
**Dr. Filip Kovacevic, University of San Francisco and author of *KGB Literati: Spy Fiction and State Security in the Soviet Union***

# Praise for *The Secret History of the Five Eyes*:

A *Sunday Times* best political and current affairs book of 2022

'Absolutely brilliant'
**Tom Holland, *The Rest Is History***

'A scandalous tale of mistrust and misjudgement'
*The Observer*

'Gripping and shocking'
**Tim Shipman, author of *All Out War***

# THE DEFECTOR

The Untold Story of the KGB agent who saved MI5 and changed the Cold War

## Richard Kerbaj

First published in the UK in 2025 by Blink Publishing
An imprint of Bonnier Books UK
5th Floor, HYLO, 105 Bunhill Row,
London, EC1Y 8LZ

A CIP catalogue record for this book is available from the British Library.

Hardback ISBN: 978-1-7894-6848-9
Trade paperback ISBN: 978-1-7894-6849-6

*Also available as an ebook and an audiobook*

1 3 5 7 9 10 8 6 4 2

Design and Typeset by Envy Design Ltd
Printed and bound in Great Britain by Clays Ltd, Elcograf S.p.A.

This book is a work of Non-Fiction. Some names have been changed to
respect the privacy of those mentioned.

The authorised representative in the EEA is
Bonnier Books UK (Ireland) Limited.
Registered office address: Floor 3, Block 3, Miesian Plaza,
Dublin 2, D02 Y754, Ireland
compliance@bonnierbooks.ie

www.bonnierbooks.co.uk

*To*
*Mum, Dad, Suzan, Sylvana and Raef*

*Marine, and also to Leo (because he made me promise)*
*and Nate (who would have made me promise, too)*

# CONTENTS

# PROLOGUE

OLEG LYALIN HAD CAREFULLY considered his next move, and about eighteen months into his role with the Soviet mission in London he entered a public phone booth ready to leap into the unknown. He was fed up with being overlooked for work promotions and wanted a new beginning, one he was prepared to trade KGB secrets for.

At thirty-two, Lyalin's career prospects at the KGB appeared bleak, despite his operational value as a prospective assassin and saboteur. A big part of his workplace qualms was the realisation that the Soviet agency regarded him as unstable – and perhaps more worryingly, open to compromise by the likes of MI5, Britain's domestic intelligence service.

Lyalin was an absent father and a bad husband, and his marriage was crumbling under the weight of his unending pursuit of mistresses. London's thriving party scene in the late 1960s had enabled his bad behaviour, but he had always been predisposed to seeking out excitement and circumventing rules.

His personality was unsuited to the rigid Soviet practices under which he was working, and perhaps if he had grown up in a more permissive society, somewhere in the West instead of a small city in southern Russia, Lyalin would never have been a government functionary. He would likely have found greater success working as an actor or a TV presenter because he was a 'bit of a character', as one of his work colleagues would attest. He was tall and vivacious with striking blue eyes, enjoyed living freely and recklessly, and was unwilling to shun the advances of beautiful women who found him humorous and 'very attractive'.

But he figured that British intelligence officials would overlook such personality flaws in return for credible secrets – and in September 1970, he activated his plan to broker a deal with them. He dialled 999 from a phone box in Highgate, north London, presumably hoping that through an anonymous call to the emergency services he would be referred to the police, and ultimately, MI5.

Whether intentionally or from nerves, he failed to specify what he was after when the call was answered – and instead asked to be connected to someone 'knowledgeable' about the Soviet Union. The operator took a literal interpretation of his request and offered him the contact details for the Soviet Embassy. Lyalin quickly hung up.

It was not until seven months later that he would try again to reach MI5. By then, however, it was virtually impossible to separate Lyalin's truth from his lies, and to distinguish his real identity from his double-life.

MI5's counter-espionage officers had been warned about his type – a supposedly disgruntled KGB officer claiming to be on a mission to betray their motherland. That warning had emerged ten years earlier via their friends at the CIA and had gone on to reframe completely their thinking about the honesty and motivations of Soviet 'volunteers'.

## CHAPTER ONE

# THE WALK-IN

FROM THE EDGE OF the front garden, where the driveway meets the street, Anatoly Klimov could see the lights on inside the house. He had carefully chosen this spot – a vantage point cloaked in the winter darkness, providing him with just enough cover to bury a plastic-bound file in the snow. His only witnesses were the two people who had accompanied him on the mission: his wife and daughter. Klimov was comforted by their presence as they stood a few feet away, even though they were forced to brave a chill of −12°C while awaiting his next move. He had informed his wife Svetlana at least six months earlier of his plan to improve their lives as a couple and create a more promising future for their six-year-old, Tatyana.

It is very unlikely, however, that he had fully explained the dangers associated with his plan – let alone whose home it was that they were standing outside of that Friday evening. Because as someone who lived his professional life in the shadows, and specialised in compromising his enemies, Klimov knew that his presence outside that very house in Westend, about six miles west of Helsinki, could have him and his two loved ones killed. Nevertheless, he led his wife and daughter to its entrance and rang the bell, hoping that the door was a gateway to the better life that he had promised them.

Inside the house, Frank Friberg was preparing himself for a night out and was in the bathroom, shaving, when he heard the doorbell. He answered, slightly bemused by the trio on his doorstep. The short, stocky man was cocooned in a thick coat, his face obscured by a fur hat. His polite, almost apologetic smile could not conceal the unease in his dark eyes. The blonde woman next to him was silent and expressionless, with a girl alongside her clutching a doll. It was ten days to Christmas in 1961, but Friberg had not been expecting guests. Perhaps more surprising was that the visitors did not appear to have lost their way en route to a party. They were standing outside with purpose – as if they belonged there. When the stranger introduced himself as Anatoly Klimov, Friberg realised that this was no ordinary house call.

On his promotion to CIA station chief in Helsinki a few months earlier, Friberg had familiarised himself with the identities of Soviet Embassy officials in the Finnish capital and had learned that a man by the name of Anatoly Klimov was among a group of KGB officers working under diplomatic cover. The Soviet operative was of particular interest to the CIA because, as far as they had been aware, he specialised in running operations against US and British interests.

He had not been seriously considered as a likely target for recruitment, because he had a reputation as a Soviet establishment hardliner with an apparent dislike of Americans. Nor had Friberg ever anticipated meeting him in person, especially not at his own home. But that evening was not the right time and place to ruminate on Klimov's approach. Instead he invited in the KGB officer and his family, hopeful that an operative of his calibre would have only been there if he were running away from his Kremlin masters, planning to betray them – or both.

On guiding his surprise guests into the living room, Friberg sensed Klimov's frustration at trying to express himself in English. The language barrier was only made worse by the American's inability to speak or understand Russian. With English their only common language and Klimov repeatedly saying one word, Friberg handed him a pencil and paper. Klimov scribbled the four-letter word he had been repeating: 'asyl'. It was two letters short of what he had intended to say, but it was close enough to confirm he wanted 'asylum'.

That had always been the typical request of prospective defectors – those who desert their homeland for a nation that is considered the enemy. And that was evidenced earlier in the year when a Polish intelligence officer, Michal Goleniewski, had sought political asylum from the United States. Yet a key difference between that case and Klimov's was that Goleniewski had already been providing the CIA with secrets for about two years before opting for political asylum. That point was not lost on Friberg.

Klimov's approach, unannounced and with his family members in tow, was very unusual. Often prospective defectors would gauge an adversary's interest in them before fully committing to treason. And in almost every case, Soviet turncoats had approached the likes of the CIA via third parties such as diplomats – and usually through US embassies. In fronting up to Friberg at his own home, Klimov had initiated a power move that suggested his confidence about the value of his own secrets outweighed any risk of being turned down by the CIA, or caught by the KGB.

He did indeed have many secrets – some obtained through his

own work, others gleaned from conversations with colleagues or stolen and kept on file in anticipation of fleeing the KGB. But the first secret he divulged that night related to his own identity. He informed Friberg that Anatoly Klimov was merely a cover name for his ostensible role as 'Third Secretary' at the Soviet Embassy. His real name, he revealed, was Anatoly Mikhailovich Golitsyn.

Anatoly Golitsyn's posting to the Soviet Embassy in Helsinki was the second he had earned in his fifteen years at the KGB and the agency's previous incarnations. The job had its ups and downs but was well-suited to his talent in counter-intelligence – an instinct his superiors had immediately recognised when he joined the Soviet security service in 1946. From there he worked his way up through a series of roles in the KGB's predecessor agency, the MGB (Ministry of State Security), including as chief officer in the Anglo-American section of the First Directorate, which focused on targeting US and British interests.

Golitsyn made a name for himself, earning his stripes through a combination of hard graft and an irrepressible sense of entitlement. Perhaps he had a chip on his shoulder about being born in Ukraine's peasant class. Or maybe his entitlement masked a belief that he should have been much more greatly rewarded for acts of patriotism dating back to his teenage days in the Komsomol, the Young Communist League, and a year of military service during the Second World War.

Golitsyn's longstanding self-regard outweighed his rank as a KGB Major and was partly the reason why he no longer wanted to be at the Soviet Embassy in Helsinki, his official workplace since July 1960. He despised his boss – or 'rezident', as those overseeing KGB bureaus stationed in foreign countries are known – and believed that he was far more intelligent and capable than his supervisor at plotting against Moscow's enemies.

Golitsyn's insatiable yearning for respect and recognition had been magnified early in his career when Joseph Stalin apparently expressed an admiration for his insights. He would recall with detail, and obvious pride, that the Soviet leader had sought him out for a discussion when he was merely twenty-six years old. According to Golitsyn, during that meeting in 1952 Stalin had accepted several 'recommendations' he had made with a colleague, including a proposal for reappointing two previously banished officials to the spy agency's foreign operations division. But the leader died before he could see Golitsyn's proposals through.

So, yes, fuelled by Stalin's recognition, Golitsyn was hardly going to be deferential to his Helsinki rezident, believing that he should be the one issuing, not taking, orders.

His attitude to work illustrated an aspirational tendency that also defined his personal life. Even when he committed to settling down and building a family, he had chosen a partner from a higher class. Svetlana was like a glamour model next to him, yet much more than her blue eyes and cascading blonde hair, she was intellectually curious and cultured. Her parents were doctors and she had studied history at university before taking a more creative route to become a screenplay editor a few years after marrying Golitsyn in August 1953. People might have wondered about this seemingly odd pairing, but Golitsyn brought adventure into Svetlana's life and through him she had seen more of the world, including Vienna and Helsinki, where he had served at the respective Soviet embassies.

She wanted what was best for her family and agreed to Golitsyn's idea of relocating to the United States. That is why she was willing to entertain the obvious uncertainty in his plan, including turning up at the home of the CIA's station chief in Helsinki. Perhaps she also knew the weight her presence would carry in Frank Friberg's mind as he contemplated her husband's request for asylum. Why would Golitsyn have brought his wife and daughter along if he had not been intending to defect? Surely they were there to demonstrate the urgency of Golitsyn's situation, of the predicament that he was in?

Friberg was a seasoned and adaptable intelligence officer and had garnered enough experience in his decade-long service at the CIA to realise the significance of the potential prize that was now sitting in his living room. On any other day, or evening, for that matter, running the agency's Helsinki station was far from glamorous or high-powered, even though Friberg's promotion to the post had been a considerable step up from his previous assignments, which had included travelling around Europe under the cover of a sales representative for a manufacturing firm. At forty-nine, Friberg was on the verge of his biggest career break, and perhaps even one of the most significant moments in the CIA's history.

The agency certainly needed a win after a series of setbacks. Its very first representative in Moscow, Edward Ellis Smith, had been exposed about six years earlier by a humiliating KGB honey trap at the hands of his 'house cleaner'. Then the CIA's woes got progressively worse when its first-ever Soviet intelligence recruit, Pyotr Popov, was executed in January 1960 for passing military secrets to Washington. Still licking its wounds from its failure to protect its sole agent from the KGB, the CIA suffered again at the hands of Moscow in the spring of that same year when its U-2 spy plane was shot down over Soviet territory while conducting a surveillance operation of missile sites.

The intelligence agency's humiliation peaked in April 1961 when it failed to protect yet another major secret – the mission to overthrow Fidel Castro's regime in Cuba, for which the CIA had drawn up the policy, gathered the intelligence, and 'trained and directed the invasion force'. When its covert operation was blown, the CIA abandoned its support for the Cuban exiles leading to the Bay of Pigs invasion. That resulted in Castro's forces capturing about 1,200 of them and killing more than a hundred.

The tragedy diminished the trust in the CIA's commitment to its allies and incensed President John F. Kennedy. He vowed to break the agency into a 'thousand pieces', fired its director, and even considered renaming it and stripping it of its covert functions. Now, just eight months on from that epic operational disaster, Friberg had a chance to turn around the agency's fortunes – all the way from Helsinki.

Of course there was no time available for Friberg to obtain, dissect and understand each of Golitsyn's secrets: that was a job for the analysts, interrogators, and Soviet experts at CIA headquarters in Langley, Virginia. But he sought enough assurances from the KGB officer to determine that the information he claimed to have would be of great value to the US agency. The American then contacted colleagues at headquarters and vouched for the KGB major and his family, saying they should be given a safe haven in the US. Friberg was given the go-ahead, and as he ushered his three guests out of the house, he witnessed Golitsyn dig up the file he had buried earlier that evening. That file alone contained twenty-three secret documents – a substantive intelligence haul by any measure.

News of the 'walk-in' in Helsinki lifted spirits among Langley's counter-intelligence staff, but their department chief, James Jesus Angleton, would have been somewhat circumspect. He believed, and perhaps with a greater intensity and conviction than his colleagues, that counter-intelligence as a craft, including recruiting, agent-running, disrupting, and degrading adversaries, was hampered by democracy. Because unlike dictatorship regimes in which the likes of the KGB were limited only by their imagination rather than man-made laws, Angleton often questioned whether a 'democratic country is capable of having an intelligence service of any great merit simply because of the built-in inhibitions'.

At forty-four, Angleton was already one of the most senior and formidable agency officials. He took his responsibilities very seriously and believed beyond any sense of hyperbole or romanticism that intelligence – as a profession and a tool for information-collection – was an absolute requirement for a nation's 'survival'. It was not in his personality and behavioural construct to accept anything, or anyone, at face value. Especially not someone from the Soviet Union belonging to the CIA's arch-nemesis.

Angleton's distrust of the KGB had framed his decision-making ever since taking charge of his agency's counter-intelligence branch in 1954, and he had long felt the Soviet organisation's presence, its spectre, its reach into the heart of the CIA; he was convinced it had penetrated his organisation. His suspicion had been reinforced by the KGB's execution of his agency's top informant in Moscow the previous year. There was no way the Soviet agency could have known about Pyotr Popov without someone on the inside betraying him, the CIA spymaster kept telling himself and his staff.

Shortly after Golitsyn arrived with his wife and daughter in the United States on 18 December 1961, Angleton was eager to gauge his thoughts on Popov's case. The Soviet defector decried the 'evil inherent in the KGB and the Soviet system' and soon presented the CIA with information that not only brought into question the US agency's competence and capability, but pointed to a nest of spies within its ranks, who had been working for years under Moscow's control.

During CIA debriefings, Anatoly Golitsyn maintained an unwavering conviction and urgency in his answers – alert that his information, and credibility, was on the line. Golitsyn was 'interrogated on his biographic data and . . . debriefed upon substantive matters within the areas of his knowledge and expertise', according to an internal memo addressed to the CIA director. He 'provided a considerable amount of information on Soviet State Security operations, methods and personalities, which has been accurate and consistent with the estimated knowledgeability of an individual with his position and experience.'

Golitsyn appeared to have blitzed the polygraph tests, bolstering his credibility in the minds of agency officials. His interrogations resulted in hours of recordings and volumes of transcripts that James Angleton studied closely, particularly intrigued by Golitsyn's disclosures about the KGB's targeting of the US, Britain, other North Atlantic Treaty Organisation (NATO) member countries, and Asian nations, including Japan. Always on the lookout for exploiting intelligence that reflected well on himself and his agency, Angleton prepared to share Golitsyn's British-related secrets with the UK's domestic intelligence agency, MI5. But above all this, Angleton's greatest focus was on Golitsyn's declaration a little time later that the KGB had planted moles inside the CIA.

Golitsyn presented a fragmented picture of the moles, short on full names and other identifying factors, but a few clues regarding one of them were easy enough for Angleton and his team to pursue. The KGB, Golitsyn said, was running a senior CIA officer who had been stationed in Germany in or around 1953, specialising in technical eavesdropping. At one point the defector had even seen internal KGB documents identifying the mole as 'Sasha' and indicating that his 'relatives or parents' lived in the Soviet Union. Golitsyn was patchy on the spy's surname but recalled that it sounded Polish, began with the letter 'K' and ended in 'ski'.

To help jog his memory, CIA debriefers drew up a list featuring staff members and contractors with 'Slavic' surnames – and on presenting it to Golitsyn, he quickly zeroed in on 'Klibanski'. There was obviously a match in the first and last three letters of Klibanski's surname, but Golitsyn's accusation needed to be thoroughly – and quietly – followed up, if only to avoid alerting the target.

The early identifiers were that Klibanski was the birth name of Serge Peter Karlow, who had been relocated from Langley to the US State Department in late 1961. His move there followed President Kennedy's order to create an operations centre that would foresee and handle foreign policy disasters and prevent another Bay of Pigs-type fiasco. Karlow was grateful for the promotion, but it was not the one he had been hoping for. His long-standing ambition was to run the agency's technical services division, responsible for developing gadgets, including bugging devices, voice alteration equipment, and even wigs to help operatives conceal their identities.

To Karlow, that role would have been far more in line with the work he had done during his posting to Germany early in his career, where he oversaw the agency's special equipment staff. He had taken that job in 1950 to coordinate a variety of operational tasks, from creating surveillance equipment to assisting agents in the CIA's Eastern European division in infiltrating Soviet-bloc countries. Perhaps more importantly during that time, Karlow and his team had identified a listening device at the US Embassy in Moscow, which had been targeting the communications of Washington's top diplomat there. The bug was buried inside a wooden carving of the Great Seal of the United States, which had been presented by the Soviet Union to the US ambassador as a gift in 1945.

Its discovery in the early 1950s hugely embarrassed the CIA,

US State Department and White House for having failed to spot it earlier. Yet it inspired Karlow to develop a similar device for his agency, codenamed Easy Chair, which was supposed to remain a top secret. But according to the paperwork Golitsyn had brought from Helsinki, the KGB was aware of Karlow's invention. Angleton and his investigators were staggered by the disclosure, reinforcing their fear that Karlow – formerly known as Klibanksi – could be their mole, Sasha.

Angleton knew Karlow well, partly because they had started their intelligence careers around the same time at the Office of Strategic Services (OSS), the CIA's wartime forerunner, before moving over to the agency upon its creation in 1947. There was no way, however, that Angleton would allow friendship to impede his pursuit of treason, and so Karlow was placed under surveillance, with a wiretap installed at his home on 15 January 1962. Determined to keep him away from secrets, and unwilling to await the investigation's outcome, Angleton asked the agency's deputy director of plans, Richard Helms, to suspend Karlow. Without giving him any reason or explanation, the CIA placed Karlow on administrative leave as the Federal Bureau of Investigation launched a secret inquiry into every aspect of his life.

Karlow was puzzled by his mysterious suspension, but Angleton and Golitsyn considered 'Sasha's' early identification a triumph. The development, within a month of Golitsyn's defection, turned the defector into a prospective superstar in Angleton's eyes and seemingly confirmed what the counter-intelligence chief had suspected all along – that the CIA had a traitor in its midst.

Golitsyn's revelations eventually inspired a witch-hunt within the agency, inflaming an existing atmosphere of paranoia that had followed a series of breaches, including the KGB's discovery that

Pyotr Popov was a CIA asset. Understanding the circumstances surrounding Popov's death was one of the agency's top priorities, because he had played a central role in educating the CIA about its primary Cold War adversary. So the timing of Golitsyn's defection in the broader context of the US agency's woes was very favourable.

* * *

The joint occupation of Austria after the Second World War, negotiated by the Allies at the Potsdam Conference following Germany's surrender in May 1945, presented its four occupying powers – the United States, Britain, France, and the Soviet Union – with a target-rich environment for espionage. Pyotr Popov had been stationed in Vienna with the Kremlin forces, among a countless number of Soviet intelligence officers operating in the Austrian capital. Much like the spies of the other occupying powers, they ranged from those who were undeclared and operating under fake identities, to others hiding behind diplomatic posts in their embassies, or blending into official roles at the United Nations.

As a Lieutenant Colonel in the GRU, the Soviet military intelligence agency, Popov had a broad range of knowledge about his nation's armed forces, including its deployments, plans and weapons systems. He understood how his access and insights could help Soviet enemies, and in late 1952 sought to provide the CIA with secrets. His approach was far less dramatic than the one that would be taken by Anatoly Golitsyn in Helsinki about a decade later, and it was also far less direct.

Popov simply slipped a letter into a car belonging to a US foreign service official based in Vienna, offering to provide secrets relating to his work in the GRU. His message, in Russian, also included instructions on where and when to meet. There was no guarantee that the twenty-nine-year-old's attempt would be taken seriously, or would even reach the CIA, but its timing was crucial. It came five years into the US agency's existence, when it had still not been able to recruit a single Soviet intelligence officer onto its books. So it was a no-brainer to leap at Popov's offer.

Popov was not after political asylum: he loved his country but despised its ruler's dehumanisation of the Soviet peasantry to which his family belonged. He wanted retribution for Joseph Stalin's genocidal acts against his community, including stealing their land and starving millions to death. The CIA recognised Popov's noble motivations from its early interactions with him, and as such, had complete faith in the information he provided, which would eventually include technical specifications of Soviet weapons ranging from tanks and personnel carriers to tactical missile systems and nuclear submarines.

He became the CIA's most precious asset – its eyes and ears within its greatest enemy during a precarious chapter of the Cold War. Over almost seven years, Popov elevated the CIA's understanding of Moscow's intentions, capabilities and targets, and largely safeguarded it against them.

Of course there were challenges associated with his safety, particularly because he was being run as an 'agent-in-place' – under the CIA's control while still fulfilling his employment obligations to the GRU both in Vienna, and later, in Moscow. The dead-drops, or hideouts created by the agency to leave or collect correspondence without bringing him into direct contact with his handlers, had to be carefully considered and were supposed to be beyond compromise. And his debriefings at safe houses, of which there were many, had been no different. Popov met George Kisevalter, a branch chief within the CIA's Soviet Russia Division, more than a hundred times.

Yet despite the agency's elaborate security protocol to protect him, Popov's cover was eventually blown. The KGB's attempt at a 'playback' – to turn him into a double-agent and feed disinformation through him to the CIA – failed to go as planned, because he alerted the US agency about his arrest. 'Popov reported that he had been arrested in February 1959 and that in the meetings thereafter he had been under KGB control and wearing a microphone,' a declassified CIA file reveals. Even before Popov was executed for treason the following year, Kisevalter and his colleague, James Angleton, were asking questions about the possibility that a CIA mole had sold him out.

Following 'Popov's then-unexplained compromise', Angleton became fixated on the idea that the KGB was running sources inside his agency. So much so that when Polish intelligence officer Michal Goleniewski defected to the United States in early 1961, Angleton suspected that he was part of a Soviet ploy intended to deceive his agency – even though Goleniewski had already been providing secrets to the CIA for about two years before his defection, including revelations about a Kremlin espionage circle in Britain operating under MI5's nose.

The circle of Soviet agents included Harry Houghton, a former Royal Navy official who had been recruited by Polish intelligence in 1951, while serving as a naval attaché at the British Embassy in Warsaw. The Poles handed Houghton's case to the Soviets on his return two years later to the UK, where he joined four other KGB agents in targeting British secrets, including information about nuclear-powered submarines at a naval base in Portland on the English south coast. The CIA provided Goleniewski's disclosures to MI5, resulting in the conviction of all five members of the Portland Spy Ring.

Goleniewski's other revelations led to the conviction of George Blake, an officer at MI6, Britain's external intelligence service, who had been supplying secrets to Moscow. And if that was not enough to prove his bona fides, the Polish spy also exposed Heinz Felfe, a counter-intelligence chief in the West German intelligence service, who was imprisoned for betraying his agency to the KGB. Yet none of that eroded Angleton's distrust of Goleniewski.

The CIA spymaster could not shake the feeling that secrets provided by voluntary defectors were elaborate deception operations designed to buttress the credibility of a 'walk-in' in the eyes of their adoptive agency. Angleton's rationale was framed by his understanding of Soviet intelligence history, including activities dating back to the 1920s when the KGB's predecessor and foundational agency, the Cheka, infiltrated agents into organisations it deemed hostile to the new Bolshevik regime.

He knew that deception had 'played a most prominent role' in the Cheka's covert actions. 'And we knew it through double agent handling and we knew it through literally thousands of cases,' Angleton would later declare. 'You don't run double agents unless you also resort to deception, and deception is internal to that because you are not going to give away all your real stuff. You give away false stuff to achieve your objectives.'

Angleton was also aware that the Cheka had exploited, and improved upon, techniques used before the Russian Revolution by the Tsar's secret police force, Okhrana. The Okhrana had wormed its spies into enemy camps to create dissent in, take control of, or completely destroy political organisations that it deemed a threat to Russia's emperor, Tsar Nicholas II. But when the Tsar was toppled, Chekists discovered Okhrana's files bursting with information about the defunct agency's tradecraft. They studied its intelligence methods, but instead of limiting their targets to dissenting political organisations as the Okhrana had, Chekists created fake resistance movements of their own to help expose 'counter-revolutionary elements'.

In 1921, under Vladimir Lenin's regime, a Tsarist organisation that had been crushed by the Cheka a few years earlier was brought back to life. The 'Monarchist Alliance of Central Russia' was reformed by the Cheka under the cover of a business conglomerate, with the apparent objective of drawing support from émigré leaders and Western spy agencies. To shore up the organisation's credibility, the Cheka recruited former Tsarist officials by threatening to kill them and their families if they refused to cooperate.

The newly recruited agents led the revived organisation and travelled abroad, including to Britain and France, to misinform émigré leaders that their alliance had penetrated the highest circles of the Soviet armed forces, intelligence community and the Kremlin, and would soon enough restore the monarchy. Although the messengers were doubted by some, they managed to convince enough émigré leaders that Communism was failing and that the ruling regime was disconnected from the revolutionary vision that had brought it to power. Alliance 'representatives' even dissuaded émigré leaders from attacking the regime for fear of rekindling its revolutionary spirit, restoring its unity, and guaranteeing its survival.

Over six years, the Chekists' mission, also known as 'Operation Trust', used disinformation under the guise of legitimate intelligence to weaken monarchist movements – and through their leaders, convinced Western intelligence agencies that the Bolshevik regime would eventually self-destruct. With such overwhelming control over opposition groups, including domestic bodies hostile to Communism, Chekists eventually arrested their members and paraded them in public trials to project an image of strength and leadership. Others, including European-based émigré leaders, diplomats, businessmen, and journalists who had been duped by Operation Trust, were blackmailed into working for the Soviet intelligence services. Decades later, Angleton closely studied the Cheka's deception mission, which profoundly impacted his mindset.

In fact, Angleton was aware of more than twenty Trust-type operations that had been conducted by the KGB's forerunner agencies, be it the Cheka or the OGPU, in the lead-up to the Second World War; well before Stalin's aggressive pursuit of military and intelligence supremacy had even reached its peak. Angleton had no reason to believe that the KGB would discontinue the operational style developed by its predecessor agencies. The Cheka's penchant for deception had infused the arteries of its successor organisation, to the point that KGB officials proudly referred to themselves as 'Chekists'.

Angleton saw the KGB as 'ten feet tall, head and shoulders ahead of [the] CIA in the intelligence profession'. He believed that there was hardly a place on the globe that the Soviet agency could not reach, and that its desire to damage Langley also included its asymmetrical methods of targeting US intelligence through the CIA's allies, especially Britain. That had become glaringly obvious following the defection of the British officials Donald Maclean and Guy Burgess to Moscow in 1951.

The pair's joint defection undermined Britain's intelligence services in Washington's eyes and brought into question its competence and trustworthiness, which still lingered now, a decade later. It also left a cloud of suspicion hanging over Kim Philby, a senior MI6 official, which Angleton struggled to come to terms with because he had considered the British officer a close friend and mentor, in whom he had confided over many years. The events only served to intensify Angleton's distrust of others, including some officials in his own organisation and within partner agencies.

While his frustration with Britain's inability to deal with the 'threat within' remained – including its failures on Burgess, Maclean, and to some extent the Portland Spy Ring – Angleton could no longer pretend that the CIA was above its partner agencies MI5 and MI6, because just as they had been directly compromised by moles, Langley was now facing the same reality. Popov's execution reflected badly on the CIA, and Golitsyn's revelation about 'Sasha' suggested that the US agency was under an unquestionable threat. Suddenly, Angleton had even more in common with his cousins across the Atlantic than the already rich history that had bound their institutions since wartime.

\* \* \*

The United States was a bit of a late bloomer in the world of espionage. While it eventually caught up and even overtook the United Kingdom in the spying game, its first civilian intelligence agency, the Office of Strategic Services, was not created until 1942 – thirty-three years after Britain's formation of MI5 and MI6. In many ways, the OSS had been an American body with a British spirit, and that was not by coincidence. The OSS's founder, William Donovan, built the wartime agency in MI6's image, with direct help from the British organisation's US representative, William Stephenson. Even its operations in Axis countries and its training and financing of opposition groups during wartime had been based on methods it learned from the British.

Many OSS officials transitioned in 1947 to its successor organisation, the Central Intelligence Agency – and James Angleton was among the first few. Along with operational knowledge, he had brought with him continuity in personal relationships, built during his wartime posting to Britain where he worked closely with, and learned a great deal from, MI5 officers. And more than a decade and a half after the war, Angleton – a calculating man with multiple agendas, who was known for withholding secrets even from his own agency colleagues to maintain an edge over them – faced with the reality of Golitsyn's defection, saw the benefit of sharing his revelations with the British agency.

Unlike the fairly seamless intelligence sharing between signals spy services across the Atlantic – Britain's Government Communications Headquarters (GCHQ) and the US National Security Agency (NSA) – their human intelligence counterparts have always operated on different terms. Some of the terms are written, others unwritten and merely agreed over a promise or a handshake. Human intelligence agencies such as the CIA and MI5, specialising in obtaining their secrets from the recruitment and running of spies, do not 'share' intelligence, but 'exchange' it.

There is a price associated with their generosity and goodwill, far beyond the personal friendships between their officers and the wartime 'Special Relationship' created by their political leaders. And that price varies because the exchange of intelligence by its initiator is based on numerous motives, including gaining better access to their partner agency's sources or source material, right through to exerting control over their counterparts. There has never been a free ride between human intelligence agencies because their relationships are largely transactional, and it was no different during Angleton's counter-intelligence reign.

Angleton dangled Golitsyn's revelations to MI5 in March 1962, each detailing humiliating security breaches to which the British were oblivious. While the CIA's counterpart organisation in London was MI6 not MI5, it dealt directly with MI5 on

UK-based counter-intelligence matters – including Soviet moles – which the British domestic agency was responsible for investigating. Angleton's nominal counterpart at the British organisation, Martin Furnival Jones, who had been overseeing MI5's counter-espionage division since 1956, was grateful for Langley's intelligence handout; much as he had been the previous year when the CIA passed on Michal Goleniewski's secrets. Furnival Jones valued Angleton's operational support, and while he shared the American's commitment to tradecraft and found him like-minded in his quiet temperament, the British intelligence official went about his work duties without a need for status, power or recognition.

In another life, Furnival Jones would have had a long career as a lawyer. But after beginning work as a London solicitor before the Second World War, he enlisted in the British army's Intelligence Corps in 1940, and a year later, joined MI5. He then worked for the US General Dwight D. Eisenhower's Supreme Headquarters Allied Expeditionary Force (SHAEF) and received a bronze star for his outstanding achievement in helping 'draw up plans to mislead Germans about the D-Day Normandy landings' of 1944. 'At the end of the war he was re-posted to MI5 and released from the Army with the rank of Lieutenant Colonel, remaining at the Security Service as a civilian,' according to a British Cabinet Office file outlining his security and military qualifications.

Furnival Jones then worked his way up MI5's chain of command, but never seemed interested in crafting an image that might fast-track his rise or make him more internally popular. In fact, while he was unwavering in upholding MI5's reputation through his work, he did not 'give a damn' about his personal image and once noted: 'Indeed I have not got an image.' He was a loner, more interested in birdwatching than socialising with colleagues, and earned the respect of his bosses through his application to the job.

That application meant facing up to the reality that he and his team were falling short at times, and Furnival Jones was willing to treat genuine security scandals as lessons to be learned rather than unwarranted attacks by the press. 'I have sympathy when the press or others say that a spy prosecution is evidence of a security scandal,' he would later state. 'It is a scandal that the man has got through the defences.'

Furnival Jones must have sensed that he was facing the potential of yet another scandal when Angleton provided him with Golitsyn's information in the spring of 1962. During his initial debriefings at the CIA, Golitsyn had pointed to a group of five British officials, referring to them as the 'Ring of Five', whom he claimed had been recruited in the early 1930s by the KGB's forerunner agency. Two of them, he said, were obviously Burgess and Maclean, who had long ago defected to Moscow. And while Golitsyn could not identify the other three, he had heard that one of them was based in the Middle East, with Stanley as his codename.

With this lead, Furnival Jones's team reopened an investigation into Kim Philby, MI6's former counter-intelligence director, who was no longer with the agency but was in fact now in the Middle East, working as a foreign correspondent in Beirut for Britain's *Observer* newspaper and *The Economist* magazine. Another Golitsyn lead informed MI5 that an apparently senior Royal Navy official, with access to top secret NATO material, had provided the KGB with detailed plans about the expansion of Britain's submarine base at Faslane, in Scotland.

With Furnival Jones devoting resources to pursue his leads and the CIA drilling him for more information, Golitsyn was on his way to making good on his promise to Svetlana and

Tatyana, his wife and daughter, that he would change their lives for the better. On 29 March 1962, a letter from the CIA's Soviet Russia Division to the agency's director recommended permanent residence for Golitsyn and his family. 'Subject [Golitsyn] has already made an outstanding contribution to the intelligence and counter-intelligence mission of the United States Government by furnishing valuable information of first priority concern to the National Security,' the letter stated. 'This Agency and the Federal Bureau of Investigation continue to exploit his knowledgeability on Soviet intelligence operations in many parts of the world.'

By then, the CIA had also confirmed that 'no evidence has been uncovered that indicates Subject was instructed by the KGB to defect for short or long term operational purposes or that his story of himself or his defection is not true'. Golitsyn was given a 'tax free' payment of $200,000 – equivalent to about $2.1m today – and new identities for him and his family to ensure their safety and protection. He became John William Stone, his wife, Irene Ann Stone, and their daughter, Catherine Marie Stone.

A new identity was not going to change Golitsyn's personality traits and hubris, however. He considered himself nothing short of a superstar and was quite pleased by the way he was valued at the CIA. Even Angleton, he felt, treated him with a level of dignity and deference that he had not shown other walk-ins. But it was not long before Golitsyn returned to his factory setting and started making outlandish stipulations. He even insisted that he had the right to a meeting with President John F. Kennedy. 'Golitsyn was very demanding and very much a prima donna from the beginning,' notes a CIA study.

Angleton was unfazed by his behaviour, however, because Golitsyn's distrust of the KGB aligned with his own. Their bond was further strengthened when Golitsyn revealed that Alexander

Shelepin, the Soviet agency leader under whom he had recently served, had created a top secret mission to dupe the West. The revelation would haunt Angleton and change the course of history for US and British intelligence over the next decade of the Cold War.

Four months after Golitsyn abandoned the KGB, word about his defection was spreading fast throughout the Soviet agency. A junior officer, Oleg Lyalin, who only knew Golitsyn by reputation, would eventually be informed about a plan to kill the 'traitor'. At twenty-three, Lyalin had demonstrated a natural inclination for trickery and deceit and was in the final stages of preparing for a deployment to the United States, where his spy career was destined to begin.

## Chapter 2

# A PROMISING RECRUIT

AFTER ARRIVING AT THE port of Klaipeda on the Lithuanian coast of the Baltic Sea on Sunday 29 April 1962, Oleg Lyalin considered the unanticipated reality he was facing; the striking contrast between the professional life he had prepared for and the assignment he was ultimately given. Only five months earlier he had been a rising star. And in recognition of the incalculable hours he had spent refining his English language skills, the KGB had provided Lyalin with a 'private flat' somewhere in Russia, in preparation for a journey to the United States. All he had to do ahead of the journey, he later recalled, was study his target country – its politics, its culture, its people – by reading 'English newspapers' and contemplating how to integrate himself into American life without having his cover blown.

Operating as an 'illegal', an undeclared KGB officer, was unlike any other job. It was an adventure filled with unpredictability, excitement, and risk. It required fast thinking, an unflinching ability to tell lies, and an instinct for dissolving into unfamiliar surroundings. Illegals were essentially human chameleons that the KGB planted in enemy nations to perform a range of counter-intelligence missions, including the theft of personal and government secrets, fomenting discord, and damaging anti-Communist networks.

Their espionage activities followed a tradition dating back decades, before the Bolshevik regime had a diplomatic presence abroad, and as such, relied on illegals to obtain information about their enemies' political, economic and military plans. Some illegals were dispatched as ostensible dissidents to seek out 'fellow' anti-Soviet elements, much like the Cheka's 'Monarchists' who were part of 'Operation Trust'. Others were given false identities, including fictitious nationalities, to portray non-Russians in language, culture and behavioural patterns, right down to perfecting accents. It was that latter pool of illegals for which Lyalin had been considered.

The KGB's illegals programme was highly selective and by invitation only. However, as Lyalin would learn, training to be an illegal required discipline far above the understanding of mission objectives and learning to speak English fluently. At twenty-three, Lyalin lacked that discipline, especially in his personal life. That may in part have been the outcome of a difficult childhood, in which he witnessed the breakdown of his parents' marriage and grieved over the death of his half-brother. Whatever it was that fuelled Lyalin's future appetite for alcohol, gambling and womanising, his lifestyle choices had already placed him on the road to his first divorce and undermined his operational capabilities in the KGB's eyes.

Which is why Lyalin was posted to Klaipeda, Lithuania, rather than to the US where he had been preparing to go and work as an illegal. Having single-handedly squandered a huge career opportunity, Lyalin was essentially demoted – provided with a regional job to spy on foreign tourists travelling to and from the seaport city. It was a task reminiscent of the work he had done when he first became affiliated with the Soviet intelligence agency in 1956. Lyalin was not merely taking a backward step by landing in Klaipeda, it was as though he had been hurled back to the beginning of his career. There was hardly anything alluring about Klaipeda, nor was there anything compelling about being in a place where the KGB's presence was reviled by locals opposed to the Soviet occupation of their country.

The KGB, and its forerunner, the NKVD, had dealt with a lot of its Lithuanian opponents over the years. They marched thousands of them into execution and torture chambers at the agency's headquarters in Vilnius, the country's capital, 200 miles east of Klaipeda. 'Local historians estimate that during the Stalinist era about 15,000 Lithuanians passed through the NKVD headquarters and about 700 were executed,' according to a CIA journal. The Soviet agency's killing spree illustrated a barbarism enshrined in its genes – a trait passed down through its culture to generation after generation of recruits.

Lyalin was not squeamish about the agency's dark history, nor its determination to punish or kill its opponents and traitors. Perhaps that was because he believed that the KGB's deeds were always in honour of the nation; in service of the regime he was proud to represent and to which his parents had devoted a substantial portion of their lives. One of Lyalin's observations of his family's commitment to the Soviet state had come from the way his father, Adolf, had maintained his devotion to the motherland even when the Communist Party had not reciprocated his loyalty.

Despite being expelled from the party for undeclared reasons in 1937, Adolf Lyalin had never abandoned his hope of one day being readmitted, and nor did he ever think of abandoning his nation. He was willing to risk his life for the country he loved, and with his career as an electrical and agricultural engineer on hold during the Second World War, Adolf took up arms against the Nazi invasion of the Soviet Union. He joined the Soviet partisans, the guerrilla warfare movements 'working in close coordination' with the KGB's predecessor, the NKVD.

It is very likely that he joined up in response to Stalin's call in the summer of 1941, when the Soviet leader ordered the formation of guerrilla groups to combat enemy forces through sabotage missions, including 'blowing up bridges and roads, damaging telephone and telegraph communications, and setting on fire woods, dumps and transports'. Three years into fighting the Nazis, Adolf sustained a battle injury and was discharged from service on 'grounds of health'. He was subsequently honoured with a service medal, reinstated into the Communist Party and given a local government job in Pyatigorsk, southern Russia.

The state had in some way repaid its overdue debt to him. Yet it was a bittersweet recognition of his patriotism, because it coincided with the death of his eldest son from a previous marriage, Aleksander, who was killed during his service with the Soviet air force several months before the war ended. That tragedy had a profound impact on Adolf Lyalin's physical health and family life. He separated from Oleg's mother in 1950 and died two years later from a heart attack, aged just fifty-four, when his son was only fourteen.

These sad events must have greatly affected Lyalin, who lost his role model and the closest person in his life. It was his father who had raised him after his parents' separation. It was his father who had generated in him an interest in engineering, and demonstrated through his own wartime service the importance of loyalty to the country. Lyalin had no choice but to move in with his mother, who relocated to Pyatigorsk to work as a geography teacher. 'After his father's death, there was very little money,' notes an intelligence briefing into Lyalin's family background, so 'he was obliged to leave school and find work.'

With a population of about 125,000 in the early 1950s, including 5,000 homeless people, Pyatigorsk was not thriving with employment opportunities. Its two key industries were a cast-iron smelting foundry where about 700 people worked, and a water-bottling facility staffed by about fifty locals. It is unknown whether Lyalin applied for work at any of those industries, nor is it known how long he was forced out of school in his early teen years.

What can be confirmed is that he maintained a hunger for education, and in 1954, he won a place at the Higher Marine School in Odessa, the port city in southern Ukraine, to study electrical marine engineering. He earned his placement at the school's English language stream after sitting competitive exams in mathematics and physics. His results guaranteed him free board on campus, as well as free uniforms and meals. It was an achievement worth celebrating and one that would obviously have made his mother proud, even though it emerged around the same time that her own loyalty to the state had come into question.

The KGB investigated Mrs Lyalin's wartime activities amid suspicion that she had been a Nazi collaborator during Germany's invasion of Pyatigorsk in August 1942. Although defeated by Soviet forces five months later, the Nazis had left a lingering darkness over the city after murdering more than 1,500 local Jews and destroying the lives of countless other residents. Lyalin's mother was suspected of being among hundreds of thousands of Soviets who had collaborated with Hitler's henchmen during wartime.

It was a very damaging claim, in part because of her

longstanding loyalty to the Stalinist regime and membership of the Communist Party. But Communist memberships did not always allay the KGB's suspicions, because it was accepted wisdom that the majority of those who had joined the party had done so for 'personal protection'.

Unlike Lyalin's father, who had remained committed to the regime after being temporarily thrown out of the Communist Party, his mother developed a resentment towards it. The accusation of being a traitor, of having allegedly assisted the enemy, weighed on her health, which had already been compromised by a likely bout of cancer that had cost her a lung. Although she was cleared of the collaboration charge in 1956, Lyalin's mother felt a lasting disdain for the KGB. She abandoned Russia, presumably to escape the local authorities who had treated her harshly, and went to live in Tsesis, a small town in north-east Latvia.

Oleg Lyalin was two years into his course at the marine school in Odessa when his mother left for Latvia. He was continuing to make an impression on his teachers, particularly in his grasp of the English language. Along with taking up engineering to follow in his father's footsteps, he had honoured Adolf's memory by maintaining his membership of the Young Communist League, which he had joined in 1951, shortly before his father's death. Life in Odessa, by the seaside and away from parental supervision, gave him an independence of mind and the ability to take up national causes and dabble in activities of which his mother would have likely disapproved, especially because one such activity would draw him to the KGB.

He sensed an adventure when a classmate working as a KGB informant told Lyalin that the agency was interested in meeting him. At eighteen, the fact that he was even being noticed, let alone singled out for an approach by an organisation of the KGB's stature, made an impression on him – and perhaps, even allowed him to see past the way it had mistreated his mother. The KGB's approach in 1956 suggested it believed Lyalin could make a suitable recruitment candidate, despite the agency's earlier case against his mother from which she had been cleared that year.

Lyalin accompanied his classmate to the school's personnel department, which had arranged for him to meet a representative of the KGB's transportation division. He impressed the Soviet agency official, and soon after the meeting he took up a junior role, alongside his studies, to become a local informant for the KGB: to keep an eye on 'Western seamen and smugglers' travelling through Odessa, one of the busiest ports in the Black Sea. 'There was nothing formal about this recruitment' and his only qualification for the job was his 'command of English', a summary of his employment record states.

Then, in the summer of 1957, Lyalin set off on a sea adventure aboard the *Tovarisch*, a three-masted barque taken from Germany by the Soviet Union as part of its war reparations. With the KGB's blessing, Lyalin joined crew members on the 'goodwill' tour of Western ports, including a fortnight stay in Portsmouth on England's south coast. It was not all smooth sailing, however, partly because the ship encountered mechanical problems during the journey. 'The Russian training barque *Tovarisch*, on a world cruise with cadets, reached Singapore yesterday for minor engine repairs after running into a cyclone after leaving Colombo,' reported *The Times* of London on 29 August 1957.

But there were far greater problems of a geopolitical nature that coincided with Lyalin's tour, including a long-established hostility between the Soviet Union and Western nations, especially Britain, which had been intensified a year earlier by the Suez Crisis. Britain had been forced to end its invasion of Egypt over its failure to secure US military and financial backing, amid fear of a potential military confrontation with Moscow. It was a humiliating climbdown by the British government, which resulted in the resignation of Prime Minister Anthony Eden. Even worse, the Suez Crisis had diminished Western influence in the region and delivered Moscow a strategic victory, strengthening its credibility and reach in the Middle East.

Such matters of global significance were far beyond Lyalin's duties to his country, let alone his service to the KGB at the time. It was not until two years after his return to Odessa from the goodwill tour aboard *Tovarisch* that the KGB tested his suitability for a more serious and permanent role. During a training exercise in Kishinev, Moldova, in 1959, he identified, cultivated, and exploited locals for information about four individuals who were of interest to the Soviet agency. He did so while using a fake name, Oleg Aleksandrovich Liabin, demonstrating an ability to operate successfully as somebody else. Lyalin's mission coincided with a major overhaul of the KGB under its new leader, Alexander Shelepin, who sought to ratchet up its attacks against Western nations.

Although still too junior to register on the chairman's radar, Lyalin embodied the qualities and skills that Shelepin desired for his agency. The chairman wanted ambitious operatives, risk-takers with a creative bent for mischief and sabotage, to help revive the Cheka's spirit in the KGB. Even before taking the agency's reins in December 1958, Shelepin believed that the KGB had been functioning as merely a domestic police force, far too limited and passive in its aims. As its new master, he wanted to weaponise it against capitalist nations, especially NATO countries, with the US and Britain at the top of that list. He wanted to damage their economies, disrupt their political systems, and foment distrust in their intelligence services. These were not delusional hopes but projections of boundless ambition.

Shelepin's presence in the Soviet hierarchy had been known to the CIA, as was his meteoric rise in the Communist Party, which continued after Stalin's death in 1953. Several months before his fortieth birthday, he had been handpicked by Soviet leader Nikita Khrushchev to run the KGB in recognition of his formidable leadership style. It was the same leadership skills that had earlier drawn Shelepin to the attention of Stalin, who had placed him in charge of the Komsomol – the Young Communist League – six years earlier.

Yet the CIA's early analysis of Shelepin's KGB takeover concluded that it would be 'in line with Krushchev's private statements that he planned to downgrade' the agency, not expand its missions. The CIA's assessment was way off the mark. Shelepin was hellbent on damaging Washington – from trying to stir up civil disobedience through KGB operations in the United States, to compromising the safety of US intelligence officials. He proposed to expose the identities of foreign-based CIA officers, and also expose the US agency's 'subversive activities . . . against some governments, political parties and public figures in capitalist countries, and to foment mistrust toward Americans in the government circles of these countries'.

It was in that climate of Soviet aggression that Lyalin was admitted in August 1960 into the KGB's 101st School, which would later become known as the Academy of Foreign Intelligence. Unlike the marine college from which he had graduated, the academy was intended to turn this junior lieutenant from an amateur operative into a fully fledged intelligence officer.

It was there that he would improve his English skills and develop a broader understanding of recruiting foreign agents, compromising Western government officials, and operating in enemy territory under an assumed identity. This was all in preparation for what, at least on paper, appeared to be a guaranteed deployment to the United States. 'This course consisted of chemistry, photography, English and tailing [keeping a target under surveillance],' an intelligence file reveals. 'Lyalin took his examination before the end of his course and graduated in October 1961.'

However, with his dream of travelling to the US reduced to ashes by his own folly, Lyalin began his new role in Klaipeda in the spring of 1962, longing for a chance to conduct the KGB's dirty work in the West. The type of dirty work that Anatoly Golitsyn was still warning the CIA about.

\* \* \*

Three months into his defection, Anatoly Golitsyn's obsessive personality was becoming increasingly apparent as he continued to drip-feed KGB secrets. In fact, his obsessive ambition to damage the Soviet agency was being embraced at the CIA, particularly by James Angleton's acolytes and the counter-intelligence chief himself. They deemed it an expression of Golitsyn's passion, not some streak of 'paranoia' as an agency shrink had flagged up in the defector's psychology report. Angleton dismissed that report because he believed Golitsyn's suspicions to be entirely justified, backed by practical experience.

He considered the idea that some therapist could pass judgement on the defector's character as an insult in itself. To the best of Angleton's knowledge, Golitsyn seemed to have proven himself time and again in exposing Moscow's sinister intentions, including its recruitment of British intelligence officials and its penetration of the CIA. How could Angleton not be overwhelmingly impressed by this man's unrivalled understanding of the KGB's political and military objectives, or his knowledge that the Soviet agency was intending to discredit and compromise Western scholars opposed to Communism in order to undermine their criticism of the ideology?

When Angleton listened to Golitsyn, he saw an oracle drawing on his understanding of the KGB's history to predict its treacherous path ahead. The cherished defector painted an increasingly horrifying picture of the long-range policies and missions activated by Alexander Shelepin, whose legacy lingered on long after his promotion from KGB chief to first deputy prime minister in November 1961.

Golitsyn told Angleton that Shelepin was determined to build the Soviet bloc's economy and military capability by stealing scientific and technical secrets from the West. He said Shelepin had created a disinformation department at the agency, focused on misleading capitalist countries, to disorient their defence policies and burden their finances and personnel with false-flag Soviet operations.

Senior counter-intelligence experts, he warned, were training the disinformation department on matters relating to US and British intelligence, NATO, aviation, rocket propulsion and other specialised subjects. And one of the department's greatest ambitions, Golitsyn revealed, was the execution of a 'Master Plan' to give Moscow an edge over its Cold War enemy through the deployment of fake defectors to the West. He told Angleton that any Soviet defector sent in his wake would be a 'provocation' and insisted that the KGB had already 'sent out multiple provocation agents to carry out this plan'.

The Master Plan's success could only be gauged with the 'penetrations of the target services to provide feedback on the effect of the efforts. Thus, it was not a question of whether the KGB had penetrated [the] CIA but rather of identifying the penetrations that were certain to exist.' This yet again confirmed

Angleton's worst suspicion that his organisation had been compromised. It even led him to conclude in early 1962 that the agency should stop targeting Soviet officials for recruitment, because new recruits risked being exposed by traitors inside the CIA who were already under the Kremlin's control.

The spring of 1962 was a difficult time for the CIA, made worse by Cuba's first anniversary celebration of its Bay of Pigs battle, which had tarnished Langley's domestic and global reputation while boosting Fidel Castro's standing as an anti-capitalist revolutionary. It conveniently played into the hands of Nikita Khrushchev, who along with admiring Castro, had offered Moscow's military support to Havana in the event of an armed confrontation with the United States.

The Soviet leader's belligerence towards Washington had escalated the previous summer, following his first in-person meeting with President Kennedy in Vienna to try to settle their differences over the post-war division of Germany and matters relating to disarmament. Instead of tempering hostilities between the two superpowers, the summit led both leaders to take drastic actions: Kennedy ramped up America's intercontinental ballistic missile forces and army, air power and nuclear reserves, while Khrushchev ordered the construction of the Berlin Wall in a 'chilling symbol of the Iron Curtain that divided all of Europe between communism and democracy', notes the JFK Library.

Their differences were further inflamed after Moscow and Washington resumed nuclear testing, breaking a moratorium that had been in place for almost three years. So it was barely a surprise in early 1962 when Khrushchev expressed his pessimism for an upcoming disarmament conference in Geneva, which had been designed to bring an end to the arms race between East and West.

The United Nations conference was set to begin in mid-March

and run for several months, but had already been undermined by President Kennedy and British prime minister Harold Macmillan refusing to attend. In reality, neither Washington, London nor Moscow were truly hopeful of making a breakthrough on the disarmament negotiations, because the transatlantic partners did not trust the Kremlin – and vice versa. Nevertheless, with all three countries committed to sending delegates to Geneva, the CIA took a keen interest in the Soviet representatives.

It is common practice for intelligence agencies to study the names of delegates assigned to international conferences, especially those involving representatives of foreign government services. They look for officials who may have been helpful in the past, or lapsed agents who had once provided intelligence but have since gone to ground to preserve their cover. Equally as important, if not more so, spy agencies cross-reference delegates' names against their own files to identify hostile intelligence officers, who may be using diplomatic cover to meet with their own agents on the sidelines of an event.

With ninety-four Soviet officials attending the Geneva conference, Angleton's team sought Golitsyn's views ahead of the March event, providing him with a list of delegates. One of the names, Mikhail S. Rogov, was a familiar pseudonym for Mikhail Tsymbal, the KGB's former rezident in Paris. But another KGB officer somehow slipped the CIA's radar. His name was Yuri Ivanovich Nosenko.

\* \* \*

The KGB had not yet come into existence when Yuri Nosenko developed an interest in joining the Soviet intelligence services. But at twenty-five, instead of wasting his time going through the usual channels of job applications or waiting to be discovered somehow, he took the familiar route of tapping into his father's contacts. In fact, it was very unlikely that without his father young Nosenko would have been invited to the New Year's Eve party at Bogdan Kobulov's dacha, or country home, in 1952.

He joined his parents at the soirée, aware of the opportunity that could come from ingratiating himself with the host. Alongside his ability to throw a party, Kobulov was a political powerhouse who had made his name in the service of Lavrentiy Beria, former head of the NKVD, by overseeing the torture and execution of countless opponents to Stalin's regime. Kobulov was also a proud Chekist who was on the up, a few months away from a promotion to become Beria's deputy at the Ministry of Internal Affairs (MVD), when Nosenko expressed an interest in becoming an intelligence officer.

Kobulov recommended Nosenko to the MGB, the Ministry of State Security – the Soviet Union's secret police and forerunner of the KGB. And by spring 1953, Nosenko was offered a role in the agency's Second Chief Directorate, which focused on domestic counter-intelligence operations against foreigners living in the Soviet Union.

The job in many ways highlighted the considerable sway Nosenko's family name carried in the Soviet Union. His father, Ivan, had been catapulted by the Russian Revolution from a shipyard labourer into Stalin's orbit, rising through a series of government positions to become the Shipbuilding Minister. And despite the post-Stalin purge in which many of his allies were executed – including Kobulov and Beria – Ivan survived. He even maintained his ministerial role under Stalin's successors, Georgy Malenkov and Nikita Khrushchev, who would later both attend Ivan's state funeral in August 1956.

Yet long before Ivan was honoured with a plaque in the Kremlin, his son had recognised his influence in the ruling hierarchy, which partly explained young Nosenko's ability to remain in the KGB, let alone qualify for the agency in the first place.

Nosenko had failed in almost every area of his life, but he always failed upwards. It took him five years to complete a four-year course at the Moscow State Institute of Special Relations after flunking an exam on Marxism. Despite that, he promptly landed a job as an English translator with naval intelligence in March 1951. He barely lasted a year before falling ill and never returning to the job 'for reasons of health'. In 1953, three months into his job at the MGB, Nosenko was elected secretary of the second directorate's Komsomol.

But his time overseeing young Communists was short-lived. He was kicked out within a year after misusing work documents to disguise his identity from a clinician treating him for venereal disease. In spite of this, and a subsequent 'poor performance evaluation' in the spring of 1955 from the newly created KGB, Nosenko was neither dismissed nor transferred. Instead, he was made a full member of the Communist Party and his record, tarnished by the Komsomol incident, was wiped clean. He capped his ascendency in the KGB with a promotion to captain in December 1959.

That was noteworthy, not because nepotism had yet again played a part in Nosenko's rise, but because it came during Alexander Shelepin's leadership of the agency. Somehow, notwithstanding all of his workplace setbacks, Nosenko had proven to be adept at attacking American interests in the Soviet Union, including the targeting of US Embassy officials in Moscow, which had been a cornerstone of the KGB's focus under Shelepin.

While Nosenko's back story had a through line in explaining his elevation in the Soviet system because of familial links, it did not explain why he had remained useful to the KGB after his father's death. The agency had no duty to keep him on its books. Surely it could have dismissed him on grounds of incompetence alone? Not to mention his chaotic personal life – with two failed marriages and a third on the brink – and his notorious drinking habits and pursuit of prostitutes. His debauched lifestyle placed him at risk of being compromised in a honey trap, much in the way that he had compromised others by deploying women to entrap them.

But in the world of espionage, where there is rarely a black and white or straightforward explanation, maybe Nosenko was safeguarded rather than hampered by his vices. Perhaps his propensity for mischief was an asset because it provided him with the ability to see bad traits in others. That could certainly go some way to explaining why he was deployed by the KGB to keep an eye on Soviet delegates at the UN conference in Geneva in early 1962.

Over three months, as Nosenko observed the behaviour of Soviet officials in the Swiss city, he was also keeping an eye on their US counterparts at the conference, but for an entirely different reason. While the event at the UN's Palace of Nations, one of the largest diplomatic conference centres in the world, may have been fertile ground for constructing a scenario for a recruitment pitch, Nosenko was not on the lookout for potential spies. He wanted to identify a way of getting to the CIA to provide his own information.

During a break in the arms control proceedings on 7 June 1962, Nosenko spotted an American delegate who had previously served at the US Embassy in Moscow. He studied his surroundings, aware that he was within sight of Soviet delegates milling around. Then, ensuring that he was no longer in view of his own colleagues, Nosenko approached the American official, shook his hand and requested an urgent meeting with the CIA.

The prospect of debriefing yet another walk-in seven months after Anatoly Golitsyn's defection was met with great excitement among some Langley officials, despite the CIA's heightened state of alertness surrounding KGB moles and the prospect of fake defectors being sent its way. Nosenko's case was handed to Tennent 'Pete' Bagley, a Soviet division expert in the agency's station in Bern, who was up to speed on the latest threats facing his organisation.

Dealing with defectors and agents-in-place was one of Bagley's great strengths. He had been involved in the events surrounding the defection of Polish intelligence officer Michal Goleniewski a year earlier and also supported the team that ran Pyotr Popov right up to the time the Soviet agent was caught by the KGB. Bagley was in his mid-thirties, held a doctorate in political science, and the twelve years he had spent at the CIA followed a wartime stint in the US Marines, which he had joined at seventeen. James Angleton liked and respected him and they had a similar worldview when it came to fighting Soviet espionage.

In preparation for his meeting with Nosenko, Bagley enlisted a young techie from the agency to rig up an apartment with microphones and a tape recorder. For chances of that nature, as his colleague Frank Friberg had discovered months earlier during the Golitsyn approach in Helsinki, might come only once – if ever – in an officer's career.

With everything set to go, Bagley informed the US diplomat who had been approached by Nosenko about where and when the meeting would take place. The KGB officer had made his own preparations, pondering the message he wanted to share, and the image he wanted to project – down to the suit and tie that he would turn up in.

## Chapter 3

# THIS MAN HAS COME TO DISCREDIT ME

PETE BAGLEY WAS SLIGHTLY bemused by Yuri Nosenko's sudden change in demeanour – his deliberate pause in the conversation as his eyes scanned the room from where he was sitting. But it was only when Nosenko clicked his fingers three times and looked at him, knowingly, to ask if the room was fitted with listening devices, that the CIA officer realised he was witnessing a performance of sorts by a man ironically signposting his familiarity with intelligence debriefings.

Bagley remained silent and expressionless. If hidden 'microphones' had been of genuine concern, then the Ukrainian-born officer would have raised his question upon entering the apartment, not halfway through the discussion. The timing of his question was odd, because only minutes earlier and in the same space, Nosenko had proposed to give secrets and discussed his operational work, claiming to be a Major in the KGB's Second Chief Directorate, which targets foreigners, especially Americans in Moscow.

On failing to elicit a reaction about the listening devices, he shrugged his shoulders, telling Bagley that it would be natural for the CIA to bug the meeting given the circumstances surrounding it. On the one hand, Nosenko appeared to want to illustrate the risks associated with his presence there, but on the other, he wanted to boast, assuring Bagley that afternoon that he had broken away from his Soviet delegation with great ease. Most intriguing was his motive for approaching the US agency. Nosenko said he had frittered away an official travel advance on prostitutes and bar tabs and needed 800 Swiss francs to settle the misappropriated funds. By Bagley's calculation, that was equivalent to a week's salary for a Soviet official of Nosenko's rank – a minuscule amount for the operative to stake his career on and to risk his life.

The American was somewhat apprehensive about Nosenko's credibility, but wanted to draw him on meaningful intelligence that could be substantiated. He particularly wanted to interrogate Nosenko's claim from a few minutes earlier that the KGB had widespread coverage of the US Embassy in Moscow, including phone taps and spies inside the building, along with surveillance teams monitoring the movements of American officials outside their diplomatic compounds.

By that point in their conversation, which was predominantly in English, with the occasional Russian word or phrase thrown in, Nosenko was already through his second Scotch and soda. He showed no sign of inebriation, still self-possessed and statesmanlike in his crisp suit and tie, his hair slicked back without a strand out of place. Aware that Bagley was studying his movements and mannerisms, awaiting his every word, he told the CIA officer that Soviet intelligence had made a significant penetration into the US Embassy in Moscow after recruiting an American sergeant who worked there.

He said the sergeant, whom he only knew as 'Andrey', was a cipher specialist who had been forced to cooperate in either 1949 or 1950, after Kremlin spooks took compromising pictures of him with a Russian woman and threatened to show them to his wife. Nosenko claimed that 'Andrey' had gone on to become such a major asset that years after his departure from Moscow, a KGB representative travelled to the US to 'reactivate' him. Yet despite the build-up Nosenko had given about Andrey, he failed to provide any specific details to help identify him. Instead, he wanted to gloat about his own accomplishments in recruiting American and British tourists, for which he claimed to have received a KGB commendation. Perhaps he was slow-pedalling, withholding key details until Bagley had made good on the money he was after.

Now well into his third drink, Nosenko looked at his watch: time was up. He needed to be elsewhere, he said, and offered to return for another conversation in two days. Bagley had hardly got started with his questions, but wanted to abide by the Ukrainian's terms and promised to have his money in time for their next meeting. With the debriefing officially over, Nosenko had something else on his mind as he got up from his armchair and headed towards the front door. In a casual manner, as if reflecting on the weather or the whisky bottle he had just defeated, Nosenko brought up the name of Pyotr Popov, the former CIA agent executed for treason by the Soviet Union two years earlier for divulging GRU secrets.

In fact, Nosenko did not even mention the GRU officer's first name, just his last, completely aware that it would resonate with Bagley. The Soviet official said he knew how the KGB had captured Popov, and there is no doubt that Nosenko's revelation was intended for late delivery, set up as a cliffhanger ahead of his next meeting with Bagley. Because despite the American's repeated appeals for more information, Nosenko insisted that he was out of time before heading off, leaving his debriefer in a state of shock. Could Nosenko have known that Bagley had been one of the CIA officers involved in handling Popov?

Being so recent, Popov's death was still reverberating at Langley, where he was fondly remembered for having 'single-handedly supplied the most valuable intelligence on Soviet military matters of any human'. His provision of Soviet secrets, according to the CIA's estimations, had 'direct and significant influence on the military organisation of the United States, its doctrine and tactics, and permitted the Pentagon to save at least $500 million in its scientific research program.'

Much like the CIA's chief molehunter, James Angleton, and George Kisevalter, Popov's handler, Bagley remained both operationally and emotionally invested in discovering how the agency's first-ever asset inside Soviet intelligence had been compromised. What if Nosenko had the answer? That was the obvious question in Bagley's mind after he closed the door behind the KGB officer and returned to the room to scrawl down his initial impression of Nosenko, in preparation for sending a coded cable to Langley.

He informed agency officials that although Nosenko had not demonstrated any knowledge of, or access to, military or political secrets, his reference to Popov and insights about the US Embassy in Moscow illustrated his insider knowledge and apparent legitimacy. Bagley requested a Russian speaker more fluent than himself for the next debriefing, to ensure that he was not missing any nuances. He was determined to milk Nosenko for every bit of information he had, and he could not have hoped for a better Russian speaker than the one Langley had in mind – Popov's former case officer, George Kisevalter.

Along with his eleven years at the CIA, and vast experience

handling agents and defectors through the organisation's Soviet division, Kisevalter was the perfect fit for the Nosenko assignment, because of the cultural authenticity and understanding he brought to dealing with Soviet agents. Born in Tsarist Russia, Kisevalter empathised with Soviet dissidents, as they opposed the very system that had forced his family out of the country after the Revolution.

At fifty-two, he was sixteen years older than Bagley and in addition to bringing a certain wisdom that accompanies age, Kisevalter was street-smart, dismissive of authority, and not easily impressed. To the extent that when Anatoly Golitsyn had started making outlandish requests a few months earlier, including a demand to meet President Kennedy, it was Kisevalter whom the agency had called on to straighten the defector out. Not because he disrespected Golitsyn in any way, but because he was not afraid of saying no to him or even upsetting him, as were many others, including Angleton, for fear of diminishing his cooperation. Now Kisevalter was preparing to do the same with Nosenko: to focus intensely on his revelations and distinguish his solid details from his fragmentary clues.

As Nosenko had promised, on Monday 11 June, two days after his initial debriefing, he arrived at the CIA's safe house in Geneva. Bagley and Kisevalter were waiting and their biggest priority was obtaining details about Popov's case. The concealed recorders were already turning and a fresh bottle of Scotch was on full display as the KGB officer walked into the debriefing room. Hardly any time was wasted on pleasantries before Kisevalter marked his authority, leading the questioning in Russian, as Bagley took notes. Of the three men, however, the person in real control was the one making the disclosures – and Nosenko had enough self-awareness to realise that, sipping on whisky as he detailed the errors of judgement made by Popov's American handlers.

It was basic, routine surveillance that had led to the GRU officer's downfall, explained Nosenko. The KGB had been tailing US Embassy officials in Moscow, including an attaché who in early 1959 was seen dropping a letter into a mailbox. A Soviet operative recovered the letter, which had been written in Russian, addressed to Popov and bearing a false return address. The KGB suspected an espionage mission and put the GRU official under twenty-four-hour monitoring.

It took just a few days for surveillance operatives to track him to a meeting with Russell Langelle, an American diplomat officially serving as the security officer in charge of the US Embassy's Marine guards. Popov was arrested sometime afterwards, said Nosenko, and made a full confession under interrogation. He was then 'played back' – turned into a double-agent to feed disinformation to the CIA during his future meetings with Langelle.

Eager to supplement this passive, long-term operational method with more immediate action, the KGB turned Langelle into its key target. It dispatched Popov to provide the thirty-seven-year-old American diplomat with ostensibly secret reports, and at some point after their meeting, five men confronted Langelle on the street. They covered his mouth, pinned his arms and dragged him into an alley before whisking him away in a car for interrogation at a nearby building. The KGB operatives laughed in Langelle's face when he claimed diplomatic immunity and threatened to harm his wife and three small children should he not provide details about his role. He refused to capitulate and also turned down the KGB's offer of money to spy.

After almost two hours of intimidation, the KGB thugs gave up and subsequently kicked him and his family out of the country.

And of course, everyone knew what eventually happened to Popov: he was tried for treason and subsequently shot.

The KGB's mistreatment of Langelle had already been reported in the Western media, so it was not surprising that Nosenko knew about it. Kisevalter was more intrigued by another element in Nosenko's outline – the details about the letter uncovered from the mailbox, which had led the KGB to Popov's scent. Those details were unknown to the outside world and had certainly never been reported. Kisevalter was among only a handful of people who had been aware that Popov informed the CIA in a secret message through Langelle that he was compromised by the ill-fated letter. Nosenko's information corroborated Kisevalter's understanding of the episode.

He then continued to impress his debriefers, revealing the KGB's proficiency at breaking into embassies in Moscow, lock-picking safes and photographing their contents without leaving any trace of tampering. In some cases, its officers planted eavesdropping devices at the diplomatic compounds, Nosenko said, even providing details about forty-two microphones that honeycombed the US Embassy in the Russian capital. Among the KGB's other methods of keeping its targets under observation was the 'litra' system, in which items such as envelopes were daubed with clear chemicals, producing a scent that could be picked up by trained dogs. Canines, including collies and shepherds, also helped surveillance officers identify foreign officials whose clothes had been contaminated with the chemicals, in some cases by their household employees who doubled as KGB spies.

Weaponising the likes of domestic cleaners did not seem too fanciful, because one had been known to have compromised Edward Ellis Smith, the CIA's first intelligence officer in Moscow who was recalled by the agency to the US in 1956. Nosenko knew that case well, and it was yet another revelation that he was proud to share during the debriefing, saying he had been working with the Soviet agency department that had targeted Smith.

Nosenko claimed that he had been running an agent, 'Valya', who worked as Smith's housemaid, and had helped devise a scenario in which the KGB could accuse the CIA officer of committing a criminal offence against her. The criminal allegation, presumably of some sexual nature, helped the Soviet agency to pressure Smith into a meeting to gauge his susceptibility to recruitment, but the Soviets failed to gain his cooperation. That also corroborated Nosenko's debriefers' understanding of the case, because Smith had confessed to the CIA that he had been ensnared in a honey trap and forced by the KGB into a meeting. On his return to the US, Smith was interrogated by his superiors about the incident and subsequently dismissed because the agency had lost trust in him.

Over several days, and with each new disclosure, Kisevalter and Bagley became increasingly confident in Nosenko's disclosures, regularly updating Langley about them. On 11 June, they sent a cable to headquarters without naming Nosenko, merely describing him as 'subj', or subject, to protect his identity from any internal leaks. 'Subj conclusively proved bona fide. Provided info of importance and sensitivity, subj now completely cooperative. Willing meet [sic] when abroad and will meet as often and as long as possible until departure 15 June.' With such reassurance, Langley provided some fresh leads, by way of names, that it wanted to run by Nosenko. One was Sasha, the codename that had been brought to the agency's attention by Anatoly Golitsyn several months earlier, sparking an internal molehunt that was still underway.

There was a bit of theatre associated with the leads: Kisevalter and Bagley were unaware that they had been sought from

Golitsyn, and Golitsyn had provided them to the CIA without knowing how the US agency intended to use them. Yet despite the secrecy surrounding them, the leads were futile because Nosenko drew blanks on all of them. Nosenko did, however, make unrelated disclosures about his agency's operations against US allies, including Canadian and British officials.

He claimed the KGB had compromised John Watkins, a Canadian ambassador to the Soviet Union in the mid-1950s, and around that time, the agency had forced a British naval attaché in Moscow to become its spy after baiting him with a lover and taking pictures of him while naked. Although he did not know his name, Nosenko said the man in question was gay, had served as a naval attaché, provided NATO-related secrets and had remained under the KGB's control on his return to London.

Kisevalter and Bagley were amazed by Nosenko's alertness and capacity for recall, despite his continuous drinking throughout the debriefing sessions. He never once slurred his speech nor struggled to explain himself, and nor did he ever seem glassy-eyed or off balance. He absorbed the whisky like it was filtered water. As the hours wore on and he became increasingly aware of the value he was providing his debriefers, Nosenko did not increase his demand beyond the money he had originally requested, even though he most probably could have done.

However, he did raise a major concern relating to his family that he felt helpless about. He informed the American debriefers that his young daughter, Oksana, was suffering from breathing difficulties, which he believed were potentially life-threatening. She required medication that was not available in the Soviet Union, he said, and nor had he been able to find it in Geneva. Nosenko's predicament placed Kisevalter and Bagley on the spot. But what better way to prove their commitment to him than to help save his daughter's life? The CIA officers sent an urgent cable to Langley to initiate a search and eventually they found the medication in Holland and had it flown by an agency pilot to Geneva.

During Nosenko's final debriefing, on the day before he was due to return to Moscow, Kisevalter and Bagley handed him the medication. Nosenko was moved by their efforts. He had been given everything he had hoped for – the medication and the money to repay his debt. Even more than he had expected, and in return for remaining in touch, Nosenko was promised an annual salary of $25,000, which would be deposited in a secret, Western bank account. Nosenko assured his American friends that he would reconnect with them whenever he was out of the Soviet Union, but stressed that he was unwilling to remain in contact while in Moscow for fear of being caught.

The CIA officials arranged a safe communication method for future interactions, where Nosenko would contact them by cable or mail via a specific address in New York and sign off his message with the name 'George'. Nosenko committed the address to memory and at the end of his final debriefing on Thursday 14 June, he embraced Bagley and Kisevalter and promised to meet them again.

The CIA officers were delighted, buoyed with enthusiasm about their big catch as they boarded separate flights the following day, each carrying his own notes and a duplicate set of the recordings of Nosenko's five debriefings. The urgency with which the pair had been summoned to Langley, and the security measures they had been asked to take, including flying separately, naturally gave them the impression that what they had in their possession was espionage gold. But even gold has variables in its purity – and it was those variables that James Angleton was struggling to see beyond.

*

A mound of files, barricading either end of James Angleton's desk, framed the private conversation between him and Pete Bagley. The young officer could see that his host was hardly listening, scribbling on notepaper what appeared to be a convoluted geometric shape. Angleton was allowing Bagley to run down the clock on his explanation about Yuri Nosenko's disclosures, even though the spymaster had already made up his mind that the KGB officer who had submitted himself to a debriefing in Geneva was a plant, a deception agent.

Angleton's respect of counter-intelligence as a craft, and his understanding of the emotional attachment case officers had towards their sources, stopped him from being too dismissive. He knew that Bagley viewed Nosenko as a career highlight – 'the biggest fish of his life'. As Bagley wrapped up his soliloquy, he watched Angleton quickly transition from doodling on the page with a pencil to ripping it from his notebook and tearing it into little pieces, before throwing it in the bin alongside his desk. The discarded paper may as well have included Nosenko's sworn testimony, because Angleton afforded it just as much, or as little, regard.

It became immediately obvious that the counter-intelligence chief could not get past Nosenko's supposed motive for approaching the CIA in the first place: the idea that he had offered so many secrets for just 800 Swiss francs to 'replenish the account from which he embezzled the money' seemed highly dubious, Angleton would later note. Amplifying his suspicions were some of the similarities between the intelligence Nosenko provided and that which Golitsyn had shared several months earlier. Of course, Bagley had no way of knowing any of that when he and Kisevalter debriefed Nosenko, because a lot of Golitsyn's material was in very limited circulation to preserve its secrecy, accessible only on a 'need-to-know' basis.

Now the timing was right, Angleton felt, for Bagley to be brought into Golitsyn's disclosures, particularly because he sensed that the CIA officer 'was of split motivation' in subjecting Nosenko's revelations to further scrutiny. It was natural for case officers to be apprehensive about submitting the validity of their sources to closer inspection, in case it brought their own judgement into disrepute. However, Bagley was up for the challenge, keen to illustrate that shielding the agency from potential disinformation was far more important than the prospect of individual glory.

As though being led into a ritual, Bagley was ushered by Angleton's personal assistant into a windowless conference room, which looked more like a walk-in closet. It was a secure location but could barely accommodate the rudimentary furniture in it – six chairs, and a shabby table that had perhaps been salvaged from the CIA's former offices in Washington D.C. before the agency's relocation to Langley in the spring of 1961. But it was there, on Angleton's orders, that Golitsyn's secrets had been sent to breathe; where his disclosures during a series of debriefings had made their way into '10 to 15 volumes of files', now plonked on the table and awaiting Bagley's judgement.

The CIA officer started going through the documents and soon realised that some contained parallel reporting to Nosenko's disclosures. When viewed against Golitsyn's material, Nosenko's secrets suddenly felt devoid of any revelatory qualities. Bagley tried to temper his unease by considering that both Golitsyn and Nosenko could have come across the same information at some point; but there were too many similarities, too many coincidences to support that view, given that KGB operations were often compartmentalised across its different sections to protect their secrecy. Even more unsettling was the fact that the parallel insights Nosenko had provided seemed to differ only marginally, as if they had been formulated to distinguish them from Golitsyn's information. The two accounts looked more like collusion than corroboration.

On reflection, Bagley found it all too convenient that Nosenko would attribute Pyotr Popov's arrest to a lucky surveillance mission in which an American diplomat was spotted posting a letter at a mailbox in Moscow in early 1959. That contradicted Golitsyn's claim that the KGB had been aware of the GRU officer's collaboration with the Americans long before it arrested him after allegedly discovering the letter. Another parallel discovery in Golitsyn's files related to the Canadian ambassador, John Watkins, who had been allegedly compromised by the KGB in the mid-1950s and the British naval attaché in Moscow who had been recruited around that time by the KGB. The only key difference in the second instance was that Nosenko, unlike Golitsyn, had identified the naval officer as a homosexual.

Bagley was completely absorbed by each discovery as he continued going through the files, only turning his eyes away from them occasionally to jot down notes in his writing pad. More and more parallels emerged as the hours wore on, including Golitsyn's leads on the KGB's targeting of the US Embassy in Moscow and his revelation that a Soviet journalist employed as a CIA informant was in fact a double-agent under the control of Moscow, just as Nosenko had revealed. After going through all of the material, it became impossible for Bagley to keep an open mind and it seemed increasingly plausible that the KGB had sent Nosenko to contaminate the information which it suspected Golitsyn had given the CIA.

'I thought it quite possible, in the view of his [Golitsyn's] statements about disinformation, that this was the beginning of a disinformation operation possibly relating to his defection,' Bagley later acknowledged. In his assessment, it would have been standard practice for the Soviet agency to have done a stocktake of its losses after Golitsyn's defection and then to have developed ways to try to discredit it. He felt completely hoodwinked.

After a sleepless night reflecting on the ruse that Nosenko had apparently drawn him into, Bagley returned to Angleton's office to deliver his final verdict. 'At the end of it all he said that there was no question about it, that they were being had,' said Angleton of Bagley's realisation that he and Kisevalter had been duped in Geneva.

Determined to get another opinion, Angleton and Bagley proposed to the agency's deputy director of operations, Richard Helms, that Golitsyn should be given access to Nosenko's material. Helms refused their proposal, but he accepted their secondary suggestion of presenting the information in the form of an 'anonymous letter [which had been] sent to the embassy by an alleged KGB person'.

When briefed on the purported letter, Golitsyn concluded that it appeared to have been sent by a person 'under control', a bogus walk-in dispatched by the Soviet agency. Golitsyn then asked to see the letter, which 'presented a situation because we didn't have a letter,' Angleton recalled. 'But he [Golitsyn] began to point out in some detail exactly what was instigating and inspiring – in terms of what he'd already given us.' Golitsyn told Bagley that there were 'serious signs of disinformation' in Nosenko's disclosures, and felt that 'such a disinformation operation, to discredit him, was a likelihood'.

Even when Golitsyn was assured that Nosenko, of whose name he was still unaware, had 'not done anything to discredit [him]' but had in fact revealed that the KGB was 'greatly upset' about his defection – the defector insisted that the Soviet agency had multiple aims, including diverting the CIA's 'attention from investigations of his leads by throwing up false scents' and trying to 'protect their remaining sources'. It was very probable that the

KGB had authorised Nosenko's meetings with the CIA to build the agency's confidence in him, said Golitsyn. But in the end, he thought, Nosenko would honour the KGB's primary objective – 'whatever the operation's main purpose might be' – to either 'discredit' Golitsyn, or even 'kidnap' him.

In light of Golitsyn's analysis, Bagley and Angleton, now convinced that Nosenko was a bogus asset, started seeing him as a major threat. Far from cutting him loose, however, they wanted to build a case against him, with any insights he had provided or action he had taken 'interpreted as part of a KGB' operation. It did not matter to them that some of Nosenko's revelations had been accurate and actionable, including one that helped the US State Department identify forty of the forty-two microphones honeycombing its embassy walls in Moscow.

Nor did it matter that the information he had provided about the British Admiralty official had allowed the CIA to assist MI5's investigation into William John Vassall. In fact, Vassall had earlier appeared in the British agency's investigation based on Golitsyn's tip-off, but had been discounted because he was deemed a Catholic of high moral character. It was only when his case was assessed against Nosenko's revelation that the naval official in question was a gay man, that he became MI5's primary target. Vassall was arrested in September 1962.

'Nosenko had . . . contributed information which materially aided in the identification and arrest,' according to a CIA investigation. However, because 'Golitsyn had previously provided similar, but less specific information, the usefulness of Nosenko's intelligence was discounted; once Vassall had been identified, it was concluded that Nosenko had been allowed to expose him in order to support his own bona fides. The argument ran that Vassall would in any case have been identified sooner or later on the basis of Golitsyn's leads.'

Vassall was sentenced to eighteen years in prison in October 1962. While MI5 toasted his conviction in Britain, its CIA colleagues were concerned about one of the US agency's spies in Moscow – not Nosenko, but a man whose achievements, many believed, justified the codename he had been given: Hero.

* * *

The street lamps lining one of Moscow's main avenues, Kutuzovsky Prospekt, were unremarkable fixtures that hardly drew attention let alone second glances from passersby. One of them, lamppost 35, had been designated by the CIA for a far greater purpose than it had originally been intended. It was on that street lamp that Hero would occasionally leave a chalk mark, signalling a package ready for collection from a prearranged secret location – a dead drop. He would then notify his handlers about it by dialling a CIA official's apartment number and hanging up after three rings. Along with Hero's two-step communication method, the CIA had implemented yet another verification process.

As a matter of daily routine, Alexis Davison, an air force attaché who also served as a doctor at the US Embassy in Moscow, would travel past lamppost 35 and subtly look for a sign. His mission became more necessary, more urgent even, after Hero went off the radar in early September 1962, leaving the CIA's Moscow station chief, Paul Garbler, questioning whether the asset's sudden absence was because he had come under the suspicion of Soviet authorities. Garbler's fear that Hero had been compromised was shared by one of the agent's handlers, George Kisevalter, who like James Angleton at headquarters, knew that their asset had unusually missed scheduled 'brush pasts' in mid-September to clandestinely hand over secrets.

Not even the potential of a nuclear disaster during the Cuban Missile Crisis in the month that followed had driven

Hero out from whichever bolthole he was in. It made no sense that the agent whose secrets had triggered warning signs in Washington, aiding in its eventual discovery of Soviet missile installations in Cuba, would remain so unreachable during the subsequent standoff between Kennedy and Khrushchev. Or had Hero been intentionally keeping his head down during those thirteen days in October that almost led to a nuclear war between the United States and the Soviet Union? He had, after all, previously expressed suspicions to his handlers that the KGB was on to him.

It was not until Friday 2 November, almost two months after Hero had disappeared, that Davison spotted the chalk mark on the lamppost that everyone had been so desperately awaiting. It accompanied the customary call in the apartment, where the phone rang three times. Given the CIA's nervousness, and with so much at stake, Garbler wanted to reconfirm the chalk mark's presence and drove past the lamppost to see it for himself.

He then instructed Richard C. Jacob, a young CIA officer doubling as an embassy 'archivist' in his official embassy role, what to look for at the dead drop. A matchbox containing a hidden message should be situated behind a hallway radiator of apartment building 5-6 Pushkin Street, Garbler told him. But in the event of an interception, Jacob was to discard the matchbox and at no point be caught with it in his possession.

Mindful of the risks involved, Jacob reached the dead drop successfully, but within seconds, KGB officers pounced on him. He had stumbled into a trap, because unbeknown to the CIA, Hero had been arrested a month earlier by the Soviet agency. On discovering that, Langley concluded that its agent – whose identity it had tried so desperately to protect – had given away his communication methods under duress. Not least because of the KGB's brutal history of beating confessions out of traitors.

The Soviet agency would have been unrelenting in extracting information from Hero, a GRU colonel called Oleg Vladimirovich Penkovsky, who had initiated contact with the CIA and its British counterpart, MI6, about eighteen months earlier.

Through his senior role at the State Committee of Science and Technology, Penkovsky had access to top-secret reports, including missile operating manuals and information relating to Soviet nuclear capabilities. He photographed the material using a miniature camera and then passed on the resulting microfilms, sometimes by way of dead drops. Penkovsky used his official trips overseas, including to Paris and London, to brief his handlers. And while in Moscow, he would perform 'brush pasts' – surreptitiously passing the microfilms to Greville Wynne, a Welsh businessman working as MI6's courier, and to the wife of the British agency's station chief in the capital. On at least one occasion, the Soviet officer concealed the material in a candy box.

Penkovksy's hatred of the Soviet regime and his fear that Khrushchev may trigger a third world war had motivated him to approach the US and British spy agencies. Even if it knew his motives, the KGB would hardly have been sympathetic. Yet the agency's thugs got enough out of him to arrest his contact, Wynne, in Budapest on 2 November; the same day its officers seized Jacob at the dead drop on Pushkin Street. While Jacob managed to use his diplomatic immunity to break free, Wynne and Penkovsky were not so lucky. They had been detained and were awaiting trial.

Yet again James Angleton was plunged into despair. Once more he was forced to reflect on another failure. Less than two years since the agency's most important spy, Pyotr Popov, was captured and killed, the CIA was now facing the prospect of the same outcome in Penkovsky's case. It seemed that with each win, a defeat was awaiting the agency around the corner. Only five days earlier, Kennedy had been able to stare down Khrushchev into a symbolic submission, forcing him to remove the nuclear missile installations from Cuba – thanks in no small part to the intelligence that Penkovsky had provided. But now, with the embers of the Cuban Missile Crisis still glowing, the CIA's asset, its 'Hero', was in the hands of its sworn enemy: the KGB.

* * *

Two days after Oleg Penkovsky's arrest, a far more junior and, at that point, less relevant KGB officer, received his first career boost. Although he shared Penkovsky's first name, this Oleg considered the West his enemy. Anyone outside the KGB's 'Sub-Division 1' in Klaipeda would undoubtedly have been oblivious to Oleg Lyalin's promotion to lieutenant on 4 November 1962. Even those within his orbit – colleagues, friends and acquaintances – most probably celebrated his latest achievement with no more than a few shots of Stolichnaya, his favourite vodka.

However, the promotion, small as it was, indicated upward movement in a career that had once shown promise before taking a sideways turn. The role of lieutenant was a welcome recognition of the operational work he had accomplished in Lithuania's port city since his deployment there in late April. Yet just as his day-to-day work of monitoring foreign seamen had remained the same, Lyalin's personal life continued its turbulence and would result in his divorce from his first wife, Tamara Ivanovna Bondarenko, five months later.

At twenty-five, Lyalin's career appeared to be average at best, and he would have been under no illusions that his dream of a posting to the United States would be revived any time soon, if at all. Nothing in his personnel record at that point could have been construed as a potential future threat for the West, nor a specific problem for Anatoly Golitsyn and James Angleton. Lyalin was as invisible to them as they were to him during that period, but he was part of a Soviet organisation known for throwing up surprises; much like the surprise it had dealt Angleton and his team after its officers took down Penkovsky.

In the autumn of 1962, between awaiting Penkovsky's fate and trying to predict future threats, Angleton was contending with another drawback. His cherished defector, Golitsyn, had become increasingly frustrated that his demands were not being met. Angleton's doting was no longer enough, and nor were the multiple meetings he had helped to organise between the defector and the CIA's boss, John McCone. As for the two discussions that Angleton had engineered between Golitsyn and the president's brother, US Attorney General Robert F. Kennedy – well, they too did not live up to the defector's high expectations.

Golitsyn firmly believed that he deserved greater access, that he needed to express his opinions and warnings about the Soviet threat to the nation's most powerful figures, right through to the president. He could not understand why, for instance, FBI director J. Edgar Hoover had turned down the chance to be graced with his presence. He also remained resentful that President Kennedy would not entertain the idea of inviting him into the White House for a meeting.

Unable to satisfy Golitsyn's stipulations, including his bid for a $10m fund (about $77.5m today) to create his own CIA sub-section to combat Moscow, Angleton and the agency's Soviet division were at a loss. Any thought that he would relent was mistaken because instead of seeing sense, Golitsyn 'went on strike and refused to be debriefed' any further, according to an in-house CIA study. Even after essentially taking him under his own care, partly to offer the agency's Soviet division a respite, Angleton struggled to satisfy Golitsyn.

In December 1962, following yet another dispute with CIA

officials, Golitsyn opted to leave the agency and the United States altogether. He did not need to look far for a new home, merely over the Atlantic where MI5's counter-intelligence director, Martin Furnival Jones, along with other senior British security officials, were still enamoured with the defector's great mind, despite his characteristically puerile antics.

It was a delicate situation for the British officials to navigate. They were aware of how jealously protective James Angleton was of Golitsyn and would not have wanted to be seen as poaching the defector, because the historical ties between MI5 and Langley outweighed the value of having him on board. Angleton was not opposed to Golitsyn's proposed relocation, perhaps hoping that it would help calm him down and eventually bring him to the realisation that the CIA had by and large treated him well. MI5's deputy director general, Graham Mitchell, intervened to ensure that Golitsyn and his family were resettled in England. As a sweetener, MI5 helped the defector obtain a licence for his revolver and even organised a 'quarantine for his Alsatian dog'.

With Golitsyn gone, Popov dead, Nosenko a suspected phoney, and Penkovsky's life in the balance, Angleton would have been forgiven to think – even by his low expectations of defeating the Soviet threat anytime in the foreseeable future – that 1963 would bring a little more fortune. Yet only twenty-three days into the new year, Kim Philby, the former MI6 officer working as a foreign correspondent in Beirut, Lebanon, fled to Moscow – plunging the transatlantic intelligence communities into yet another crisis.

## Chapter 4

# THE BETRAYAL

JAMES ANGLETON WAS CONTENDING with the prospect of two betrayals: one by his former friend, Kim Philby, and another by MI6, which had withheld from him the traitor's confession before his escape. Hoping to make things right, the British agency tasked Nicholas Elliot, who had obtained Philby's confession after confronting him in Beirut in January 1963, to bring Angleton up to speed in a courtesy call. Yet no grovelling apology over the delayed notification was going to appease the CIA spymaster, especially after discovering that MI6 had briefed the FBI about Philby's defection before him.

Ironically, as someone who resented being kept out of the loop, Angleton was a prolific hoarder of secrets whose office vaults contained documents and pictures – including actionable material requiring investigation – which he withheld from everyone. That did not temper his fury during the telephone briefing, however, because he was a man of double standards, an authority of such stature that normal rules would only apply to him if he so decided. Perhaps he was also overcome by emotions over something far deeper and more personal than MI6 informing the FBI before him about Philby's defection. As the phone call came to an end, Angleton would undoubtedly have reflected on his own relationship with Philby, which had been lurking in his mind for twelve years.

The suspicion that had engulfed Philby right after his friends Donald Maclean and Guy Burgess fled to Moscow in 1951 had given Angleton some hope, however small, that the supposedly wiser of the three British officials had not committed the same sin of devoting his soul to the enemy. Although Angleton had severed all contact with him after his loyalty fell into question, he had seen Philby's supporters protest his innocence, not least of all Britain's foreign secretary and future prime minister Harold Macmillan, who exonerated him in Parliament in 1955. But now, with Philby's treachery confirmed, Angleton was torn by regret and self-blame for having failed to see through the man he once deemed a friend, a sounding board – even a mentor.

Flashbacks of his deep conversations with Philby must have been painfully vivid. Highlights of some of those discussions had even been recorded in memos and kept in one of Angleton's vaults. There was no escaping the reality of his time with the turncoat, including their frequent drinking sessions at Harvey's restaurant, one of their hangouts in Washington D.C. Such outings had often followed operational meetings at the CIA's offices, which Philby had 'visited 113 times' between 1949 and 1951 during his time as MI6's US station chief, an in-house CIA study reveals.

Angleton, who at that time was the CIA's liaison to Western counterpart services, met the British officer on at least twenty-two of the visits, most of which had been followed by 'long lunches over cocktails' during which they would likely have discussed the US agency's vulnerabilities, fears and shortcomings relating to the Soviet threat. With Philby's escape behind the Iron Curtain, the authority and respect that Angleton had built over many years risked being compromised. So he quickly snapped into damage limitation mode, determined to defend his reputation as a man of shrewd judgement who could not be outplayed.

MI6 was an obvious target of his vitriol, and an easy one, too. It had accumulated such a humiliating catalogue of intelligence failures in the previous decade or so that it now resembled a dessicated figure of a once formidable espionage body. Angleton vented over its inability to stop its latest traitor from fleeing. Had the British agency learned nothing from its incompetence and mishandling of the Burgess and Maclean cases? The CIA molehunter, who had been outfoxed, wanted everyone to believe otherwise: if he had been in charge, he would have placed Philby under surveillance from the minute he suspected him.

Not only was that disingenuous, but it also conflicted with an agency record in which Angleton had floated the possibility of Philby's innocence rather than his probable guilt. 'The one piece of evidence that does exist is Angleton's observation recorded in 1956 that although Philby may not have been a KGB mole, his close association with Burgess might have resulted in the loss of secrets to the KGB,' a CIA analysis noted. Those who knew Angleton directly or through his work felt that he became even more distrusting and disenchanted following Philby's defection. 'It seems almost certain that the revelation of Kim Philby's duplicity . . . had a profound effect on Angleton and his views of the KGB's capability and his propensity to believe it likely that [the] CIA had also been penetrated at high levels,' according to the analysis.

In some ways, Angleton's anger with the intelligence community across the Atlantic was an exercise in cognitive dissonance.

Not only because of the post-Second World War security ties binding Washington and London, but because he was an anglophile in his formative education and security tendencies. He had attended Malvern College, a private independent school in Worcestershire, in the West Midlands of England. The selective secondary school was a world away from his birthplace in Boise, Idaho, in Northwestern United States, but it meant that he could spend summers with his parents in Italy, where his father ran the American Chamber of Commerce in Rome.

In 1937, on the eve of his twentieth birthday, young Angleton had enrolled as an undergraduate at Yale University where he studied English literature and poetry, eventually serving on the editorial board of its prestigious literary magazine. He then returned to Britain in the early 1940s as an OSS counter-intelligence officer, and while there, he learned about compartmentalising and securing intelligence. He was highly regarded and trusted by British colleagues, cleared to receive raw intercepted German military communications, codenamed ULTRA.

In addition to analysing the decrypts obtained by Bletchley Park's codebreakers, who had broken Berlin's cypher machine, the Enigma, Angleton was also briefed on MI5's Double Cross system, in which Nazi operatives had been recruited and 'turned' to deliver a combination of real and false information to their German controllers.

Those lessons would help shape his thinking on deception, double-agents, and turncoats. They made him more cautious, calculating, and distrusting – qualities that were as necessary as they were justified in Angleton's mind. As the agency's counter-intelligence czar, he believed he was better equipped, more knowing, more competent, and more intellectually capable to deal with certain threats. His impressive counter-intelligence staff of almost 200 people did not reflect the overall influence he had over the CIA. In the eyes of his agency admirers and critics, Angleton 'viewed himself more as chief of an operational entity' than a chief of staff.

His obsessive personality was not selectively applied to spy hunting, however. It seeped into his hobbies of writing poetry, raising orchids and fishing on weekends. In the words of the CIA's historian, Angleton 'surrounded himself and his staff with an aura of mystery, hinting at dark secrets and intrigues too sensitive to share' and he even 'ran vest pocket operations and compiled extensive files that he kept out of the regular Agency records system. He believed the values of Western democracies left them vulnerable to intelligence attack – especially deception – and so he sat on some actionable information if he thought it was unverifiable or counterfeit.'

Angleton had been a different man entirely at the time he had dealt with Philby. It was not that he had been naive, but his job requirements as the agency's liaison officer, essentially managing its interactions with Western agencies, had been to cultivate partnerships rather than to look for moles. He believed that defeating the Soviet threat required close working relationships with partner agencies, including MI6 and MI5, which were built on trust and mutual interest. Trust was paramount in that arrangement, because although Langley's partners looked to it for operational support, including leadership, research and analysis, Angleton believed that 'they must also be confident that we can give a full measure of protection to secrets shared with us'. And while he had been busy protecting secrets, Philby had been feeding them to the enemy.

As Angleton contemplated his future interactions with the British intelligence community after the latest defeat to the KGB, the mood was equally if not more sombre on the other side of the pond, where the realisation of Philby's treachery had exploded like a landmine under Harold Macmillan's feet. It coincided with a spy scandal involving one of the prime minister's own cabinet secretaries, and a secret investigation by MI5 into its own deputy director general, which had been largely inspired and guided by the one and only Anatoly Golitsyn.

\* \* \*

Arthur Martin must have been slightly unnerved when he got into Roger Hollis's car, unsure how to interpret a one-on-one meeting they had held only minutes earlier at Leconfield House, MI5's headquarters in central London. Over the duration of that half-hour briefing, Martin had expected the British agency's director general to make a meaningful comment, or even challenge him, about his claim that the organisation's second-in-command – Hollis's very own number two, Graham Mitchell – was most probably a Soviet spy. But instead, Hollis had sat hunched at his office desk, his face drained of colour and almost expressionless but for a half-smile, as though he had been in a trance.

As MI5's head of Soviet counter-espionage, Martin had been suspicious for some time that whispers from within the British agency were being filtered to the KGB. He believed that someone embedded in the organisation, and likely at quite a senior level, was acting on the orders of their Kremlin controllers to help divert MI5 away from moles in the civil service. What else could explain the widespread treachery over more than two decades and the delays in identifying traitors including Guy Burgess, Donald Maclean, John Vassall, members of the Portland Spy Ring, George Blake – and the latest, Kim Philby? And the majority of such cases had only been uncovered with the help of defectors, including Anatoly Golitsyn.

The KGB's success in penetrating British intelligence had to have been guided from within, Martin felt. His preoccupation with that thought had been solidifying since his promotion to run the agency's Soviet counter-espionage section in January 1960, but it took on a new urgency after Golitsyn's relocation to London, because the defector was determined to help prove that MI5, much like the CIA, was compromised.

During the Leconfield House meeting on the evening of 7 March 1963, Martin had even told Hollis that he feared for Golitsyn's safety in the UK. That stood to reason because it was Graham Mitchell, the man Martin suspected of being the plant within the agency, who had played a pivotal role in recommending the relocation of Golitsyn and his family to Britain. What if that in itself was part of a bigger play that Mitchell was plotting? But having laid out his theory about Mitchell, and the unprecedented internal security risk facing MI5, Martin had received barely any feedback from Hollis except a proverbial pat on the back for raising the issue and an assurance that he would mull it over.

It was a strange reaction that Martin could not absorb, and so during the short drive to the Travellers Club, the gentlemen's club on Pall Mall where Hollis had invited him for dinner that evening, Martin quipped that he admired the director general's apparent calmness given the magnitude of the problem on MI5's hands. It was only then that Hollis snapped out of his pensive mode, immediately reassuring Martin that he was taking the allegation very seriously – and he did, as demonstrated five days later when he authorised a low profile probe into Mitchell's background.

The probe vindicated Martin's intuition but was also a huge coup in Golitsyn's favour, proving once again his sway over matters of counter-intelligence on both sides of the Atlantic. The defector's influence over Martin and other senior MI5 officials enabled him to gain almost unfettered access to the British agency's files, including raw and speculative intelligence, which in some cases contained uncorroborated allegations against people. The Soviet defector was being treated like counter-intelligence royalty, and was being paid thousands of pounds a month, by some estimates, for his analysis and brainstorming.

Along with having a front-row seat as the agency launched its investigation into Mitchell, Golitsyn was even given the honour of selecting a codename for it – PETERS – which had once been the defector's own codename. Much like the investigation that he had inspired into 'Sasha' at the CIA, Golitsyn was now largely responsible for placing Mitchell's life under a microscope. MI5's deputy director general was followed home from work every evening by a team of watchers, and a closed-circuit television camera was fitted through a pinhole in his office wall to keep him under visual and audio observation whenever he was at his desk. Everything about him started to appear suspicious, right down to his tic of muttering to himself when he was alone in the office, a supposedly safe space that MI5 investigators also searched numerous times in his absence.

In the spring of 1963, the Mitchell case was becoming of such great concern that Hollis briefed Harold Macmillan about it on three occasions. It was yet another disaster that the prime minister had to endure, on top of the embarrassment surrounding Philby's defection and a controversy embroiling his secretary of state for war, John Profumo, over lying about his affair with a woman romantically linked to a Soviet intelligence officer. The spy scandals deepening Macmillan's political trauma were compounded even further after the loss of Oleg Penkovsky, one of the greatest MI6 and CIA Cold War assets, who was put on trial in Moscow that spring and subsequently executed.

So it was unsurprising that the British prime minister was horrified about the allegation against MI5's deputy chief, even though it had not yet become public and was known by only two other government cabinet members, including Foreign Secretary Alec Douglas-Home. The flurry of espionage disasters left Macmillan fighting for his political survival. Yet even then, he had the good sense to ensure that Britain's closest ally was informed about the internal menace dogging his nation's security service.

Shortly before the 'Profumo Affair' saga, which had already claimed the career of Macmillan's war secretary and was soon to force the man himself out of office, the prime minister authorised Hollis to travel to Washington D.C. to brief the CIA and FBI about MI5's investigation into Mitchell. It would have been reasonable for Hollis to think that officials there would be equally astounded, given their long-held views about the Soviet threat. But they were not. In fact, they were sceptical that Mitchell could be a culprit because he was fully briefed on ongoing American and joint US–UK operations, which they felt he would surely have compromised had he been under the Kremlin's control. Nevertheless, the case against Mitchell was briefed up the US chain of command, all the way to President Kennedy.

The heat surrounding Mitchell provided Golitsyn's theory of an insider threat the sort of lifeline that another of his tip-offs desperately needed but was now lacking. Despite more than a year-long investigation into his allegation that Peter Karlow was 'Sasha', the FBI was forced to drop the case after finding no supporting evidence against the CIA official. Naturally the absence of evidence was a major setback, but it did not hamper Golitsyn's determination to uncover who else could fit the Sasha mould at the CIA, and nor did it stop James Angleton from maintaining his suspicion about Karlow.

'Reportedly at the urging of Angleton,' an in-house agency study later found, 'the decision was made to pressure Karlow to resign, which he did.' The timing of Karlow's resignation in July 1963 coincided with Golitsyn's return to the US that month. Perhaps predictably, Golitsyn had eventually fallen out with MI5, the trigger being the agency's failure to kill a story in the British press exposing his presence in the country. The *Daily Telegraph* article, resulting from a tip-off via its Washington bureau, had incorrectly named the defector 'Dolitsyn'. It was later suspected to have been leaked with Angleton's blessing, because he wanted his man back in the US, focused on CIA moles rather than MI5 ones.

Along with a CIA welcome-home bonus of $200,000, Golitsyn was given more freedom to be a part of, but apart from, the agency, and he elected to live in New York instead of Washington D.C. to 'have more privacy and separation from the CIA'. Long gone was the bureaucratic resistance with which he had at times been met during his initial stint at the agency. Now, Golitsyn's theories were being embraced with unquestioning enthusiasm and even an overwhelming deference inspired by the agency's counter-intelligence chief.

With Angleton's authorisation, Golitsyn was given access to the organisation's personnel records to identify potentially shady patterns in staff profiles that, in his judgement, corresponded with the attributes of the mole-at-large – Sasha. It was a slow burner but one that he relished, and it bestowed him with the air of authority that he so craved. 'Golitsyn also began to insist that he be accepted as an equal by CIA and FBI, not as a Soviet defector, and be given full access to appropriate CIA and FBI files to uncover high-level KGB penetrations of the US government and other Western intelligence services,' according to an agency record.

He demanded 'total access to relevant materials – i.e., personnel and operation files' to 'apply his KGB background and experience to analyse these materials'. Golitsyn wanted to 'combine his analysis with what the CIA or other Western intelligence services knew about the KGB and its operation . . . [and] provide his analysis and recommendations for action'. The defector's ambition of creating his own CIA sub-section to combat the Kremlin threat, which had been turned down by the agency's Soviet division in 1962, was set to inspire another investigative format that would sate Golitsyn's ego, bring him closer to the FBI, and deepen the hunt for Sasha.

Indeed, a breakthrough relating to the mysterious Sasha appeared to emerge in early 1964 in a place far from Langley, courtesy of a Soviet official who was also eager to provide insights into what was fast becoming a defining moment of US twentieth-century history – the assassination of John F. Kennedy. With the country still mourning the president's death in November of the previous year, the FBI and CIA were desperate for any details that could illuminate the events leading up to the shock assassination.

\* \* \*

In January 1964, Yuri Nosenko was again in Geneva on official duty as a security officer to monitor delegates involved in another series of disarmament talks. He organised to meet his two CIA case officers, Pete Bagley and George Kisevalter, and much like eighteen months earlier when he first came into contact with the two American officials, Nosenko arrived at a safe house in the Swiss city bearing KGB secrets. It was at a different location to the one in which he had previously met them, but the Scotch whisky was still in the same place – in a glass, on ice, and in hand.

He seemed upbeat, thrilled to see the pair whom he regarded as confidants, and eager to inform them about his new mission. He was hoping for a change, a break from serving his KGB bosses, and the chance to escape the mundanity of domestic life. Pete Bagley and George Kisevalter were caught off guard to learn about Nosenko's proposed new mission, not because they secretly suspected him of being a deception agent, but unexpectedly he wanted to defect to the United States without his family.

His intention to abandon his wife and children, including young Oksana, whom Bagley and Kisevalter helped provide life-saving medication for in 1962, seemed as callous as it was calculated. Yet the KGB officer talked about it as casually as he would later discuss a job promotion, even assuring his hosts that his loved ones would be 'okay' without him. This assurance puzzled the two Americans, because they knew that the Kremlin typically prevented family members left behind from ever reuniting with a Soviet turncoat and generally made their lives difficult, deeming them traitors-by-association.

Instead of openly passing judgement, Bagley and Kisevalter wanted Nosenko's disclosures to keep coming, hoping that his dissatisfaction with his new role as deputy chief of the KGB's Tourist Department, which had inspired his search for a new life, would result in some major intelligence breakthroughs for the CIA. It was their chance to 'learn from him the details of his mission and its relation to possible penetrations of the US intelligence and security agencies', a CIA assessment of the meeting later revealed. 'Ideally our interest would be best served if Subject [Nosenko] were broken as early as possible but . . . our actions must be conceived and carried out in a manner which contributes to our basic goal without alerting Subject unduly at any stage'.

By giving Nosenko the impression that they believed him and were willing to entertain his request for defection, the Americans encouraged the Soviet official to divulge new secrets. First, he revealed his knowledge of past interactions between the KGB and Lee Harvey Oswald, who two months earlier had been charged with the assassination of President Kennedy. Nosenko would have been keenly aware that nothing would be of greater interest to the CIA than information about the shooting, which had traumatised the United States and damaged the reputation of its intelligence and law enforcement agencies for failing to protect the president.

Unlike the previous tips Nosenko had provided, which were predominantly second-hand, he told Bagley and Kisevalter that he had personally reviewed the KGB's entire file on Oswald – from the US Marine veteran's first stay in the Soviet Union in the late 1950s to his attempted return there in September 1963. He said the KGB had deemed Oswald mentally unstable, partly because the former Marine had tried to kill himself when the Soviet Union initially rejected his attempt to defect there in 1959. But more to the point, Nosenko dismissed suggestions which had been circulating since Kennedy's death that Oswald may have pulled the trigger on Moscow's orders, assuring them that there was no truth in that.

In between disclosing other secrets and pouring a fresh drink, Nosenko said the KGB had recruited a US army captain in Germany and codenamed him Sasha. He had no more details about the case, somehow forgetting when or even how he had heard about it. Nor did he remember that Bagley and Kisevalter had asked him about a 'Sasha' during the debriefings in Geneva in the summer of 1962.

Nosenko's new revelations were suddenly raising more questions than they were answering, but his CIA hosts wanted to buy time, asking him to continue with his delegation duties until they had sought feedback from Langley about his proposed defection. They wanted to play him like they felt he had been playing them, to reel him in with the promise of a 'solid career with a certain personal independence' that awaited him should he go through with the defection. 'Because of the very great assistance you've been to us already and because of this desire to give you a backing,' he was told, the CIA 'will give you a little additional personal security' by way of a salary.

With so many doubts at CIA headquarters about Nosenko's claims and perceived motives, Bagley and Kisevalter did not consider him an ideal candidate for defection. They figured he would be more useful remaining a conduit of information from inside the KGB, if only to get a better understanding of how the Soviet agency may have been trying to use him to mislead the CIA. However, Nosenko was adamant that he wanted to flee the Soviet Union, and on Tuesday 4 February 1964, he reappeared at the CIA safe house looking distressed and convinced that his contact with the Americans had been compromised. His fears, he said, followed a cable sent to the Soviet Embassy in Geneva demanding his return to Moscow. Langley could not overlook the development, and although it agreed to his defection request, it was unsure whether to relocate him to the US or another country.

Nonetheless, Bagley and Kisevalter disguised Nosenko in an American officer's uniform and smuggled him out of Geneva in a car to a CIA facility in Frankfurt, West Germany, where he underwent further interrogation. Still convinced that he was a 'dispatched defector', the CIA flew him to the US on 12 February and took him to a safe house near the capital. As agency officials developed ways to force a confession from Nosenko, who was deemed by one of his case officers to be a 'small-time con-man', the CIA's other defector, Anatoly Golitsyn, retained his stardust in the eyes of James Angleton and Co, and continued to theorise with impunity.

Golitsyn's wish of being treated as an equal by agency officials was truly coming to fruition, to the point that he was even provided with 'full access to the Nosenko material', including interrogation transcripts, biographical data, and information surrounding the initial approach he had made to the CIA in Geneva. After combing through the files for four months, Golitsyn met with Angleton and two other senior officials to divulge his findings. 'I would like now to make known my conclusions,' he said during the meeting on 29 June 1964. 'He is a provocateur who is on a mission for the KGB ... to mislead.' Golitsyn's revelation was very much in line with Angleton's thinking, convincing the counter-intelligence chief that his own judgement about Nosenko had been correct all along.

While Nosenko maintained his innocence during a series of interrogations, insisting that he had not been 'sent', some aspects of his story eventually fell apart. He confessed to lying about his rank, saying that on his first encounter with the CIA in Geneva, he had inflated his seniority to be taken more seriously, describing himself as a major when he had in fact been a captain. He also revealed another lie from that first debriefing. The 800 francs he had requested to settle the money he claimed to have embezzled was merely a ruse he concocted amid concerns, ironically, that an offer to provide information for free may not have been taken seriously by the CIA.

Nosenko's confessions were yet another huge coup for Angleton and Golitsyn, providing the apparent evidence they had long hoped for – that the KGB was indeed dispatching deception agents. While Golitsyn had yet to deliver on the elusive 'Sasha', that did not matter so much, because he had apparently struck gold again in identifying Nosenko as an imposter. Golitsyn's assessment further strengthened the confidence in his work, both at the CIA where he was producing results to Angleton's satisfaction, and at MI5, where the investigation he helped launch into the agency's deputy director general was in full steam.

It was becoming difficult to bet against Golitsyn, and an earlier lead he had given MI5 – about the KGB's ambition to install a mouthpiece at the helm of British politics – was suddenly re-energised in late 1964. By then, Harold Macmillan's resignation as prime minister at the height of the Profumo Affair spy scandal had left his Conservative party on shaky ground, and attention was turning to the newly appointed opposition leader, Harold Wilson, as the man who could unseat the Tory government.

The defector claimed the KGB had engineered Wilson's appointment as Labour Party leader in February 1963 following the death of the previous party leader Hugh Gaitskell. He also insinuated that the Soviet agency may have been responsible for 'killing' Gaitskell – even though Lupus Erythematosus, an autoimmune disease that attacks the immune system, was the recorded cause of his death.

Golitsyn based his hunch on his past interactions with the KGB's 13th Department, which specialised in assassinations. The department excelled in using 'poison rather than guns or explosives,' according to the CIA, 'because murders can be accomplished more surreptitiously in this manner and in some instances without leaving easily recognisable traces of foul play.' Golitsyn had heard of the 13th Department's ambitious plan to kill a high-profile political figure in Europe and fill their place with a Kremlin stooge.

Although unaware of which country it planned to target, Golitsyn said Britain seemed like a plausible setting because the department's chief, General Nicolai Rodin, had served in London as the KGB's rezident in the 1950s and had been responsible for handling British spies, including the Admiralty's John Vassall and MI6's George Blake. Golitsyn's lead was admittedly more of a loaded gun than a smoking gun, but it was far too important for MI5 to sleep on. In a step toward developing it, an agency official contacted James Angleton for advice.

The CIA molehunter eventually reported back with a clue from a Soviet scientific journal that had revealed the result of a chemical experiment in which lab rats were successfully induced with lupus. It seemed somewhat circumstantial, because the chemical had only worked when it was delivered regularly and in large doses, so it was unlikely to have been the cause of Gaitskell's death – unless he had been subjected to repeated poisoning attempts, which he had not. Still, MI5 did not totally dismiss the chemical assassination theory, because the science experiment cited had been conducted seven years earlier, raising questions about whether Moscow had persisted in developing the chemical to produce the same results in smaller doses and through a single shot.

Complicating MI5's questions about Gaitskell's death was Harold Wilson's entry into Downing Street in mid-October 1964. It is unknown whether Golitsyn had been aware that MI5 had already had its own concerns about Wilson when he made the allegation against the Labour leader the previous year. In fact, the British security service had taken an initial interest in Wilson almost two decades earlier, shortly after he had become a Member of Parliament in 1945 and then quickly been promoted a couple of years later to run the Board of Trade in Clement Attlee's government. At thirty-one, he had been the youngest member of the British cabinet and an apparent rising star, drawing attention from the Communist Party of Great Britain.

When MI5 picked up chatter from Communist civil servants about the apparent similarity between Wilson's political mindset and theirs, the agency opened a file on him. From then on, Wilson, or Norman John Worthington as MI5 codenamed him, was on the security service's radar. But although Gaitskell had provided the British agency with a list of sixteen suspected Communist MPs in his party shortly after he had become leader in 1961, Wilson's name had not been among them. It was one thing for MI5 to have had concerns about Wilson as a young cabinet member, but for the British security service to be actively questioning the loyalty of a sitting prime minister was unprecedented.

That sensitivity would not have been lost on the CIA, but Angleton's attitude towards it was typically more aggressive. His concerns were heightened after Golitsyn informed him and the agency's chief, John McCone, in no uncertain terms that Britain's new prime minister was a KGB spy. 'Golitsyn told the DCI [McCone] that British prime minister Harold Wilson was a KGB agent', a partially redacted in-house CIA journal reveals. Angleton was spooked by the prospect that the leader of the US's most important political ally could be a Kremlin asset. So much so that he travelled to London to inform MI5 officials about it in person, illustrating the delicacy and magnitude of the perceived security threat and the trust he had placed in Golitsyn's information.

Although a little sceptical about Angleton's tip-off, MI5's Martin Furnival Jones was familiar enough with the KGB's modus operandi to know that recruiting a senior politician with a promising career was among its highest operational objectives. 'If Russian intelligence can recruit a backbench Member of Parliament and he continues to hold his seat for a number of years and climbs the ladder to a ministerial position, it is obvious the spy is home and dry,' Furnival Jones would later declare while commenting on Moscow's targeting techniques.

But to justify a probe into the prime minister's alleged KGB ties required evidence far beyond generic insights and supposition. And while Angleton claimed to have the evidence against Wilson, he wanted to disclose the information on his own terms. The CIA official refused to reveal his source – later revealed to be Golitsyn - and insisted that he would only provide the evidence if MI5 assured him that it would keep it to itself and not tell anyone in the Labour government. British agency officials objected to his ultimatum, especially since evidence of that nature would require immediate investigation as a matter of national priority.

The other challenge MI5 faced was that Wilson, shortly after his ascension to office, had expressed concerns that the agency spied on members of parliaments. At one point even Wilson suspected that MI5 had monitored his own communications before he entered Downing Street. The prime minister eventually banned the agency from eavesdropping on parliamentarians or snooping on their mail – in what became known as the 'Wilson Doctrine'.

MI5 was in a bind. While Angleton's proclaimed 'evidence' against Wilson was a prerequisite for a meaningful investigation, the CIA molehunter withheld the supposedly incriminating material because the British agency rejected his stipulation about how it should be handled. With some frustration, Angleton left London and returned to Langley, where the atmosphere around security breaches became even more intense. Golitsyn finally convinced the CIA and FBI to form a joint investigation into the 'Sasha' scare. Much like he had been honoured by the British two years earlier in selecting the codename for MI5's investigation into its deputy director general, Golitsyn's ego was stroked by the coded portmanteau chosen for the joint FBI and CIA investigation – HONETOL – combining letters from J. Edgar Hoover's last name and Golitsyn's first name.

'HONETOL was formed in November 1964 to work on Golitsyn's assertion that at least five and possibly as many as thirty Agency officers or contractors were Soviet penetrations,' an in-house CIA study notes. 'Golitsyn insisted that Hoover participate directly in the task force, but the [FBI] director refused. Instead a senior FBI officer and Angleton were the most senior representatives. The five people Golitsyn had specifically named as KGB moles became the prime subjects of the HONETOL investigations.'

Among those named was Richard Kovich, a CIA counter-intelligence veteran in the Soviet Russia division, who had helped run the agency's prized asset, Pyotr Popov, in the 1950s. Golitsyn had closely reviewed Kovich's personnel file and found that the US-born officer, who had worked at the CIA for fourteen years, was the son of Serbian immigrants, born Dushan Kovacevich. Clearly a Slavic name. Igor Orlov, a CIA contractor, was another suspect. Under the name of Aleksandr Kopatskiy, Orlov worked for the agency in Germany in the 1950s against Russian émigrés. 'Sasha is a common nickname for Aleksandr, and the last name Kopatskiy fit Golitsyn's original description of the agent's surname,' said the CIA study.

As the HONETOL operation started sweeping up evidence against suspected CIA officials, a KGB officer almost 4,000 miles away was still entrenched in the mundane activity of monitoring foreign seamen travelling in and out of Lithuania's port of Klaipeda. Oleg Lyalin seemed to be going through the motions on the work front in a seemingly unremarkable fashion, occasionally getting the same recognition that thousands of other Soviet service personnel received, such as a medal he received in May 1965 to commemorate the twentieth anniversary of his nation's 'victory in the great patriotic war'. However, on a personal level, his life had taken a remarkable turn – one that would soon reshape his career prospects.

\* \* \*

On paper, at least, Oleg Lyalin was coming of age. His first marriage to Tamara Ivanovna Bondarenko had ended in divorce in April 1963, but he did not seem to dwell long, as his love for a new woman was blossoming. There were similarities between her and his first wife: both had the same first name – Tamara – and both were in their late twenties, and were charmed into marrying him. Two years after tying the knot with the second Tamara, the couple welcomed their firstborn, naming him Alexander in honour of her father and Lyalin's half-brother, who died in battle during the Second World War. Lyalin's home life had never been better. And his work life, though not quite as he imagined it would be, was also flourishing like never before.

Whether by design or default, Klaipeda would turn around his career fortunes, becoming the setting for yet another promotion in late 1965. Lyalin was made senior lieutenant on 17 December, putting him on course for a second chance at the work life he had missed out on five years earlier: operating on the KGB's orders in the West. The KGB's 'special action' taskforce, Department V, which specialised in the art of abduction, sabotage and assassination, took an interest in him.

The selection process would undoubtedly have assessed his operational and personality traits against the kind of mission Department V chiefs had in mind for him. He met the criteria, and in February 1967, Lyalin bade farewell to Klaipeda and made his way back to Russia to await his training. The training centre in Golitsyno, west of Moscow, was run by Department V, which had been created in October 1966 to replace the KGB's 13th Department, the very unit Anatoly Golitsyn had warned MI5 about five years earlier in connection to Hugh Gaitskell's death.

There was no ambiguity about the type of executive action that the 13th Department had been set up to pursue during the interwar years. It had been Stalin's very own hit squad, created in December 1936 for 'terror purposes', according to a CIA study into its operational background. At first, it was based within the NKVD, a forerunner to the KGB, eventually evolving to conduct missions that included political murders and kidnappings.

The department's 'principal enemy' was the United States, with Britain as a close second. 'Secrecy about the work of this department is maintained through the careful selection and training of its personnel; its officers do not discuss their experience among others; department documents are not circulated,' the study reveals. The training its operatives underwent, including in the use of 'small arms, jujitsu, code, wireless, driving, surveillance', had been developed and perfected by its successor organisation, Department V, which became known notoriously as the 'wet affairs' department for its proficiency in 'liquidating' targets.

Among its top priorities was the targeting of defectors. 'The Soviets have gone to great lengths in the past to silence their intelligence officers who have defected,' the CIA study noted, as evidenced by the unexplained 'suicide' of military intelligence official Walter Krivitsky, who had defected to the US shortly before the Second World War, alerting the FBI and MI5 to Kremlin spies. Krivitsky was suspected to have been killed by the NKVD when he was found in a hotel room in Washington D.C. in February 1941 with a single bullet in the head, and three suicide notes by his bedside.

On Wednesday 1 March 1967, as Lyalin checked in to the Department V centre in Golitsyno to begin his intensive training, he had been affiliated with the KGB for eleven years. But if he ever had any reservations about committing sabotage or murder for the sake of the motherland, he was about to be brainwashed out of them.

## Chapter 5

# THE EXPORT AGENCY

TO BE AMONG THE elite, the most carefully selected KGB officers, must have filled Oleg Lyalin with personal satisfaction and validation each time he set off on a practical training assignment. His enrolment at Department V's academy did not guarantee a high-flying career, but it did guarantee the chance for one.

He had already once failed to fulfil his superiors' expectations of him, and having tasted the resulting personal regret and professional regression, Lyalin must have been determined to clinch a far better outcome this time around, particularly now with a young family to support. And to enjoy the ride as well, because if there had ever been an adventure park tailored for adrenaline junkies with a bent for sabotaging the West, he was now through its front gates; surrounded by endless activities in which to immerse himself, including lessons in bomb-making and parachuting into enemy territory.

Lyalin's new adventure was driven by a singular purpose.

Whether he was in the field or at his desk, he was furthering his understanding of breaking Soviet enemy nations through the penetration and ultimate destruction of their central nervous system: their critical national infrastructure, ranging from their food supply warehouses to their electricity grids.

On some of the practical missions he was assigned, Lyalin joined a group of six students to break into a simulated 'factory, rocket base, power station or something similar', as he would later explain. 'The group would have to locate and identify the target, give a full description, including plans, details of security measures and how entry might be affected, and an assessment of its value as a target.' In another exercise, for which he was selected to lead a group of students, they 'blew up a bridge', presumably in preparation for future missions to destroy overpasses used by enemy armies.

There was a lot to take in during his course, right down to recruiting foot soldiers; men and women willing to put their lives on the line for Moscow. He learned all about 'partisan warfare, including organising a small army from a small group, and how to maintain security and prevent penetration by the local secret services of army intelligence,' a document outlining Lyalin's training reveals. He was taken through the intricacies of assembling and handling explosives, or the 'basic principles and precautions', as he described them, but felt that bomb-making was as easy to forget as it was to learn. 'Because everybody understands that, as soon as you leave the school you will forget about it, but it won't take you that long to renew it again.'

In September 1967, on completing his six-month course, Lyalin understood how to spread fear and panic in enemy territory. He was alert to the common vulnerabilities in a country's national infrastructure, including its train stations, government buildings, and military bases.

When he returned to Klaipeda later that autumn as a fully-fledged sleeper to await Department V's deployment orders, civil unrest a few hundred miles away in Czechoslovakia had gathered momentum, threatening the Communist model that had ruled the country for almost two decades. Young Czechs, led by students fed up with Soviet rule and their country's economic decline, demanded widespread reforms including freedom of expression and self-determination.

Their voices evoked the spirit of the Hungarian Uprising of eleven years earlier, in which revolutionaries called for free elections and the withdrawal of Soviet troops. That had not ended well for the Hungarians, when the Red Army invaded in November 1956 and crushed the rebellion. Yet amid the deadly clashes, Yuri Andropov, the Soviet ambassador in Budapest who had advised Moscow's defence leaders on the ground, revelled in the military incursion, which killed more than 2,500 Hungarians.

In the decade that followed, Andropov sought to make a greater contribution in suppressing Czechoslovakians through his new role as KGB chief. Claiming that dissent in the country was the result of subversive Western activities, Andropov urged Soviet leader Leonid Brezhnev in early 1968 to approve a military invasion to stamp out what became known as 'The Prague Spring'. Andropov also took proactive measures by authorising a counter-intelligence mission, Operation Progress, in which KGB 'illegals' posing as Western journalists, tourists or students, were deployed to the Czech capital to penetrate, disrupt and discredit revolutionary groups.

Some of the illegals posed as British, Austrian or West German, and there were plans for another ostensible Westerner to join them sometime later. 'On 2nd May 1968, Lyalin was sent to Moscow and instructed to prepare himself for his mission to Czechoslovakia posing as an American tourist of American origin,' an intelligence file outlining his proposed assignment reveals. 'This mission did not materialise as the situation in Czechoslovakia was brought under control and Lyalin returned to Klaipeda.'

It was an unexpected setback: his mission fell victim to the Soviet invasion of Czechoslovakia in August of that year, but he only had to wait three months for his next opportunity. And when it did, Lyalin was again recalled to Moscow to prepare for the new assignment, which promised to be the crowning promotion of his twelve-year affiliation with the KGB.

While his two previous assignments with the illegals department had never materialised, this new assignment appeared to be a sure thing, yet one that required further training to perfect the cover role that was being created for him. He was to become a fashion connoisseur to help sate the Soviet Union's growing infatuation with Western clothing brands; a credible businessman specialising in the export and import of 'knitwear'. The cover was engineered to appear low-key, and was intended to exploit his English language skills. It would give him an officially declared role within a Soviet Union trade delegation to supplement his undercover work for the KGB.

Lyalin's makeover into one-part saboteur, one-part fashionista fast-tracked him through the meeting rooms of the state machine to acquaint him with business affairs, including 'instructions from the Foreign Trade [ministry] for his cover position', and he was eventually introduced to most of the KGB's departments in Lubyanka, the agency's headquarters in Moscow.

By the end of his training, Lyalin was expected to return to a country that he had visited briefly eleven years earlier as part of his maritime college's 'goodwill' tour of Western ports – the United Kingdom. Lyalin had some idea of what to expect of its climate, culture and people, and would come to discover through his research that a few things had changed about the country since 1957, including the political persuasion of its government, which was now under the Labour Party. The Kremlin deemed Labour to be less hostile towards Moscow than its political rivals, the Conservatives. But despite that, MI5 had stepped up its suspicion of the KGB because of its fears of Soviet moles in its ranks.

With no diplomatic immunity to hide behind, Lyalin realised that he could be arrested for espionage if his cover were ever blown, potentially imprisoned, or at the very least, become the cause of a diplomatic showdown between London and Moscow. Also aware that MI5 officers would run a background check on his visa application, he waited in hope for his paperwork to be approved. Once he had that, it would be a gateway to a fresh adventure.

Overcoming visa restrictions was one of the KGB's major operational challenges at the time. The anti-Soviet mood in the West, heightened by Moscow's crushing of the Prague Spring, had further reinforced MI5's attempts to hamper Soviet spying in Britain. Another major factor in the British agency's thinking was the fact that there had been a 700 per cent increase in the number of Kremlin intelligence officers in London over two decades – and that only accounted for those who were known to MI5.

'The identified intelligence personnel rose from 15 in 1950 to 120 in 1970,' noted a US government security briefing into the espionage phenomenon plaguing Britain. But even that figure would prove to be an underestimation. 'The number of intelligence officers was far in excess of the number which the resources of [MI5] permitted to investigate.'

Through the 1960s, as MI5 increasingly grappled with Kremlin espionage, including investigations into some of its own current and former members of staff, the agency tried to limit the Soviet Embassy's head count. Moscow countered the restrictions by inflating the 'number of working wives as well as the numbers in other organisations' with representation in the UK, including its national airline Aeroflot and the Moscow Narodny Bank, which were suspected of providing cover roles for intelligence operatives.

It was accepted wisdom within MI5, and more generally among Western intelligence agencies, that between 30 and 50 per cent of Soviets operating out of Western-based embassies, consulates and trade delegations were involved in espionage in some way or another. And even that did not represent the full scale of the West's security burden, because the USSR also outsourced its spying to Eastern bloc partners, including Hungarian, Bulgarian, East German and other satellite embassies and their respective trade bodies.

'Communist companies abroad provide an opportunity for Communist penetration of society,' a CIA examination into the Kremlin's foreign commercial ventures revealed. 'For example, the covert transfer of funds from Moscow to local Communist businesses for transfer to national Communist parties or front organisations represents a means of direct control of Communist "active measures" [such as espionage and sabotage] abroad.' So with Western intelligence agencies, including MI5, already highly suspicious of Soviet diplomatic and commercial missions, Lyalin's assignment needed to overcome vetting obstacles from the get go.

In the autumn of 1968, as Lyalin continued preparing for his deployment to the UK, the transatlantic intelligence community was still tangled in a series of investigations into insider threats, which had been predominantly instigated by Anatoly Golitsyn's leads. In the ensuing fallout, a landscape of paranoia was being established. Now, a few questions surrounding Golitsyn's analysis were beginning to emerge, and perhaps a few too many for his liking. 'Sasha' remained invisible, a spectre still haunting James Angleton.

The case against Yuri Nosenko, which only a few years earlier had concluded that he was a false defector, now appeared far less certain. And MI5's investigation into its former deputy director general, which was ultimately expanded to engulf the agency's former chief himself, produced far too much smoke with no apparent fire.

\* \* \*

Almost a decade had passed since the loss of the CIA's super-spy, Pyotr Popov, whose capture and execution sent Langley on the path of heightened alertness for enemies within. But James Angleton was still unable to find the culprits who had compromised Popov. Even with Anatoly Golitsyn's seemingly invaluable insights throughout the 1960s, and the expanding list of CIA suspects that the defector had identified, Angleton failed to satisfy his central counter-intelligence objective – finding the moles. None of the five CIA officers who had been the 'primary subjects' of the agency's joint HONETOL operation with the FBI had left any fingerprints proving their alleged treachery. Of course, there was some seemingly 'circumstantial' evidence that Angleton weaponised to drive the five suspects out of the agency, but that was not what he was after. He wanted hard and indisputable evidence that would see them locked up, preferably in isolation and for the rest of their lives for daring to betray their country.

It would have been well within his scope of reasoning to deem HONETOL's conclusions as unsatisfactory, and to raise questions about them, too. Had the case against the CIA suspects been intentionally hampered by J. Edgar Hoover's men, the

FBI officers appointed to HONETOL, to discredit Golitsyn's analysis and recommendations? Angleton must have been suspicious that the FBI did not share his, nor Golitsyn's, passion and determination for rooting out the CIA moles. Perhaps in Angleton's mind that also went some way to explaining why Hoover's men pulled the pin altogether on HONETOL in February 1965 – a mere three months into the joint mission – and left him to run it as his own 'internal' project.

Was their decision genuinely the result of an absence of evidence as they had claimed? And if so, how could they not see it the way Angleton did: the absence of evidence was merely an indication of how well the KGB had penetrated his agency? The FBI's conclusion in the Sasha saga was not dissimilar to its view about Yuri Nosenko. It completely contrasted with Angleton's findings.

Somehow, and in a way that Angleton could neither relate to nor understand, the FBI had become convinced that Nosenko was a genuine defector within days of his arrival in the United States in early 1964. By essentially dismissing the CIA's suspicions of him, the FBI had presented Angleton with a 'serious problem', because Langley's lead molehunter had already drawn up an action plan to deal with the defector, 'which would not be appropriate if CIA were forced, as a result of inter-agency consultations, to treat Nosenko as a bona fide defector'.

As extensive as it was aggressive, the plan included efforts to 'break him' under interrogation and publicly discredit him through a press briefing that would characterise Nosenko as a pawn in a KGB operation, orchestrated by the Soviet agency 'as an act of desperation following a decade of deception and disloyalty to the regime on the part of a score of senior Soviet intelligence officers'. There was no way that Angleton and his acolytes were going to allow the FBI's positive opinion of Nosenko to jeopardise their tough measures against him.

Perhaps to the FBI's surprise, the CIA's interrogations appeared to bear fruit in late 1964 after Nosenko was found to have 'shown in the present sessions and over the past months that he is unable to support his legend', or his suspected cover story. But that was still not enough. It fell short of the evidence Angleton wanted from Nosenko – an admission that he had been 'dispatched by the KGB'. Having held him as a 'virtual prisoner' in a safe house in Clinton, Maryland, south of Washington D.C., since shortly after his arrival in the country, the CIA relocated Nosenko in August 1965 into a purpose-built 'jail' at an agency training site in Williamsburg, Virginia, where he was 'literally confined in a cell behind bars with nothing but a cot'.

The new detention facility, codenamed Loblolly, had been 'designed and staffed with the intention of engendering in Nosenko a feeling of hopelessness, from which the only escape would be through confession that he was a KGB agent and revelation of the full details of how he had been briefed and dispatched by the Soviet authorities. With the exception of being allowed certain books, carefully selected for him by the Covert Action Staff of SR [Soviet Russia] Division, Nosenko was confined under conditions which were as close to stimulus-free as was consistent with maintaining him in good physical health.'

Within a month of his detention at Loblolly, Nosenko was stripped of privileges, including books, and each time he was deemed uncooperative, 'soap, towel and toothbrush were temporarily denied him'. As his mental and physical condition deteriorated, and he started hearing 'voices emanating from various objects, such as his shoes and his spoon', a CIA medical assessment dismissed his psychological decline, saying that 'if Nosenko actually does hear voices, it could normally be expected that they would speak to him in his native language, rather than in English as he told the base medical technician'. On one hand, the CIA regarded Nosenko's complaints as 'contrived', and on the other, 'hopeful signs that the isolation is beginning to have an effect'.

The setting to which he had been confined, combined with the hours of relentless interrogations and repeated accusations of lying, ground Nosenko down by autumn of 1966. He admitted that he had lied to Pete Bagley and George Kisevalter about the telegram recalling him to Moscow from Geneva in 1964. 'On 4 February 1964, I told my CIA contact in Geneva that a telegram from Headquarters in Moscow had been received in the KGB residency in Geneva recalling me immediately to Moscow,' Nosenko confessed to his interrogators in October 1966. 'No such telegram ever existed. No telegram was received in Geneva. I admit that the story was a lie. I myself invented this telegram in order to hasten my defection.'

That admission had significantly strengthened Angleton's case against Nosenko, but despite that and his confession to other lies, Angleton was still unable to convince the FBI that he was a false defector. It proved, if nothing else, that Angleton had limited sway over the US law enforcement organisation. Yet his influence over other partner agencies was stronger, especially across the Atlantic, as he had demonstrated earlier that year during a secret visit to London.

On the morning of 14 March 1966, shortly after Angleton had landed in the British capital with Anatoly Golitsyn, he requested an urgent meeting with the heads of MI5 and MI6. Langley's molehunter and his Soviet confidant had intentionally showed up uninvited and announced, hoping to underscore the gravity and secrecy of their mission, which had not even been shared with the CIA's own London station chief.

Much had changed at MI5. Martin Furnival Jones, once the British agency's counter-intelligence chief before a promotion to deputy director general to replace Graham Mitchell in 1963, had reached the peak of his career. Furnival Jones was now in charge of the organisation, but despite the greater status and responsibilities that came with being the boss, he was still fully aware of his agency's setbacks and struggles against the Kremlin and committed to finding ways to overcome them. And there were perhaps no two greater bearers of bad news regarding MI5's failings against the KGB than Angleton and Golitsyn. Furnival Jones cleared his diary to meet with them when they arrived in London that Monday morning. His MI6 counterpart, Sir Dick White, hosted them at his flat.

Angleton's urgent message was largely a repetition of his usual concerns, including the Soviet penetration of Western intelligence agencies and the KGB's disinformation campaign. The CIA official also stressed the importance of closer collaboration on counter-intelligence investigations between his agency and its British partners, such as the pooling and distribution of investigative outcomes. Furnival Jones and White felt that Angleton's overall message was rather familiar and repackaged, but they took it seriously due to its timing. By then, MI5's probe into Graham Mitchell, who had since retired, had been expanded to question the loyalty of the agency's former director general Roger Hollis, who had first come under suspicion shortly before his retirement three months earlier in December 1965.

Angleton had been kept up to date on both cases, and two months before his latest visit to London, a joint investigative committee set up by MI5 and MI6, codenamed FLUENCY, concluded that Hollis and a 'middle grade spy' were the most likely moles. Yet Furnival Jones dismissed the allegations against Hollis from the outset. Unwilling to accept the findings against his predecessor, he asked for an investigation into the 'middle - grade spy', who had been brought to MI5's attention by Polish defector Michal Goleniewski.

Mitchell was unlikely to be that spy because he had been too senior to fit the description, however a serving MI5 officer, Michael Hanley, did. Furnival Jones took it upon himself to interview Hanley, a future director general of the agency, and quickly declared him innocent. So, with the 'middle grade spy' still unidentified and potentially lurking within the agency, it was no wonder that the heads of MI5 and MI6 dropped everything they were doing to hear what Angleton and Golitsyn had to say during the pair's visit in the spring of 1966.

The following year, Angleton, in coordination with MI5 and MI6, created a counter-Soviet intelligence forum beyond transatlantic boundaries to include officials from Australia, Canada and New Zealand. While it was billed as a top secret initiative to broaden discussions surrounding KGB threats, Angleton typically tried to turn it into an opportunity to inflict his vision on a much larger captive audience.

About twenty of the most senior counter-intelligence officials from the five countries attended a conference, codenamed CAZAB, that was hosted by the Australian Security Intelligence Organisation (ASIO) in Melbourne on 6 November 1967. It was the first meeting of its kind that brought together human intelligence (HUMINT) officials from the Five Eyes – the intelligence network made up of the US, UK, Australia, Canada and New Zealand. Not only did Angleton invite Golitsyn to the four-day event, but the defector attended as a 'guest of honour'.

Details of the event remained secret for almost six decades, but in an interview with the author in March 2025, ASIO's director general, Mike Burgess, revealed its importance. 'This was a significant meeting that very few people knew about,' said Burgess. 'This was counter-intelligence liaison. So it's only those agencies involved in either penetrating or finding the penetrations, not the signals intelligence agencies ... Think of it as a like-minded small group of people getting together who are showing a high degree of trust because of the common problem they're looking to address.'

KGB moles and Soviet disinformation campaigns were among the topics of discussion, as were questions relating to bona fide and sent defectors. 'When there are defectors, you've always got to keep your mind open to, is that defector giving you everything that is true and helpful, or is it designed for other reasons, such as to misdirect you?' Burgess said. Unlike British intelligence officials at MI5 who embraced Golitsyn and deferred to him for guidance, ASIO is understood to have been wary of him. The Australian agency's dealings with the defector were indirect and through the CIA.

The Melbourne conference was deemed a success, and in September 1968, a second CAZAB meeting was held, this time in Washington D.C., where discussions focused on concerns surrounding senior Soviet moles operating inside of Western intelligence agencies. The concerns were of particular interest to MI5, because the British agency was still embroiled in its hunt for the 'middle grade spy' alongside its investigation into Graham Mitchell. But it was not until the following year, in the summer of 1969, that Martin Furnival Jones authorised an investigation into his agency's 'high-level' Soviet penetration, which had allegedly taken place several years earlier – the case of Roger Hollis.

MI5's increased preoccupation with its molehunts in the late 1960s, however, may well have compromised its operational focus and distracted it from the KGB threat outside its own inner circle. In early 1969, the British agency was unable to spot the KGB's fingerprints on a Soviet trade official's visa application. Foreign Office records reveal that 'Oleg Adolfovich Lyalin . . . applied for a visa in February 1969 in order to join the staff of the Soviet Trade Delegation in London.' His application was waved through without question.

\* \* \*

Ahead of his departure for Britain, and with his cover role training still wrapping up, Oleg Lyalin was briefed on his trade delegation responsibilities; how to split his time between his 'import and export' work and his operational priorities. A visa approval was a positive sign, but by no means unshakeable proof that his cover was sufficient. What if the British authorities had decided to clear his entry into the country in order to track him from the second he landed at the airport, and through him, identify his colleagues, his targets, and his recruits?

Operational countermeasures, including taking protracted routes to shake off physical surveillance, were one way to divert MI5's watchers from his espionage duties. But another way to maintain a low profile was by moderating his behaviour. There were many behavioural rules uniquely relating to foreign postings that he was required to observe, including how Soviet operatives were to conduct themselves in social situations. In theory, there were no outright bans on drinking, partying, gambling and dating, because they were common realities among Soviet officials on foreign assignments. Yet the Soviet agency wanted its personnel to be wary of how a reckless indulgence in such activities could embarrass their employer, or even worse, turn them into honey trap targets.

At the KGB's London residency (or *rezidentura*), Lyalin's

arrival was awaited with huge expectations, commensurate with his recent promotion to captain. First and foremost, his imminent mission was to advance Moscow's stance against its enemy, Great Britain, through the identification of its political, military and economic weaknesses – all in preparation for a potential future war. That meant understanding Britain's social landscape, its coastline vulnerabilities, and ways of demoralising its civilian life. Unlike his time at sabotage school, where there was some margin for error associated with operational thrills and drills, Lyalin's London assignment was going to be an unforgiving test in a hostile territory, where a slip-up could potentially damage him and Department V as a whole.

Far from intending to throw him into the fire from the outset to see if he could fend for himself, the KGB's London residency, to which Lyalin would report, wanted to ensure that he would be well prepared upon replacing one of Department V's representatives in the British capital, Aleksander Savin, whose posting was coming to an end. So the outgoing spy started preparing his locally recruited agents for a customary handover. Savin's British agents were far from ideologues, driven predominantly by money, occasional gifts, and the thrill of spying – so they were seemingly predictable, easy to handle and did not object to following orders from a new spymaster. One of them, a failed law student, had become a crucial KGB asset over the previous two years.

The two closest male figures in Siroj Abdoolcader's life had academic abilities that seemed way out of his reach. His father advised the government of Malaysia and was a distinguished lawyer, whose services to the legal profession had been honoured with a knighthood by King George VI after the Second World War. And his brother had graduated with first class honours from a law school in London before embarking on a distinguished career that culminated in his appointment as a judge.

Abdoolcader had a lot to live up to when he left the family home in Penang for London in 1957 aged nineteen, hoping to follow in the footsteps of his two role models. 'Abdoolcader was brought up in Penang and was never politically active,' a record of his migration to the UK would later reveal. 'When Malaya was granted independence in 1957, he was sent by his father to England to study law because [his] father believed there would be openings in the new independent country for qualified lawyers.'

It was not long before Abdoolcader's intellectual limitations became an insurmountable barrier: he failed multiple bar exams at Lincoln's Inn, the association for barristers in London, and turned his back on full-time study three years later. He blamed Britain's legal establishment for his unfulfilled ambitions, deeming it rigged against people of his ethnicity. But his flawed logic failed to take into account that it was from the same British legal establishment that his father and brother had derived their careers and success.

Instead of accepting responsibility for his own failure, Abdoolcader became so embittered against the UK that he scribbled 'British English bastards, English swine' across his passport. He claimed to be a victim of the British class system 'because of his colour', but his father, Sir Hosein, refused to indulge Abdoolcader's excuses and effectively disowned him. 'There are no openings in Malaysia for unqualified people,' Sir Hosein informed him in a letter. 'You let the family down by failing your bar examinations . . . You can jolly well make the best of it. There is no place for you in Penang.'

The option of returning to his native Malaysia to plead for his father's forgiveness was no longer viable, so instead, in October 1960, Abdoolcader settled for a job at the motor licensing department at County Hall, home of the London County Council, and later of the Greater London Council. As a clerical officer specialising in the registration of trade vehicles, Abdoolcader knew his way around the thousands of folders crammed inside the Greater London Council's vehicle registration department.

The folders were intended to look virtually identical, not only for the sake of bureaucratic uniformity, but for the purpose of protecting the most sensitive ones: those marked 'Special'. It was a label distinguishing cars registered to the Royal Family, Metropolitan Police, and MI5. Details identifying the exact ownership of those cars were not kept in the folders, however, but remained secret, closely held by the department head. As an added layer of protection, the special folders were 'distributed randomly along the shelves' and could only be accessed by staff members with the authorisation of their boss.

Abdoolcader had the 'occasional legitimate reason' to access the special folders, and in those instances, at least, he sought his manager's approval. He explained those aspects of his job to Aleksander Savin when they met in a supposedly random encounter at a pub in Archway, north London, in 1967. It did not occur to him at the time that Savin, a KGB officer operating under the cover of a Soviet trade delegate, had actually targeted him for information, nor did he walk away when the Soviet official expressed an interest in recruiting him. In fact, Abdoolcader, who had grown up in the shadow of his father and brother and now led an unfulfilling life as a junior clerical officer, was buoyed by the prospect of being sought out – and of being useful. It made him feel recognised and important.

Over the next two years, Abdoolcader regularly met Savin to provide information about vehicles the KGB suspected were tailing Soviet spies in London. Such insider knowledge was of great value to the Soviet spy agency by helping it to run 'false flag' missions to sap MI5's surveillance resources, while undercover KGB officers ran their operations in parts of the capital from which the 'watchers' had been diverted. That was one of many problems MI5 faced as it tried to crack down on the Kremlin's espionage missions in Britain. The agency rightly suspected that a growing number of KGB operatives were using the trade department for their cover, but struggled to collate hard evidence about their activities, some of which were by now being aided by Abdoolcader's work.

The KGB knew exactly how to appeal to Abdoolcader's mindset, and having spent a few years running him, Savin made him feel like a 'friend' rather than an asset. He dined with him and gave him the occasional gift, including a watch that Abdoolcader wrote about proudly in his personal diary. In the spring of 1969, with his London posting coming to an end, Savin informed Abdoolcader that he would soon be reporting to a new KGB handler.

# Chapter 6

# WATCHING THE WATCHERS

EVERYTHING APPEARED TO HAVE gone to plan when Oleg Lyalin landed in the United Kingdom in 1969. His dream of breaking through the Iron Curtain to experience life in the West was finally realised, and he was pleased with his cover role as a so-called 'textiles specialist'. He was, after all, to be based in London, the world's fashion capital. Along with setting global trends in dress code and music, the city was also in the midst of a cultural revolution that was sweeping the country. The social inhibitions that had long afflicted the British had made way for baby boomers entering young adulthood to join the nation's growing tolerance for sexual expression, drug-taking, and unrestrained partying.

No amount of research about Great Britain, or discussions with colleagues about what to expect from living there, could have measured up to the experiences that Lyalin was about to have. He was now officially a guest of the country that had given global audiences not only the Beatles but also James Bond, the fictional

MI6 officer who had become a cultural icon for defeating Soviet villains, and whose travails had already been the subject of five blockbuster movies with a sixth set for release later in the year.

Fortunately for Lyalin, there was no Bond-like immigration official to intercept him upon his entry into the country, to pierce through his cover and raise last-minute suspicions. In fact, it appeared to be a nasty joke at the expense of Britain's intelligence community, and particularly MI5, that when Lyalin breezed through customs on bogus paperwork, the Soviet 'Trade Delegation official' who was there to welcome him was actually an undercover KGB officer. The officer's bold move to greet Lyalin would undoubtedly have been authorised by the KGB's London residency, but it seemed less of a careless step than an expression of self-assurance that Soviet operatives could get around unhindered and unchecked in their host country.

MI5 was oblivious to the embarrassing events surrounding Lyalin's entry into Britain on Friday 11 April, perhaps proving that it was never too far from KGB-orchestrated humiliations during that era. One of the latest in a long list of embarrassing episodes was the drama surrounding former MI6 officer George Blake, whose audacious prison escape three years earlier remained in the headlines amid a court case to bring his accomplices to justice.

The KGB asset had been merely five years into his forty-two-year custodial sentence for treason when he scaled Wormwood Scrubs prison's perimeter wall with a 'ladder made of rope and knitting needles', before eventually fleeing Britain for Moscow on false documents to reunite with his Soviet handlers. While Blake's jailbreak was an impressive coup for the KGB, it was of far less operational importance than what the agency expected Lyalin to achieve on his posting.

At the Soviet Trade Delegation in Highgate, north London,

Lyalin was among more than a hundred officials whose mission, at least according to their job description, was to aid Moscow's increasing participation in the world economy by building closer ties with British trade partners. That also meant finding creative ways to overcome the trade barriers that hampered Soviet manufacturers, including buyer unfamiliarity with Soviet products and a general hostility to Soviet goods, which were often associated with poorer quality than their Western alternatives.

Yet as much as he had to maintain the facade of a man serious about commerce, Lyalin's individual performance would not be measured by his ability to improve Moscow's export and import relations with London. The trade mission's headquarters was merely his stage for keeping up appearances. It allowed him to mix with genuine delegates, both in the office and during social occasions, if for no other reason than to bolster the credibility of his cover. It also spared him from the thirty-five-mile travel limit outside London that had been imposed on Soviet diplomats a few years earlier, in retaliation for the same Soviet restriction on British diplomats in Moscow. So Lyalin was geographically unrestricted in going about his 'commercial' business, while at the same time familiarising himself with briefings about the KGB's local operations.

Aleksander Savin, the outgoing Department V representative in London, introduced the new arrival to his recruits as part of the asset handover. It was a delicate process, in which an agent needed to be assured that their new handler would treat them with the same regard as the old, protect their identity at all times, and even be there for them as a 'friend'. Whether driven by ideology, grievance, greed, a penchant for risk-taking or a combination of all such qualities, agents are generally emotional quagmires that require careful handling, regular praise for their bravery, and recognition of their loyalty. But by definition, espionage agents are inherently disloyal because they have chosen to side with the enemy, to steal and cheat and misinform, and no amount of operational success could ever fully dispel their handler's distrust of them.

Having been informed about what to expect from Savin's assets, including Siroj Abdoolcader's ability to identify MI5's surveillance vehicles, Lyalin wanted to ensure that the transition of all the agents to his control was as seamless as possible. Equally, he wanted to bring them up to his own operational standards: to broaden their targets, teach them new communication methods and deception techniques, and turn them into talent scouts.

Two of the agents brought under Lyalin's control were brothers-in-law, who had been recruited in the first half of the 1960s by a KGB handler codenamed Alex. When Savin inherited them upon his posting to London in 1965, he also became known to them as Alex – even though that was merely an abbreviation of his first name rather than an alias to protect his identity. So perhaps it was in the interest of continuity that Lyalin adopted Alex as the codename that the agents would also come to know him by. Most of them, including the brothers-in-law, required little motivation to go about their work because they had already been through several years of on-the-ground tradecraft training and relished the excitement associated with espionage, especially the use of gadgets.

The three-word inscription on a green pencil, 'Made in England', had been intended to look generic, to normalise the writing instrument and help it blend in with other stationery items in Kyriacos Costi's bedroom. Lying in a money box by the sideboard cupboard next to Costi's bed, the sharpened pencil was seemingly indistinguishable from any other. But it was neither made for writing nor a product of England: its flat top unscrewed to reveal a cavity for microfilm storage. The KGB had given Costi this piece of 'craftsmanship' along with other spycraft tools, including ostensibly American-made batteries – even featuring the Eveready brand logo – that also contained hollowed-out cavities for hiding messages.

Costi's bedroom at the home he co-owned with his parents in Finsbury Park, north London, resembled a miniature espionage outpost. He spent some of his time there monitoring call sign transmissions from Moscow for his new handler Oleg Lyalin. The messages were encrypted through a virtually unbreakable numerical system known as the one-time pad; essentially a pad of paper with pages on which five-digit groups of random numbers were printed. To safeguard the encryption, each set of codes was strictly used only once, and only the message sender and recipient had matching codebooks to decrypt them. Observing that decryption model, Costi would plug his headphones into a portable shortwave radio and go about decoding the transmitted communication.

Unlike his spymaster Lyalin, who had sharpened his tradecraft through intense theoretical and practical training over the years, Costi had been given a crash course in cryptography before being left to get on with the job. Most interestingly, his collaboration with the KGB had not come from a direct approach but through a family connection. In 1965, Costi, known as 'Ken' to his close friends, had been recommended to the Soviet agency by his brother-in-law, Constantinos Martianou, who had been recruited four years earlier during his time as a teenage member of the Young Communist League of Britain.

The Cypriot-born pair, in their twenties, lived about a mile apart, and both seemed to enjoy spying for Moscow far more than their actual day jobs as tailors. But in some ways, they made a seemingly reliable team, not because of their family ties and shared interests, but based on their different skill sets. Costi was an aspiring techie, a quasi-cipher clerk who was somewhat capable but far from impressive at handling code, while Martianou was a field operative who cleared dead drops – including 'holes in walls, dumps or containers such as packets or cans' used by agents and their controller to exchange secret messages. He also helped Lyalin identify other prospective targets for recruitment.

Having demonstrated a knack for spying during his early days as an agent, Martianou was sent by his first agent-handler to Kent, south-east of London, to identify the voltage output of the Northfleet Power Station, and he succeeded. On another mission to the south-west of London, Martianou obtained intelligence about the size and layout of the Fawley Refinery, owned by the US multinational oil and gas company, Esso. As a junior operative, Martianou was not given the exact reason for the KGB's interest in targeting Britain's critical national infrastructure sites. Yet it was assets of that nature which Lyalin had been sent to Britain to target and plot against.

Alongside juggling meetings with his agents, cultivating fresh talent and fulfilling his official day job obligations, such as negotiating with British textile sellers, Lyalin made a point of mixing business with pleasure. He developed a huge liking for socialising in Soho, the liveliest entertainment area in London's West End, often spending afternoons drinking at pubs and bars there. He was 'a natty dresser who bought his clothes in Regent Street [central London]', as someone would later remark. 'Oleg was known as a big spender who, according to one restaurateur, "thought nothing of picking up an £80 tab",' worth more than three times the average weekly earnings of a male manual worker in London.

He also frequented expensive restaurants in Soho, splurging on 'French cuisine and champagne' and spent at least one night a week in Mayfair, attending nightclubs with Soviet businessmen from the Moscow Narodny Bank. Lyalin's behaviour, including such regular nights out, was not typical of someone who could be trusted with secrets, let alone operational work. But it was completely within the KGB's code of conduct, presumably because it helped to maintain his cover.

In the summer of 1969, as Lyalin became increasingly accustomed to London's fast life, he continued reporting to his KGB station chief, taking instructions on potential targets, including government officials worth recruiting and military bases vulnerable to attack. Until that point, Lyalin had remained virtually invisible to MI5, which was on the verge of being consumed by a major investigation that its director general, Martin Furnival Jones, had resisted authorising for quite some time.

\* \* \*

Four years into his leadership of MI5, Martin Furnival Jones was being hounded by an incessant chorus of suspicion surrounding his predecessor – the man who had championed him, vouched for him, promoted him to be his deputy for two years and blessed his rise to the organisation's top office. Furnival Jones had to contend with the prospect that his former boss, Roger Hollis, had betrayed him, his colleagues and the agency, which was an uneasy position for him to accept.

It was equally mind-boggling to consider that the now six-decade-old agency, which had played a pivotal role in hunting spies during two world wars, could ever have been manipulated at the highest level by its Soviet enemy. That would mean accepting that in the nine years that Hollis served at its helm, between 1956 and 1965, the Kremlin had effectively steered MI5. If he really were an enemy asset who had helped neutralise the agency's mission against Moscow – for instance, diverting his staff's attention away from the KGB's operations in the UK – then how many other Soviet spies had Hollis planted in MI5, and how many remained 'in place'?

Difficult questions needed to be asked in search of evidence against Hollis, and as a qualified lawyer with a forensic instinct who had previously overseen MI5's counter-espionage division, Furnival Jones was willing to do that. But he must have been torn between his personal doubts about the allegations against Hollis and the need either to prove or discredit the rumours surrounding his former boss.

The known Soviet assets who had penetrated Britain's security apparatus in previous decades, including Burgess, Maclean, Blake and Philby, had all been recruited by Moscow in the 1930s before they had entered Britain's intelligence community. As had Anthony Blunt, who was already under Soviet control when he joined MI5 in the early days of the Second World War and avoided exposure as a traitor for more than two decades. So by that recruitment pattern, Hollis's pre-service days would become a focal point of any inquiry, including the nine years he had spent in China from the late 1920s working in advertising for the British American Tobacco Company before joining MI5 in 1938.

Despite the obvious differences between his advertising experience and the counter-subversion and counter-espionage missions that he went on to specialise in, Hollis had made an immediate impression on MI5's leadership. Some of his career highlights within his first decade included debriefing Igor Gouzenko, a Russian cipher clerk whose defection in Canada in 1945 arguably marked the beginning of the Cold War. Another was Hollis's deployment to Australia to help that country create a spy service in MI5's image – the Australian Security Intelligence Organisation (ASIO). His experience, judgement and likeability fast-tracked him through MI5's ranks and within two decades of joining the organisation, he was in charge of it.

Furnival Jones was certainly not alone in his huge respect for Hollis. Sir Dick White, another MI5 former chief who had personally handed Hollis the agency's reins in 1956 before moving on to run its sister agency, MI6, was effusive about his former deputy's achievements. 'The personal qualities responsible for his rise,' White would later note, 'were those of integrity, objectivity and imperturbability in times of crisis. They were qualities he greatly needed when he became head of the service . . . and faced a decade of almost continuous national security problems.' Such problems, of course, included Philby's defection to Moscow, the Profumo Affair that claimed Harold Macmillan's prime ministership, and Blunt's confession in 1964 to being a Soviet asset.

In some ways, it could be argued that Hollis faced nothing but security setbacks during his tenure, because MI5 had failed to land any substantial hits against Moscow – except for those that had resulted from leads provided by Eastern Bloc defectors to the CIA, including Michal Goleniewski and Anatoly Golitsyn. However, perceiving MI5's intelligence failures under Hollis's leadership as potential confirmation that he had collaborated with the enemy was a huge risk for the agency's reputation. Because even if he were eventually cleared of any wrongdoing, the investigation itself could forever stain the agency's legacy.

Those who distrusted Hollis undoubtedly deemed Furnival Jones as spineless for his initial reluctance to have him investigated. But he was not going to throw the agency's ex-boss to the lions for the sake of appeasing his accusers, especially because he remained very sceptical of the allegations against Hollis. It was not just because Furnival Jones was biased in favour of his old colleague, but because the claims against Hollis were being made by the same intelligence officials who had previously suspected, but had failed to yet prove, that MI5's former deputy chief, Graham Mitchell, had also been a Soviet spy.

One of those officials was Peter Wright, a counter-espionage veteran who chaired FLUENCY, the joint MI5 and MI6 investigative committee to root out British moles. He viewed the KGB threat to MI5 with the same fixation that had long gripped James Angleton at the CIA, and was convinced that Mitchell and Hollis had been aiding the enemy. Wright was unrelenting in the pursuit of his two priority targets and wanted Furnival Jones's authorisation to conduct a no-holds-barred inquiry into them.

He was also not alone in sounding the alarm about Hollis and Mitchell: Wright had the support of two cheerleaders in Langley – Angleton and Golitsyn – who still held a remarkable sway over MI5's counter-Soviet strategy. While the three were on the same page about the need for a broader and more aggressive inquiry into MI5 moles, Angleton was a late adopter of the theory that Wright and Golitsyn had been pushing for several years.

It was no surprise that Golitsyn suspected Mitchell. Golitsyn had been in London, working alongside MI5's head of Soviet counter-espionage in 1963, when the investigation was first launched into Mitchell. Yet despite his close involvement in it, which included personally bestowing the internal probe with its codename PETERS, neither Golitsyn nor MI5 had been able to convince Angleton about its importance. In fact, the CIA's counter-intelligence boss had initially dismissed the possibility of Mitchell being a traitor because he felt that if he were a spy, he would not have been able to resist warning his Kremlin controllers about MI5's operations and secrets, or at the very least, about some of Langley's shared secrets.

But we know that Angleton was susceptible to embracing

Golitsyn's theories, even if in some cases his suspicion took some time to take hold. One of those theories, which had been touted by both the defector and Wright, was about Oleg Penkovsky, the prolific Soviet spy who had forewarned Washington about Moscow's military installations in Latin America before the Cuban Missile Crisis. Golitsyn and Wright became convinced that Penkovsky had been a plant. It was a difficult theory for others to embrace, including Angleton, because Penkovsky had provided thousands of pages of military secrets to his joint handlers at the CIA and MI6, and ultimately paid the price for the leaks with his life.

But anything seemed possible under the KGB's new direction that Golitsyn had been warning about since his defection. Had Penkovsky simply been hoodwinked by the KGB's deception operation? Had the Soviet agency turned him into a sacrificial lamb, dangling him to the CIA and MI6 so that it could achieve its overall strategic goal of burrowing deeper into Western intelligence agencies?

Golitsyn suspected that Penkovsky had been planted on the West as part of the Soviet 'Master Plan', the KGB's strategic mission to falsely cast loyal Soviet officials as defectors. And he feared that while Penkovsky may have initially set out to be a genuine spy for the West, his leaks had been brought to the attention of the KGB by a senior British or American mole, allowing the Soviet agency to drag him back under its control and manipulate him, as it had done several years earlier in the Pyotr Popov case. The theory about Penkovsky was as much, if not more of a stretch as questioning whether Mitchell or Hollis had been the moles who had tipped off the KGB about his work for the British and Americans.

But the pressure that Wright, Angleton and Golitsyn had imposed on MI5 finally pushed Furnival Jones into approving a full-scale investigation into Hollis and Mitchell in the summer of 1969. Unlike the early stages of the 1963 probe into Mitchell, which MI5 had flagged to some senior members of Macmillan's government, the investigation into Hollis, codenamed DRAT, was so secret that its whole existence was withheld even from the British prime minister himself. Despite that, however, MI5 saw fit to update the CIA regularly about both investigations and even sought Angleton's advice about them.

Still reigning supreme over the CIA counter-intelligence domain he had been leading for thirteen years, Angleton's tenure had survived three White House administrations and was into its fourth following Richard Nixon's entry to office in January 1969. His relationship with the Oval Office was conducted through the agency's director, Richard Helms, whom Nixon had been advised by his predecessor, Lyndon B. Johnson, to keep in place.

However, Angleton's real focus in the new administration was its German-born national security advisor, Henry Kissinger, who favoured détente with the Soviet Union as a way of reducing tensions between Washington and Moscow, and resolving security concerns, including arms control. Angleton, with some input from Golitsyn, became increasingly hostile to Kissinger's approach to Moscow and started contemplating whether even the president's security czar was a Soviet spy.

A clash between Kissinger and Angleton was on the cards, but instead of playing out over the issue of détente, it would be triggered by a major development at MI5. Meanwhile sometime before that, while MI5 was bogged down by the drama surrounding the investigations into Hollis and Mitchell, less than a mile away, a business venture was being finalised to scale up trade between Moscow and London.

\* \* \*

Beside the doorway at Marcol House, nameplates identified the corporate tenants and their floor numbers in the five-storey building. The fourth floor's plaque read: Razno and Co. The firm had been set up to give the Soviet trade mission a footprint in the exclusive Regent Street area of central London, right by the capital's most glamorous fashion strips. Unlike other tenants of the office block, including the Menswear Association of Britain, there was no clue in Razno's name about the nature of its business. But in many ways it was defined by its name, which in Russian means 'different'. And it certainly was.

It was different because the firm was officially registered in late October 1969 as Ableville Limited, so Razno did not really exist on paper but was merely the company's trading name. It was also different because, according to its registration records, it appeared to be limitless in its trade objectives, claiming to specialise in the import or export of a vast number of products, including 'textiles, leather, clothing and wearing attire, fancy goods, farm produce, animal seed, agriculture and horticulture machinery'. And it was different because it was actually a front in the KGB's mission to shore up Oleg Lyalin's cover and justify his regular travel to central London, where he met his agents from time to time.

To keep on top of the latest fashion trends, Razno's management immersed its staff in the glitzy local environment, encouraging them to seek inspiration for the newest looks and styles by frequenting retail stores around Soho, including Carnaby Street and Oxford Circus, which were packed with avant-garde men's and women's clothing brands catering to celebrities, tourists, and general victims of fashion labels.

Razno's management style was far ahead of its time, too, focused on keeping its office morale high. Local British staffers, mainly employed in secretarial roles, were treated no differently from the predominantly Russian employees, often invited for in-office lunches paid for by Moscow. And in the lead-up to Christmas, each staff member was sent home with a hamper loaded with exotic Soviet delicacies, including caviar, cream cheese and vodka.

Razno's official purpose, its raison d'être, was succinctly articulated by one of its lawyers to showcase the transparency of its commercial objectives. He said it had been 'established to promote and develop trade between the UK and [the] Soviet Union' and handle 'negotiation of exports to the Soviet Union of ladies' and men's clothing, [and] ladies' and men's shoes'. Regardless of the KGB's own agenda, Moscow had high expectations of Razno, entrusting it to plough millions of pounds into British exports that would appeal to the Soviet markets.

As one of Razno's advisors and negotiators, Lyalin did not have a desk at its Regent Street headquarters but he was often seen there, always in a suit and tie, for business discussions with the firm's managers. In one instance he helped close a deal on women's stockings, which were in huge demand in Moscow, and reportedly netted the Soviet trade mission a profit of twenty times their purchase price. While each stocking cost 20 pence in the UK, it would reportedly sell for £4 in the Soviet capital. 'Lyalin set up a deal for shipping tights worth £250,000 in Britain to Russia,' according to a report highlighting his 'sharp eye for a good business deal'.

However, Lyalin's work for Razno was not driven by commitment to its operations or a desire to win employee-of-the-month. The company was simply a means to an end. It offered him a crucial smokescreen, allowing him to bounce between its office and his meetings with assets, including the two brothers-in-law, Constantinos Martianou and Kyriacos Costi, who among other places, had a longstanding habit of being debriefed or instructed at Tottenham Court Road Underground station.

By late 1969, Lyalin's juggling of business deals and espionage assignments had become second nature, and he was pushing his agents to take greater operational risks. He provided Siroj Abdoolcader with more vehicle registration numbers, to check whether they belonged to MI5's surveillance officers. And spotting an opportunity to turn Abdoolcader into more than a one-trick pony, he trained him in recruiting civil servants, eventually asking him to target a Ministry of Defence (MoD) employee whom Lyalin believed had access to sensitive military secrets.

It was a dangerous move. A failed approach could potentially trace Abdoolcader's footsteps back to Lyalin and it was well known in the intelligence community that some MI5 officials publicly identified themselves as 'MoD' staffers to protect the secrecy of their security service roles. Even when the British agency's director general had been knighted by the Queen two years earlier, his name appeared in the public Honours List as 'Jones, Edward Martin Furnival, attached to the Ministry of Defence'. So Abdoolcader's planned approach to an MoD official risked triggering warning bells at MI5.

Thankfully for Lyalin, MI5's warning bells had been muffled for years, and the agency was now hobbled by the investigation into its two former top officials – Graham Mitchell and Roger Hollis. In fact, in early 1970, Martin Furnival Jones would have to search for inspiration and guidance across the Atlantic yet again. There, the Soviet defector advising the CIA on its molehunt and still staking his reputation and relevance on weeding out Soviet plants, agreed to come to MI5's rescue after Furnival Jones requested – in writing – his assistance 'with the problems of penetration of British intelligence'.

# Chapter 7

# SPYCATCHER

AT SOME POINT BETWEEN the car park and the hotel reception desk, Anatoly Golitsyn felt that a few of the staff members knew who he was, as though the Kremlin had pre-positioned them in Bournemouth, on England's south coast, to keep him under close observation. Golitsyn was unnerved by the premises' setting, the staff's unwelcome presence, and a general sense of unease. He became convinced that he was being spied on and that his safety was compromised. No assurance from MI5, which had carefully chosen the hotel after undoubtedly running security checks on its employees, could have changed his mind or eased his paranoia.

Perhaps Golitsyn placed little value on MI5's security assurances because he had long known that the British agency's record of identifying spies, let alone catching them, had been sketchy at best. Testimony to that was his arrival in the UK at MI5's invitation to help identify suspected KGB moles in its service. MI5 had essentially elevated Golitsyn to a prophet-like figure by appealing for his help, looking to him as the saviour it needed to overcome its own existential challenge. Far from his years demanding to be treated as an equal by intelligence officials on both sides of the Atlantic, Golitsyn was now on the verge of being worshipped.

He had been overdosing on the fumes of his self-worth for almost a decade since fleeing the KGB and had developed the kind of prima donna antics that would make a Broadway performer blush. Throughout the 1960s, the demands he had placed on the CIA, MI5 – and even CIA and MI5 – even the FBI for a brief period – appeared to be limitless. Golitsyn seemed to have an almost pathological disposition to bearing grudges, much as he had after President Kennedy and J. Edgar Hoover refused to meet him years earlier, or when the CIA turned down his proposed creation of an agency sub-division under his control that would step up the spy war against Moscow.

But in the sphere of real influence, at the top echelons of management where operational directions were approved, Golitsyn remained the most highly sought after Kremlin insider – cherished by arguably the two most powerful spymasters at MI5 and the CIA, Martin Furnival Jones and James Angleton. Golitsyn's star status placed him at the forefront of transatlantic intelligence discussions about countering the Soviet Union's hostility.

Apart from frequently seeking his insights, the CIA and MI5 also imposed Golitsyn on their partner agencies, as had become evident three years earlier when he accompanied Angleton to the CAZAB security conference in Melbourne, Australia. While there had been the occasional murmurs among Five Eyes officials about Golitsyn's reliability and competence, they appeared to be outweighed by intrigue about his apparent instincts to sniff out KGB moles.

On matters of personal safety, however, Golitsyn had become a walking contradiction. While he never missed an opportunity to play up the ongoing KGB threat against him, his behaviour suggested he was not really that worried. He was somehow unconcerned, for instance, about dining at restaurants – especially ones near where he lived in New York – that were frequented by Kremlin officials, including those working at the United Nations. Since at least a third of foreign-based Soviet officials were undercover spies during the Cold War, with dozens of KGB operatives planted in Manhattan at the Soviet mission to the United Nations alone, it could have been argued that Golitsyn was intentionally flirting with danger. Not once, however, did anyone attempt to tamper with his meals, intimidate him, or follow him – a fact that somehow failed to pique the interest of American and British intelligence officials until years later.

Golitsyn's inconsistent approach to the perceived threat on his life was apparent upon his arrival in England in May 1970, where shortly after being taken to the hotel in Bournemouth, he demanded safer accommodation. Aware of his temperament, and his tendency to go on 'strike' whenever his demands were not met, MI5 relocated Golitsyn to a rented house about seven miles further west – and when that did not ease his safety concerns, transferred him to the home of an MI5 official where he lived with the officer and his family. Even then, he maintained his irrational behaviour; only leaving the house in the evenings to avoid being seen, and insisting on drinking Perrier sparkling water because he worried about being 'poisoned'. As if his imagined assassins would only poison fizzy water of the cheaper variety.

His behaviour was nothing short of theatre, but Furnival Jones still approved his access to MI5 files – even authorising their transportation from the agency's London headquarters to a safe house near Golitsyn's temporary residence. 'On the basis of their past research the Security Service intend to provide you with briefs covering the individuals who have fallen within their field of scrutiny in the context of penetration,' Furnival Jones had noted in a letter to Golitsyn ahead of the files' transfer. 'Each case will be identified by a serial number but the full names of the individual concerned will be supplied on request . . . The briefs which will be supplied initially will be prepared in summary form.'

MI5's provision of files followed in the CIA's footsteps after the US agency had years earlier granted Golitsyn access to its own documents in its pursuit of 'Sasha', the mole that was still undetected in the American intelligence agencies. In Britain, the defector applied himself to the task with the same rigour he had at the CIA, poring over the files to spot any hint of betrayal, hoping to rid MI5 of its alleged mole infestation. And much like his futile search in the US, Golitsyn's hunt for treachery in Britain appeared to go nowhere. Some MI5 officials even perceived it to be a 'complete waste of time' and resources, bringing into question Furnival Jones's judgement in authorising the defector's involvement in the first place.

But the MI5's director general had taken that step at a time of crisis, during a dark period in the agency's history when its former boss and deputy boss were still under investigation for allegedly betraying their country. Furnival Jones was desperate to resolve MI5's internal dilemma and refocus the agency on its core mission of targeting, and irreparably damaging, the Soviet intelligence machine. Perhaps it was that desperation – coupled with MI5's confidence-sapping security failures over the previous ten years – that forced Furnival Jones to turn regularly to Langley for answers, seeking Angleton's wisdom and Golitsyn's insider perspective.

If he had been more questioning in his later judgements, Furnival Jones would have figured out that the operational closeness between MI5 and the CIA, as important as it was in the face of the Kremlin's persistent threat, was somewhat blinding his organisation. That closeness, which could be traced back to the defections to the CIA by Michal Goleniewski, Anatoly Golitsyn and Yuri Nosenko in the early 1960s, had produced some good results in the way of leads that helped to capture British spies. But many of the other leads, especially Golitsyn's, which had raised suspicion about MI5 officials and even the British prime minister, Harold Wilson, up until that point had predominantly stirred up panic and hysteria but little else.

A year after Furnival Jones had authorised the full investigations into Roger Hollis and Graham Mitchell, their cases appeared to be wrapping up amid a tumultuous political climate that, according to most of the electoral polling in 1970, looked certain to reinstate Harold Wilson in power for a second term. Yet opinion polling, much like intelligence assessments, is not a perfect science.

* * *

An economic crisis had plagued Harold Wilson's government in the second half of the 1960s, resulting in high interest rates, increased taxes, and union strikes. Compounding his political distress was a currency devaluation, which had been intended to boost exports but backfired, ratcheting up import costs and inflation. The spring of 1970, however, brought with it an astounding turnaround – a revival of Labour's fortunes and its leader's future prospects, as British exports were nursed back to better health and average wages were increased. Opinion polling put the incumbent prime minister comfortably ahead of his Tory rival, Ted Heath.

Wilson had already once trounced Heath in the 1966 general election, and although his challenger subsequently appeared to present a threat, he seemed confident about defeating his rival yet again at the ballot box. Buoyed by the nation's apparent mood change towards his leadership, which for several years had been pilloried, Wilson called an election in May 1970 with the expectation of remaining at 10 Downing Street.

'Taking the general trend of all the polls together, the signpost now plainly points to a Labour victory of some dimension,' a column in *The Times* noted on 4 June 1970. 'Even the pre-election wages boom theory does not really explain it, since so many people are still feeling the pinch of the rising cost of living, for which recent wage increases are merely regarded as belated compensation.' Over the course of the election campaign, Wilson presented himself as the presumptive winner and the media largely bought into his hype.

MI5 was also keeping an eye on campaign developments, partly because questions around Wilson's historic links to the Soviet Union remained unresolved. The British agency had first taken an interest in Wilson's interactions with Moscow more than two decades earlier, when shortly after entering Parliament, he travelled there for a series of negotiations as president of the British government's Board of Trade. MI5 seemingly had no concerns about three official visits he made to the Soviet capital in the late 1940s, but was intrigued about his subsequent trips between 1952 and 1959.

During that seven-year stretch, with Labour in opposition following a Tory election victory in 1951, Wilson made several trips to Moscow as an advisor to Montague L. Meyer Ltd, a British company that imported timber from the Soviet Union. MI5 became increasingly interested in his trips, and while it did not suspect him of being a secret Communist, its officers did wonder about the connections he developed on his travels, which culminated in meetings with Soviet leader Nikita Khrushchev and other top Kremlin officials.

Perhaps even more intriguing was Wilson's regular contact in the 1950s with Ivan Fedorovich Skripov, a KGB officer working under diplomatic cover in London. MI5 concluded that although he was apparently unaware that Skripov was a Soviet intelligence officer, Wilson must have suspected that he was, but continued meeting with him anyway.

Wilson may have been blinded by his political aspirations, because his contact with Kremlin officials and leaders was largely to position himself as Labour's Soviet expert and a potential foreign secretary in his party's future government. In the service of that goal and in the interest of preserving his close ties to Moscow, he refused to align himself with other left-wing Labour MPs in condemning the Red Army's invasion of Hungary in October 1956, in which more than 2,500 people were murdered. Wilson's position did not go unnoticed by MI5, nor the KGB. In fact, that same year the Soviet spy agency started considering him for potential future recruitment. It even opened an 'agent development file' on him, codenamed OLDING, but his recruitment never materialised.

In 1962, the ambitious politician joined Hugh Gaitskell's shadow cabinet as shadow foreign secretary after failing to beat him in a leadership challenge. At that point, Wilson's public displays of affection for Moscow, which in the previous decade had seen him write gushing newspaper articles in praise of Khrushchev and his economy's 'modernisation', very much came to an end. His Communist admirers in Britain and the USSR, including KGB officials who had once hoped that he would be a torchbearer for the cause, seemed to give up on him.

So when questions about Wilson's loyalty were then raised

by Golitsyn and Angleton upon his election as prime minister in 1964, MI5 naturally took them seriously; but with no hard evidence to support such claims, could not move them forward in any meaningful way. In a twist of irony, the MI5 official who had initially raised concerns about Wilson in the 1940s and opened a 'permanent file' on him was the agency's then top expert on Communism – Graham Mitchell, the man who would rise to become MI5's deputy chief and fall under suspicion himself.

Fast forward six years from Wilson's first-term victory and the prime minister appeared to be on the brink of re-election. His opponent, Ted Heath, put on a brave face in public, but behind the scenes his Conservative colleagues and trusted aides were preparing to commiserate with him on his anticipated defeat. Labour had made a remarkable comeback in the polls, after more than two years of performing badly in local elections and by-elections.

Compounding Labour's improved fortunes were Heath's own setbacks: he was not personally popular among voters and had been embroiled in controversies within his cabinet, including when he was forced to sack his shadow defence secretary Enoch Powell in 1968 over his anti-immigration 'racialist' comments in what would become known as a the 'Rivers of Blood' speech. So there were ample reasons to convince Heath and his party that the Conservatives were headed for electoral defeat.

On judgement day, however, in a monumental upset to Wilson and yet another confirmation that electoral polls are unreliable, Heath was elected prime minister on 18 June 1970 in a surprise victory that was epic by all measures. Having dethroned seventy-six Labour MPs and gained a thirty-seat parliamentary majority, Heath was in a state of political dominance and determined to follow through on campaign pledges, including his promise to crush trade unions he suspected of being Communist bedfellows with reprehensible sympathies for Moscow. He was eventually also persuaded to take aggressive action against the Soviet threat on home soil; a threat which had triggered political scandals in the vein of the Profumo Affair and damaged two Tory governments before his.

The politician Heath appointed to oversee the Foreign Office was Sir Alec Douglas-Home, an old hand at the role having previously served as foreign secretary about a decade earlier. Douglas-Home was still scarred by the Profumo Affair of the early 1960s, because he had a front-row view of that scandal during his time in Harold Macmillan's cabinet. Even after Macmillan collapsed on his sword and Douglas-Home was appointed prime minister to restore the Conservatives' standing, the new leader could not overcome the spy scandal's fallout. He lasted two days short of a year in office before losing the election to Harold Wilson.

Determined to rehabilitate his political legacy, in a complete turnaround from only six years before, Douglas-Home was now set to place Moscow firmly in his sights and take a keen interest in the Kremlin's diplomatic and trade missions in Britain. At MI5, Martin Furnival Jones would have been watching this with interest and anticipating a sea change in the government's approach to the Soviet Union. On the same day that Heath was elected, the MI5 director general was eyeing a major development in his agency's joint investigation into Roger Hollis.

Four years after suspicion about Roger Hollis was first brought to Martin Furnival Jones's attention, and about a year since he had approved an investigation into him, MI5's chief was confronted with the inquiry's preliminary findings on 18

June 1970. The case against Hollis rested on three allegations surrounding his wartime service, including a tip in the winter of 1945 from Konstantin Volkov, the Soviet consul in Istanbul, alleging that up to seven people in British intelligence were in the Kremlin's pay. Among them, Volkov said, was the 'acting head' of a counter-intelligence department.

Volkov said he would provide the British authorities with information about the Soviet spies in return for money and political asylum. He also insisted that his proposal should not be raised with London by telegram, because he feared that the Kremlin had penetrated Britain's cipher communications. So the British Embassy in Istanbul instead sent his proposal by diplomatic courier to MI6 where Kim Philby – secretly under Moscow's control at the time – was appointed to follow up on the case. Volkov was subsequently 'kidnapped by the Russians, carried on to a Soviet plane and carried back to Moscow', according to an MI5 file. Philby, it would later emerge, had informed his Soviet handlers of the consul's plans. Volkov was never heard from again and was most likely killed.

Twenty-five years on, Volkov's tip about the 'acting head' of a counter-intelligence department had been exhumed by the joint MI5 and MI6 investigation, or FLUENCY, and was put forward as a key allegation against Hollis. Both agencies had counter-intelligence departments during the period in question, but Hollis had not been in charge of either of them. In fact, he had been running MI5's counter-subversion division for the previous five years, and his agency's counter-intelligence branch had been under Guy Liddell's authority.

At MI6, a restructure had placed Philby as 'acting head' of the agency's counter-intelligence department, also known as Section V. So the person whom Volkov had warned about had been Philby all along. To this day it seems astounding that those investigating Hollis had even considered Volkov's tip as 'evidence' against him, rather than further confirmation of Philby's treachery, according to the authorised history of MI5.

The second allegation against Hollis centred on a lead from Vladimir Petrov, a former intelligence chief at the Soviet Embassy in Canberra. Before defecting to Australia in 1954, Petrov had been told by a colleague in Switzerland that a serving MI5 officer had been in a position to show the British agency's files to his Soviet controllers. But when that lead was re-examined in the context of Hollis's case, investigators somehow disregarded a confession by Anthony Blunt in 1964, who by then had long left MI5 to become the Surveyor of the Queen's Pictures. The former MI5 officer had confessed to smuggling files out of his agency's headquarters during the war, which fitted the timeline in question.

The third lead against Hollis was equally thin, citing information from an American code-breaking programme, the Venona Project, set up during wartime to decrypt Soviet communications. A September 1945 decrypt identified an agent in London codenamed JOHNSON. Yet that, too, was later revealed to be Blunt, not Hollis – but only after numerous people were suspected of being JOHNSON.

Now, with the preliminary findings in hand, Furnival Jones remained sceptical of the so-called fresh evidence against Hollis, but instead of killing the case, he authorised an interrogation of the former director general. And just as he had withheld knowledge of the Hollis case from Harold Wilson, Furnival Jones also kept it secret from Ted Heath, steering well clear of it when he met the new prime minister shortly after his entry into Downing Street. Heath had called that meeting with Furnival Jones and other security officials, including Sir Dick White who had left his MI6 directorship and become the Cabinet Office's

Intelligence Coordinator, to discuss his concerns about the Soviet threat in Britain.

In his previous role as Lord Privy Seal at the Foreign Office, Heath had dealt with White in the early 1960s on matters relating to spy scandals, including George Blake's case, and was hugely impressed by him. The prime minister did not feel the same admiration for Furnival Jones nor, as he would later note in his autobiography, did he find MI5's boss convincing.

By Heath's assessment, London needed to restore its high-level political interactions with Moscow, which had been downgraded after Britain rightly condemned the Soviet invasion of Czechoslovakia in 1968. His approach, however, was less about extending an olive branch to the Kremlin than confronting it about Soviet spying in the United Kingdom, which in the autumn of 1970, British officials told him had become widespread and blatant.

Heath's previous experience in dealing with Soviet espionage would have told him that resolving it through diplomatic channels alone was unrealistic, particularly because of Moscow's tendency to deny any knowledge of, or involvement in, spying in foreign countries. Yet since diplomacy offers an avenue for registering a concern in good faith before taking drastic political action, Heath ordered his foreign secretary, Sir Alec Douglas-Home, to raise the espionage problem with his Soviet counterpart, Andrei Gromyko.

Shortly before that happened, Heath was alerted to a different kind of security dilemma that required his immediate attention – one involving Britain's closest ally, the United States. President Richard Nixon, one of the first world leaders to congratulate him on his election to office, was embarking on a European tour and wanted to schedule a brief stopover to meet the prime minister in early October. Unwilling to accept Britain's safety assurances around the proposed visit, a US Secret Service team arrived a fortnight ahead of Nixon to evaluate the security risks and protocols at the prime minister's country residence, Chequers, and its surrounding estate.

It became startlingly obvious that the Americans had different standards when they were meticulous enough to take an interest even in the safety of the house's water supply. To accommodate their concerns, Heath's head of security staff walked them to a spring on a hill nearby, informing the Americans that the water probably came from there. He then walked them halfway down the hill to a water tank, before taking them to the junction at the base of the hill through which the water supply came into the residence. The Americans remained concerned about the water's protracted route, and having initially considered placing a security guard at each of the three points to prevent a potential poisoning of the supply, they then scrapped the plan and decided to fly in bottled water from the United States.

The informal lunch at Chequers on 3 October 1970 went smoothly, and Nixon enjoyed his afternoon tea with the prime minister as much as he enjoyed emphasising the importance of discussing their policies with complete freedom and transparency. Yet it was not until that evening, shortly after Nixon's departure, that Chequers' staff realised they had committed a major security breach when a cook raised questions about the bottled water stored in the kitchen.

It turned out that they had completely forgotten to enact the special security measures that had been put in place for the president, and had served him normal water instead. While the mishap drew chuckles among staff, it would later emerge that the US Secret Service had perhaps been right in its fears about the water supply, because the KGB had around that time tasked Oleg Lyalin to identify ways of poisoning Britain's water.

While Lyalin remained below MI5's radar, he had seen a few colleagues from the Soviet Trade Mission get kicked out of the country for espionage activities. And espionage was the central point that Britain's foreign secretary wanted to raise with his counterpart, Andrei Gromyko, in late October 1970. Gromyko's visit to London was an opportune time for such a discussion, Douglas-Home figured, but during his meeting with the Kremlin's foreign minister on Wednesday 28 October to raise his objection about illegal Soviet activities in Britain, he was confronted by a moment of irony.

After denying the spying accusations against locally based Soviet officials, Gromyko appealed to Douglas-Home to approve the visa of a Soviet official who had been assigned to the embassy in London, but whose application had been rejected after British authorities rightly suspected that he was an undeclared spy. While the British foreign secretary humoured Gromyko and promised to study the case 'carefully', he ultimately stood by the decision that the official in question was 'unacceptable for any appointment' in the UK.

Still hoping for a diplomatic solution over the 'inadmissible Soviet activities' in Britain, Douglas-Home wrote to Gromyko five weeks later, urging him to take immediate action. In a letter dated 3 December 1970, he stated:

I find myself constrained to write to you about the scale and nature of the intelligence activities conducted by Soviet officials in this country and about the frequency of the attempts which had been made in recent months to introduce to this country officials who in the past have been engaged in such activities.

While diplomatic in tone, the letter underscored the foreign secretary's eagerness to stop Soviet spies being manoeuvred into Britain under the guise of embassy or trade officials. He also reminded his counterpart that four Soviets had been made persona non grata that year for that very reason:

> In 1970 alone we have refused the visas to more than half a dozen Soviet officials assigned to this country because we have every reason to suspect on the basis of what we know about their previous activities, that if they were admitted to this country they would not restrict themselves to work which we regard as legitimate and conducive to the maintenance and development of good relations.
>
> Most of the men whom we have refused had been appointed to the Soviet trade delegation. I know that the Soviet trade delegation is not directly subordinated to your Ministry, but since you, as Minister for Foreign Affairs of the USSR, are concerned with all the matters which affect the foreign relations of your country, I wish to invite to your attention the number of cases which have come to light of late in which members of the Soviet trade delegation have been found to engage in totally inadmissible activities. This year alone permission to stay in this country has been withdrawn from four members of the Soviet trade delegation.

The tussle between Douglas-Home and Gromyko was happening in a different stratosphere to the one Oleg Lyalin inhabited, but the tensions between the Heath government and the Brezhnev regime certainly filtered down to the Soviet mission's rank and file in London. Lyalin had become increasingly alert to the more aggressive approach that the new British government seemed to be taking against Soviet officials, and subsequent events were set to shake him even further.

* * *

Eighteen months into his posting to London, Oleg Lyalin started to wonder seriously if his cover had been blown, and whether MI5 was allowing him to continue operations in order to get a broader understanding of his network. An obvious question in his mind would have been whether the British agency knew about his sources, including Siroj Abdoolcader, and to what extent it was aware of his habits, including all the drinking and partying that was fuelling his social life. His concern was not a product of an overactive imagination or paranoia, but in reaction to a call from Kentish Town police station to the Soviet delegation in September 1970. A police officer had called to ask for him by name, and on discovering that Lyalin was out of the office, left a message for him with his colleague.

With no diplomatic cover to hide behind and no way of ignoring the inquiry without raising further questions, Lyalin attended the police station in north-west London, only to discover that an officer there merely wanted to confirm his postal address. That only heightened Lyalin's suspicion and it would not have been far-fetched for him to think that the whole episode was part of an MI5 ploy. If he really were compromised, then a change of behaviour might mask his future operations, but it could not undo anything he had already been caught doing. Without knowing for certain if he were being watched, he carried on with his operational work including meeting with his agents, and continued socialising, yet with a sense of foreboding that he was a marked man.

Already onto his second marriage by the time he had arrived in the UK, Lyalin had never felt shackled by the bonds of matrimony, and was not planning to change his ways in his early thirties. He was aware, much like his colleagues at the Soviet mission in London, that there were endless affairs going on between officials, both married and single. 'There is of course a good deal of assorted sex within the Russian community, and provided that this is reasonably discreet no one will pay too much attention to it,' he would later reveal. 'If matters, however, get out of hand and there is any danger of a public scandal, then people are sent home . . . The general Russian attitude over women is that it is the fools who get caught and they are the ones who deserve to suffer.'

Soviet officials with a taste for hedonism had to avoid unintended pregnancies, the contraction of a venereal disease, or anything else that publicly embarrassed the embassy. Womanising was an important part of espionage in Lyalin's view, and in some ways he felt liberated, rather than constrained, by the KGB's rules around affairs, because he knew exactly how to break them. He declared each fling with a British woman to his bosses as part of his operational work.

'In theory any relationship with a local woman would lead to repatriation of the official concerned,' according to a note of Lyalin's recollection. 'The intelligent KGB officer will of course declare his interest in a woman by suggesting that she is a potential intelligence recruit, and provided he has already reported this contact he can usually get away with it, provided again that reasonable discretion is shown.'

Under KGB rules, even excessive drinking was condoned, providing there were no 'complaints from neighbours'. Beyond such rules, it was Lyalin's infectious charm and likeability that helped him to get away with mischievous behaviour. His colleagues endured his flamboyant lifestyle and even overlooked the fact he had a wife and child who spent their time between

England and Russia. He was the master of playing the class clown, as though he wanted his non-KGB colleagues to focus on his sense of humour and clumsiness, to avoid arousing any suspicion about his undercover identity. 'He would drop pencils, upset teacups and even trip over the doormat,' a colleague at Razno declared about his work behaviour.

The hectic pace of darting around London's West End attending dinners, discos and dates, and generating secret funds by fiddling his work expense accounts, did not seem to interfere with his mission – his operational schedule was as busy as his social diary. He had been tasked by head office to make 'contingency plans' for assassinating British politicians and causing starvation by sabotaging the UK's 'emergency food supplies'. Other KGB targets included 'public utilities, the railways, government and military communications, government offices and shelters'.

The Soviet agency's long-term ambition had been the 'demoralisation of the civilian population' in Britain and 'the complete disruption of the political and economic life of the country'. It believed, for instance, that a sabotage attack against railways would generate a lasting security scare, dim the population's willingness to travel and eventually 'paralyse the economic life of the community'.

Lyalin also wanted to damage British–US relations, one of the aims of his posting, and took an interest in the US Navy base at Holy Loch on Scotland's west coast. The base had been of major importance to Washington since the late 1950s, when President Eisenhower had convinced Britain that the US needed a secure location in European waters within striking distance of the Soviet Union.

American naval officials favoured the Scottish location because it would fast-track the replenishment of crews, ensuring vessels would no longer need to return to the United States after each patrol, a round trip that would take up to a fortnight and cost as many days in each operational cycle. Each submarine that sailed into the US base was to be armed with Polaris nuclear missiles, far deadlier than any bombs that had been dropped during the Second World War – and the vessels, their weapons, and sailors, were to be of great strategic significance to the US.

However, the arrival of American naval crews aboard the support ship USS *Proteus* at Holy Loch in 1961 prompted a series of anti-arms demonstrations at the site – a public opposition to the British and US government agreement that Moscow wanted to exploit and, almost a decade later, Lyalin was eager to act on. The controversy surrounding the loch would have been of great help to Lyalin and his KGB colleagues in London, as they analysed the plausibility of targeting the base. Lyalin knew that the site, which sits in an inlet of the River Clyde, would be out of bounds to anyone without a security clearance. Naval officials there kept a close eye on technical and operational secrets, precisely the information Soviet spies had specialised in targeting in the race for military supremacy against the West.

However, stealing nuclear technology was not part of Lyalin's mission, because in the spring of 1967, the Kremlin had obtained a secret submarine manual from the Holy Loch site. It had appeared to be a tradecraft coup, until three KGB agents, including an American serviceman, were arrested and jailed. As a result, US and British vigilance around Holy Loch increased significantly, deterring future KGB attempts to infiltrate it. It was an embarrassment for Moscow and a wake-up call for the Soviet spy service, forcing it to rethink its operational methodology when targeting US Navy assets in Britain.

As someone trained in circumventing security restrictions and avoiding detection, Lyalin considered a more subtle approach. Along with his Department V colleagues, he drew up plans for targeting the waters at the base instead, proposing to pollute the River Clyde with radioactive waste. By doing so, they believed they could stoke the ongoing fears held by anti-nuclear protesters, who had been warning for years about the potential release of radioactive debris from the operation and maintenance of nuclear submarines in the Firth of Clyde.

Though Lyalin's operational commitments seemed to be ever-expanding, between developing plots to kill, sabotage and poison, and working out new missions for his agents, his fast-paced double-life was becoming a recipe for stress. And while he thought he was subtle in his extramarital affairs, he had developed a reputation at the Soviet trade mission as a serial womaniser with a habit of propositioning colleagues. Complicating his marriage, which was already on life-support by late 1970, were Lyalin's feelings for a colleague's wife.

Chapter 8

# THE KGB'S RULEBOOK ON EXTRAMARITAL AFFAIRS

AT THE SOVIET TRADE delegation's headquarters in north-east London, most men and women went about their daily work stoically and in administrative uniformity, like automated functionaries operating to the Kremlin's programme setting. They were there by invitation, guests of a country that had cautiously accepted them in the name of economic diplomacy. But above all, they were embodiments of the hammer and sickle who had proven their loyalty, if not their merit, to mother Russia – and in some instances landed their postings with the help of family links. Aside from top management that interacted with British government officials, other trade delegates were supposed to remain faceless, faithful servants.

One stood out in the eyes of her colleagues, however, for having an undeniable presence, even when stationed at her desk examining sales product descriptions. Some say it was her 'husky Russian voice' and blonde hair that drew the 'stunningly beautiful'

Irina Georgiyevna Teplyakova to Oleg Lyalin – and that she, in turn, had been swept away by his carefree nature, sense of playfulness and charm.

Whatever sparked their romance, their professional paths were destined to intersect because they both worked as import experts, on the lookout for British sellers offering great deals. Lyalin and Teplyakova were also in their early thirties, known to assist colleagues with English translations, and had been some of the first officials drafted to help the delegation's affiliated export firm, Razno, when it was set up about a year earlier. But it was their interactions outside of work, where Teplyakova had become Lyalin's 'constant companion' at 'fashionable Mayfair or Soho nightspots' in London's West End, that were being noticed.

Even at the trade mission, their behaviour – the banter, the glances, the knowing smiles – suggested that they were lovers. Their office colleagues suspected that much, but somehow Teplyakova's husband, Anatoly, who also worked in the same office, had no idea. Anatoly's ignorance of what his wife was up to may have been a result of his travel back and forth to Moscow for work and to check in on their seven-year-old son, Ivan, who attended school in the Russian capital and lived with Teplyakova's parents.

Teplyakova confided in a curious work friend that she was having an affair, but did not mention her lover's name. 'I knew both Irina and Oleg quite well,' a Soviet trade official would later recall. 'Irina was a tall, good-looking . . . woman and it was very awkward for her, of course, because she was married . . . Irina talked to me about the affair she was having, but she never told me that it was [with] Oleg – although, of course, I knew too well. They were never outrageous together in the office, but I and the other girls knew what was happening.'

In late 1970, while Lyalin was already informing friends that he wanted to divorce Tamara, there was nothing to suggest that Teplyakova was in the same place in her relationship with her husband. In fact, she had just celebrated her ninth wedding anniversary in September and her husband adored her. While she trusted that Lyalin would keep their affair a secret, it is unlikely that he trusted her enough at that point to inform her that he was merely pretending to be a trade delegate and was in fact a KGB operative. Even if he had told her, it may not have come as a shock. Her own father, a former Soviet foreign service official named Georgi Stetsenko, had served as a correspondent with the Soviet News Agency, or TASS, in Sweden in the 1950s, but had himself been a Kremlin intelligence official working undercover.

Stetsenko, aka 'Gergii', had been posted to Stockholm in 1951 to run a Swedish naval official, Ernst Hilding Andersson, who had been recruited by Moscow five years earlier. Andersson provided a range of secrets, including those about the 'defences of Swedish naval bases [and] the readiness of the fleet', and also boarded British ships visiting the Nordic country to obtain briefings about them before producing a 'report written with invisible ink' for his handlers. Andersson had likely known Stetsenko by another name. When he was arrested for espionage offences in late 1951, Andersson confessed to his crimes and gave up his Soviet handlers, but Stetsenko's name did not feature in prosecution records, so he managed to continue operating in Stockholm.

Stetsenko also maintained his connection with Soviet intelligence officials in the wider Nordic region, including one in Finland with whom he was a close family friend – Anatoly Golitsyn. But it seems that Golitsyn had lived his cover well as 'Anatoly Klimov', to the extent that when Teplyakova had met his spouse, she was introduced to her as Svetlana, the wife of

Mr Klimov. Teplyakova would later recall that during a trip to Finland to see her parents, she met Svetlana, and heard that her husband had taken up his post at the Soviet Embassy in Helsinki in July 1960.

'She heard his story when she visited her parents in Finland and, while there, she met Golitsyn's wife who called on her mother,' a recently declassified intelligence file reveals. 'Irina Tepliakova [*sic*] however also knew of Golitsyn as Klimov.' Teplyakova only learned that the Klimovs were in fact the Golitsyns after the KGB officer and his family defected to the US in December 1961.

Teplyakova's tangential links into the world of espionage, whether through her father's work and friendship circles, or via Lyalin's own operational activities that she was about to discover, would not have been uncommon, because of the sheer volume of Soviet foreign service officials directly or indirectly affiliated to the likes of the KGB. But those involved in the business of stealing secrets were often also proficient at leading double lives in their domestic affairs – as Lyalin had been doing behind his wife's back, and also Teplyakova's.

At one point Lyalin was reportedly dating five women at once. The impulse for *joie de vivre* that had blighted his early career and cost him a deployment to America, appeared to have been revived with irrepressible force with each week he spent immersed in London's vibrant lifestyle. He seemed to become more extroverted with age, more vocal and more flirtatious, as a newly hired colleague at Razno learned.

Susan Woodthorpe joined the Soviet firm as a receptionist in late 1970, mainly performing administrative duties such as welcoming visitors and taking and transferring calls. Having grown up working at her father's pub in Tottenham, north London, the attractive nineteen-year-old knew how to make a great first impression. She exuded confidence, barely wore make-up aside from mascara to frame her large blue eyes, and her blonde bob appeared more windswept to the right side than styled. Woodthorpe looked people directly in the eyes during conversations and was not opposed to flirting.

Soon after she started working at Razno, she found herself having to entertain, and be entertained by, a 'handsome' and vibrant man who would burst into the office 'always in a suit', speaking in an 'American-style' accent and often bearing gifts. 'Oleg Lyalin used to come to the office and bring caviar sandwiches, caviar and cream cheese,' Woodthorpe recalled fondly more than fifty years later during an interview with the author. 'I don't know where he got them from, maybe from the trade delegation.' And he often showed up at the office with another gift in hand – vodka. 'Stolichnaya vodka,' said Woodthorpe. 'That's what he used to bring in. I don't know if he gave anybody else any, but he certainly gave me some. He'd give me the entire bottle.'

Woodthorpe was about thirteen years his junior, and was rather familiar with older men trying to overwhelm her with charm. Lyalin had done exactly that even during their very first interaction in the office. 'He was a very friendly person, very chatty, very flirty, and loud, very loud,' she said. Woodthorpe did not know that he was married, as he never mentioned having a spouse and child during their many conversations and after-work drinks. She was also under the impression that he was in his mid-twenties rather than early thirties, because he was youthful in spirit, looks and demeanour.

'I went out a couple of times [with him] just for drinks,' she said, and the pair became close enough colleagues that she invited him to her father's pub, where she introduced him to members of her family. 'He was a bit of a clown . . . a bit of a character.' Woodthorpe said Lyalin was like she had been in her early twenties, 'here, there, and everywhere', always on the lookout for excitement. 'He was very much like me, an adventurer,' she said. And he could have been a 'potential lover . . . had I been more forthcoming.'

About eighteen months had passed since Oleg Lyalin arrived in England and inherited Siroj Abdoolcader through his predecessor. While Abdoolcader continued supplying the registration details of MI5 surveillance vehicles, he was falling short of Lyalin's growing demands. As someone who instinctively shirked responsibility, blaming anyone but himself for his setbacks, Abdoolcader was presumably in denial about the obvious mismatch between his versatility as a spy and the missions Lyalin gave him. Of course, he wanted to impress his handler and at times he even lied about the accuracy of information he provided, including vehicle registrations, to feel more valued and hard-working.

In his relentless drive for validation and belonging, Abdoolcader had earned 'rewards' at Lyalin's discretion, including a 'transistor radio', a 'toiletry set' and 'various sums of money, the largest of which was about £100' – equivalent to about a month's salary for a manual worker. He was also given thoughtful birthday presents, and in one case, an electric razor inscribed, 'To our dearest Siroj on his birthday'. The KGB had effectively replaced his family, and Abdoolcader was thrilled to feel he had a home again. He had found his social tribe, as evidenced by his musing in diary entries that described Lyalin as a 'good friend' and occasionally reflected on the 'lovely' evenings that the two had spent together.

It was a problem in the making, however, that Abdoolcader's motivation for spying came from a place of personal insecurity and need for acceptance, rather than an inherent passion for espionage or a natural inclination for it. His brain was not fast enough, his ploys were not clever enough, and winning was not in his nature. Even worse, he was uncoachable to the point that his application of Lyalin's instructions invariably misfired when it came to turning operational rehearsals into field realities.

To further his own interests and garner praise, Abdoolcader had provided Lyalin with the contact details of a Ministry of Defence (MoD) official that he claimed was an acquaintance with 'access to classified information'. Pretty quickly, however, it became apparent that Abdoolcader knew little about her work. The MoD official had merely told him she 'could not talk about' her work because it was 'confidential'. He also completely overplayed to Lyalin how well he knew the official, because instead of being a friend as he had claimed, she was just someone he had once met at a party. So in the test of cultivating a potential new source for KGB exploitation, Abdoolcader pretty much scored zero.

Perhaps sensing early on that a different approach was required, Lyalin pointed Abdoolcader towards another MoD official, Marie Theresa Antoinette Richardson. She was a personal assistant to the Royal Navy's deputy director of supplies and support staff, whose details had been provided to Lyalin by Moscow. Richardson's name had been flagged during her holiday on a Baltic cruise through Denmark, Finland and Leningrad in 1969, when Soviet officials spotted that she had written 'Ministry of Defence' as her place of work on a customs form. A female Soviet customs official then tried to befriend her on the trip, but Richardson saw through the cultivation attempt and on her return home informed British naval authorities, who then alerted MI5.

Unaware that Richardson had briefed the British authorities about her travel experience, the KGB planned to target her in London and, through Lyalin, gave Abdoolcader her name and photograph. Lyalin believed that because Richardson 'was born in India', she would somehow be willing to betray her British employer and be a 'likely contact'. A supposition that was not only racialist but operationally naive, as was Abdoolcader's approach of adopting an 'Indian name' to try and ingratiate himself with her.

Abdoolcader phoned Richardson, presumably to arrange a meeting, claiming his name was 'Siroj Ali'. It is very likely that he was nervous, and painfully aware that the task he had been handed was well beyond his limited capabilities. His story quickly unravelled, and on failing to convince Richardson about his assumed name, Abdoolcader switched his story and committed the greatest espionage faux pas of all by revealing his true identity. But even then he was unconvincing.

'He told her his real name and place of work, passing himself off as the friend of Siroj Ali,' according to an outline of the comical episode. The fact Abdoolcader had broken cover in a single call and drawn unneeded suspicion to himself could only have diminished Lyalin's faith in him. But Lyalin's demands towards him remained unchanged, perhaps believing – or even hoping – that the clumsy agent would improve over time.

However, he continued to disappoint. Far from accumulating espionage victories as he and his handler had hoped, Abdoolcader kept proving to be largely incompetent, including when asked to organise a basic dead drop in a vehicle parked in Portsmouth, on the English south coast. Lyalin must have been left scratching his head in dismay when Abdoolcader returned from the mission with the suitcase in hand, because he 'couldn't find the car'.

Compounding Abdoolcader's setbacks in the field was his mindless disregard for concealing his Communist sympathies and his collaboration with the KGB. His apartment in Cricklewood, north-west London, was littered with Communist literature, a biography of British turncoat Kim Philby by his wife called

*The Spy I Loved*, and documents listing the registration numbers of MI5 vehicles.

Abdoolcader's shortcomings conveyed the KGB's flawed recruitment objectives. In its push to expand its reach in Britain, the Soviet agency seemed more interested in increasing its number of agents than ensuring that they were the right fit. It somehow believed that such recruits would shed their intellectual deficiencies by learning on the job, or in the worst-case scenario, handlers could milk them dry for what they could provide and eventually burn them – an approach known as 'pumping and dumping' in espionage vernacular.

As Lyalin soon realised, a few hours of tradecraft training here and there were largely insufficient when it came to his London agents in general. Abdoolcader was not alone in his incompetence. Lyalin had operational challenges when training Kyriacos Costi, too – the tailor who had been recruited by the KGB through his brother-in-law, Constantinos Martianou.

While he found it easy enough to instruct Costi on how to shake off potential surveillance 'in the streets, on buses and trains' and how to 'meet with him without being followed', Lyalin struggled to teach him Morse code. Perhaps he expected way too much from Costi, who had left school aged twelve to work as a tailor. But Lyalin refused to give up. He disregarded Costi's cognitive gap when it came to encoding and decoding messages for secret communication, and kept trying to turn him into a professional.

At some point in mid-1970, Lyalin met Costi in Soho and drove him in his car to a 'very quiet road' in Hammersmith, around seven miles away in west London. 'He switched on the radio and tuned it into Morse signals,' and then over two hours, Lyalin 'explained . . . Morse code', Costi later recalled. The second tutorial was similar in tone and setting to the first. 'He met me as arranged and we went in his car,' Costi said. 'This time he gave me more lessons in Morse code and gave me a tape with Morse code on it . . . I practised with the tape and later gave it back to him.'

Lyalin maintained his calm when Costi still failed to grasp Morse code and figured the spy needed to decompress, to escape the espionage drills for a bit of sunshine on the continent. He instructed Costi to go on holiday to Italy, and encouraged him to visit Rome, Pisa and Portofino. He even financed Costi's trip with £140 in 'single £1 notes'. On 15 November 1970, Lyalin met Costi after his return from the six-week jaunt.

'He said now that I had been on holiday and was rested, I should work harder at practising at receiving and decoding the radio messages. At first after my holiday he didn't show any annoyance, but afterwards he started getting fed up with me because I couldn't learn decoding.' Yet somehow, amid all of their capability blunders and general operational ineptitude, Lyalin's agents, including Abdoolcader and Costi, managed to remain invisible to MI5, whose central purpose was to bust agents like them – but whose officers were still erratically chasing their tails in the hunt for traitors in their own ranks.

* * *

As the chief protector of MI5's reputation and operational mission, and the primary key holder to vaults containing its unpublicised achievements and unforgiving failures, Martin Furnival Jones had become enslaved by his organisation's greatest secret, and it was entirely his own doing. Perhaps he had felt that inviting non-agency officials into a briefing about Roger Hollis could potentially prejudice the case against him, when Furnival Jones himself had remained uncertain about the allegations against his old boss. But with a major development set to unfold in the former director general's matter – one that would draw Hollis directly into the firing line – Furnival Jones had a change of heart.

He informed the nation's most senior civil servant, Cabinet Secretary Sir Burke Trend, and the head official at the Home Office, Permanent Secretary Sir Phillip Allen, that Hollis had been under investigation for some time and was about to be subjected to an interrogation. Having become Britain's top civil servant in 1963 while Hollis was still serving as MI5's chief, Trend knew him well, yet there is no evidence suggesting that he challenged the agency's handling of Hollis's case. Allen did, on the other hand, and appealed to Furnival Jones to inform Ted Heath, saying the prime minister should not be kept in the dark about a matter of such national security significance.

It was indeed extraordinary that Heath had not been brought into the picture, even though by February 1971, when Hollis was first interrogated by MI5, the former agency chief had been under suspicion for about five years, and under investigation for almost two years. Could Furnival Jones have taken that stance because he felt there would have been too much explaining to do? One could imagine that after receiving a briefing on Hollis, Heath's first question would have been about why he had not been informed earlier.

Other questions would undoubtedly have followed, including ones about who else had known before him, and perhaps even what justified keeping him, the nation's elected leader, out of the circle of trust when the CIA – a foreign entity – was regularly being updated through its counter-intelligence director, James Angleton. And since Furnival Jones had taken the unilateral decision to keep the prime minister uninformed, and the one before him, then what else was he likely to withhold from Heath? Surely that question alone would have jeopardised Heath's confidence and trust in MI5's top official and potentially cost Furnival Jones his job. So in part it may have been the fear of facing up to such questions that helped to convince Furnival Jones to stick to his guns and leave the prime minister in the dark.

Furnival Jones's continued scepticism about the allegations against Hollis could only have been heightened by the resolution of Graham Mitchell's case several months earlier. The two cases had some obvious similarities, but the most common thread between them was FLUENCY, the joint MI5 and MI6 investigations unit overseeing them. A major problem was that the unit was being run more like an active prosecution by its chairman Peter Wright than a considered, level-headed and independent investigative body. Anyone who was dragged into its net seemed to be presumed guilty, rather than being given the benefit of the doubt and then assessed on the basis of solid evidence.

Despite a seven-year ordeal, during which the former MI5 deputy director general was at times subjected to wiretaps and followed by surveillance officers to determine whether he was a Soviet mole, Mitchell was cleared of any wrongdoing by Furnival Jones, and the FLUENCY case against him was finally closed in August 1970. In some ways, Furnival Jones was relieved by the outcome, but must have been very embarrassed that he had authorised a case that was somewhat meritless, built on the back of a paranoid hunch in 1963 that had been championed and amplified by Soviet defector Anatoly Golitsyn.

Golitsyn's toxic influence on MI5 since his defection, from the false accusation against Mitchell to his unsubstantiated claim that Harold Wilson was a KGB spy, had taken their toll on the British agency, destabilising its assessments and analysis and undermining its self-confidence. It was absurd that Furnival Jones always felt the need to reach across the Atlantic for advice from Golitsyn and Angleton. And in early 1971, he must have arrived at that very conclusion, or one similar, because he was about to change his approach to dealing with US agencies, especially the CIA.

Conveniently, or perhaps serendipitously, the forthcoming transformation in MI5's dealings with Langley was set to happen independently of, but around the same time as, Ted Heath's step change in his interactions with the Nixon Administration. The prime minister had started to question Anglo-American relations the previous year and was determined to reframe them more favourably towards Britain's foreign policy goals.

Greeted by a full military guard of honour on his first official visit to the White House, Ted Heath stood alongside Richard Nixon on the South Lawn, at the back of the presidential residence, as the leader of the free world paid tribute to the closeness between their two nations. 'Our countries have a Special Relationship which we often refer to,' Nixon said on the morning of 17 December 1970. 'That relationship can be described in terms of a common language, of our adherence to the common law, and of the various institutions of government which we share in common.'

During his brief welcoming remarks at the beginning of the prime minister's two-day visit, Nixon evoked the Special Relationship twice – and that was twice too many for Heath's taste. Because unlike Nixon, he saw the Special Relationship as a potential obstacle for Britain's relationships with other countries, some of which were wary of London's closeness to Washington. So while the prime minister gritted his teeth politely during the South Lawn address, and in his response praised the 'courage of American people' and the US's post-war generosity in helping to 'rebuild Europe', Heath waited until the pair were in a private setting to air his real views about the ties that bound Britain to the United States.

While there was obviously some prestige and value associated with London's historical links to Washington that Heath wanted to preserve, he understood that the 'Special Relationship', the phrase popularised by former British prime minister Winston Churchill after the Second World War, was a broad concept rather than an operating framework. Heath wanted Britain also to have a series of strong relationships with others, including European and Latin America nations.

Europe was a key economic attraction that had eluded Britain for more than a decade. An application by Harold Macmillan's Conservative government to join the European Economic Community, which later became the European Union, was blocked by French President Charles de Gaulle in 1963 because he distrusted the UK's foreign policy intimacy with the US and 'feared that British membership would weaken the French voice' on the continent. A second membership bid was made under Labour's Harold Wilson, but that too was vetoed by de Gaulle in 1967 for similar reasons, including that 'Anglo-American relations would lead to the United States increasing its influence in Europe'.

Yet even after de Gaulle's resignation in 1969 and his death eighteen months later, Britain remained conscious of the persisting distrust that the late leader had fomented about its closeness to Washington. Heath wanted to overcome that hurdle, chiefly because a third application was in play for EEC membership – and the prime minister wanted to succeed where two British leaders before him had failed.

He could not let Nixon's comments about the Special Relationship remain unchallenged, and shortly after the official pleasantries on the South Lawn, Heath expressed his views in another brief speech at the White House, but to a more intimate gathering, including Nixon and his wife. The prime minister said he was not in favour of a special relationship between their nations, because such a bond risked being broken by either party and could also offend other allies. Heath said he preferred a 'natural relationship' instead.

'I believed in a natural relationship, the result of our common history and institutions, which nobody could take away from us,' he later recalled in his autobiography. His speech was diplomatic speak, because what the prime minister had intended to say but did not articulate was that he wanted to ease the perceived love affair between the transatlantic countries in order to secure Britain's entry into the EEC. But his approach ultimately worked; Nixon got the message.

'This was fully accepted by President Nixon, who always got on well with the British, and indeed, with most Europeans,' Heath noted. 'He firmly believed in the creation of a strong European community as the basis for an effective NATO [the North Atlantic Treaty Organisation of which Britain was a founding member in 1949].' A month after Heath's White House visit, Nixon sent him a letter to yet again honour the relationship between their two nations. But notably, Nixon had changed his tone in line with the prime minister's earlier suggestion.

'When on 22 January 1971 Nixon sent his "warm personal regards",' Heath recalled, 'my advisors and I noticed with interest his statement that "I look forward to continuing our dialogue and to further strengthening the natural relationship between our countries and ourselves; and I hope you shall always feel yourself at home here in Washington".'

Heath felt appeased and one step closer to his hopes of a more united front with Europe. However, an unexpected event that year would test the sincerity of their platitudes and bring into question the meaning of political transparency between Heath and Nixon. That event would involve a KGB officer who had been plotting against both their nations during his time in London – Oleg Lyalin.

* * *

As spring approached in 1971, Oleg Lyalin was feeling increasingly unsettled at work, trapped in a psychological minefield that he had single-handedly constructed. At one end, he was contending with the incessant lies he had told his wife – and on the other, he was a slave to his sexual proclivities and multiple love affairs. Having so desperately craved an international posting and overcome professional hurdles to attain his goal, Lyalin wanted to resolve his personal dilemmas without compromising his career. He wanted a reset. To bring an end to his failing marriage and begin a new chapter away from the chaos that he had dug himself into during his two years in London.

One idea he had been considering to resolve his personal conflicts was to return to Moscow, seek an official divorce, and then start afresh in a new job at Lubyanka, the KGB's headquarters. His operational work in Britain had been satisfying but not without problems, especially because the three agents he had inherited were not performing as he had hoped. Siroj Abdoolcader was a dud, and the two brothers-in-law, Kyriacos Costi and Constantinos Martianou, were average at best. But abandoning ship and leaving Britain was a long shot, because Lyalin's career prospects were out of his hands.

The KGB was under no obligation to shorten his posting, into which it had invested money and training and would typically have expected to get three or more years from. It would have also expected Lyalin to land some breakthroughs, including new recruits, which were not materialising. So he was not really in a position to ask his bosses for any special privileges. Lyalin's domestic problems were solely his.

By April 1971, he was set on a plan that he thought could guarantee his return to Moscow. It was a scheme that could even improve his professional standing among his colleagues, he figured. Much like his undercover work, it required careful consideration, patience and, most of all, good timing.

Lyalin knew about the notoriety garnered by KGB officers who were expelled by their host nations. While the KGB's leadership at Lubyanka resented dealing with the logistical headaches and diplomatic tussles associated with compromised officers, it was also quietly proud of the mischief they had committed before being caught spying. So Lyalin thought if he could create the pretext for his own expulsion, then he too could return to a hero's welcome at central command in Moscow.

# Chapter 9

# A SUSPICIOUS WALK-IN

AN AUDIO ARCHIVE OF Oleg Lyalin's voice was being created, and he could see, close up on the recorder, the tape strip winding itself around the take-up reel. Placed in front of him to ensure the sound quality of each word it picked up, the recording device was also a constant reminder that what he was saying could never be unsaid and that all of his disclosures would subsequently be checked for clues and accuracy. He had not been informed about a second recorder, concealed somewhere in the room to produce a backup audio in case the first malfunctioned, but he must have presumed from his years of espionage work that the MI5 safe house to which he had been invited was as wired up as an electric store.

Lyalin had assured his MI5 debriefers, Harry Wharton and Tony Brooks, that no subject was off limits, essentially daring them to ask about his operational work, cover duties and personal life. And he appeared determined to stand by that pledge when the pair brought him in for questioning. He knew little about his hosts, and most probably not even their real names, but he did know that they would be sceptical about every secret he was sharing. They had no reason to believe him, given the circumstances under which he had sought them out on 21 April 1971.

Only hours earlier that Wednesday, Lyalin had approached a duty officer at Hampstead police station in north London, identified himself as a Soviet trade representative, and asked to speak to counter-intelligence specialists with whom he could share important information. It was part of a plan that he had been ruminating over for several months, Lyalin would later claim, but one that had coalesced in only weeks, if not days, before. Within moments of introducing himself to specialist officers at the police station, Lyalin revealed that he was a KGB officer using the trade delegation as his cover. He rightly anticipated that the officers would alert MI5, because the spy agency has primacy on matters relating to domestic espionage.

The British security service was seasoned in managing voluntary Soviet spies, as it had done so at the end of the Second World War when Russian cypher clerk Igor Gouzenko defected in Ottawa and Canadian authorities invited MI5 to debrief him. But the British agency's direct experience with 'volunteers' was now a little outdated. And while some of its senior officials had been involved during the 1960s in debriefing Soviet turncoats and Bloc operatives, including the Polish intelligence officer Michal Goliniewski and KGB official Anatoly Golitsyn, they had done it at the invitation, and under the supervision, of the CIA.

Lyalin's case was unique, because MI5 had never before been presented with a Soviet volunteer of his calibre on its own turf, and nor had it been aware that the KGB's Department V even had officers at the Soviet agency's London residency. So when Hampstead police informed MI5 about Lyalin, Wharton and

Brooks were dispatched to meet the KGB captain to determine whether he passed the sniff test. Martin Furnival Jones must have awaited an update with trepidation and contained excitement.

Lyalin's approach via a police station had been a bold move and it was intended to appear that way, since he had voluntarily broken cover. His action seemed a little too carefully considered and calculated, bearing all the hallmarks of a 'dangle' – an intelligence official dispatched to provide secrets mired in disinformation for the sake of damaging an enemy service. Exactly what MI5 and the CIA had been fearing for more than a decade. The timing of his approach that spring would also have raised questions among MI5 officials. The Heath government had declared its intention to place the Soviet trade delegation in its sights only five months earlier, when the foreign secretary, Sir Alec Douglas-Home, wrote to his Soviet counterpart and accused the trade mission of facilitating the KGB's espionage activities in the UK.

It would have been reasonable for Wharton and Brooks to suspect that Lyalin had been sent on KGB orders to expose some aspects of the Soviet agency's work in London for the sake of concealing far more sensitive ones. Or had he been sent to gauge MI5's attitude to the Soviet trade delegation, which the KGB was desperate to preserve as a safe haven for some of its undercover officers? Such a question would have been in line with MI5's suspicion of 'walk-ins', because the agency had heard enough from Golitsyn and Angleton about the KGB's intention through its 'Master Plan' to dispatch fake volunteers. How could Lyalin be any different to, say, Yuri Nosenko, whom the CIA's most important arbiter on espionage, James Angleton, still believed was a KGB plant?

Lyalin's willingness to be so forthcoming and transparent in sharing secrets, when he had not been given any guarantees, was suspicious in itself. A central element of his supposed desire to spy for MI5 was especially difficult to believe, because it seemed to have been scripted and rehearsed to bolster a backstory – a legend.

He told his MI5 debriefers that he had intended to begin spying for the British service seven months earlier, in September 1970. He said he had called the 999 emergency hotline from a public phone booth in Highgate, north London, in an attempt to reach British intelligence authorities, but had hung up when the operator misunderstood his request. Yet if he had genuinely been so eager to divulge secrets in September 1970, why had he not called back there and then, or in the following days or weeks, instead of waiting seven months to approach MI5?

Could it be because seven months would be just about long enough to help him build the legend, to give a credible impression that he had tried to contact the British authorities through an anonymous call but had failed to get through? Had he even made the call in the first place? And if so, why had the 999 operator taken the bizarre step of offering him the number of the Soviet Embassy, as Lyalin was now claiming, when the embassy had nothing to do with the emergency hotline? Why had Lyalin not simply asked the operator to connect him to the police? Surely he had the requisite language skills to do that given that his posting to the UK was almost entirely based on his fluency in English? Such questions would have been obvious for MI5 to consider when Lyalin professed his long-standing desire to provide KGB secrets.

Another of Lyalin's early admissions would also have raised some red flags. He informed the British interrogators that he genuinely believed his cover had been blown by MI5 shortly after his arrival in the UK in the spring of 1969. Yet if that were true, and the KGB also believed it to be so, then why had the Soviet agency not sent him back home to avoid compromising his agency colleagues in London? Or had the KGB kept him in place in anticipation of eventually sacrificing his identity in a pre-meditated walk-in scenario?

Everything about must have Lyalin seemed way too con-venient, way too odd, and there was a lot to unpick in his disclosures, which in some instances appeared to be tailored to establish his candour. He went so far, so fast, and eventually exposed all his covers and revealed the multiple assumed names under which he performed his KGB duties, including 'Oleg Aleksandrovich Liabin, Aaron Adolfovich Stromvasser, Makarov, [and] Gutch'. Lyalin informed MI5 that he spoke 'good English, some German and a little bit of Spanish and French' and demonstrated that he was well-travelled, despite London being his 'only foreign posting' with the KGB. He said he had previously visited 'Bulgaria, Turkey, France, Italy, Gibraltar, Sweden, Denmark, Poland and East and West Germany' among other countries.

Yet of all his disclosures, Lyalin's overall motive presented the biggest credibility problem. Because he was not driven by some kind of ideological awakening, nor by money or even a desire to defect when he came knocking on MI5's door. He said he simply wanted the British service to arrange for his expulsion from the country, so that he could return to Moscow to divorce his wife without hampering his KGB career. In return, he said, he would spy for MI5 from Russia as an agent-in-place. The last two high profile Soviet agents-in-place, Pyotr Popov in the 1950s and Oleg Penkovsky in the 1960s, had become cautionary tales at the KGB after the agency uncovered their treachery and had them executed. So the fact Lyalin wanted to expose himself to such a risk was another reason to doubt his honesty or even question his mental stability.

'Lyalin originally approached [MI5] in 4/71 and reported that he was having matrimonial problems and was not progressing as well as he wanted in the KGB,' reveals a document citing an MI5 briefing. 'He proposed furnishing information if the British would have him declared persona non grata. He claimed such action would bring him praise from the KGB and would also permit him to return to Russia where he would institute divorce proceedings against his wife.'

While Lyalin's motive for returning to Moscow seemed peculiar at best, if not totally absurd, his detailed outline of the KGB's mission in Britain must have left Martin Furnival Jones questioning the competence of his officers who had been largely blind to the Soviet agency's local operations. The KGB, Lyalin revealed, had been planning multiple attacks against the country's critical infrastructure through its Department V section, to which he belonged.

'In his intelligence role, Lyalin's task was to make contingency plans for sabotage against military, political and economic targets in the United Kingdom,' his MI5 debriefers noted. 'Although according to Lyalin specific targets have not yet been allocated as between the KGB and the Chief of Intelligence Directorate (GRU).' Lyalin disclosed that since arriving in Britain two years earlier he had focused on identifying targets around the country, including Hayburn Wyke, a small cove on the north Yorkshire coast, that could be used by Soviet saboteurs as dropping zones for sea and airborne landings.

He said the Soviet regime, as part of its contingency planning in case of a future war with the UK, had ordered the KGB to plot a series of sabotage missions, including the destruction of railways, flooding of the London Underground, and the identification of high profile political figures that it could assassinate. The KGB was also preparing for the infiltration of military sites, as an intelligence document reveals:

Lyalin was in the process of selecting and reporting on sites to be used for the infiltration by air and sea of Soviet sabotage groups into the UK during the period of crisis preceding the outbreak of conventional war. He had submitted a comprehensive plan for the seaborne landing of a group (or groups) on the North Yorkshire coast and consideration was being given to the selection of a dropping zone for an airborne landing north of the Caledonian Canal [which stretches 60 miles between Scotland's east coast at Inverness to the west coast near Fort William]. He was also building up a group of UK-domiciled agents. The group which had already been equipped with a radio, was, when the time came, to have provided Lyalin with a self-contained operational base and to have been used to prepare for and subsequently to support the arrival and operations of the Soviet sabotage groups.

If MI5 had anticipated some change in Lyalin's motives during a series of debriefings that Wharton and Brooks conducted with him in the spring and summer of 1971, then the agency would have been disappointed. He remained unchanged, uninterested in asking for anything more than what he had first requested. An MI5 analysis into his disclosures revealed that he had been frank and transparent – and he had even sacrificed the identities of his local agents, including Siroj Abdoolcader, whom MI5 then placed under surveillance.

Lyalin's information covered a broad canvas, in some cases unlocking secrets far outside of his direct involvement but which he had picked up throughout his career, including matters relating to the GRU's presence in the UK. He also revealed at a later debriefing that the KGB was cultivating Joseph Kagan, a British businessman well known for his friendship with Harold Wilson.

Kagan's textile firm made the raincoats that had become a part of Wilson's image. He funded Wilson's private office and had even been knighted on the former prime minister's recommendation.

MI5 interrogators were staggered by Lyalin's allegation that his colleague at the KGB's London residency, Richardas Vaygauskas, was in regular contact with Kagan. When Brooks questioned Kagan about the claim, the businessman admitted that he had visited Vaygauskas's flat almost every week since 1964, the year Wilson was elected to Downing Street. Kagan said he and Vaygauskas bonded because they were both of Lithuanian origin and they would regularly gossip about the prime minister's extramarital affair, along with other matters relating to politics. Kagan revealed that he had also introduced Vaygauskas to a number of MPs, but insisted that he had no idea that he was a KGB officer.

With so many leads to pursue, and all materialising in intelligence gold, MI5's faith in Lyalin's disclosures was firming up. But the agency was still unwilling to take any chances. It kept Lyalin under surveillance, with 'watchers' following him around to observe his pattern of movements and the people with whom he was mixing. MI5 deemed him unpredictable in his behaviour and turned down his initial proposal for an orchestrated expulsion, worried that he could be compromised if he were allowed to return to Russia to spy from there for MI5.

Instead, the British agency devised an alternative plan to bolster his credentials within the KGB through the creation of a bogus Ministry of Defence source, codenamed AFT, whom he could 'recruit'. The so-called agent would have access to ostensibly secret information that would appeal to the Kremlin and elevate Lyalin's standings among his peers.

Despite MI5's tradition of informing the CIA about its local investigations, including the one into its former chief Roger

Hollis, the British agency opted to take a road less travelled in Lyalin's case. In a true about turn, and a move that defined the changing transatlantic relationship, instead of seeking Langley's advice and James Angleton's blessings, MI5 intentionally kept the Americans out of the picture.

Martin Furnival Jones was now six years into his leadership of MI5, and he had been overwhelmed by the security dilemmas apparently inflicted by the KGB, many of which remained unresolved and continued draining his agency's resources. Suspected leaks, prospective in-house Soviet spies, and multiple investigations into the Kremlin agency's apparent dominance over his organisation had all become familiar themes. And while he maintained a far healthier scepticism than the likes of James Angleton and Anatoly Golitsyn about the KGB's reach and abilities, he never fully dismissed the theories that the pair embraced, including those involving the Soviet agency's penetration of Britain's intelligence community.

In fact, Furnival Jones had often gone against his better judgement and approved probes into accused officials and former officials based on hunches that had either been generated or enabled by colleagues on the other side of the Atlantic. Oleg Lyalin, or GOLDFINCH, as he was codenamed by MI5, changed all of that.

His emergence on the scene must have empowered Furnival Jones to rethink his approach. The British chief resisted the characteristic temptation of seeking the CIA's advice about MI5's dealings, which in the context of Lyalin's approach and disclosures, would have meant allowing it to pass judgement on the credibility of this newly acquired British asset. While not driven by any sudden distrust of the US agency, Furnival Jones was perhaps unwilling to inform the CIA because on balance a lot of the guidance that Angleton and Golitsyn had provided had come to seem increasingly flaky. Based on their propensity to misinterpret shadows as apparitions, Angleton and Golitsyn would almost certainly leap to the assumption that Lyalin was a 'plant', as they had done with other walk-ins before him.

Aiding Furnival Jones's decision to exclude the Americans from the Goldfinch case was the loose framework of the Five Eyes alliance of intelligence agencies in the US, UK, Australia, Canada and New Zealand. Since its official creation in 1956, the alliance had involved intelligence-sharing agreements that were not legally binding and were at times completely disregarded. There is even a designation within the Five Eyes for doing exactly that: in the US, it is known as NOFORN – 'not for release to foreign nationals'; in the UK it is known as UKEYES ONLY. Such classifications allow member agencies to withhold intelligence from their alliance partners.

So while Furnival Jones would have known full well that playing the UKEYES ONLY card risked infuriating Angleton, he still followed his instinct. The veteran British spymaster recognised that MI5 may well have stumbled on a goldmine when Lyalin offered himself to the agency, and it would not have been lost on him that his agency's unawareness of Lyalin during his two years in Britain was in itself a security failing. But on the upside, the MI5 chief would have perceived the KGB captain as a godsend, who, if proven to be a genuine asset, could end his organisation's disastrous run against its Cold War enemy.

Much like the close interest taken by senior CIA officials in Golitsyn's case after his relocation to the US, Furnival Jones would have felt the weight of responsibility on his shoulders in ensuring that all decisions regarding Lyalin were considered and correctly judged. So the MI5 boss would have personally examined interview summaries and transcripts to try to understand the character and background of this Department V officer, who had been a lifelong Soviet regime loyalist, a Communist 'party member since 1960 and [. . .] the Young Communist League leader in his group' during his college days in Odessa.

'From what Lyalin has said, there can be little doubt, that whilst taking account of the risks of attribution and escalation, the Department V are making dispositions to commence sabotage operations in the UK in a period of possibly prolonged crisis, leading up to the outbreak of war,' debriefing notes revealed. 'During such a period, a variety of sabotage measures would be taken, including in their objectives the demoralisation of the civilian population and the complete disruption of the political and economic life of the country.'

While the KGB had 'not engaged in industrial sabotage in the UK in peacetime', Lyalin revealed that 'on one occasion a proposal was submitted to headquarters for an operation to contaminate Holy Loch with radioactive material with a view to implicating the US Naval Forces.' He also disclosed a KGB scheme to infiltrate Whitehall, Britain's political heartland that hosts government buildings, including the Palace of Westminster. Under that plan, Lyalin said, local agents would pose as delivery men and couriers to gain access to the targeted site, and then scatter colourless poison capsules that would kill anyone who stepped on them. It seemed like a far-fetched plan that MI5 did not take too seriously, but it reinforced the KGB's evil intent towards Britain.

As Furnival Jones kept an eye on Lyalin's case, he gave careful consideration to strategically exploiting it through a counter-espionage and political offensive. Because unlike withholding information from the political top brass as he had done in the case of Roger Hollis, Furnival Jones needed buy-in from Downing Street to go properly after the KGB. And in that instance transparency very much worked in his favour, because instead of approaching the prime minister with allegations of MI5's shortcomings against the KGB, he would be submitting direct evidence from an active asset about the Soviet agency's treachery on home soil.

As MI5's officers continued mining Lyalin for information, its surveillance teams were on his tail, trying either to catch him out or confirm his disclosures.

\* \* \*

The shouting and gesturing indicated from a distance that Oleg Lyalin and his wife, Tamara, were locked into a domestic dispute that had spiralled out of control and spilled onto the street. An undercover MI5 officer assigned to follow Lyalin around London could see from the pair's impassioned exchange and body language that the one-time sweethearts were at their wits' end.

It seemed that the multiple affairs, alcohol binges and constant lies that had destroyed Lyalin's marriage could no longer be ignored. But his public display of anger placed him in a dangerous predicament, which could easily have derailed his posting and seen him recalled to Moscow by the KGB. Matrimonial disputes were supposed to be private matters, not for everyone to see. Displays of such domestic chaos were a clear breach of the KGB's rules: the Soviet spy agency specialised in fomenting chaos and disorder among its enemies, but strongly disapproved of disorder in its own circle.

On that day in May 1971, a few weeks after he had first approached MI5 to offer his services, Lyalin tried to end his verbal showdown with Tamara by getting into his car to drive off. But she refused to let him go, determined to hold him to the type of accountability from which he had been running for several years – if not most of his life. Tamara stood in front of Lyalin's vehicle to stop him from driving off. While he eventually managed to get away, Tamara remained furious and unbeknown to him, she informed one of his KGB colleagues about his behaviour.

From MI5's perspective, at least, Lyalin's public dispute supported his claims about the deterioration of his marriage. He had shared enough information about Tamara during his debriefings, even confessing to the numerous affairs he was having – including the one with Irina Teplyakova – that MI5 officials could not have been overly shocked when they read the surveillance report into his street clash with his wife.

They were not there to provide moral wisdom, relationship advice, or a shoulder to cry on, but Lyalin's debriefers would have regarded his personal dilemmas as exploitable vulnerabilities and, with his help, tried to identify similar vulnerabilities in the KGB cadre. In future debriefings, MI5 'asked GOLDFINCH to consider ways and means' in which Western agencies 'could harass selected intelligence officers in the Russian community, mainly with a view to forcing the withdrawal of selected individuals,' an intelligence record reveals. 'GOLDFINCH considered the matter and gave us his views on two cassettes of tape.'

A 'distilled account of his [Lyalin's] views' reveals a series of KGB rules and guidelines to deter its officers from over-indulging in inappropriate behaviour, including excessive drinking, dating, financial loans, and misappropriation of agency funds through the abuse of work expenses claims. 'GOLDFINCH isolates the susceptibilities of intelligence officers and others into the three great evils of drink, women and money,' the intelligence summary reveals. Lyalin told MI5 that all such 'evils' could be weaponised to disrupt and degrade the KGB.

While the Soviet agency tolerated excessive drinking, alcohol was still a useful tool to use against its officials, he said. One way of damaging the KGB would be to circulate 'stories in the press about wild parties and bottle throwing' and 'if the stories could be substantiated by the production of Russian bottles then so much the better'. Another alcohol-related method to discredit Soviet spies would be by spreading disinformation accusing them of profiting from the sale of Russian liquor obtained through the KGB 'canteen'.

'A fair amount of Russian drink – vodka, wines, and spirits – is sold through the Co-Operative shop,' Lyalin said, 'but it is always limited in order to reduce the amount of drinking which is always a problem within a Russian community. Nevertheless it is fairly readily available and the selling of such drink to locals would be a major crime. From time to time IOs [intelligence officers] would give presents of such drink, but in this case an official note would be made of it, and it would not therefore be possible for anyone found selling to non-Soviets to get away with it. A very damaging ploy would be to suggest that an intelligence officer had bought electronic radio equipment or cameras through selling Russian liquor to the locals.'

For such a ploy to succeed, said Lyalin, MI5 could sell a Soviet intelligence officer 'Hi-Fi equipment at a very cheap rate', with 'no receipt', and then circulate rumours about how the individual had obtained it 'through selling off drink from the KGB canteen'.

Much like any other intelligence organisation, the KGB was alert to the use of honey traps by its adversaries, and so its officers were supposed to be discerning about selecting their romantic partners to avoid being caught out. That meant the creation of rumours about unintended pregnancies was a far more subtle and less resource-intensive 'disruption' method, said Lyalin. And to prevent the KGB from 'hushing up' such rumours, MI5 would need to circulate them through the 'clear community' – non-intelligence officials, including trade delegates, or the Communist Party.

'If a Russian IO [intelligence officer] were to cause a girl to become pregnant, then the matter would be treated very, very seriously,' he said. 'This would be even more important if the girl attempted to demand marriage or to be taken to Russia. A careful and detailed investigation would be mounted and of course the officer might get away with it in the end. It would, however, stop any intelligence work by the officer concerned, and even an unproven rumour of this nature might hang over the individual concerned for some time. It would be very important in circumstances such as this for rumours to be passed through the "clear community" or the [Communist] Party organisation.'

Lyalin's insights were invaluable in arming MI5 with operational strategies and tactics against the KGB at a time when Martin Furnival Jones had started liaising more closely with the prime minister and foreign secretary about the prospect of expelling Soviet officials from the country. While recognising the value he brought to his handlers, Lyalin would every now and then accept a small payment of between £10 and £20 (equivalent to about £150 and £300 in today's money), but never appeared to be driven by money. Nor did he demand special privileges, as Golitsyn had been doing in the US and Britain for almost a decade.

Of course, Lyalin's handlers would have known that his candour during debriefings was self-serving, because it helped diminish the British agency's early suspicions about his bona fides. But it became increasingly apparent to them that his desire to spy for MI5 was genuine; that he relished devising new methods that could be used by his controlling agency against the Soviet organisation.

By late May, as Lyalin continued providing evidence of the KGB's mischief in Britain, MI5, in coordination with senior government officials, started developing a robust plan to strike back at the Kremlin.

Of the dozen officials gathered at the Foreign Office to strategise against the Soviet spy problem in Britain, no one was better armed with actionable intelligence than Martin Furnival Jones. By that point, Oleg Lyalin had been under his agency's control for just over a month, and having closely examined his asset's disclosures about KGB activities in the country, the MI5 chief was certain about the best course of action to take. Furnival Jones had attended the interdepartmental meeting on 25 May 1971 to argue for a mass expulsion of Kremlin operatives, suggesting that the removal of 100 Soviet officials from the country would diminish the security threat and deliver an unequivocal statement about the UK's intolerance of espionage.

It was natural that Furnival Jones's proposal was tailored in favour of national security, but others at the meeting that Tuesday afternoon were concerned about the long-term impact that a mass expulsion could have on Anglo-Soviet relations, trade, and more generally, public opinion. The view that the 'commercial stakes involved appeared very high', as Cabinet Secretary Sir Burke Trend had contended, was unconvincing, because British exports to the Soviet Union had been stagnant since 1968, hovering in the order of 1.2 per cent of total British exports, with no signs of improving at any point in the near future.

Sir Denis Greenhill, the Foreign Office permanent secretary who was hosting the meeting at his office, was alert to the security concerns surrounding the 'disproportionate size of Soviet establishment in this country compared to our major allies . . . [and] the number of trade officials bore no relation to the actual trade'. But he favoured a more diplomatic approach in confronting the issue, saying the 'most defensible basis of action was to go for parity between embassies', in case, as another official argued, the public asked 'why one hundred spies had been allowed to operate [in Britain] in the first place'.

Along with demanding parity, Greenhill argued that Britain could also stipulate a limit on the number of Soviet citizens engaged in commercial ventures. 'On the commercial side, we should limit the Russians to a figure which would be related to the actual and intended business to be done in this country.' That, he said, would allow the British government to 'keep our list of 100 identified agents in reserve as evidence of misbehaviour.' Furnival Jones rejected his proposition, saying it was 'far less attractive from a security point of view' and that the 'aim should be to get rid of the people we know to be spies'.

Furnival Jones must have resented the idea of being forced into a dance-around for the sake of appeasing the Kremlin. It was the very attitude that had been championed by the previous government. And it was the same attitude that was largely responsible for the presence of 550 Soviet officials in London in 1971 – more per capita than in any other Western nation, including the United States. Of those officials, about 200 were suspected spies.

The MI5 spymaster told the interdepartmental attendees that 'however we went about reducing the Soviet establishment, the Russians would react badly', whereas the 'British public would understand the ejection of identified spies more readily than the principle of parity and negotiations of the Soviet Trade Delegation.' Sir Burke Trend suggested that a way to circumvent, or at least temper, any public outrage regarding MI5's failure to stop 100 Soviet spies from roaming around the country in the first place, was to take immediate steps and frame them as a corrective measure to the previous government's unwillingness to act against the Soviet threat. 'Provided action was taken soon, there would be little difficulty in explaining that the present situation was to some extent a legacy of the last government,' he added.

Along with the domestic calculations around expelling spies en masse, there were other considerations Britain needed to navigate to avoid hampering its foreign policy objectives, including the longstanding Quadripartite negotiations between itself, the US, France, and the Soviet Union. Between them, they were attempting to resolve the status of Berlin, which had been divided into East and West zones after the Second World War, and subsequently administered by the four nations involved in the multilateral talks. As it stood, the three allies refused to recognise the German Democratic Republic and the Soviets considered the Federal Republic of Germany its enemy.

Compounding such matters were the difficulties faced by Berliners and occupying authorities, including those relating to the movement of goods, access by road and air, and the political status of the East and West zones. The Quadripartite negotiations were expected to conclude early in the second half of 1971, so in the view of the intergovernmental officials discussing the expulsions of Soviet spies from Britain, it made sense to postpone any action till then.

None of those who attended the meeting with Furnival Jones expected the perfect outcome that day, because the discussion had been called at the prime minister's request not to find an immediate solution, but instead to give careful consideration to the potential advantages and setbacks of the proposed expulsions. And while neither Ted Heath nor any of his cabinet members attended, most if not all of the officials in the room understood that the prime minister favoured a mass eviction of Soviet Embassy and trade staff, because history had shown that previous officials declared persona non grata were merely replaced by Soviet officials who were next in line.

As summer approached, further discussions were held to determine how Britain should handle its Soviet problem, and in June, as if to test the Kremlin's appetite for retaliation, the Foreign Office expelled two Soviet Embassy officials from London. The pair 'had been detected in active intelligence operations against the United Kingdom'. Lyalin was very likely to have identified them to MI5, and as feared by Foreign Office officials all along, the USSR quickly countered by expelling as many British diplomats from Moscow, accusing them of engaging in 'activities incompatible with their diplomatic status'. Each side denied the other's accusation.

By late July, the British home secretary Reginald Maudling and foreign secretary Sir Alec Douglas-Home approached the prime minister to determine the final course of action against the Soviets. Maudling maintained his objection to mass expulsion while Douglas-Home argued in favour of it. Despite the potential impact on Anglo-Soviet relations, Ted Heath, who had now run out of patience, agreed with Douglas-Home that the best way to confront the Kremlin's espionage hostility was not through negotiation but aggressive action. The prime minister ordered the mass expulsion for October, after the anticipated conclusion of the Quadripartite negotiations. Heath's decision, final and defying the objections of several government officials, was a huge win for Furnival Jones, who had been adamant all along about taking such a stand.

Around the time the prime minister was setting an expulsion date, Oleg Lyalin informed MI5 of a KGB plot to murder Anatoly Golitsyn. He said his agency headquarters had renewed its efforts to track down the Soviet defector whom the KGB had vowed to 'kill . . . as soon as they could find him', ever since Golitsyn had been sentenced to death in absentia in 1964. Lyalin told his MI5 handlers that one of his colleagues at the Soviet agency's London residency received a telegram ordering him to establish a method of reaching Golitsyn, whom Moscow was aware had 'visited England several times'. And while Soviet agents had 'established his place of residence' in the United States, it did not have a way of getting to him.

'Moscow required detailed information about where he was living, his habits and activities,' according to an intelligence report citing Lyalin's disclosure of the KGB plot. 'From the working of the telegram source [Lyalin] deduced that the object of this order was to remind [the KGB's London residency] of a standing instruction that the highest priority was to be given to obtaining information about him [Golitsyn].'

With increased KGB hostility being planned in Britain, and a looming deadline for the expulsion of the Soviet agency's operatives from London, the prime minister's office and MI5 were confronted with an unexpected turn of events that threw their respective political and operational plans up in the air.

Chapter 10

# NO WAY BACK

SHORTLY AFTER MIDNIGHT ON the bank holiday weekend in August 1971, a Hillman saloon veered in and out of its lane while heading down Tottenham Court Road. The popular central London thoroughfare, famous for electronics outlets specialising in stereo equipment, was a busy traffic artery into Soho, through which revellers flowed in and out of the nightlife district. The Hillman was travelling in that direction, but its driver was obviously struggling to keep the steering wheel steady.

Constable Charles Shearer was in a police vehicle with another duty officer that Monday morning when they spotted the Hillman with its lights off. 'It was about 1.30 a.m. and we were driving in the Warren Street area of Tottenham Court Road when we saw this car being driven a bit wobbly,' Shearer later recalled. 'We followed and eventually stopped [it].'

Its driver was venting, and eventually started 'shouting and swearing' when Shearer told him to turn off the car's engine.

A blonde woman in the Hillman's passenger seat, seemingly desperate to avoid the furore, left for a taxi nearby. The driver's attitude remained unchanged, and to avoid further confrontation with him, Shearer cuffed his wrists and placed him in the back of the police car, as he would have done in other similar instances.

'Before we drove off he was lying back in the seat with his feet up on my shoulder,' said Shearer. 'I turned round and said, "What are you playing at? Take your feet off the back of my seat." And he replied, "You cannot talk to me, you cannot beat me, I am a KGB officer."' As a seasoned policeman who had dealt with enough drunks on previous patrols, Shearer was no stranger to people 'claiming all sorts of things', so he gave little consideration to what the self-proclaimed spy was saying. 'At the police station, he refused to give a breath test or any samples of blood or urine,' Shearer noted, after arresting the driver on 30 August 1971. In a further act of disobedience, the offender gave the Soviet Trade Delegation's address instead of providing his own as he had been asked – although he did give his real name: Oleg Lyalin.

Lyalin was charged with 'driving while drunk', and during the seven hours or so that he was held in a cell at Tottenham Court Road police station, he worked out a plausible storyline to present his bosses when the time came; one that would paint him as an innocent victim of anti-Russian hostility. Just after 9.00 a.m., he briefly appeared at Marlborough Street Magistrates Court and was subsequently bailed on a £50 surety, provided on his behalf by a Soviet Embassy official.

On any other day, the appearance of a drunk in court would have been quickly forgotten as hardly a newsworthy affair. But with the British news agenda heavily attuned to Soviet skullduggery during that period of the Cold War, it was unsurprising that there would be an element of intrigue about a

Russian 'trade delegate' being hauled before a magistrate. The next day, a ten-line news item appeared on page five of the *Daily Express* newspaper under the headline 'Russian bailed over B-test'. The brief report noted that the Soviet official, whose last name the newspaper spelt 'Lialine', had been bailed to reappear in court the following month.

Hoping to dispel any blame that could be levelled against him by the KGB, Lyalin told his supervisor that his arrest had been a cheap shot by British authorities – a stage-managed intimidation tactic. He was confident that his explanation played to his agency's preoccupation with conspiracies, and the day after, on 1 September, Lyalin met with his MI5 handlers to assure them that the KGB had bought the lie he had constructed around his police encounter. It seemed like an easy win, yet there was another matter that he wanted to alert his controllers about – a far more complex problem that neither he nor MI5 could have foreseen.

Lyalin's love life, complicated by any metric, had become even more so, and he had heard that his estranged wife posed a serious danger to his career. Tamara's contempt for his behaviour, previously witnessed first-hand by the British agency's surveillance officers in London, was becoming fairly well known. But in a new development, Lyalin had heard that Tamara wanted his colleagues to know that he could not be trusted, because he was a liar and a cheat who appeared to be turning his back not only on his family, but also on his employer.

Lyalin was certain of her intention, he told MI5, because a colleague in Moscow had warned him in a letter that Tamara had claimed he 'was dissatisfied with his work in the KGB'. Unfortunately for Lyalin, the letter was delivered in error to another official at the London residency. 'A personal note to him from a friend at the KGB Headquarters was inadvertently delivered to another KGB agent in London with the result that

Lyalin was informed by his superior that he would have to return to Moscow with every indication that severe administrative action might be taken against him,' an intelligence memo reveals. The KGB instructed him to stop his local duties and prepare to head back home.

Two days after briefing MI5 about his dilemma, Lyalin felt the net was closing in on him at work; his time was up. But he was also confident that he was at least one step ahead of the KGB, which was still unaware that he was collaborating with MI5 – and as such, had not placed him under surveillance. Instead, the KGB 'told him to return to his residence [and] pack his bags' in preparation for his return to Moscow, an intelligence briefing notes. 'No guard was assigned to him, with the result that he returned to his office, collected all his own papers together with a number of documents dealing with the work of other KGB agents', with the intention of handing the material to MI5.

One of the documents contained thirteen pages and fifty-four photographs of a sabotage plan in which KGB operatives 'could be landed at a point on the Yorkshire coast and then make their way inland.' That coastal location had been chosen because of its close proximity to the RAF's early warning radar installation, which was jointly operated by the British and Americans to detect approaching ballistic missiles. 'A marked map attached to this document indicated why this particular place would be selected: it was only a few miles from the Early Warning Station at Fylingdales.' Along with the documents, Lyalin also snatched the keys to one of the trade mission's cars and used it for his getaway.

It was to be one of the most important decisions in Lyalin's life up to that point. The Department V captain took such drastic action with the full knowledge that he was preparing to abandon the Soviet Union forever. He had readied himself to take a leap

*Right*: Oleg Lyalin, a KGB officer, arrived in London in 1969 to join the Soviet trade mission under the cover of a 'textiles specialist'. MI5 was completely oblivious to his espionage work until he approached the agency.

*Below*: Vladimir Putin briefly served as the head of the FSB, successor to the KGB, before he became Russia's prime minister in the late 1990s and, ultimately, its president. He revived Moscow's mission to hunt down defectors.

*© Harry Myers / Shutterstock*

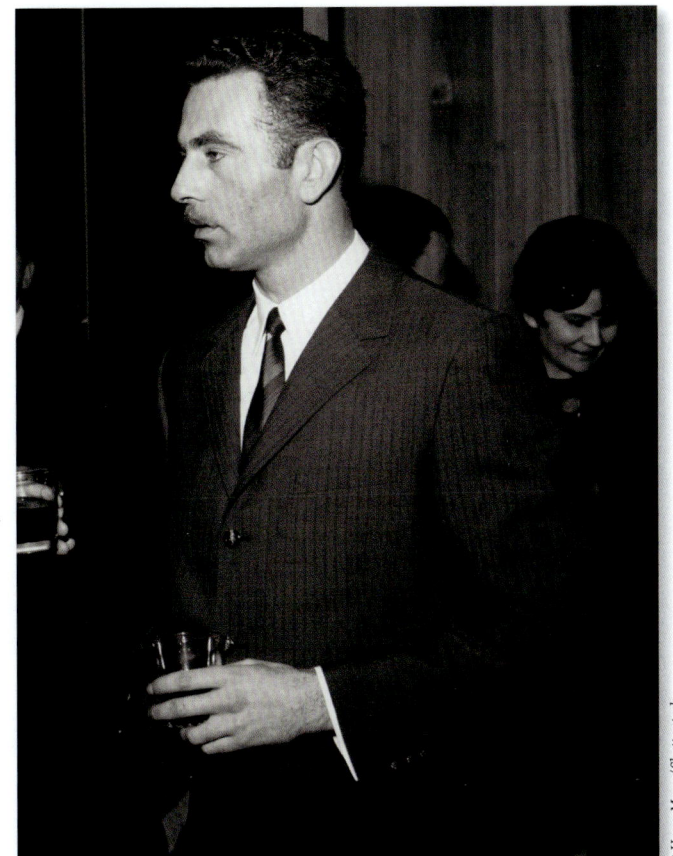

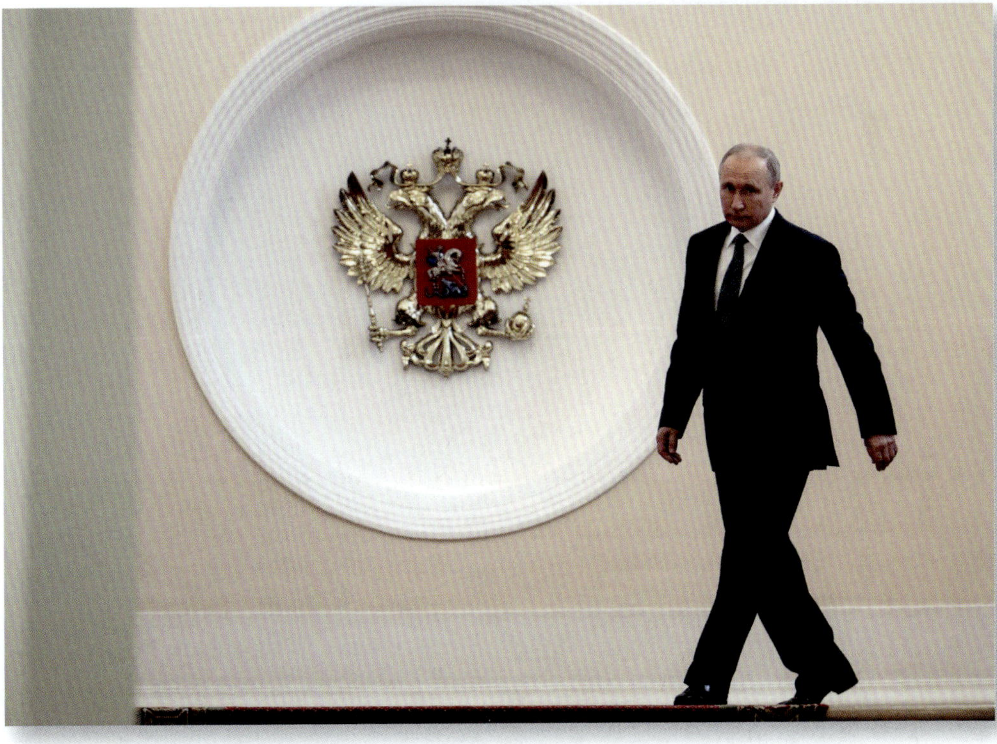

*© Photo by SERGEI BOBYLYOV / SPUTNIK / AFP via Getty Images*

© Photo by Hulton-Deutsch/Hulton-Deutsch Collection/Corbis via Getty Images

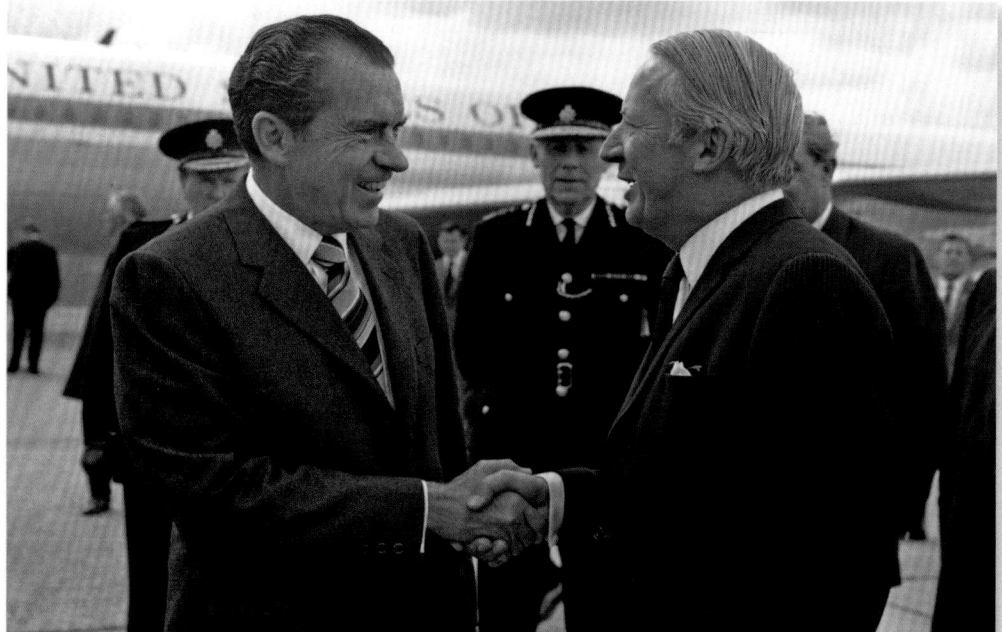

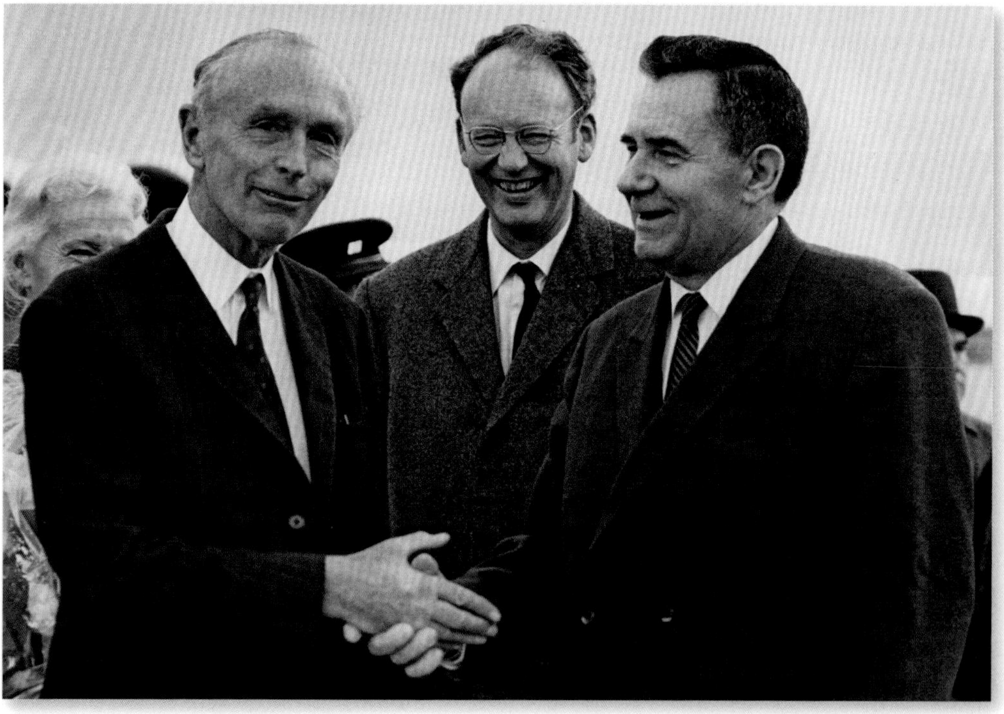

© Photo by Ian Showell/Keystone/Hulton Archive/Getty Images

*Top*: British Prime Minister Ted Heath, here with US President Richard Nixon, wanted to reframe the 'Special Relationship' between London and Washington into a 'Natural Relationship' to avoid offending their allies.

*Bottom*: British Foreign Secretary Alec Douglas-Home repeatedly warned his Soviet counterpart, Andrei Gromyko, to scale back Kremlin espionage operations in the UK before the Heath government expelled them en masse.

*Left*: One of the many newspaper headlines about Britain's 1971 purge of Soviet spies - the biggest expulsion of Kremlin spies by any single country to date.

*Right*: Lyalin's defection with Teplyakova, especially after their identities were exposed in the press, dominated the news agenda in Britain for months.

*Left*: Irena Teplyakova, Lyalin's colleague at the Soviet trade mission, tried to keep their affair a secret after friends recognised that she was his 'constant companion'.

*Right*: After nine years at MI5's helm, Sir Roger Hollis retired from the agency in 1965 under a cloud of suspicion that he had been a Soviet spy. MI5 withheld its investigation into him from two prime ministers.

*Below*: GRU colonel Oleg Penkovsky was an MI6 and CIA asset who supplied Kremlin secrets, including missile operating manuals and information relating to Soviet nuclear capabilities.

*Above*: Donald Maclean was a senior British Foreign Office official who defected to the Soviet Union in 1951 with Guy Burgess, a former MI5 and MI6 intelligence officer. Both had been recruited by the Kremiln in the mid-1930s and, along with Philby, would become members of the 'Cambridge Spy Ring'.

*Below left*: Anthony Blunt was already under Soviet control when he joined MI5 during the Second World War and was not exposed as traitor until he confessed to his treachery two decades later.

*Below right*: Kim Philby, a former MI6 officer responsible for hunting moles within his service, would eventually be exposed as a Soviet spy. His defection to Moscow in 1963 exposed years of British intelligence failures.

*Above*: Susan Woodthorpe, at her father's pub in Tottenham, appeared in a TV interview in October 1971 to discuss her friendship with former Razno colleague, Oleg Lyalin. She was shocked to learn that Lyalin was a spy.

*Right*: In July 2025, the author joined Susan Woodthorpe on a journey to Regent Street in central London to visit locations she once frequented during her employment at Razno more than fifty years earlier.

© Bettmann / via Getty Images

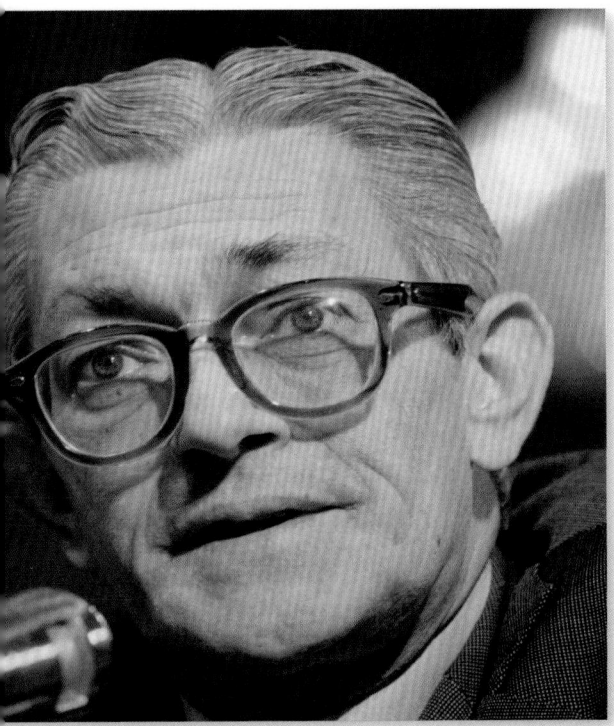

*Left*: James Jesus Angleton, who ran the CIA's counter-intelligence staff for two decades, imposed his will on partner agencies, including MI5 and MI6.

*Below*: After many years of turning to the CIA for advice, MI5's director general Martin Furnival Jones transformed his organisation's fortunes when he kept the US agency out of the Lyalin case.

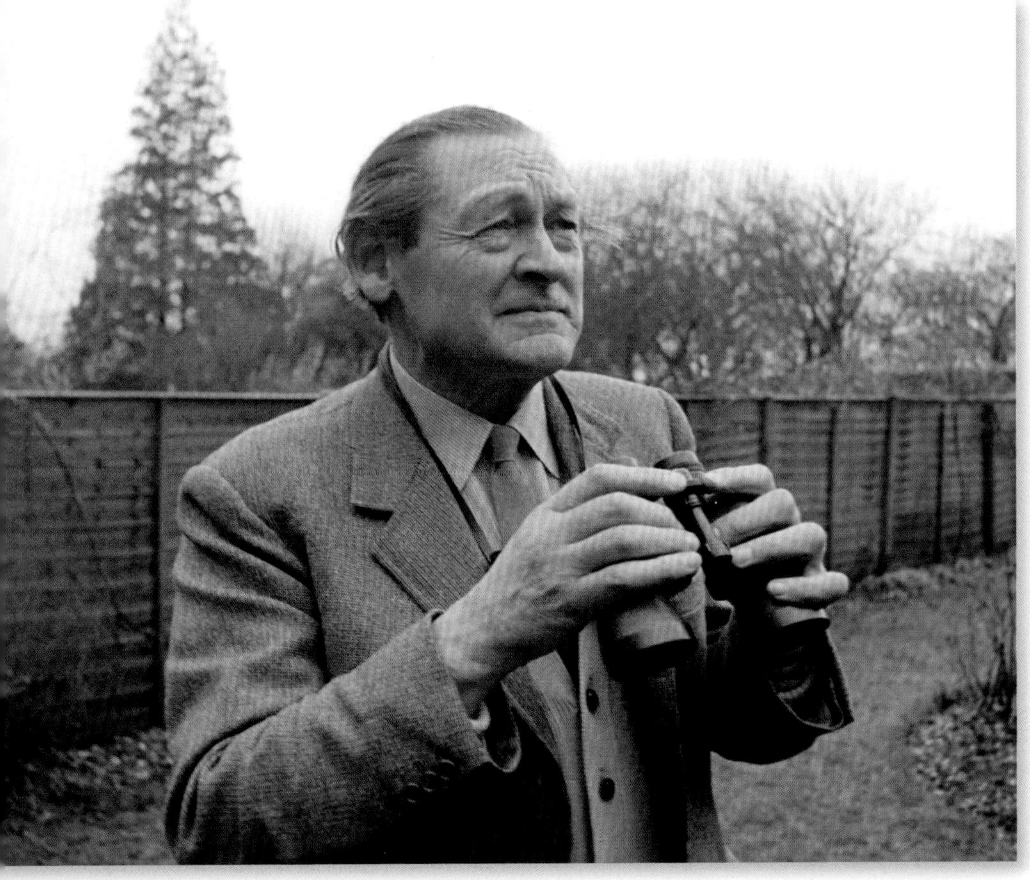

© Photo by WATFORD/Mirrorpix/Mirrorpix via Getty Images

*Above*: The FBI's director, J. Edgar Hoover eventually lost faith in the CIA's counter-intelligence methods after committing resources to a joint investigation with the agency into Soviet moles.

*Right*: Yuri Andropov was Moscow's ambassador in Budapest during the Hungarian Revolution before he became the KGB's chief, and ultimately, leader of the Soviet Union.

of faith without first informing his British handlers, yet was somehow confident that they would be there for him, as he had been for them over the previous four months or so.

Defection was the only way out of the mess, and while Lyalin was committed to it – and by that stage had no other viable option – he wanted to co-opt someone else onto his journey. Perhaps he realised that a life on the run, living under a new identity and always having to watch over his shoulder, would be made a little easier in the company of a familiar face. And with at least four women in his life, including a Czech student, a married English woman, and his trade delegation colleague Irina Teplyakova, Lyalin felt he had options.

So at 9.50 a.m. on Friday 3 September, he called his English lover to try and convince her to leave her husband for him. She refused. Lyalin then hung up and dialled the next number on the list.

In the summer of 1971, after a trip to Russia to spend time with her son, Ivan, and her parents, Irina Teplyakova had been reluctant to return to London. The thought of spending another school term away from her eight-year-old boy was a test in itself, even though she was comforted that he would be in his grandparents' good care. 'She did not want to go back to London,' her mother, Yelizaveta Stetsenko, later recalled. Perhaps Teplyakova sensed that Britain had burdened her with too much emotional baggage: a husband she now no longer loved and a playboy who probably did not love her back. Weighed down by such thoughts and feelings, she returned to London, if only to fulfil her work obligations at the Soviet trade mission.

However, on 3 September, six days before she was due to celebrate her tenth wedding anniversary with Anatoly Teplyakov, she received a phone call that was going to upend her life. It was

Oleg Lyalin informing her that he was effectively in pursuit of a new identity, a new home and a different future. There was no ambiguity about his intent. During the brief call, Teplyakova could tell that Lyalin had made up his mind about abandoning the fatherland, his career, his wife and his six-year-old son, Aleksander. He told Teplyakova that he wanted her to spend the next chapter of his life with him.

She had no time to mull over the offer, to reflect on the real cost – and insanity – of deserting her own child, whom she missed daily and whose voice she had not heard since returning to London a month earlier. Along with that, Teplyakova would be abandoning her mother and father, to whom she owed so much for looking after Ivan. But the horror of the predicament that Lyalin had placed her in – of choosing a life of uncertainty in a country she had never anticipated, nor ever desired to make her home – could not be dealt with rationally. Because to do so would mean rejecting his proposition outright.

Within hours of speaking to Teplyakova, Lyalin called his MI5 handlers. He informed them at 2.15 p.m. that he wanted to defect with a 'friend', and shortly thereafter, arrived with Teplyakova at one of the agency's safe houses. They signed applications for political asylum and were immediately taken into hiding amid fears that the KGB would soon enough discover their disappearance and begin hunting them down. MI5's security arrangements for the pair was a crucial part of the overall intelligence forecast that the agency's chief, Martin Furnival Jones, had to consider and authorise.

A greater challenge he faced was how the pair's defection would impact the October deadline that the prime minister had given for expelling Soviet spies from Britain. Furnival Jones would not have wanted the new defections to give the Soviets a pretext to withdraw from the Quadripartite negotiations – and thus blame Britain for obstructing the anticipated agreement over Berlin's status.

MI5 could probably have kept Lyalin's and Teplyakova's defections under wraps through the ensuing weekend, but at some point thereafter, the Soviet trade mission would undoubtedly have started questioning British authorities about the whereabouts of its two missing officials. That much could have been anticipated. What could not have been predicted was that Lyalin's sudden and unexpected decision to defect, for which he had never previously expressed a desire, would coincidentally and conveniently dovetail with the resolution of the Quadripartite negotiations. Because on the same day that he and Teplyakova signed their asylum forms, Friday 3 September, the four nations involved in the negotiations signed their own agreement.

That evening, as Lyalin and his lover tried to acclimatise to their new living arrangements in a hiding place, and Furnival Jones was mulling over with his top officers and government officials how best to handle the likely fallout of the day's events, Teplyakova's husband, Anatoly, arrived back from work to an empty house. He became seriously concerned when his wife did not return home that evening nor the following day and knew that something was amiss. 'He spent the weekend searching for her, then, on the Monday had to go to Moscow,' it would later be revealed, most likely for work and to be alongside his son.

The following day, after discovering that Teplyakova had defected, the Soviet mission informed Anatoly about his wife's status. 'On Tuesday, 7 September, two days before their 10th wedding anniversary, it was announced that Irena [sic] had asked for asylum,' according to a newspaper report.

Neither Anatoly nor Teplyakova's parents could believe that she had run off with another man, let alone forsaken them and her son for a life in hiding. 'I knew Lyalin,' Anatoly would later disclose. 'We worked together. My wife also used to work at the Soviet trade mission in London where he had his office . . . She was a foreign correspondent, which meant that she would buy supplies for the trade mission and sometimes act as translator as she did when the new premises [Razno] were opened . . . But these reports of an affair are untrue: they are the invention of the British authorities.'

Teplyakova's father, Georgi Stetsenko, who must have reflected on his own agent-handling work while dealing with the family tragedy, was convinced that his daughter was the victim of an MI5 conspiracy, even though he was 'sure she did not have information of any interest to the British'. Her mother, Yelizaveta, was overwhelmed and in tears after learning about her daughter's decision to flee. She was also unwilling to accept the reality of Teplyakova's defection with Lyalin. 'My daughter would never choose her destiny with such a man,' she told a British reporter. 'For ten years we have been such a happy family . . . [And] now this terrible news. We are sure our daughter has been kidnapped and is being held by threats by the British authorities.'

The KGB may as well have scripted the threat and kidnap allegations made by Teplyakova's family, because they laid the blame at Britain's door instead of criticising the Soviet agency's failure to deter its own from fleeing to the enemy. Even before the defections became public, the KGB's London residency was naturally panicked about the wider implications the episode could have. Lyalin's bosses expected that he would inform MI5 about his own agents, including Siroj Abdoolcader and the Cypriot-born brothers-in-law, but were more worried about how much else he would disclose about the KGB's active and future operations, personnel, communication methods, and ties with Bloc agencies.

'KGB Headquarters [continued] the analysis of Lyalin's operational activities while assigned to London' and 'also review[ed] the files to which he had access,' an intelligence briefing from a Soviet officer reveals. But there were also reputational matters the London residency had to face – and be answerable for – because Lyalin was the first Department V official ever to defect to the West. His understanding of the sabotage unit's operations alone, the KGB feared, was enough to damage, if not totally destroy, its Western operations.

It was perhaps anticipated that the KGB would hide the circumstances surrounding Lyalin's disappearance from its own rank and file, yet the agency's top officials could not pretend there was nothing to fear. So through limited and secure briefings, the agency's headquarters informed their rezidents – or foreign-based bureau chiefs – about Lyalin, ordering them to question their operatives about whether they knew him, and if there was any way that he could compromise their identities or operational work.

'Facts relative to the defection were made known to the various Branch Chiefs,' the briefing states. 'KGB officers within each Branch were questioned concerning the possibility of Lyalin's knowledge of their KGB affiliation,' yet 'the basis for this questioning was not disclosed to the KGB officers.' The Soviet agency's chief in New York was among the senior officials alerted to the defection, and by his assessment, the security implications surrounding it were of such enormity that he anticipated Yuri Andropov, the KGB chief, would fire all of the officials assigned to the agency's London residency.

Little did he know that the FBI had already penetrated the KGB's residency in Manhattan.

* * *

On failing to return to the London residency after he had been instructed to pack his belongings and prepare for his departure back home, Oleg Lyalin's sudden fall off the radar left the local KGB chief in no doubt that he may have sought protection from the enemy. The clues had been there. The letter citing his wife Tamara's claims about Lyalin's dissatisfaction with the KGB; Lyalin's stop by the trade mission to gather paperwork; and his decision to steal one of the mission's cars to get away, all signalled that the Department V official had committed himself to crossing the proverbial Rubicon.

Three days after the KGB had lost track of Lyalin, MI5 informed the FBI about his defection and supplied a 'brief document' based on his disclosures of the 'possible leads and cases' linked to Soviet operations in the US. Yet aside from informing the FBI that Lyalin was a Department V officer, MI5 revealed little else about his operational background and nothing about how long he had been cooperating with the British agency.

That same day, on Monday 6 September, the KGB's headquarters cabled its New York bureau about Lyalin's defection to place its colleagues there on alert, and cushion the impact that its compromised British mission could have on the agency's US operations. A KGB officer working under the FBI's control learned about Lubyanka's cable, and on 10 September, passed on the information to his American handlers.

Most intelligence from human assets is generally never complete, often provided in fragments that require context, analysis and interpretation – and the FBI's material in this case was no different. Its coverage was somewhat patchy, because the FBI's source neither knew Lyalin's first name, nor his motive for defecting, but did have accurate insights into his educational background and service record. The source also knew that prior to beginning his London assignment in 1969, Lyalin had been part of the 'KGB's S Directorate' – its 'illegals' division.

'Source learned that, concerning the reaction of KGB Headquarters regarding the defection, the NY Residency's opinion is that all KGB personnel assigned to the London Residency will be replaced,' reveals the FBI intelligence memo, dated 10 September 1971. 'Concerning those KGB officers assigned to the NY Residency who might be known to Lyalin, source indicated that the prevalent opinion in the NY Residency is that no immediate action is necessary regarding possible replacement of these officers since the possibility exists that Lyalin might not recall specific names and identities.'

While operational conversations and cordialities were ongoing between the FBI and MI5 in the first two weeks or so of September 1971, at no point did either side discuss everything it had on the defector and Teplyakova. And just as the British agency had at that stage effectively categorised intelligence relating to Lyalin and Teplyakova as 'UKEYES ONLY', withholding it from all foreign nationals including their closest Five Eyes allies, the US law enforcement organisation had taken a similar approach in regards to its KGB asset in New York.

Another certainty at that point was that the leaders of both agencies, Martin Furnival Jones at MI5 and the FBI's J. Edgar Hoover, had lost faith in the CIA's bad judgements on counter-Soviet action, especially those bearing the fingerprints of James Angleton and his sidekick, Anatoly Golitsyn. During that period in September, neither MI5 nor the FBI shared anything about the London defections with Langley.

But in Moscow, as developments around Lyalin's case continued to unfold, the KGB's headquarters was increasingly getting jittery about its operational exposure and the extent to which it could ever be remedied. 'Source stated that, as a result of

Lyalin's defection, it is the consensus of opinion within the NY Residency that at the present time, the Department of Personnel, KGB Headquarters, is conducting an analysis to determine who might be acquainted with Lyalin and vice versa,' the FBI learned through its Soviet asset. 'This analysis would develop where Lyalin had been trained, where he had previously served, the extent of his activities abroad, the files to which he had access, the operations of which he had knowledge, etc. Only upon completion of this analysis, would KGB make a determination, concerning of security abroad who might have to be recalled to the USSR for security purposes.'

By all accounts, the KGB's chief, Yuri Andropov, had underestimated the intelligence dilemma on his hands, despite instructing his departments to obtain the facts surrounding Lyalin's background and motive, while simultaneously developing a narrative to discredit him in the event that his defection became public. Andropov was essentially going through the motions, without the sense of urgency that would have followed the defection of a more senior official to an adversary of greater abilities. The KGB chief did not deem MI5 as KGB-equal – neither in its manpower, resources, recruitment capabilities, nor operational risk-taking. Perhaps that was because Andropov hoped or believed, the British were hampered by their own quaint morality and the rules under which they operated.

Unlike Andropov's operatives, MI5 and its sister agency, MI6, would never knowingly march their officers or agents to their deaths for the sake of operational gains. The British did not have the KGB's ruthlessness, the Cheka bloodline harking all the way back to the 'Trust' missions of the 1920s. And along with Andropov's disregard for the safety of his rank and file in pursuit of Cold War supremacy, and the general indifference to human rights and international laws, he had long been emboldened by the wins that his agency had racked up against Britain under him and his predecessors. The KGB's success against MI5 and MI6, including its recruitment of the country's most damaging turncoat, Kim Philby, had fostered among its leadership a feeling of invincibility.

How could Andropov have any respect for a British intelligence community on which he and his predecessors had trampled for decades by funnelling hundreds of operatives into the Soviet Embassy and trade mission in the UK, most often undetected? Sure, Britain got Lyalin, but the USSR had got Burgess, Maclean, Philby and Blake – not to mention all the other Soviet assets who did not defect, including Vassall and Blunt. On any score sheet, the Soviets were way, way ahead.

And therein lay the problem: the Kremlin, much like its spy agencies, did not expect much from the country it considered America's junior partner and the prime beneficiary of the US's intelligence capabilities. It did not regard the new British government's allegations of Kremlin espionage, which had been raised verbally and in letters by the country's foreign secretary with his Soviet counterpart, even worthy of a reply – let alone an explanation or a feigned attempt to scale back the activities of Soviet spies.

In one of those letters, Sir Alec Douglas-Home's tone, which by any reading appeared to be hardened and resolute, had hinted at Britain's willingness to take action against Moscow. 'The Soviet Union conducts espionage against Great Britain on a large scale,' the British foreign secretary had huffed to his Soviet counterpart in a letter dated 4 August 1971:

Even if I were to mention only those cases which have become public knowledge during the last few years, the list would be a long one. Many more cases, some of them very serious, are known to me and doubtless to you also. Governments which engage in intelligence activities on such a scale as this must expect that the authorities in the countries attacked will take such precautions and counter-measures as may be open to them.

However, the obvious threat of 'counter-measures' had not even elicited an acknowledgment from the letter's recipient.

While Andropov grimaced in the shadows about the London defections, hoping they were nothing more than a minor setback, Martin Furnival Jones and Ted Heath became increasingly certain that the October deadline for the proposed mass expulsion needed to be brought forward. With political discussions between the prime minister and his top tier well underway, Furnival Jones made a move that he knew the KGB had been expecting: he authorised his team to take down Lyalin's agents and provided Scotland Yard with their details.

Detective Chief Inspector Gordon Fryer appeared at 44 Upper Tollington Park, north London, certain that the man he was there to arrest was home that evening. Having been briefed by MI5 on where to locate the incriminating evidence at the terraced property, Fryer turned up with a search warrant and two colleagues intending to raid Kyriacos Costi's family home, where the KGB asset lived with his parents and siblings. The detectives introduced themselves at the front door before charging up the stairs to Costi's bedroom on the first floor.

Realising that he had locked himself in there, they yelled at him to come out. 'We are police officers – open up!' Fryer's partner shouted. After just a few seconds the detectives forced their way through with 'bodily pressure' – presumably shoving and kicking the door in – to find Costi standing in silence, with no place to hide, let alone time to contemplate his next move.

'On the sideboard between the windows I saw a radio with the aerial fully extended, connected to the radio was a tape recorder,' Fryer noted shortly after the raid on the evening of 9 September 1971. 'The radio and tape recorder had single ear pieces connected. In front of the radio was paper bearing groups of figures.' When asked about the equipment, Costi stalled, certain of the trouble ahead, but far too rattled to think of a way out of it. 'I have nothing to say,' he replied, before quickly realising that there was little sense in being defiant or denying his offences since his room was virtually a crime scene, with some of the spy gadgets on full display and many others tucked inside a brown briefcase by his bed. 'Everything you want is in my briefcase,' he confessed.

On searching the briefcase, Fryer found two Eveready SP2 batteries, and even before he asked about their use, Costi offered to show him how they worked. 'He then unscrewed the tops of both batteries revealing cavities inside, which in one disclosed two pieces of paper bearing writing, a blue plastic pen cap, a piece of white plastic tubing and a small roll of film. Inside of the other battery, I found two pieces of paper bearing writing. Also in the briefcase were fifty-one pieces of paper, some of which bore various writings and figures.'

A subsequent decryption of the messages hardly illuminated their meaning, but confirmed that they had been sent from the 'general Moscow area', according to Costi's interrogation file. One message partially read: 'Please speed up establishing friendship with Lucy customers. Trousers for Alex do not fit.' While another from 2 June 1971 read: 'Basing on previous discussions arrange trip to REDCAR on 5th June. Stay there till 6th. Returning back home late in the evening of 6th. Necessary instructions get from Alex. Trousers for ALEX do not fit. Good luck. End. No. 4.'

Another curious item among the tradecraft gadgets that Fryer inspected during the raid was what appeared to be a lead pencil. 'Let me show you,' said Costi, before unscrewing the 'top of the pencil revealing a hollow interior'. Eager to appear cooperative, Costi explained its function: 'I got it for [storing] film but haven't used it, it's too difficult.' With an almost instant admission of guilt by Costi and multiple spy gadgets confiscated and in their possession, the detectives placed him under arrest for espionage offences and drove him to Scotland Yard's headquarters on Broadway, Westminster, for further interrogation.

Costi initially lied that he had been working under the control of the Polish intelligence service, rather than the KGB, and claimed that he had reported to two agent handlers called 'Mike'. But when pressed for more clarity, Costi came clean, saying, 'I think it better I tell the truth,' before providing a written statement laying out his espionage activities.

In it, Costi revealed that the KGB had recruited him in January 1967 at the recommendation of his brother-in-law, Constantinos Martianou, and that he had initially reported to a man he knew as Alex before a 'second Alex' came along. 'After knowing Alex for about a year, he told me he was going to Russia and arranged to meet me at Warren Street Underground station and introduced me to another man who said he was also named Alex and said I should work for him,' Costi said. 'After I had met the second Alex a few times, he told me he wanted to train me to read Morse code.' That Alex was the person Costi had identified in a photograph the police had shown him. Scotland Yard and MI5, however, knew the person featured in the photograph by another name: Oleg Lyalin.

About two hours later, at 12.50 a.m. on 10 September,

Fryer's colleague, Detective Chief Inspector Donald Ginn, was interviewing Costi's accomplice, Constantinos Martianou, in a nearby room at Scotland Yard. Ginn was determined to prise a confession out of him, especially since he had lied about knowing 'Alex' earlier that evening after police had raided his tailor shop in north London.

'You remember at the shop,' said Ginn, 'I asked you if you had known or heard of a man, a Russian, named Alex. You said "No".'

Martianou replied: 'Yes, I said "No".' He claimed to have fallen out with Costi in a dispute over their joint tailoring business and maintained his denials about knowing any Russians or receiving any money from them.

'You realise if we were not sure that I wouldn't be asking questions,' said Ginn.

'Yes,' replied Martianou.

'You realise your brother-in-law, Kyriacos Costi, is here?'

Aware that he had been cornered and that Costi's likely confessions in another interrogation room would be used against him, Martianou realised that he would be best served by telling the truth. 'I'm sorry,' he said, 'I'll tell you the whole story.'

It was not how Martianou had envisaged his day would turn out, because his interrogation file reveals that only hours earlier he had been celebrating the birth of his first child, a 'baby son born on the day of his arrest'.

Martianou admitted working for three Soviet handlers since his recruitment a decade earlier, all named 'Alex'. He also owned up to introducing Costi to the KGB but said he 'didn't know how deep he was in', because he had been instructed by his handlers to never discuss espionage work with his brother-in-law. The treachery of his espionage work only dawned on him when he started reporting to 'Alex number three' – Oleg Lyalin.

'I realised how wrong and stupid I had been to get involved in this like this. To be truthful, I was frightened to tell them straight away I didn't want to do anything for them although they must have realised this, because I was afraid they might have harmed me or my family. I realise now that the proper thing to do was to go to the nearest police station and tell everything. I have never regretted anything so much in all my life.'

Costi and Martianou were unique recruits in a sense, because although they had never been jointly deployed on KGB missions, they knew one another through family links. The Soviet agency generally kept its British-based assets apart, to help ensure that if one was compromised they could not compromise others. Which is perhaps why Siroj Abdoolcader had no idea about the unpublicised arrests of Costi and Martianou – much less about Lyalin's defection – before detectives charged through County Hall on Friday 17 September and arrested him on suspicion of espionage.

Detectives found 'three lists of registration numbers' while questioning Abdoolcader at his office, and a 'card carrying the name Oleg Lyalin, with the address of the Soviet Trade Department in Highgate', according to police notes. For a split second, Abdoolcader took responsibility for his actions, saying he had been a 'bloody fool' for getting tangled with the KGB and that he had only been spying 'for fun'. However, on being taken to the police station for an interview, he resorted to a more characteristic line of defence: blaming others.

'The dirty rotten Russian swine blackmailed me into it,' he told detectives. A police search of his home uncovered Communist literature and pieces of paper bearing car registration details. Abdoolcader was charged with three espionage offences, including providing information through his work 'that was intended to be directly or indirectly useful to an enemy, namely the registration numbers of vehicles belonging to the Security Service [MI5].'

Abdoolcader later confessed to his crimes, even telling detectives about the gifts he had received for his treachery, including the 'electric razor, a wristwatch, a toilet set and about £140 to £150' with the 'largest single amount being £100'. It would later transpire that Lyalin had 'rewarded' Abdoolcader for his efforts with similar gifts to those he had given to his other two agents – Costi and Martianou.

With the agents now in custody, and the KGB still trying to understand the extent to which Lyalin had compromised it, there was now a growing consensus among British officials that the deadline for expelling Soviet spies must be brought forward. Ted Heath was on the verge of approving a plan that aimed to be more devastating to KGB operations in Britain than the Soviet agency had ever encountered – a plan codenamed Operation Foot.

Sir Alec Douglas-Home arrived at a meeting in Downing Street on 21 September eager to push on with Operation Foot despite resistance from some Foreign Office officials who favoured a less hostile, and more diplomatic approach. He shared the prime minister's view that a light-touch resolution with the Kremlin was out of the question and that the risk of damaging Anglo-Soviet relations, trade, and upsetting détente between East and West was a risk worth taking.

There were several last-minute considerations that the foreign secretary and Ted Heath needed to make before setting an expulsion date, including the expected publicity that would follow the government's action. Sir Denis Greenhill, the Foreign Office permanent secretary, who also attended the meeting that Tuesday afternoon, could see the potential for exploiting the anticipated media hype once the news broke and suggested that they get ahead of it. It was not uncommon for government officials to provide attributable and unattributable background briefings to journalists on sensitive matters, including national security, to help shape narratives in their favour.

An overwhelming preoccupation with how Soviet spies had entered the country and why they had been allowed to remain for so long, for instance, would obviously have been far from ideal. For the expulsion to be a publicity coup, the media would need to focus on the overall triumph rather than the mishaps and failings. The British government wanted to emphasise the embarrassment it had dealt its adversary in deciding to upend KGB operations in the country. That would have suited MI5 and Downing Street, of course, by creating friendly and compelling TV, and favourable newspaper headlines.

Yet in the event that reporters were to interrogate the government about why it had not taken action earlier, an advisory note that had been prepared for Douglas-Home suggested the following answer: 'We wanted to exhaust to the limit the possibilities of peaceful settlement. It is only recently that we have reached the conclusion that this is impossible.'

A second advisory note urged the government to draw on the 'Lyalin material in order to make the maximum impact'. It also advised in favour of publicising the 'precise numbers of those expelled', but warned against releasing their names, at least initially. 'Lyalin's name must also be held back.' Another consideration that emerged during the Downing Street meeting was about whether the government should inform its allies about the imminent expulsion. Sir Burke Trend, the cabinet secretary, who regularly met with intelligence community leaders, including Martin Furnival Jones, was of the opinion that the allies should be notified before, rather than after the Soviets. Douglas-Home disagreed.

On fielding the arguments and taking in all the advice, the prime minister called for Operation Foot to be implemented seventy hours after the meeting and tasked the Foreign Office to deal with the usual formalities. Soviet intelligence officials at the KGB and GRU, oblivious to Britain's next move, were still dealing with the mess that Lyalin had left them in.

On 23 September 1971, all KGB personnel were 'exhibited a picture of Oleg Lyalin and the woman with whom he had defected,' notes an intelligence file. 'Lyalin's picture was also exhibited to all GRU personnel and [those] assigned to the New York GRU Residency.'

## Chapter 11

# OPERATION FOOT

AS THE FOREIGN OFFICE'S permanent secretary, its most senior civil servant, Sir Denis Greenhill knew the gravity of what he was about to do, when he summoned the Soviet chargé d'affaires to a meeting. As instructed by the Heath government, he was on the verge of pressing the diplomatic nuclear button on London's already frail ties with Moscow, to reclaim an authority over the UK's national security status that Soviet intelligence operatives had abused for far too long. Even Greenhill's guest, Ivan Ippolitov, the main communication conduit between his host nation and his fatherland, personified such espionage abuse because he, too, was a KGB vassal – a 'co-optee', as Oleg Lyalin would later reveal.

Greenhill had been overseeing Britain's diplomatic service for a little over two years and was attuned to the USSR's aggressive tendencies towards the West, and particularly the UK. Not least because he had attended seemingly endless discussions with cabinet ministers, as well as MI5 and MI6 spymasters, to address the Kremlin's thirst for stealing Britain's secrets and plotting to undermine the country's security and military and technological capabilities.

The subject of spying had even arisen during Greenhill's visit to Moscow to meet Soviet foreign ministry officials in May 1971. They confronted him about what they claimed were spurious accusations that Sir Alec Douglas-Home had previously raised with his counterpart. During the meeting, officials decried the foreign secretary's repeated slurs about Soviet espionage in Britain, saying they were baseless and unnecessarily hostile, because Moscow deemed spying as reprehensible behaviour that its foreign-based representatives would never engage in. The officials then warned Greenhill that Britain would be 'well advised' to refrain from taking any aggressive steps against the Soviet mission in London, according to his record of the meeting.

Greenhill had informed London about the warning, yet four months on he was about to throw caution to the wind on the afternoon of 24 September 1971. All of the high-powered talks that he had attended with other British officials, all of the strategic posturing, and the expected consequences of proposed retaliatory attacks against the KGB, had now boiled down to the moment he sat across from Ippolitov to deliver a message that was set to become a defining chapter in the Cold War. A chapter that the British government anticipated, and even accepted, would potentially plunge London's relationship with Moscow to unprecedented lows.

Presenting unsavoury news to the heads of embassies in London was just part of Greenhill's role as permanent secretary at King Charles Street, home of the Foreign Office. In June, three months earlier, he had served the Soviet mission with an expulsion notice for two officials caught spying. But that had been easy work in a sense, hardly the type that threatened to upend Soviet–Anglo ties, and it had resulted in two British diplomats being expelled from Moscow in a tit-for-tat. The implementation of Operation Foot, however, was on a different scale altogether, expected to be far bigger, far noisier, and far less likely to produce a predictable retaliation.

For Greenhill, the mass expulsion would bring with it an element of undeniable personal satisfaction, even more poetic than the political dividends that Ted Heath and Douglas-Home were betting on. Because Greenhill himself had been a victim, or perhaps a survivor, of Kremlin skullduggery in the early days of his career. On his very first foreign posting, the Bulgarian regime had accused him of spying shortly after he arrived in Sofia to join the British diplomatic mission. The Soviet satellite state provided no evidence to back its claims, nor any meaningful avenue for recourse. Instead, it threw him out of the country in April 1949 despite the Attlee government's protestations and denials.

Two decades or so later, Greenhill was on the other side of the divide, largely directing the diplomatic theatre that began to play out when Ippolitov arrived for the 3.15 p.m. meeting that Friday. He told the Soviet representative that the British government had designated dozens of Soviet officials for expulsion, because it believed they were working directly or indirectly for Kremlin intelligence agencies, including the KGB and GRU.

Greenhill expected Ippolitov to dismiss the allegations – as the Kremlin had done for years – and perhaps even protest the British government's decision as a belligerent act timed to inflame anti-Soviet sentiment in the West. But the Soviet diplomat remained silent, calm, and expressionless, Greenhill would later recall. It was as though Ippolitov were contemplating a chess move, rather than dealing with a diplomatic and political crisis that was about to overwhelm him and the regime he served.

Greenhill pressed on with his message and told Ippolitov that everyone named in the expulsion order would have to leave Britain within a fortnight. And to prevent those in the firing line from dodging the coming bullet, Greenhill provided the Soviet official with a breakdown of their names and job descriptions. An abridged outline of the expulsion revealed that of the Soviets earmarked for removal, 'forty-three of them will be diplomatic officials, fourteen Soviet Embassy officials [with no diplomatic immunity], twenty-eight from the Soviet trade delegation, and six from ancillary establishments' including Aeroflot, the Soviet airline. Ultimately ninety officials would be expelled, along with fifteen others who were stripped of their accreditation while on leave in the Soviet Union.

During the dressing-down at Greenhill's office, Ippolitov's face 'betrayed no emotion of any kind whatsoever', the permanent secretary recalled, but the Soviet diplomat acknowledged that the expulsion order was a 'serious matter'. Ippolitov had not recovered from the hand grenade that had exploded in his face when Greenhill lobbed another in his direction, announcing a fundamental difference between this expulsion order and previous ones.

In the past, the Soviet foreign ministry had simply replaced its expelled officials with new ones and while the process had been an administrative nuisance and somewhat operationally disruptive, the diplomatic replacements had often picked up from where their predecessors had left off and got on with the job of spying. But not anymore. Greenhill calmly informed Ippolitov that Moscow 'would not be allowed to replace' those expelled and warned him that 'any retaliation against British diplomatic personnel assigned to Russia' would result in 'other definitive action'.

Of all the diplomatic wrangling that Ippolitov had faced in

his career, that afternoon at Greenhill's office would undoubtedly have been one of the worst professional experiences he had ever faced. And for it to have taken place on a Friday, towards the end of play, made it that little bit worse, because Ippolitov was forced to return to the Soviet Embassy and deliver the grim news to his staff, as well as to regime and agency leaders in Moscow. An MI5 surveillance officer positioned near the Soviet mission's headquarters at Kensington Palace Gardens, west of central London, noted the panic among Soviet officials entering and leaving the embassy. The officer even witnessed an official sprinting into the embassy from the GRU's residency across the road, after undoubtedly being ordered in for a briefing.

The anxiety that gripped Soviet diplomats and spies in London was in contrast to what was unfolding about two miles west at Leconfield House – MI5's headquarters. Martin Furnival Jones celebrated with his staff, toasting the momentous occasion around the same time that the Foreign Office was hosting a press briefing. Foreign Office officials informed reporters that the spies targeted for removal had been involved in a 'hive of intelligence activities', including 'efforts to obtain military and industrial secrets' such as 'data on the supersonic airliner Concorde' and the Kremlin's contingency plans to land saboteurs along the north Yorkshire coast near Britain's ballistic missile warning system.

With the print and broadcast media briefed, and the Soviets in a state of utter dismay, the British government's anticipated outcomes were running like clockwork, by that point at least. The press pack largely bought the well-executed government spin instead of focusing on MI5's past failures to insulate Britain against the Soviet threat. Journalists and commentators parroted the Foreign Office's news lines, saying that the long overdue action against Soviet spies had been hampered by a lack of evidence, but that thankfully, Britain's new defector had come to its rescue – and he had.

Oleg Lyalin had provided the crucial information, correspondents were told, which exposed the vast number of Soviet intelligence operatives who had been masquerading as diplomats, trade delegates, and even bank and airline executives, not to mention other cover roles they had adopted. The *Evening Standard* that night summed up the government's action succinctly in a front page story titled: 'KGB defector betrays London espionage ring: Britain Expels 105 Russians for Spying.'

It then quoted a Foreign Office statement revealing that the 'number of Soviet officials in Britain and the proportion of them engaged in intelligence work has been causing grave concern for some time.' Without naming Lyalin, the Foreign Office acknowledged his contribution. 'The man, an officer of the KGB, the Soviet secret service police, brought with him certain information and documents in eluding plans for infiltration of agents for the purpose of sabotage.'

Having briefed the press, the British government's next move was to inform its allies. And while the prime minister's earlier decision had been to withhold any details about the expulsion until the Soviets had been notified, MI5 officers alerted the FBI about Operation Foot an hour before Greenhill's meeting with Ippolitov, according to a declassified intelligence briefing. That heads-up for the FBI underscored the fact that MI5 seemed to have lost the operational intimacy it had once enjoyed with the law enforcement's sister agency, the CIA.

A cable to the FBI's New York office references MI5's briefing in which the British agency explained that the expulsion had been 'under consideration for some time but for various reasons could not be carried out'. MI5's explanation appeared to be tactical, an attempt to head off any harsh criticism of its failure to alert the US law enforcement agency earlier. However, there is no evidence that the British agency took similar measures to appease the CIA – and perhaps testament to that was James Angleton's reaction to the expulsion and a message from Martin Furnival Jones to the US agency's London station that MI5 kept Langley out of the loop because it 'didn't want any interference'.

Having once been MI5's first port of call when it needed operational answers, guidance or wisdom, the CIA's counter-intelligence chief was furious to discover that the British agency had withheld from him Lyalin's existence until after his defection. And as a longstanding advocate of removing Soviet spies from Western countries, Angleton was equally enraged that MI5 failed to consult him about its government's mass expulsion plans ahead of time. His reactions were typical, and instead of taking time to reflect on MI5's changed approach toward him – at least to ascertain whether its actions were a bureaucratic blip or a systematic shift in its behaviour – Angleton fell into his usual pattern of thinking.

The first question in his head was not whether Lyalin could explain the KGB's latest strengths and vulnerabilities, or offer insights about the potential Soviet penetration of the CIA that Angleton was still desperate to resolve. No, Angleton's first thought was about Lyalin's bona fides. After learning about his approach to MI5 and the circumstances surrounding his defection, he immediately drew parallels with the earlier KGB volunteers, including Yuri Nosenko, whom Angleton still believed had been 'sent' on Soviet orders. As Angleton considered the best strategy for presenting MI5 with his scepticism about Lyalin, a parallel power struggle was taking place between the political leaders on either side of the Atlantic.

The British prime minister had taken an impersonal approach in belatedly alerting the White House about Operation Foot, essentially leaving the uncomfortable work to his underlings. Having reframed Britain's ties with the United States from a Special Relationship to a 'natural relationship', Ted Heath proved to be less deferential to the Oval Office than his predecessors. That was particularly true on matters of British foreign policy, such as the spy expulsion. Heath saw no point in directly alerting Richard Nixon ahead of the purge, because the president's priority was the preservation of détente with Moscow, not Britain's espionage problem – so informing him ahead of time would have risked the president opposing Operation Foot.

Instead, the prime minister instructed his top diplomat in Washington to inform the president's team. In a letter to national security advisor Henry Kissinger, delivered shortly after Sir Denis Greenhill had informed Ivan Ippolitov of the expulsion order, Britain's US ambassador passed on Heath's 'sincere regrets' for not having informed Nixon ahead of time, claiming a press leak had forced the government to move swiftly on the decision.

Nixon was irked by Britain's reasoning when Kissinger briefed him of it, and neither he nor his national security advisor deemed it sincere. The president would have been forgiven for thinking that Heath's unilateral decision to trigger the mass expulsion was at odds with the verbal agreement from their very first meeting, in which the prime minister and Nixon pledged to discuss their policies with complete freedom and transparency.

Yet, while the Nixon Administration was irritated about the circumstances surrounding the expulsions, its détente counterparts in Moscow were totally outraged.

* * *

Kremlin officials from Soviet leader Leonid Brezhnev through to Foreign Minister Andrei Gromyko and KGB chief Yuri

Andropov were still in a state of shock, unable to comprehend Britain's attack against Moscow. Gromyko, who had all but disregarded his British counterpart's repeated warnings about Soviet spying, knew that he had been outplayed by Sir Alec Douglas-Home and caught flat-footed. While he had long admired Douglas-Home's politeness and quiet manner, the Soviet official had underestimated his political nous.

Three days after London's bombshell, Gromyko confronted the British foreign secretary about the expulsion order on the sidelines of a 27 September United Nations meeting in New York, but to no avail. And with the world's media desperate for an update on the unfolding saga, Douglas-Home was willing to share some of the details of his almost ninety-minute conversation with the Soviet foreign minister. 'Mr Gromyko made a protest, a vigorous protest about the action we'd taken and I replied to that protest,' the British foreign secretary told reporters. He ruled out reversing the government's decision, and in a conciliatory tone, said the expulsion had been 'designed to remove an obstacle to good relations'. To which Gromyko later retorted: 'That's a fine way to improve relations.'

Back in London, Soviet officials and their families were busily packing their suitcases for their imminent departure. Among them was Richardas Vaygauskas, the Soviet intelligence officer whom Lyalin had exposed for cultivating Harold Wilson's close friend Joseph Kagan. But the KGB, while still wobbly on its feet after the expulsion order had placed its London residency on the brink of decimation, was preparing to strike back.

Its primary target was none other than the man it now reviled – the man it deemed a traitor, an inconsequential operative and a promiscuous drunk: Oleg Lyalin. It wanted to change the news narrative away from the Kremlin being stunned and impotent in the face of Britain's unforeseen move. Moscow saw the media circus around the expulsion as a major public relations disaster, because it taunted the Kremlin about its great defeat and underscored the damage Lyalin had caused. It wanted to redress the balance at the very least.

Correspondents and broadcasters continued pontificating about the extent to which the defector's insights had helped MI5 and the British government to blindside the Kremlin. But the scoop that everyone wanted – from regional and national newspaper reporters in Britain to those on the *New York Times* and *Washington Post* – was the defector's name. His and Irina Teplyakova's names had remained a mystery, largely because MI5 always sought to protect the identities of its informants, agents, and defectors. Such protection, part of the security service's operational standards, was to encourage operatives from enemy camps to break ranks with their agencies and exchange their secrets for a safe haven in Britain. But spycraft is unpredictable at the best of times, let alone when dealing with an adversary like the USSR.

After five days with no sign that Britain was reconsidering its expulsion notice or willing to negotiate a less humiliating ejection of Soviet citizens from the country, the Soviet Embassy's second secretary, Vladimir Pavlinov, agreed to a newspaper interview with two reporters from the *Daily Express*. While the Soviet Embassy had received a deluge of interview requests from journalists around the world, it specifically targeted the *Daily Express* for reasons far more compelling than the so-called transparency that Moscow wanted to project.

Pavlinov had only been in Britain for a week, so it seemed curious that the Kremlin would offer him up for an interview. But, in retrospect, it appears that he had been chosen for his ability to manipulate the press. He understood the benefits of playing journalists in order to deploy Soviet counter-narratives, if for no other reason than to irritate the British government. The single question he had rightly anticipated – and prepared for – before greeting the reporters and settling in for the interview, was the one pertaining to the KGB defection in London.

He toyed with the reporters at first, pretending that disclosing the defector's identity would be improper; a breach of diplomatic decorum. And he maintained that posture for a little while, showing self-restraint and parrying the reporters' questions about the mystery defector with a knowing smile, before finally offering a hint. Pavlinov said the man in question was a 'trade official' who had recently been involved in a traffic incident that had been covered by the *Daily Express* on 31 August. 'His name, gentlemen, was in your newspaper,' he said, holding up his thumb and forefinger an inch apart to indicate a small story. It took the reporters barely any time to locate the newspaper edition that Pavlinov cited – and there, on page five, was Lyalin's name, with a variation on its spelling, 'Lialine'.

The KGB would have had at least a hand in coordinating the timing of Pavlinov's 29 September interview, because the Soviet agency knew that Lyalin was due to appear in court the next day on the drink-driving charge. Unlike his brief appearance at Marlborough Street Magistrates Court, which had been largely ignored by the media, Lyalin's scheduled appearance at the same premises on the morning of 30 September drew journalists from around the globe, because the *Daily Express* had revealed his name that morning.

It also drew the ire of MI5 and the Foreign Office, because Moscow had ruined their hopes of keeping Lyalin's identity secret. And in a move to aggravate the Foreign Office even further, a Soviet Embassy spokesman refused to discuss Lyalin's identity with other newspapers despite Pavlinov's deliberate leak. 'I am not in a position to confirm or deny the report, but personally I have never heard the name Oleg Lialine [*sic*] before,' the spokesman said. Discerning journalists knew that was a lie. 'The name of the Russian turncoat, Oleg Lyalin, was leaked on Wednesday night to the *Daily Express*, almost certainly purposefully by a Soviet Embassy official who himself arrived here [in London] only last week,' the *Washington Post* reported.

On the morning of Thursday 30 September, correspondents who had expected to catch a glimpse of Lyalin in court were left disappointed. While his name was the first one featured on a list outside the courtroom, the defector was nowhere to be seen. 'Moments after 10.30 a.m. No. 1 Court was opened to the press and public,' *The Times* reported. 'The jailer called out: "Remand number one, sir." Then, in almost the same breath, he added: "No answer".'

In such instances, the police would seek an arrest warrant for an accused who had failed to attend a scheduled court appearance, but they did not. As would later be revealed, Lyalin's absence had been authorised by the Attorney General, Sir Peter Rawlinson, amid MI5 fears that the KGB would attempt to kill him. 'I received categorical advice from the security services that there was personal danger to Oleg Lyalin,' Rawlinson told Parliament. 'I was told that the anxieties of it were of bringing him to the court and taking him away from it, and the safeguarding of the concealment of his whereabouts before trial and where he went after trial.'

Lyalin's court absence robbed journalists of a news break-through, but it especially shocked Charles Shearer, one of the police officers who had booked him for drink driving the previous month. Shearer's court attendance was a run-of-the-mill matter for him, and until that day he had not a clue that the Russian he had arrested on Tottenham Court Road in late August was the mystery KGB operative that everyone was desperate to hear from.

'Up until this morning, I did not know that the man I arrested that night was a spy,' he told reporters outside the court. 'It was only when I read the papers today that I twigged.' On reflection, Shearer recalled that Lyalin had been apprehensive about leaving court with a Soviet official following his first court appearance in August. 'We attended the court for the hearing – it was very brief,' Shearer said. 'There were Russian people there from the trade delegation who put the money up for his bail. At this point I wasn't quite sure who he was bailed to, because somehow I felt he didn't want the Russian representatives to take him.'

As reporters conflated evidence with conjecture to drum up sensational headlines and manufacture scoops, Shearer had to contend with the accusation that he had been deliberately deployed to arrest Lyalin as a pretext for the government's expulsion plans. 'There were all sorts of rumours flying that I was put in place to stop him,' he later said. 'That was nonsense, because he was Joe Bloggs [an ordinary person] as far as we were concerned.'

With September's court proceedings failing to live up to the media's expectation, the press turned to the Foreign Office for more answers, where officials scrambled behind the scenes to determine an approach that would strike a balance between protecting Lyalin, exploiting his defection, and reclaiming control of the story. The Kremlin's weaponisation of the unfolding events since planting Lyalin's name in the British press was relentless. It even included a KGB initiative to deploy one of its greatest wartime assets, Kim Philby, for an interview with *Izvestia*, a state-run newspaper, to castigate Britain's 'large-scale . . . provocation' and the 'false accusations against Soviet officials in London'.

The Moscow-based traitor also took a swipe at London's press pack, accusing 'dozens' of journalists on reputable newspapers, including the *Sunday Times, Daily Telegraph, Financial Review,* and *Observer* – his own previous place of work – of being 'paid agents' of the British intelligence services. 'On each of these news organs the recruited journalists and publishers have a British secret service dossier on them, listing their "strong and weak points, their vices and human failings",' Philby ranted. It was by no means surprising that the Soviet asset, who had worked as a 'correspondent' for British publications from Beirut before his defection in 1963, suspected other journalists of also participating in espionage work.

With so much at stake in trying to keep Britain ahead of its rivals in Moscow, the Foreign Office issued a press statement around midday on Thursday 30 September, which would undoubtedly have been approved by MI5's director general Furnival Jones. The statement confirmed Lyalin's identity, and it 'did so with what seemed to be some reluctance or annoyance,' the *New York Times* reported. While partly serving its purpose in showcasing Britain's willingness to be decisive and hit back at the Soviet Union yet again, the statement failed to deter Kremlin officials from stepping up their character assassination of Lyalin.

Less than twenty-four hours after the defector's name was on every journalist's lips, he was being described in the Western media as a 'man about town' with a 'fatal weakness for . . . liquor and ladies'. All accurate, of course, but from the KGB's perspective, such disclosures intended to paint him as an unserious and incapable Soviet operative hardly worth his rank. A phoney who could not be trusted.

Even when Lyalin's picture was leaked to the press the following day, it featured him in a profile angle looking glassy-eyed and expressionless, with a glass of liquor in his hand. The picture had reportedly been taken at an event he had attended to celebrate the opening of a Soviet trade delegation building in north London. Under the headline, 'This is Oleg the so elegant spy', a report in the *Evening Standard* described the 'partygoer' as having a 'vodka glass' in hand. 'It was revealed how his charm, soft manners and his playboy world of expensive restaurants and West End clubs attracted the ladies,' the report added. 'Two blondes and a brunette figured prominently in the London life of Lyalin, who was married with a wife and a . . . son back home in Russia.'

With the Kremlin attributing Lyalin's motives to financial rewards, even security officials who were culturally opposed, and almost pathologically wired to loathe engaging with journalists, agreed that the British government should do its own aggressive press briefings. Those briefings went a long way to discredit the accusation that Lyalin had been bought by MI5. In a page-one story deriding the 'smear campaign by Moscow', Britain's *Daily Telegraph* said regime officials in the Russian capital were 'telling journalists that he [Lyalin] was a "playboy" and a "Casanova" . . . To give the impression that Lyalin was a figure of no importance – another routine Russian reaction in the cases of defectors.' The newspaper added: 'Reports that he has been paid £25,000 by British security for his information about Soviet spies in Britain are being discounted.'

As the media's obsession with Lyalin continued to grow, questions about his girlfriend, Irina Teplyakova, soon emerged. Her job with the trade mission lacked the kind of glamour and excitement that surrounded intelligence roles, but the KGB still managed to exploit her story by portraying her as having callously betrayed her husband and disowned her only child. It wanted to cast her as a vixen with a faulty moral compass, and instead of forbidding trade delegates and her other colleagues from discussing her case, the KGB appears to have given them the green light.

An unnamed colleague from Razno, the Soviet trade mission's outpost in central London, revealed that there was 'talk' about Lyalin and a 'beautiful blonde Russian woman' of whom he was 'quite fond'. A front-page headline in the *Evening Standard* on Friday 1 October screamed: 'Beautiful blonde Russian seeks asylum: Oleg girl defects'. While correctly described as Lyalin's 'constant close companion', Teplyakova was wrongly described as the KGB captain's former 'secretary'. But many Fleet Street journalists were unburdened by any need to be accurate in their pursuit of salacious stories about her affair with Lyalin.

A feature article in the *Daily Mirror*, headlined 'Irina: the beautiful blonde who fell for a spy', expounded the difficulty she had faced when making 'the decision of her life'. When forced to choose between staying with her husband or running away with 'the KGB mystery man', she had chosen 'happiness', the newspaper opined. The *Mirror* quoted an unnamed trade delegation colleague saying: 'It must have been very difficult for her. She would have had to decide overnight between whether to stay here in Britain with Oleg – or go back.' In fact, Teplyakova had to make that decision in an instant, not overnight.

Fuelled by an interwoven narrative of KGB operatives, British officials awaiting Moscow's reprisal, and a playboy's love affair with an assumed Jezebel who had ditched her son and husband, it was hardly surprising that the people on both sides of the Iron Curtain were absorbed by what the press quickly dubbed 'spy mania'.

Watching the unfolding saga was the former Razno employee, Susan Woodthorpe, who had left the firm earlier that year to spend the spring and summer in Spain. Within weeks of returning to London to work at her father's pub in Tottenham, north London, the now twenty-year-old spotted Lyalin's name and picture in the newspaper. At first she dismissed reports about his KGB connection, because she 'couldn't imagine him doing anything sinister and underhand', thinking he had probably defected simply because he 'just wanted to stay in England'.

She asked herself could the man she had considered a colleague and friend, with whom she had shared numerous vodkas and had once even invited to her family's pub, really be a spy? Surely he was far too casual and unrestrained to fit the part. More than five decades later, Woodthorpe told the author about an incident she had overlooked that may have been connected to the British security service's interest in the KGB's links to Razno.

In early 1971, a few months into her job as a receptionist at Razno, and shortly before leaving for Spain in March, Susan Woodthorpe had returned from work to her father's pub to find a message from a British intelligence representative. 'I came back from work one day and my dad says to me, "Well, you'll never guess what happened." He said, "I had either MI5 or MI6 here wanting to get your information to contact you."' Woodthorpe was excited from the minute she had received the message to the instant she dialled the number that had been left for her. Even though she had never previously encountered the British security service, she knew that she needed to be discreet, choosing a phone booth in the basement of a pub around the corner from Razno to make her call.

'He was a British gentleman,' Woodthorpe said of the brief conversation with the apparent security official, whom she never met in person nor spoke to again. 'He just asked if I would be prepared to help them if I was needed and I said, "Yes" . . . It was quite a short phone call; he didn't go into depth about what was going on.'

Till this day Woodthorpe does not know why she had been sought out by the British authorities. But the approach coincided with MI5's renewed determination to roll up the KGB's operations in the UK after Ted Heath's election to office, and came before Oleg Lyalin volunteered his services in April 1971.

Just as MI5 had suspected the Soviet trade mission of providing cover for Kremlin operatives, it had also viewed its affiliates such as Razno with suspicion. And while it would have made sense for MI5 to target a locally hired British woman for recruitment to keep an eye on Razno's staff, Lyalin happened to approach the spy agency a few weeks later to volunteer his services, eventually providing pretty much all MI5 wanted to know about his multiple places of employment.

So while British intelligence authorities never approached Woodthorpe again, they would undoubtedly have seen her name and picture pop up in the newspapers on Saturday 2 October 1971, after she had taken the initiative to get in touch with the press to tell her own story.

'He always had money for a drink, but never threw it around,' Woodthorpe revealed about Lyalin during a TV interview, which was then cited by newspapers. 'He often took me and the other two girls in the office to a pub. We all liked him and used to say what a laugh he was. He was always cracking corny jokes, like swaying into the office saying, "Oh dear, I'm drunk again." You could have got the impression of him being a playboy, but a lot of it was just joking – he is not a very serious person at all. He was rather clumsy, tripping over the mat and things like that.'

More than fifty years on, Woodthorpe still wonders whether Lyalin would have been more open about his double-life had she fallen for his charm. 'I now wonder what would have happened if I had gotten on with him as a lover or a partner,' she told the author. 'He was quite a charmer.'

The news saturation surrounding Lyalin served another Soviet objective that could not have been fulfilled by the KGB officials in London, now that their covers had been compromised and MI5 was closely watching their movements. The headlines inadvertently alerted the KGB's locally hired agents that anyone who had been connected to Lyalin now risked being rounded up by MI5. 'It was a way of telling agents through the pages of the press that only those associated with Lyalin were in danger,' one security analyst revealed. 'But even those agents not associated with Lyalin are in a state of confusion, because they cannot be sure whether their contacts in the Russian Embassy are about to be expelled.'

The mass exodus was to begin. On the first weekend of October, many Soviet officials swept up by the purge were on full public display as they left their homes in London for the final time.

Chapter 12

# THE FALLOUT

SOVIET EMBASSY AND TRADE representatives, more used to luxury transportation than budget travel, were crammed onto three coaches with their families, work files, and suitcases. Their drive through London's autumn mist that weekend was destined to become as memorable as it was miserable, and their mud-splattered shuttles featured 'School Bus' signs on their windscreens, although not because the passengers were students of a new dawn of British diplomacy. The signs were intended to deflect attention, but were an unconvincing cover, much like the diplomatic identities that many of the buses' passengers had hidden behind for months, or in some cases, years.

Upon arriving at Tilbury Docks, one of the country's main ports in south-east England, the buses and several cars accompanying them quickly made their way into a gated area signposted 'No Entry Except on Business'. It was yet another cover to protect the dozens of sour-faced men and women as they disembarked to gather their belongings like displaced people in search of shelter.

All of them appeared to be overcome by the realisation that the comfortable London lifestyles they once took for granted were now no more than a memory.

In tribute to that, perhaps, some passengers brought along consumables such as Coca-Cola and Western cigarettes – some of the small luxuries that they had come to enjoy in their host country. 'They must have cleared out the embassy's whole duty-free stock,' a dock worker quipped after helping the Soviets with their luggage.

In preparation for the final leg of the journey, dozens of the Soviet officials, surrounded by a dreary backdrop of rusted cranes and dilapidated sheds, convened on the quayside. They were united in frustration and a feeling of unfairness. Even their children were downcast, several clutching teddy bears and wooden toys for comfort. In all, about 200 Soviet nationals, including the spies' families, had been directly or indirectly swept up by the British government's purge – about twice the number of individuals who had been targeted for expulsion. And in anticipation of the media interest that had not let up since the Foreign Office's announcement of the expulsion order ten days earlier, police 'guarded every entrance of the dock area', as reporters later noted.

But in reality, the press exclusion zone was largely a public relations exercise. On one hand it showcased British law enforcement authorities as being apolitical in protecting the privacy of foreign officials and their families, while on the other, it amplified the government's goodwill in managing the mass diplomatic exit with apparent respect, rather than a sense of retribution.

For all intents and purposes, the expulsion's masterminds, from the prime minister and foreign secretary to Martin Furnival Jones at MI5, could not have scripted a more humiliating send-off for the Kremlin functionaries even if they had tried. Government and security service officials expected – even hoped – that well-placed journalists would figure out a way to circumvent privacy guardrails in the name of 'public interest'. And the press pack did not disappoint.

Enterprising photographers, who had been tipped off to arrive at the port early that weekend, bypassed the police barriers to get a closer look at the expelled subjects. The snappers trained their lenses in the Soviets' direction, occasionally jostling to find a better frame before taking one shot after another. A reporter who witnessed the frenzy would later report that as 'press cameras clicked away, one Soviet shouted: "Stop those stupid things!",' but the Soviets were powerless to do anything else aside from demand to be left alone as they counted down for their cruise ship to arrive and whisk them to Leningrad.

'It was no jet set, James-Bond style farewell,' the reporter said of the Soviets' humbling exit. Nothing seemed to go their way, and even the vessel they were awaiting was mired in controversy. The Second World War troopship, *Baltika*, had been at the centre of another scandal about a decade earlier, when it had ferried Soviet premier Nikita Khrushchev to the United Nations general assembly in New York in 1960, and one of its crewmen promptly defected to the US, causing the Kremlin considerable embarrassment.

The *Baltika* became a talking point yet again on Sunday 3 October 1971. The ageing vessel, with a red hammer and sickle plastered across its exhaust funnel – way above its deck for everyone to see – arrived two hours late for its pick-up. 'It was past midday with a watery sun breaking through the mist before the expelled officials and their families . . . finally walked up the gangplank amid tight security precautions,' a journalist observed. Bundles upon bundles of luggage were craned onto the ship, and even a few Russian cars, including a Moskvitch and a Volga, were hauled aboard.

'No one else was allowed beyond the departure gates in the terminal hall,' a report revealed. 'Boarding passes already issued to news men were declared invalid . . . [And] the Soviet Embassy apparently had bought up every empty berth. Even some bona fide Russian passengers were barred from boarding until the purged KGB corps had taken their places.'

With roughly one-fifth of the Soviet mission now out of the country, the British government was still anticipating the Kremlin's retaliation against its own presence in Moscow, where seventy-eight officials, including forty diplomats, were assigned to the UK Embassy. A proportionate expulsion was expected to wipe out fifteen to twenty postings from the British mission, which was around the number that Kremlin officials had earlier touted in the Soviet press.

The Foreign Office and Downing Street, however, were more concerned about the KGB's intimidation of other British citizens in Moscow. The Soviet agency had placed some of them under 'ostentatious surveillance', keeping a close watch on all their movements, and in some instances, leaking their names to local media outlets under the accusation that they were 'agents of British intelligence', according to a Foreign Office official.

Far from merely harassing diplomats, Soviet henchmen also targeted British journalists, businessmen, and others. 'For its sinister aims, British intelligence uses employees of British institutions in the USSR – businessmen, journalists, and scientists,' declared a senior commentator on *Pravda*, the nation's biggest-selling newspaper and a renowned mouthpiece of the Soviet regime. The intimidation tactics did not even spare British families, including parents going about their ordinary daily activities such as collecting their children from day care.

'A policeman barred many English mothers from a nursery school where they had gone to pick up their children,' the Foreign Office official revealed. 'The policeman refused to admit mothers who did not have their passports with them.'

With little to no diplomatic leverage to help ensure the safety and privacy of its citizens in the Soviet Union, the best the British government could hope for was a swift and proportionate retaliation against its embassy head count. Ted Heath was keen to neutralise the prospect of further escalation with the Kremlin, especially as he had already won the tussle against his country's greatest foe.

The prime minister's next play was especially important, because his allies in Europe, including France, whose support he had sought and still needed in Britain's bid for entry into the European Economic Community, were worried that a full-scale diplomatic and intelligence war between London and Moscow could hinder wider East–West security cooperation, which was already feeble. France's concern was shared by the Nordic countries neighbouring the Soviet Union.

Adding to Heath's distress were Labour Party MPs, including the man he had unseated the previous year, Harold Wilson, claiming that the expulsion had been a political, rather than a security operation, timed to bolster the prime minister's ratings. 'I think the whole thing is a bit phoney,' Wilson said in a radio interview. It was a rich accusation from a former leader who had been blamed for completely failing to address the KGB threat in Britain during his six years in office. Wilson also took a swipe at Lyalin, saying: 'My experience of these matters is that no nation, least of all the Russians, would have one man, so junior and so utterly stupid anyway, with a list of 105 people.'

Heath was unwilling to remain silent in the face of such insults. 'It really is a contemptible attitude,' he said, 'for a man who was once prime minister and had to handle national security himself, and who knew this position perfectly well but did not deal with it, to make a suggestion like that on a matter of the highest importance to the security of this nation.'

Thankfully the domestic political skirmish did not cloud the government's focus on Moscow's retaliatory plans, and after days of deliberation, the Kremlin delivered its response, which appeared to be largely face-saving instead of the aggressive strike that some British officials had feared. Eighteen British citizens were expelled from Moscow, including four diplomats from the embassy. Another ten former embassy officials were declared persona non grata, forbidden from ever returning to the Soviet Union.

Moscow's counterattack also resulted in the cancellation of three ministerial visits, including that of the foreign secretary, Douglas-Home. However, by and large, the Kremlin accepted its fate, including Britain's order that expelled Soviet officials could not be replaced. No longer would Britain accept a one-out, one-in scenario.

No amount of venting, political posturing, or threats were going to restore the freedom that Soviet intelligence officials had once enjoyed in Britain. Reality overtook the KGB much more quickly than the agency could figure its way out of the Lyalin problem, to the extent that its senior officials were succumbing to the kind of paranoia that the CIA and MI5 had come to know far too well. Gone were the days when KGB spymasters could recline in their thinking chairs, congratulating themselves for having outsmarted the American and British spy agencies, which had squandered endless resources chasing enemies within – 'moles'.

Suddenly, the Soviet spy agency was in the grips of a new and unforeseen era, one that would shatter its self-assurance and bring into question the judgements of its chief, Yuri Andropov, who until then had taken for granted the KGB's superiority over its adversaries.

On any given day, between arriving at KGB headquarters and strolling to his third-floor office, Yuri Andropov was greeted by a monument outside the building that was designed to inspire – a tribute to the defence of the motherland and the crushing of its rivals. At twelve metres, the height of an average three-storey building, the monument immortalised a man who had been much larger than life in character and deeds. The statue, depicting a man in a trench coat staring valiantly ahead as if contemplating the spoils of his victories, had been a centrepiece at Lubyanka Square for nine years when Andropov took over the KGB. Instead of lionising the usual Soviet icons such as Vladimir Lenin or Joseph Stalin, the steel sculpture paid homage to the KGB's founding father – Felix Dzerzhinsky.

He was idolised by generations of Kremlin intelligence officers for the unrestrained ruthlessness that spanned his leadership of the KGB's forerunners, including the Cheka and the OGPU. Even after his death in 1926, his influence on espionage and sabotage endured, as did his legacy of overseeing the mass killing of regime opponents in the name of 'organised terror', as he had called it. It would have been natural for his successors, from the infamous Lavrentiy Beria and Alexander Shelepin right through to Andropov, if only introspectively, to compare their career achievements to Dzerzhinsky's, to see if they could hold a candle to the man who had been celebrated as the Russian Revolution's 'devout knight'.

Andropov's route into the intelligence community had not been by way of espionage missions but via policy, political and diplomatic work. However, his career as a spymaster, at least in its early days, could well have lived up to Dzerzhinsky's legacy. Like his hero, Andropov relished punishing dissidents, favoured totalitarianism over multi-party systems, and was not opposed to turning on loyalists who were suddenly deemed inconvenient. But he was self-aware enough to balance his hard-man persona with an air of refinement. Despite the influential part he had played in the crushing of the Hungarian Revolution and the Prague Spring, which had killed thousands and dashed the hopes of millions, Andropov cultivated the image of a shrewd, sophisticated thinker with a diplomatic veneer, to avoid being seen as basically a thug.

Like all KGB chiefs before him, he welcomed praise and was inclined to talk up his achievements, as he had done in the agency's first annual report after his takeover. Presented to the Communist Party leadership on 6 May 1968, the top secret report – revealed forty-three years later by the Woodrow Wilson International Center for Scholars – features Andropov boasting about his organisation's infiltration of the 'enemy's special services' through the recruitment of foreign agents, along with uncovering dozens of 'double agents planted by the enemy' and preventing the 'compromise of 22 officers and agents of the KGB and GRU' by adversaries:

> We also succeeded in obtaining data on some modes of communication between the enemy's intelligence and agent networks in spotting specific intelligence officers engaged in enemy activities against the USSR, and in passing to the enemy advantageous information and disinformation, [even] regarding operational activities. More successful fulfilment of the task of penetrating the enemy's special services has been facilitated also by measures of recruiting foreigners. During 1967, 42 agents

were recruited, among them 8 diplomats. The counter-intelligence service carried out special measures which resulted in photocopying 54 documents of ambassadors from member countries of NATO, annual reports of some embassies, reports of military attaches, and other classified materials on political, military-economic, operational and other matters.

By Andropov's estimation, serving the USSR was not just a job but a lifetime commitment, and he was at a loss as to how some fellow citizens did not share his devotion to the motherland. Even though he was less brutal than the likes of Dzerzhinsky and Beria, deep down, Andropov believed that Soviet dissenters, the men and women who failed to conform with Communism, were afflicted with personal insecurities, including 'ideological delusions, religious fanaticism' and warped opinions of Moscow that needed to be firmly addressed. He detained the luckier ones in psychiatric asylums to be 'cured', and had his henchmen torture or execute those who were less fortunate.

In reforming the KGB's domestic operations, Andropov had no regard for legal constraints, moral barriers, ethical dilemmas, or hiccups surrounding civil liberties and human rights. He wanted to preserve the agency's Chekist lineage, and in so doing, upscaled its activities, including its core business of espionage and sabotage, right through to arming anti-Western militants in the Middle East and Africa. He also targeted the 'influence of the Catholic Church', which he deemed subversive and incompatible with Communism, discrediting its officials through fabricated rumours.

But above all this, in prosecuting the KGB's foreign mission, Andropov reserved his greatest animosity for his agency's rivals, with the CIA at the top of the list, and MI5 not too far below.

Described by a Soviet bloc general as the 'godfather of Russia's new era of deception operations aimed at improving the badly damaged image of Soviet rulers in the West', Andropov wanted to continue weakening MI5 and the CIA through disinformation campaigns – and he also wanted their intelligence. He prioritised the theft of Western secrets by burgling embassies, compromising diplomats, and recruiting officials with Communist sympathies as well as embittered intelligence officers with axes to grind.

Despite the brutality and operational acumen that had assured Andropov's rise, his credibility suffered enormously in the autumn of 1971 after Oleg Lyalin's betrayal and Britain's purge. Adding to Andropov's woes was the embarrassment he endured upon briefing Leonid Brezhnev about both cases and confessing to the Soviet leader that Lyalin's cooperation with MI5 would likely compromise the global espionage network that had taken the Soviet Union decades to build. No explanation regarding the expulsion could have mitigated Andropov's shame, especially since Brezhnev had been compelled to cut short an Eastern European tour and race back to Moscow to deal with the crisis.

It was one thing to be overwhelmed by the perceived injustice of Lyalin's betrayal, but to have overlooked the threat MI5 posed against the KGB's interests in Britain was foolish and unprofessional. Had Andropov become too complacent and self-assured? Had he carelessly disregarded Britain's numerous written and verbal threats regarding Soviet espionage in the UK, simply brushing them aside as empty and unenforceable diplomatic intimidations? Or worse still, had MI5 suddenly clambered out of its years of introspection and insecurity to become better at playing the spy game?

The mass expulsion had not only diminished Andropov's access to British secrets and demolished his agency's sabotage plans against the UK, it had also seriously limited his access to US intelligence. It had been an accepted fact since the Second World War that the transatlantic countries shared more information with one another than with any other ally. And Moscow had repeatedly and successfully exploited that information-sharing from its inception, including through its recruitment of British scientists working on the Manhattan Project, who leaked nuclear secrets in the 1940s. And, of course, through former MI6 officer Kim Philby, who had supplied CIA-related material thanks to his closeness to the likes of James Angleton.

There was no denying it: Andropov's colossal failure at the hands of MI5 in 1971 threatened to stain his reputation and forever render him outplayed by his British counterpart, Martin Furnival Jones. But instead of shouldering the blame, he directed his anger at the KGB's rank and file. It was they who were the problem, Andropov felt – they who needed to be disciplined, they who needed to be reminded of the KGB's remorselessness in its mission to reach anyone it deemed an enemy, including rogue officers in its ranks.

He wanted to shed his agency's internal decay in the quest of restoring its honour. He was incensed and disenchanted that any KGB official would choose to sell out their nation rather than commit themselves to weakening its enemies. So, in his determination to stop other officers from following in Lyalin's footsteps, Andropov focused his attention on the agency's activities in the country hosting the KGB's largest overseas presence – the United States.

Of the 1,500 or so Soviet nationals officially working there, about half were Kremlin intelligence officers and their working wives, some operating out of the embassy in Washington and others, including Mikhail Mikhailovich Antipov, posing as UN diplomats. Antipov's official role as 'first secretary' to the Soviet

Union's UN mission allowed him to oversee the KGB's sabotage and assassination planning against the US, because he was the head of his agency's Department V in North America. In the same way that he had evaded US security screenings when he arrived in the country in 1969, Antipov had successfully done so on a stint earlier that decade, proving what the CIA's James Angleton had long suspected, that 'diplomatic access and immunity make the United Nations a spy nest'.

Bolstering the Soviet espionage cadre in the US were dozens working under the guise of trade delegates, tourism advisors, and press correspondents – and 'illegals' operating under deep cover, who were said to exceed the total number of Soviet officials on working visas. 'There are also hundreds each year who come in and out [of the US] on temporary duty to attend trade, cultural and scientific conferences,' noted the *New York Times* in the wake of Lyalin's defection. 'Many are known, identified KGB or GRU officers.'

As the agency's overlord, Andropov wanted to preserve the KGB's strategic interests in the US. But he understood that American security officials would have been determined to capitalise on Britain's mass expulsion by identifying KGB vulnerabilities in Washington and New York. Especially since at least seven of those who had been expelled from London had previously been based in the US under diplomatic cover. Fearing that tougher US action against his operatives in North America risked enticing Soviet officials to the other side of the Iron Curtain, Andropov issued an order in mid-October 1971 that rattled KGB staff and became a flashpoint for generating paranoia and discontent.

He instructed KGB officers in Manhattan to raise any suspicions they held of disloyalty within their own ranks, regardless of whether or not they had any evidence to back such allegations. There was no threshold for suspicion to deter disgruntled employees from making false accusations against colleagues. Andropov was simply on the hunt for targets, people to go after – prospective turncoats whom he could punish and make an example of. In a top-down organisation where the director is akin to an emperor, no one dared to challenge him, least of all the KGB's rezident in New York, who sought unsubstantiated claims from his staff to assure Andropov that ruthless steps were being taken to help redress insider threats.

The Soviet agency's sudden change of approach in the US was supposed to be kept secret. But a Soviet official working under the FBI's control in New York informed his handlers. 'Since the defection of Oleg Lyalin, there has been one noticeable innovation concerning the security measure within the KGB NY Residency,' according to a debriefing of the FBI's Soviet source. The debriefing memo also reveals that in a series of one-to-one conversations with the KGB's employees in New York, top Soviet spies directed their officers to provide 'any suspicion' which they 'might have about a fellow . . . officer'. One of the rezident's demands was that such information should 'be furnished to him personally and in secret, irrespective of the officer's KGB rank'.

Turning Soviet operatives against each other did nothing to restore the KGB morale, which had been pummelled by the British purge. Instead it 'caused a great amount of apprehension among the officer personnel', the FBI source revealed. If KGB officers had been uneasy about spying on their colleagues, they were even more concerned and unnerved that they themselves could become surveillance targets should a workmate misconstrue their own behaviour.

With a complete disregard for the heightened paranoia among his US-based staff, Andropov then planned to introduce an even more draconian measure – or 'service', as it became known – to deter prospective turncoats. He wanted to deploy an undercover surveillance team at the New York residency, 'which would analyse the activities, behaviour pattern, etc, of the Soviet personnel in order to prevent a potential defection'. The FBI's Soviet source believed that the 'KGB Headquarters will initiate this "service" within the NY Residency in the future but added that the implementation of this procedure will necessarily take time.'

Along with monitoring its US personnel, and banning 'intelligence meetings between KGB officers and their most important American agents', Andropov was also prepared to swap out his Manhattan-based operatives in the event that Lyalin blew their cover. 'The NY Residency has assumed a "wait and see" attitude, and will take no action unless personnel at the Residency are publicly identified by Lyalin or unless Headquarters so directs,' the FBI's source revealed.

Andropov's hunch about Lyalin's ability to compromise his officers was partly obvious and largely correct, because within days of his defection, the estranged KGB captain started providing the FBI with investigative leads through his MI5 debriefers.

\* \* \*

With the KGB after his head, the media preoccupied with his love affairs and MI5 determined to exploit his recollections, assessments and tactical evaluations, Oleg Lyalin relished his newfound purpose and mission inside his hiding place. He had as many opinions as he had secrets and was uninhibited in offering operational advice. During hours upon hours of debriefings, which would be conducted over weeks, months and years, Lyalin fielded questions regarding the KGB's mission in and outside Britain, providing crucial insights into the Soviet agency's state of play in Europe and the United States.

Anticipating Lyalin's vendetta against his former colleagues, the KGB recalled its Department V operatives, including those serving in Asia and South America, but it was a little too late. By then, Lyalin had very likely exposed the identities of Soviet saboteurs who fled back to Moscow from their field offices, including those from Mexico City, Helsinki, Montreal, Bonn, Bogota, Lagos, Athens and Paris.

By avoiding any affiliation with Department V's recall of operatives from global cities, Mikhail Mikhailovich Antipov maintained his diplomatic cover at the Soviet UN mission and remained in New York until the following year. His case was exceptional, though, because any other KGB official who had ever enjoyed a 'diplomatic' or 'foreign trade' cover could presume that their operational role was blown, or likely to be as a result of Lyalin's defection.

Martin Furnival Jones and his officers at MI5 rejoiced about each setback they dealt the KGB with Lyalin's help, and were now eager to help their allies. The British agency provided his disclosures to their partners, and especially helped the FBI in its mission to undermine Soviet espionage in the US. MI5 gave Lyalin's biographical details to its US partner, with a breakdown of his upbringing in Russia, educational background, entry into the KGB, the career setbacks that he had faced ahead of his deployment to the UK, and the intricacies of the Department V training and sabotage methods, which the defector had detailed in his early debriefings.

MI5 also supplied the American law enforcement organisation with the names of Soviet operatives whom Britain had expelled in the mass purge, along with each of their photographs, and they were willing to help more. '[MI5] has offered to service any requests we may have for questioning Lyalin,' notes an FBI memo. 'Each office should consider this offer and submit any questions it feels should be submitted to Lyalin concerning the information he has already furnished or any information he may have which would be of interest to the Bureau.'

Over a series of interviews at an MI5 safe house, Lyalin identified Soviet officials working with the Kremlin's mission to the UN – and also provided and corroborated information regarding KGB illegals operating in New York. 'GOLDFINCH has furnished a great deal concerning illegal operations regarding the US,' notes a partly-redacted FBI paper, citing Lyalin by his MI5 codename. 'It is therefore possible that with a review of the material and the furnishing of the photographs, GOLDFINCH would be able to possibly identify or furnish some information concerning these individuals.'

By analysing photographs of US-based Soviet officials supplied by the FBI, Lyalin helped identify forty-five 'new KGB officers in the NY area', who were part of the Soviet mission to the United Nations. He also identified Nikolay Alekseyevich Kuznetsov, the KGB's former head of Department V in the US, who had successfully operated under UN cover until his return to Moscow in late 1969. While the FBI had been aware that Kuznetsov had tried unsuccessfully to recruit a chemist during his deployment, it had been unaware that he had 'recruited a technician connected with electronics and computers for which he received a very high decoration'.

Even though some of Lyalin's 'intelligence identifications' had been previously known to the FBI, there was a 'substantial number of new identifications of personnel', an FBI document reveals. 'Initial review indicates that a number of these latter individuals reside within Soviet establishments and we have, therefore, not developed a sufficient amount of information about their activities to date to confirm or negate Lyalin's identifications. This initial review indicates that some of these individuals may well have either security or radio monitoring assignments within Soviet establishments.'

But despite stepping up its counter-espionage investigations into Soviet intelligence officers and agents in the US, the FBI never appeared to consider a British-style mass expulsion.

Even so, the prospect of such an event happening would have loomed large at the time. As the security crises continued to unravel across the Atlantic, one of Yuri Andropov's greatest fears was realised when a Soviet 'trade' official in Brussels went missing in October 1971. Anatole Thoibev suspected that his longstanding friendship with Lyalin would eventually draw the KGB's attention and trigger his recall to Moscow for questioning. Refusing to take his chances, Thoibev stole a diplomatic car from the Soviet trade mission's headquarters in the Belgian capital and raced to a police station for help. 'It was thought . . . that Thoibev might have defected for fear of reprisals and as a result of his close friendship with Lyalin,' a press report revealed.

Thoibev's defection was instructive, because it proved that Andropov's mission to prevent KGB officers from escaping to the West was somewhat unworkable. No surveillance systems could totally dispel the threat of Soviet turncoats, and while Andropov understood that, he persisted with his internal security clampdown. But he also realised that to return the KGB to its glory days, proactive measures had to be taken to make it look attractive to prospective defectors from the West.

'Lyalin has disgraced our organisation,' Andropov told an acolyte. 'We should have a programme that would entice Western spies to come to us. We need to seduce them into coming here with financial remuneration, a better life, perhaps ideological reasons. Spare no effort.' As part of that mission, Andropov turned to a familiar bedfellow who was the KGB's craftiest Cold War recruit – Kim Philby.

Yuri Andropov had long admired Kim Philby's commitment to the Soviet cause and felt that Moscow owed him a great deal for the risks he had taken for the KGB. But little had been done to utilise properly the Englishman's skills since he had defected in 1963, aside from parachuting him into the odd Soviet press interview to rail against the Kremlin's adversaries, and most of all, his former peers in Britain's intelligence community. Andropov decided to change that. He wanted to revive Philby's tradecraft weaponry, with all of its mischief and cunning, and provide him with a central role in the KGB's renewed fight against Britain and the United States. No one at the spy agency, or anywhere in the Soviet Union and its satellite states for that matter, could claim to know more than Philby about MI5, MI6 and the CIA.

Andropov's intended redeployment of Philby's skills was not welcomed by some senior KGB officials, who remained suspicious that he was a British double-agent. And their suspicion was far from passive: the agency had bugged Philby's phone and apartment, opened his mail and screened his visitors. It was hardly surprising that the former MI6 officer sensed a lack of warmth from his Soviet masters after defecting, and as such, was disillusioned. He felt cast aside, isolated, and that he was in effect living under house arrest. He spent most of his days in his rundown Moscow apartment drinking away his sorrows. The KGB had failed him and perhaps in so doing, it failed itself by not fully exploiting his skillset much earlier.

Wielding the power to transform Philby's situation at a moment of his choosing, Andropov scaled back the surveillance operation against him, but retained the KGB's phone taps to keep eavesdropping on his calls. Overall, however, the agency remarkably improved Philby's living arrangements, fully renovated his apartment at his request and to his liking, and provided him with a housekeeper and a monthly credit of 100 rubles to spend at a grocery store reserved for the Soviet elite. The veteran spy was also given books, clothes, transport and theatre tickets, and even flown around to Kremlin-friendly nations, including Cuba, where he was treated like a celebrity and showered with gifts.

'The goal set out by Andropov was to significantly improve Philby's life and show other potential collaborators in the West that he was living happily in the Soviet Union,' noted a former senior KGB official tasked with looking after the British defector.

Philby's reactivation delivered immediate dividends, giving him the sense of purpose that Andropov had hoped for. With endless time on his hands, Philby's espionage knowledge was drawn on from across the agency. He coached KGB trainees, as well as young intelligence officers bound for the West, including Australia and New Zealand, in how to conceal their spying and adapt to their host nations' security procedures and social norms. He helped the KGB analyse and assess Western secrets, including stolen US State Department and CIA documents. He also reconnected with foreign correspondents with the intention of providing information and disinformation that would damage Soviet adversaries.

While Philby's direct knowledge of the British intelligence agencies and the CIA was now somewhat dated, it still proved to be useful. He instructed the KGB's foreign counter-intelligence section on how to improve its work against US and British spies and also advised the Soviet agency to reconsider the approach of an Australian volunteer, whom it had suspected of being a double-agent. The Antipodean operative, thought to be with ASIO, the country's domestic spy agency, proved Philby's hunch to be correct. He ultimately provided the KGB with intelligence relating to Australia and its two closest allies, the US and Britain.

Philby's contributions, along with the Australian operative's secrets and the KGB's clampdown on potential dissidents in its US cadre, were largely tactical measures rather than strategic moves. They were knee-jerk reactions to a problem beyond repair; a way for Andropov to reclaim a sense of control over the KGB's destiny after his irrevocable loss in Britain. But somehow, the CIA's counter-intelligence supremo, James Angleton, was oblivious to the KGB's devastation and its leader's insecurity and struggles.

In fact, far from realising that the Soviet agency had been weakened by Britain's purge, Angleton was convinced that it had succeeded yet again in exercising its 'Master Plan' – its deceitful mission to plant yet another of its loyal officials in the West. And he was desperate to make his new findings known to MI5.

## Chapter 13

# 'WHAT REPORTS?'

WHETHER ARRIVING IN LONDON by invitation or completely unannounced, James Angleton's visits to MI5's headquarters were generally marked by a tone of caution and contrived urgency about the Soviet threat that, by his own estimation, was omnipresent but barely visible. It was in that tone that he had informed MI5 about his suspicion of Harold Wilson shortly after he had been elected prime minister in the early 1960s. It was also in that tone that a few years later Angleton had reasserted his belief to Martin Furnival Jones that the KGB had penetrated MI5's senior ranks.

The CIA spymaster enjoyed leveraging his gravitas across the pond because MI5 had, for more than a decade, regarded his authority as an adequate substitute for solid evidence. But despite Angleton's stubbornness in ignoring the reality that his warnings and operational leads were still failing to produce meaningful results, he must have sensed that his authority was diminishing in Furnival Jones's eyes. Nothing else could really explain why the MI5 director general had not told him about Oleg Lyalin's approach to the agency before his defection. And equally, nothing else could answer for MI5's unwillingness to seek Angleton's advice, let alone apprise him ahead of time, about Britain's purge of Soviet spies.

The twin issues were at the forefront of Angleton's mind when he arrived in the British capital in the autumn of 1971 to provide what he thought MI5 needed – his unsolicited verdict about its defector. He declared to the agency's top brass that having reflected on Lyalin's backstory and the circumstances under which he had approached the organisation, he was convinced that the KGB volunteer was an imposter.

Yet of all the outlandish claims that Angleton had resolutely stood by over the years, Lyalin's alleged connection to the Soviet agency's 'Master Plan' was the easiest to disprove. Because if it were true, it meant that the KGB had staged Lyalin's cooperation with MI5 despite knowing that it would compromise the identities of local Soviet operatives and risk a massive British retaliation, such as the subsequent expulsion of more than a hundred of them. If Angleton were right, then that meant the KGB had willingly allowed Lyalin to expose some of its most secretive sabotage plans, force the recall of its Department V officers from around the world, and even encourage other Soviet officials to defect.

Angleton's attempt to discredit Lyalin was so off the mark that it could not simply be dismissed as a quirk of his longstanding suspicion of the Soviet system. It brought into sharp focus his state of mind; his inability to see beyond the distorted and self-absorbed microcosm that he had long dwelled in. Angleton's baseless claim about Lyalin was also invalidated by his poor track record on matters that had required unbiased analysis – from the molehunter's failed crusade to categorically identify the CIA's mole, 'Sasha', to his character assassination of KGB defector Yuri Nosenko. The one thing that the latest London visit was set to underscore in Angleton's mind was that he was no longer seen as a bastion of global counter-intelligence, nor held in the same high esteem by his peers and one-time acolytes.

After failing to convince British intelligence officials of his Lyalin theory, Langley's counter-espionage boss returned to the US unswayed in his thinking, still determined to undermine MI5's KGB defector. To the point that when the British agency shared Lyalin's leads through the FBI, Angleton locked away the files instead of circulating them to the US National Security Council and President Nixon, as he was supposed to do. Somehow he had failed to see that his desire to damage Lyalin's credibility could have been better served by circulating the intelligence with the caveat that it should not be taken at face value.

One reason he may have opted against that strategy was perhaps that he had come to the quiet realisation that no one was taking him seriously any more. That his magic touch had lost its lustre, not only among MI5 officials as he had earlier discovered, but more broadly among those in Washington and Langley who had the authority to decide the future of his career.

Angleton's failure to circulate Lyalin's intelligence unravelled several months later when FBI director J. Edgar Hoover expressed his excitement about it in a phone call with Richard Nixon. 'How do you like the British reports from their source Lyalin, Mr President?' Nixon, who was on holiday in Florida, could not recall ever seeing the material in question. 'What reports?' the president asked, before realising that the intelligence had been withheld from him. Nixon then contacted Henry Kissinger to ask if he had been aware of Lyalin's files, but the national security advisor had also been kept out of the loop.

Nixon and Kissinger realised that the missing information

was more likely to have been blocked intentionally rather than accidentally withheld because of some administrative oversight. Kissinger demanded answers from the CIA, and soon enough, the agency's head of plans, responsible for overseeing covert operations and recruitment of foreign agents, tracked the intelligence files to one of Angleton's safes. Senior CIA officials were horrified by Angleton's actions and reprimanded him over the breach of protocol. The episode marked the beginning of Angleton's end.

A CIA inquiry was launched into his handling of intelligence and found that Angleton was an habitual hoarder, who had gone 'overboard' in withholding information from his superiors. He stockpiled thousands of operational leads in brown envelopes and cardboard boxes that he stowed in vaults, safes and cabinets, refusing to log them into the agency's central filing system because he feared they would be vulnerable to moles. His stashed secrets featured intercepted mail, briefings on investigations by partner agencies such as MI5, and even material outside the scope of his departmental responsibilities, including an autopsy report on the former Secretary of State Robert Kennedy, who was killed in 1968.

'The paper-and-records problem was high on the agenda of issues that needed to be addressed,' the agency's inquiry notes. 'The quantity that the Angleton vaults and safes contained was almost overwhelming, and much of this had never been made available outside the [Counter-intelligence] Staff.'

The inquiry also concluded that Angleton's fear of insider threats did not justify his safekeeping methods. 'Whether for reasons of bureaucratic style or fear of penetration of the Agency, information of all kinds and from all kinds of sources had been held privately,' according to the CIA's findings. 'In a more serious vein, files were found on the assassinations of President

John F. Kennedy and his brother Robert F. Kennedy. These included autopsy pictures of the remains of Robert Kennedy.'

The CIA investigators gave careful consideration to that particularly 'bizarre finding'. And while they thought that Angleton's interest in the JFK case related to Yuri Nosenko's insistence that the KGB had not assassinated the president, they could not understand why the counter-intelligence chief 'had the pictures' in his vault. 'Neither could they think of any reason why it was appropriate for CI Staff files to contain them. They were accordingly destroyed.'

Another file discovered in one of Angleton's vaults contained a memorandum from a meeting at Langley between MI5's chief Furnival Jones and his CIA counterpart Richard Helms. During that meeting in early 1971, the British official had revealed that he had personally interviewed MI5's former deputy director general, Graham Mitchell, after a lengthy investigation into his alleged ties to the KGB, and had cleared him of any wrong-doing. Furnival Jones was so confident in his findings that he had flown to the US on a surprise visit to alert Helms in person and to provide a separate face-to-face briefing to J. Edgar Hoover at the FBI.

At Furnival Jones' request, Helms then ordered a typed memorandum of the director general's statement, essentially to put Mitchell's exoneration on the official record. The memo was then sent to Angleton so that he could share it with relevant staff members, including the CIA's London station chief. But Angleton never did.

By deliberately keeping some of the most secret and sensitive intelligence records to himself, Angleton had effectively ring-fenced them from the agency's executive control, exercising a near-totalitarian authority over how they would be handled and exploited. By his own judgement, no one was better able to adjudicate on such matters. Where he did stand apart from his colleagues was in the extent of his unrelenting suspicion of the Kremlin threat, the prism through which he viewed every aspect of the Cold War.

'Unlike the Emperor and his imaginary clothes, Angleton's fantasies were never vulnerable to objective examination, simply because he surrounded such data as existed with a wall of secrecy,' the CIA inquiry concluded. 'His "facts" were available in full only to a minimal number of trusted apostles; to the rest of the intelligence community, both American and foreign, he doled them out selectively – seldom in written form – to prove whatever point he was trying to make at the time.'

Described by the CIA's inquiry as 'a man of loose and disjointed thinking', Angleton harboured suspicions that held no bounds. He had even kept a file on Kissinger because he had suspected him of being a Soviet spy. Following the National Security Advisor's trip to Beijing to restore US relations with China in 1971, Angleton had wondered 'whether the KGB had its arm on Kissinger'.

By then Angleton had long been wedded to Anatoly Golitsyn's theory that the 'Sino-Soviet split' – the breakdown of the post-Second World War military and economic relationship between Beijing and Moscow – was merely a disinformation operation to dupe the West. 'His contention that the Sino-Soviet schism was a disinformation project carried out under the direction of the KGB was subject to ridicule even by some of his friends and supporters.'

Angleton formed his impressions of people according to his preconceived, unshakeable opinions of them – and believed at his very core that everything he had done was for the greater good, regardless of whether it had violated the CIA's code of conduct, like his safekeeping habits. The power and influence he drew from helming the agency's counter-intelligence operations had been magnified by Anatoly Golitsyn's arrival on the scene in 1961 because the KGB defector completed him in some ways; bridging the gaps in Angleton's own operational shortcomings.

It was as if having Golitsyn by his side had somehow made up for Angleton's inability to speak Russian, his lack of first-hand experience in agent-running, and his apparent disconnect with field work. But now, in late 1971, that partnership was proving his downfall.

While Anatoly Golitsyn's tight partnership with James Angleton was mutually beneficial, it was of far greater value to the defector. It helped him to circumvent scepticism, placed him at the top table of counter-intelligence deliberations, and provided him with unfettered access to Western secrets. Golitsyn had an impassioned cheerleader in Angleton, a supreme advocate and enabler, a resolute anchor to relationships within and outside of the CIA, including with MI5. With Angleton's stamp of credibility, Golitsyn's most far-fetched hunches and theories had been rendered convincing and enlightening.

Yet Angleton's most prized asset became his greatest liability, because the CIA veteran had repeatedly failed to see the writing on the wall, refusing to heed the early warnings about Golitsyn's self-serving inclinations and mental instability, which had emerged in psychological screenings. Within days of Golitsyn's arrival in the United States in late 1961, the agency's psychologists had subjected him to a series of tests probing his character, honesty and state of mind. One of the examiners, clinical psychologist Dr John Gittinger, warned in an official report that the defector was 'mentally ill' with a propensity to 'exaggerate'. He also concluded that the 'primary reason' underlying Golitsyn's defection had been to 'gain status'.

A subsequent CIA inquiry revealed that Golitsyn was diagnosed with a 'paranoid personality' in early 1962. But instead of taking that highly relevant diagnosis into consideration when assessing Golitsyn's credibility, Angleton and his acolytes had downplayed it because they wanted him to keep divulging secrets.

'Although account was given of this [Golitsyn's] psychological problem, it was considered in the light of a threat to the continuity to the debriefing process rather than as a factor reflecting on the validity of the purported intelligence he gave us,' the inquiry report notes. 'It was apparently felt that, if we could maintain his stability, we could depend not only upon the objectively verifiable facts he gave us, but also upon his often very theoretical generalisations.'

Angleton was convinced that he knew better than the mental health specialists. He effectively regarded their conclusions as being worth less than the clipboards that they carried during psychological testing. He especially resented the CIA's psychologists and denounced them for 'accusing' Golitsyn of being paranoid, saying their negative diagnosis of 'one of the finest analytical minds' had played into the KGB's playbook. 'I find that kind of accusation the kind that must have set off the greatest peals of glee in the KGB of the many statements of his defection,' Angleton later told a congressional hearing.

While lambasting the psychologists' 'imprecision and unprofessionalism', Angleton praised the Ukrainian defector for supplying 'several thousands of pages of very hard core information, which had resulted in perhaps the most major counter-espionage cases in . . . the whole Western world.' But that proclamation in itself was a complete delusion, because Golitsyn's information was riddled with fantasies.

With the countless errors that came to be chalked up to Golitsyn's leads, the CIA was determined to set the record straight in the mid-1970s and tasked investigators to unearth and dispassionately re-examine his disclosures. They were immediately staggered by the inconsistencies in his backstory and the disproportionate amount of resources that Angleton had devoted to his shoddy operational leads. Not to mention the way in which the counter-intelligence chief had embraced some of the defector's most improbable boasts, including that he had personally advised Joseph Stalin in 1952 and that the Soviet leader had accepted his recommendations.

Angleton had accepted that claim as proof of Golitsyn's 'analytical mind', as he would later declare. But the claim turned out to be completely unfounded. 'On the face of it, it seems highly unlikely that Golitsyn, at the time a twenty-six-year-old junior officer in the KGB, would have gotten an audience with Stalin, much less been able to convince Stalin to reinstate banished KGB leaders,' an in-house CIA paper notes. 'In any event, the [sic] Golitsyn's recounting of the [event] is consistent with his later demands for personal audiences with President John F. Kennedy and FBI director J. Edgar Hoover so that he could offer changes in US policy towards the USSR.'

Of far greater concern, however, were Golitsyn's repeated claims that the KGB had penetrated the CIA through its 'Master Plan', with a mole called 'Sasha' being the central suspect. Golitsyn's first victim, Serge Peter 'Klibanski' Karlow, was cleared by the FBI following an intense investigation, but only after his career had been ruined. Instead of reassessing their thinking about that failed outcome, Golitsyn and Angleton doubled down. The defector then went on to identify another potential suspect, and another, and another.

The CIA was for some time convinced that Igor Orlov, who had served as one of its contractors under the name of 'Aleksandr Kopatzky' in Germany in the 1950s, was Sasha. But even he did not fit the bill because he had never become an officer, had never been given access to top secrets, had never served at Langley, and had left the agency in 1961. So he could hardly have been the high level CIA penetration that Golitsyn had warned about. Over two decades, a series of FBI and CIA investigations into Orlov turned up no prosecutable evidence. He died in 1982.

Overall, the CIA's 'Sasha' pursuit resulted in more than forty senior CIA officers being intimately investigated, including fourteen who had been deemed top suspects. Some were fired without explanation, others had their reputations ruined and careers stalled, or were forced into professional exile in a molehunt that ultimately failed to uncover a single Soviet penetration, let alone result in any prosecutions.

It would become one of the most shameful and embarrassing episodes in CIA history. And while those who had been wrongly accused took legal action against their former employer, the CIA only compensated three of them – fewer than 10 per cent – including Karlow, under what became obscurely known as the 'Mole Relief Act'. Future CIA generations would go on to ridicule the 'Master Plan' as the 'Monster Plot'.

Another victim of the 'Master Plan', Yuri Nosenko, had been wrongly subjected to harsh interrogation, cruel mental and physical treatment and detained for more than three years, largely because Golitsyn had accused him of being a KGB plant who had been sent to 'discredit' him. Nosenko was also paid out by the CIA. He confronted Angleton in 1975 after finding the former spymaster's number in the phone book, perhaps hoping for an explanation for the way he had been mistreated during his 1,277 days in detention. 'It was a brief and fruitless exchange, with Mr Nosenko rising in his passions and Angleton cool and adamant about his judgment,' the *Washington Post* would later reveal. 'I have nothing more to say to you,' Angleton reportedly said. 'And Mr Angleton, I have nothing further to say to you,' Nosenko replied.

A re-examination of Golitsyn's actions in Nosenko's case in the mid-1970s found that Golitsyn's accusations had been typically self-serving. 'It can be argued that Golitsyn had two interests,' the CIA review concluded, '(a) to discredit Nosenko in order to maintain a position of pre-eminence as advisor to CIA (and other Western intelligence services) on Soviet intelligence matters, and (b) to promote his contentions as to how the West was being deceived by the Soviet Union in political and strategic matters, and thus to enhance his positions as advisor to governments on overall Soviet political matters.'

Alarmingly, all of Golitsyn's leads about the KGB's penetration of the CIA – except for one, which would also turn out to be untrue – had been based on his misconstrued analysis of the US agency's personnel files. One of his greatest abilities, it would later transpire, had been to formulate theories based on information he had gathered from those files, claiming it had aligned with similar material that he had already seen while at the KGB.

'Remarkably and tragically, all of Golitsyn's "leads" to the KGB moles in the CIA . . . were based not on sensitive information he had acquired as a KGB officer, but from postulations based on his knowledge of the KGB modus operandi and his review of CIA personnel and operational files,' a partially redacted study into Golitsyn's 'Master Plan' reveals. 'Moreover, in view of the fact that upon his defection, Golitsyn had claimed to be unaware of any penetration of CIA beyond Sasha, it seems reasonable to speculate that Angleton's own predilections about KGB deception operations and penetration were the foundation of Golitsyn's assertions.'

Christopher Andrew, who authored MI5's official history, said the 'Monster Plot' conspiracy theory that Golitsyn and Angleton pushed throughout the 1960s overstated the KGB's operational capability. 'As well as relying on historical myth, the monster plot conspiracy theories, which emerge in the early 1960s, also make assumptions about a truly astonishing level of operational efficiency by the KGB during the early Cold War,' he said. 'That is quite impossible to square with what we now know about its actual performance.'

By feeding each other's paranoia throughout the 1960s and early 1970s, Golitsyn and Angleton crippled the CIA with fear and cost it potential intelligence breakthroughs that had been disregarded out of extreme caution, said David Robarge, the CIA's official historian. 'By fixating on the Soviets, Angleton largely ignored the threat that other hostile services posed – notably the East Germans, Czechs, Chinese, and Cubans,' Robarge noted years later. 'His operational officers were so deeply involved with defensive CI [molehunting] that they did not contribute nearly enough to offensive [counter-espionage] operations. He became far too dependent on Golitsyn and consequently mishandled some cases.' Robarge observed that Angleton's 'security consciousness became self-consuming and stultifying for his staff.'

Of all the CIA officers whom Angleton had handpicked to join the CIA's molehunt, Clare Edward Petty became the most sceptical. The seasoned counter-intelligence officer found it impossible to overlook Golitsyn's flimsy leads and came to suspect that he had been under KGB control, dispatched to sow discord and confusion at the CIA and undermine its relationships with other Western agencies, including MI5.

What Petty recognised, but no one else around him had appeared willing to acknowledge or question properly, was how Golitsyn had convinced Angleton that any Soviet defector or prospective defector who had emerged after him had been a KGB plant. By and large, however, CIA case officers who eventually shared Petty's scepticism of Angleton's and Golitsyn's objection to Soviet volunteers were still unwilling to challenge the pair's rigid thinking for fear of coming under suspicion of being Kremlin assets themselves.

Petty felt that if Golitsyn had in fact been dispatched, then he had certainly succeeded in imposing the KGB's anti-defection strategy onto the CIA – and in so doing, had managed to turn himself into the ultimate vessel through which the Soviet agency could feed its misinformation. Angleton, in consultation with Golitsyn, rejected at least twenty-two prospective Soviet defectors because he suspected that they were 'dirty' – sent on the KGB's orders.

CIA investigators who later reviewed Angleton's rejections were confounded by his logic, since the agency's greatest historical achievements against the Kremlin had come from Soviet volunteers, including Pyotr Popov in the 1950s and Oleg Penkovsky in the following decade. It had been to Langley's great disadvantage that under Angleton's counter-intelligence leadership, the CIA had not given prospective Soviet volunteers the 'benefit of every reasonable doubt', the Agency investigation found.

The 'Master Plan' thesis set the CIA's 'counter-intelligence programs back by a number of years,' the inquiry report added. 'And though we may be tempted to look back and say that this is now water over the dam, there can be no assurance that such is the case. For if one poses the question of how many additional Soviet agents and defectors we might have gained had our handling of those who did approach us been better calculated to encourage, rather than discourage them, the only answer is: nobody knows.'

Perhaps it was just as well that Oleg Lyalin had missed out on his posting to the US as part of the KGB's illegals programme in the early 1960s. Because if his career path had taken the same trajectory – but in Washington, rather than London – then Angleton would absolutely have rejected Lyalin's approach, too. One could only hope that in such an alternate universe, Lyalin would have had the wherewithal to turn to the FBI for help, in part because the law enforcement agency saw the value in the intelligence he had provided MI5 from the very beginning, unlike Angleton who tried to discredit him.

Angleton's past was set to catch up with him, and Petty, who became increasingly suspicious of Golitsyn's backstory, was determined to make that happen. As that all played out at the CIA, the KGB's director Yuri Andropov continued reeling from Lyalin's defection, which by December 1971 was on its way to impairing almost every crucial facet of his Soviet agency. Not even the crackdown on potential moles and aspiring defectors at the KGB, nor his reactivation of the English spy, Kim Philby, could save Andropov's agency from the coming storm.

The West's security scrutiny and suspicion of Soviet officials, which had been gradually building through the 1960s, was now at its peak. Kremlin diplomats, working wives, so-called military attachés and trade representatives, and saboteurs posing as UN delegates – the people Andropov once relied on for foreign operations – now may as well have been walking around with three big letters branded on their foreheads: KGB.

It was in that precarious atmosphere that a former British intelligence officer, who had once specialised in breaking spies, would get his chance to settle an old score with the Soviet agency.

As Mr Justice Milmo took to the bench at the Old Bailey to sentence two traitors, the High Court judge brought with him several decades of experience in dealing with Britain's enemies. Because in his former professional life as a wartime officer at

MI5, Helenus 'Buster' Milmo had been regarded as one of the British agency's most forensic and capable interrogators, often tasked with prising the truth out of Nazi spies. When the Second World War came to a close and the Soviet Union emerged as the West's new adversary, MI5 again turned to Milmo to question a suspected turncoat whom the agency feared was working for Moscow – Kim Philby.

After a four-hour interrogation on 12 December 1951, Milmo delivered his verdict in a detailed, twenty-five-page report that should have eliminated any doubts about the former MI6 official's treachery. 'I find myself unable to avoid the conclusion that Philby is and has been for many years a Soviet agent,' Milmo wrote. Sir John Sinclair, MI6's director who had been Philby's boss, dismissed Milmo's findings, attributing them to a 'mass of selected circumstantial material without a crumb of positive evidence.' Sinclair was wrong.

Twenty years later, Milmo witnessed the public degradation Britain had inflicted on the KGB through its spy purge, and must have felt some degree of quiet satisfaction in being able to play a small but personally meaningful part in holding the Soviet agency to account. The two men in the witness box whose cases he was now adjudicating were nowhere near Philby's calibre, but they had served the same enemy. Kyriacos Costi and Constantinos Martianou, whom Oleg Lyalin had earlier exposed as KGB assets, had already pleaded guilty. But the fate of the brothers-in-law was at the mercy of the British justice system – or perhaps more satisfyingly, it happened to be in Milmo's hands that Tuesday, 7 December 1971.

In passing sentence, Milmo ruled that the pair had been 'acting for those who have evil intent towards' Britain. 'I am satisfied that neither of you falls into the category of major foreign intelligence agents,' he told the court. 'On the other hand, I am equally satisfied that it would be quite wrong to regard you as insignificant offenders, if only because the presence in our midst of secret agents for foreign powers is something which may be regarded as calling for severe punishment.' He sentenced Martianou to four years in prison and Costi to six years.

In a separate court case the following year, Lyalin's former agent Siroj Abdoolcader, who had become known in the media as the 'car numbers spy' for leaking MI5 vehicle registration details to the KGB, vigorously played down his espionage activities, claiming he had spied under duress. It was as though he had totally forgotten about the thrill and validation he had sought from spying; experiences he had detailed in a daily journal that detectives found in his home. 'I was threatened and blackmailed into this because they told me I would get fixed up and get into serious trouble if I did not do what they asked,' Abdoolcader claimed in a statement to court. 'I meant no harm to Britain.' He was sentenced to three years' jail on 8 February 1972.

Almost two thousand miles away from the London court hearings, Yuri Andropov was in Lubyanka, helplessly grappling with the mounting struggles tormenting his beloved KGB. Even his revenge plans for Soviet traitors, some of which had been carried over from his predecessor, appeared to be in doubt. His kill list seemed unachievable, barely worth the paper it was written on. The KGB's hunt for the defectors Anatoly Golitsyn and Yuri Nosenko had failed and its pursuit of Lyalin seemed unlikely to be more successful. So it was with some frustration that Andropov surrendered to another unrealistic, but ostensibly 'legal' path in going after MI5's asset, submitting Lyalin's case to the Supreme Court of the Soviet Union. Lyalin was sentenced to 'death in absentia' on 27 July 1972.

It was a hollow victory and far from where Andropov wanted to be. It was also another uncomfortable reminder of how the

KGB's misfortunes of the previous year had shown no sign of abating. And as Andropov considered the future of his agency's sabotage and assassination arm, Department V, Martin Furnival Jones was about to sign off from a career that had appeared quite underwhelming until a Russian volunteer became both his – and his agency's – greatest saviour.

There is no doubt that a confluence of good timing and great luck had played into Martin Furnival Jones's hands when Oleg Lyalin came knocking in the spring of 1971. The timing and unforeseen fortune, however, could have been easily squandered had the MI5 chief not corrected a bad habit, the need for CIA feedback, which had long been his personal and institutional reflex. Furnival Jones clenched an historic breakthrough largely because he had exercised two security measures. Firstly, he had blocked out Langley's contaminated thinking and contagious paranoia, which had permeated MI5's core through the 1960s and the beginning of the following decade. Secondly, he had created an inner circle in which Lyalin's existence prior to his defection became known to only about ten senior MI5 officials.

That move would ultimately serve a dual purpose. It protected Lyalin's identity, and disproved James Angleton's claims that MI5's top tier had been compromised. Because if the agency's senior leadership had in fact been compromised, surely someone would have given up Lyalin at some point during the process.

It does not bear thinking about what would have happened if Furnival Jones had resorted to briefing Angleton about Lyalin's approach – as he had done in many previous cases, including the top secret investigation into Roger Hollis, which he had even withheld from two British prime ministers. If that had happened, there is every chance the Russian volunteer would have been turned away and Britain's spy purge would have been much different and most likely far less damaging to the Soviet Union.

Perhaps Furnival Jones's greatest error of judgement of his MI5 leadership was in failing to act earlier to properly re-evaluate his agency's relationship with the CIA. He was far too charitable in his deference to Angleton, treating the overhyped molehunter as some sort of infallible figure. By cutting him loose, however, Furnival Jones transformed his own legacy from one that could have remained mired in mistakes to one that would become noteworthy. Shutting out Angleton's opinions had completely changed MI5's fortunes and realigned its post-Second World War intelligence exchanges with the CIA into a relationship that was no longer based on submission and unilateral concessions.

In effect, Furnival Jones had taken a similar approach to the CIA to that which Ted Heath had earlier taken to the White House, when he reframed the Special Relationship into a 'natural relationship' – one marked by mutual respect and deep friendship rather than unquestioning loyalty. But while every spy chief is answerable to their political master, Furnival Jones's changed approach to Langley appears to have been autonomous; based on his own experiences and frustrations with the US agency's counter-intelligence czar rather than any desire to conform with the British prime minister. Testimony to that was Furnival Jones's willingness to put MI5's reputational and operational safety ahead of his obligations to Downing Street.

Towards the end of his tenure, Furnival Jones had restored his staff's morale for the first time since the beginning of the Cold War, turning MI5 into a difficult target for Lubyanka. As an added bonus, he had left his Soviet counterpart, Yuri Andropov, wounded and unsteady on his feet. Nothing would undo that humiliation for the KGB. And while Andropov succeeded in turning Lyalin into a 'hate figure' within the Soviet agency, with an internal investigation that emphasised the defector's treachery and promiscuity, that was of absolutely no operational consequence.

What Andropov really wanted in the wake of the spy purge was some way of reviving his agency's sabotage and assassinations arm, Department V, but he failed to achieve that and eventually shut it down. 'The expulsion of 105 Soviet intelligence officers from London in 1971 marked the major turning point in Cold War counter-espionage operations in Britain,' MI5 has since acknowledged. '[It] made Britain a hard espionage target for Soviet intelligence for the first time. For several years most Soviet agents in Britain were put on ice and the KGB was forced to ask Soviet Bloc and Cuban agencies to help plug the intelligence gap.'

In 1972, after a thirty-one-year career at MI5, Furnival Jones left the spy world aged sixty to work in the private sector as a security consultant and spend more time on his hobbies, including birdwatching. His old friend at Langley, James Angleton, was in a far less happy place. The cracks in the formidable Angletonian image, many of which had started forming after he was found to have hidden Lyalin's intelligence from the White House, had now grown into hideous fractures. The counter-intelligence chief was also about to be embroiled in a more troubling inquiry as Clare Edward Petty combed through files relating to Anatoly Golitsyn's operational leads and overall influence at Langley.

Petty's attempt to unmask Golitsyn as a KGB plant galvanised in his mind a question that became difficult for him to see past. What if Angleton himself was a Kremlin asset, who had been Golitsyn's handler inside the CIA? On the face of it, Petty's question could have been seen as the same kind of paranoia that had apparently blinded his two big targets. But his question seemed less far-fetched when viewed through the lens of what MI6 had experienced three decades earlier, when Soviet spy Kim Philby had worked his way up the British agency's management to run its counter-intelligence branch – essentially playing the same role that Angleton would go on to land at the CIA.

If Angleton had in fact been a Kremlin asset, according to Petty's fears, then that would go a long way to explaining the protection and favourable treatment Golitsyn had enjoyed in comparison to others who had defected to Langley before and after him. It would also explain the remarkable generosity Angleton had afforded Golitsyn in his working and living arrangements, which read like a list of security measures that the CIA molehunter should have cautioned against rather than approved. And the list was extensive.

Golitsyn had been allowed to live 'where he wished and had no security protection' during the time he spent in Britain in 1963, according to the CIA's mid-1970s inquiry. All that MI5 had asked of him was to 'keep his whereabouts to himself, not stay in one hotel for any length of time, and to call MI5 when he wanted to meet'. Those lax security measures, which had probably helped in 'maintaining a cooperative attitude on his part', had set a precedent for the 'manner in which he would live' in the US on his return to the country in July 1963.

'Upon his return here, he was given complete freedom to set his own pattern of living and working, following the British example,' according to the CIA inquiry. 'He obtained his own residence in New York, the location of which was unknown to the CIA for some time. He moved several times, developed the concept that he was the best judge of his own security, and at times lived "almost under the eaves of the Soviet Mission" in New York, while simultaneously refusing to talk to CIA officers because [the] CIA was penetrated.'

Along with these unprecedented freedoms and privileges, Angleton had authorised Golitsyn to take secret CIA files home for analysis. 'Classified materials, in quantities that filled several packing boxes, were eventually found in Golitsyn's possession at his upstate New York farmhouse,' another recently declassified CIA paper reveals. 'Some of this material consisted of personnel-type files on CIA staff officers. Golitsyn, who resisted returning these documents . . . maintained that Angleton . . . had given these files to him to review and to keep as long as he needed them, and he was not finished with them yet. Ultimately, all the files that were found were retrieved from Golitsyn, though it has never been possible to be certain that this represented all the files that he in fact had.'

Casting even more concerns about the Angleton–Golitsyn nexus was the fact that the Ukrainian had 'controlled his own interrogations' upon his defection, 'withholding information if he chose, refusing to answer questions according to his own whim, and on occasion refusing to talk to CIA officers'. Angleton had been aware of all of this and had done nothing to question it, let alone challenge it. Nor had he acted on the 'inconclusive test results' from Golitsyn's polygraph examinations. 'No further attempt was ever made to establish Golitsyn's bona fides during Angleton's tenure as Chief, CI [Counter-intelligence] Staff.'

Even before the CIA's curious findings emerged in its internal investigation, Petty's historical review left him convinced that both Angleton and Golitsyn were moles. His circumstantial evidence against the pair was compelling, and while it was taken seriously by the agency's director, it fell short of conclusively proving that Angleton and Golitsyn were Kremlin assets.

In the lead-up to Christmas 1974, having served twenty years as the CIA's counter-intelligence overlord, Angleton was dismissed from the agency under the guise of voluntary retirement after the agency learned that an investigation by the *New York Times* was set to accuse him of overseeing illegal CIA domestic activities, including 'amassing files on as many as 10,000 Americans and opening private mail', despite congressional statute forbidding the agency from intelligence operations within the United States.

When the *New York Times* published its story on 22 December 1974, a throng of television reporters appeared at Angleton's house to question the circumstances surrounding his departure. Asked by one reporter if he had been 'induced to resign', Angleton stared at the ground for a few silent moments. He appeared exhausted and in complete despair, as if grieving the loss of the only thing that had ever given him a sense of purpose. He then looked up and said: 'I'm very unhappy to leave the agency.'

Seymour Hersh, the journalist who led the *New York Times* investigation, would later reveal that it was only a 'coincidence' that Angleton had been forced to resign around the time his first story about the CIA's domestic illegalities had appeared. 'William E. Colby, the Director of Central Intelligence, had been pressing for Angleton's retirement for months,' Hersh said.

Angleton's successor, George Kalaris, was determined to overhaul the CIA's counter-intelligence division. He also authorised an investigation into Anatoly Golitsyn in March 1975 to resolve the suspicions that had continued looming over the Soviet defector. The question was simple: was Golitsyn a genuine defector, or was he a deception agent, the most successful such 'plant' in Cold War history? The investigation ran for four months and resulted in an eighty-page report, which picked apart Golitsyn's shoddy theories and failures.

The fact that it was only eighty pages is remarkable in itself, given the scale of damage that Golitsyn caused the CIA – not to mention MI5 – from instigating the futile 'Sasha' molehunt in search of the alleged Soviet penetrations of the US agency, to his fanciful theories about the KGB's creation of fake defectors through its 'Master Plan'. By comparison, the CIA conducted countless reviews into Yuri Nosenko's case to establish his bona fides, resulting in thousands of pages.

While the Kalaris-authorised investigation concluded that Golitsyn was a bona fide defector, the fact that the CIA twice felt it should investigate him is a reflection of his dubious motivation, and his perpetually flawed intelligence leads, which may as well have been scripted for him by the KGB. The investigations into Golitsyn were of an era when the CIA was largely unaccountable and predisposed to covering up its embarrassments, misjudgements and criminal activities, as the Church Committee – a bipartisan Senate inquiry into illegalities committed by US intelligence agencies – would reveal in 1976.

But five decades on, with the CIA now subjected to far more scrutiny, it would be worthwhile to re-examine Golitsyn's case with fresh eyes, without any direct or perceived interference from the old guard, which has long moved on. Given that the second Trump Administration in Washington, for example, came to office in 2025 vowing to expose past misjudgements of the US intelligence community, few cases could be more important than Golitsyn's.

Surely it would be worth taking a dispassionate look at the remaining doubts surrounding the bona fides of the most disastrous defector in history – doubts that former and current agency chiefs within the Five Eyes have expressed to this author. Perhaps a re-examination would cast much needed light on at least some of the confounding factors surrounding Golitsyn's defection. Should more questions not be asked about Golitsyn's remarkably bold 'cold' approach to the CIA's station chief's home in Helsinki with his wife and daughter in tow?

That high-risk approach, when analysed in hindsight, seems

out of character for someone who had claimed to be hyper-alert about his fear of the KGB. Why had he placed himself and his family in the firing line that evening in December 1961 without so much as seeking a predetermined CIA consideration, let alone a guarantee, that he and his loved ones would be granted political asylum?

Should more questions not be asked about why further polygraph tests were not conducted when Golitsyn's initial CIA examination produced inconclusive results? Should not more questions be asked about why Golitsyn had somehow been allowed to oversee his own security and living arrangements in New York near the UN headquarters swarming with KGB officials, despite his repeated claims that his life was in grave danger . . . from the KGB? Although Golitsyn repeatedly denounced and tried to discredit defectors who came after him, none of them, ironically, questioned his bona fides. Oleg Lyalin even told MI5 that 'Golitsyn's defection was convincing and that he had never heard any rumour that it was not genuine,' according to an intelligence report declassified more than five decades later in mid-2023.

Yes, Lubyanka did send a telegram to the KGB's London residency in the summer of 1971, which Lyalin told MI5 had been sent by head office to illustrate its committed pursuit of Golitsyn's whereabouts because it wanted him dead. But did that prove that Golitsyn had been a genuine defector? Or did Lubyanka send the telegram in the hope that its message would filter out through intelligence chatter and maintain the facade Golitsyn had created about the looming KGB threat?

The answers to such questions could either reaffirm Golitsyn's bona fides, or reveal that he had been the chief emissary of the KGB 'Master Plan' that he warned about. If he was a fake that would mean that the biggest KGB penetration of the intelligence agencies across the Atlantic during the Cold War had never been the likes of the wrongly accused – Mitchell, Hollis, Wilson and the string of supposed 'Sashas' – but that it had actually been Anatoly Golitsyn all along.

Numerous factors contributed to Angleton's dismissal and Golitsyn's loss of status. But there is a poetic irony that the beginning of their downfall was triggered by a so-called threat that they had spent more than a decade warning about – a volunteer, a walk-in Soviet defector. Except in this case Oleg Lyalin had not been sent by the KGB, he was running away from it.

Oleg Lyalin remained an active and productive source for MI5 for many years after his defection, sharing insights and assessments on the Soviet threat. In 1977, he provided the British agency with further methods to exploit KGB vulnerabilities, which MI5 then shared with the FBI. He suggested planting incriminating material in the personal luggage of Russian diplomats nearing the end of their tour by targeting the removal firms they use. 'All Russians who return to their country usually have their possessions packed by the same firm,' Lyalin said. 'If a considerable number of consumer goods, e.g. nylon raincoats, were to find their way into [an official's] luggage, he would be in considerable trouble if this was found by the customs in Russia . . . for which imprisonment is a certainty.'

Lyalin also suggested other methods of compromising Russian officials, including posting them 'presents or gifts from a local company to the embassy with a request that they should be delivered in Russia for the individual concerned'. That, he said, would immediately cast suspicion upon the target. 'The intelligence officer in Moscow will have the greatest of [*sic*] difficulty in extricating himself from this one, and would be unlikely to return to this country.'

MI5 never lost sight of the operational value that Lyalin continued to generate, and through an array of security measures, it wanted to ensure that he and Teplyakova remained safe. The new identities that the British agency gave them soon after they defected must have provided them with some sense of calm and anonymity.

According to some unsubstantiated reports, the lovers even underwent plastic surgery to change their appearance. But nothing would have completely obviated the persistent threat that they faced from the KGB, however distant and diminished it was. The pair could never have felt truly free and would have had to accept, begrudgingly or otherwise, the reality that they would most likely spend the rest of their lives in effective hiding. One can only imagine the emotional trauma, longing and guilt that Teplyakova felt over abandoning her son, Ivan. Or the way Lyalin dealt with his inability to lock eyes with his son, Alexander, at least to try and explain why he had turned his back on him when he was only six years old.

On 12 February 1995, Lyalin died at his home in an undisclosed location in northern England after a long illness. In contrast to the blanket news coverage given to his defection, his death was barely reported, despite brief obituaries in *The Times* in London and the *New York Times*. It remains unknown what became of Teplyakova. Her file, along with Lyalin's, remains sealed at MI5.

Soviet defectors became a centrepiece in bolstering Western capabilities against Kremlin espionage after the Second World War. Three stood out for providing highly valuable secrets. Russian cipher clerk Igor Gouzenko alerted the West to the Soviet Union's duplicity after defecting to Canada – arguably triggering the Cold War. Vladimir Petrov, the spy chief at the Soviet Embassy in Canberra, helped transform Australia's standing among intelligence officials in London and Washington in the early 1950s – without which the Five Eyes network could not have been formed. But no other Cold War defector came close to matching the damage Oleg Lyalin caused KGB operatives in the West.

Despite all that, however, the Soviet agency's director, Yuri Andropov, managed to avoid enough of the blame in the Kremlin's eyes to rise to the very top. In November 1982 he became the first former spy chief in Soviet history to become the nation's leader. His rise, despite all the hiccups along the way, would undoubtedly have made his revolutionary hero, Felix Dzerzhinsky, proud. But it also turned Andropov himself into a hero in the mind of a young KGB officer. An officer who would follow a similar career trajectory and go on to revive the business of assassinations through a post-Soviet incarnation of the KGB.

His name is Vladimir Putin.

# DIFFERENT RESET, SAME OUTCOME

AS HE STROLLED TOWARDS Yuri Andropov's grave during a ceremony to commemorate the Soviet leader, Vladimir Putin was there to fulfil a personal objective that eclipsed the official duty he was assigned that day. He wanted to honour the memory of a man he cherished; a man whose legacy he mythologised as a symbol of Russian exceptionalism. It was a national characteristic that Putin believed had been in decline since the collapse of the Iron Curtain, and while he was not yet in a position to revive it personally, time was on his side.

He had already transformed his career prospects beyond what he could have imagined after joining the KGB at the height of the Cold War during Andropov's reign at the agency. And now at forty-six, Putin's achievements in and outside of the espionage business placed him within earshot of Moscow's political elite.

Within three years of Boris Yeltsin drafting him into his government from relative obscurity in 1996, Putin had charted a quick path into the Russian president's inner circle. He briefly served at the helm of the FSB, Russia's domestic spy agency and successor to the KGB, before Yeltsin appointed him as the nation's security czar in March 1999. It was in that capacity, as Secretary of the Security Council of Russia, that Putin attended the Kremlin War Necropolis three months later to lay a bouquet of flowers at Andropov's grave – not to memorialise his hero's death fifteen years earlier, but to celebrate the eighty-fifth anniversary of his birth.

He would go on to pay several more tributes to Andropov to keep his spirit alive, including the commissioning of a ten-foot statue of the late leader. Yet Putin's greatest honour to Andropov's memory was ultimately to follow in his footsteps on a march to rekindle the Soviet spirit, crush domestic dissent and pursue enemies of Mother Russia, including dissidents and defectors.

Andropov's mission to target defectors in the West had been crippled early on in his fifteen-year reign at the KGB after Oleg Lyalin exposed his organisation's sabotage and assassination plans in 1971, along with the identities of the operatives assigned to diplomatic posts to help implement them. The extent of the damage that Lyalin inflicted on the KGB's pursuit of defectors was revealed in an FBI intelligence document decades later. An FBI informant told the US law enforcement organisation that Lyalin's hit against the KGB brought an end to the Soviet agency's mission to kill defectors. 'Such actions, if they ever occurred, certainly ended after Oleg Lyalin's defection to England in 1971,' says the FBI document, which was not released until forty-six years after Lyalin's defection.

Although Lyalin's case predated Putin's rise through the Kremlin's security apparatus, he would have been well-versed in the defector's treachery, because it offered a cautionary preview of the damage future defectors could cause. Putin had a quiet, and initially unpublicised aspiration to revitalise Andropov's mission to target defectors, because he too despised traitors. However, Putin's choice of putting personal grudges ahead of his nation's wider geopolitical goals would eventually backfire and expose his ruthlessness and recklessness. Time and again Putin's campaign against defectors provoked a backlash that frustrated the Kremlin's resets with the West.

Alexander Litvinenko, a former FSB lieutenant colonel, would become the first of many Putin targets in the West. Litvinenko had publicly accused the FSB of corruption while it was under Putin's leadership and told journalists that it was plotting to kill a prominent Russian business tycoon who had fallen out with the Kremlin. Litvinenko was subsequently arrested and detained on charges of 'abusing his office' – and although he was later acquitted, he recognised that his safety was at risk. He knew all about the state's weaponisation of the FSB to lock up dissidents or make them disappear. So in October 2000, seven months after Putin was elected president, Litvinenko fled Moscow for London. Feeling protected by the political asylum that Britain granted him and his family, Litvinenko maintained his vocal opposition to the FSB and Putin.

In Putin's binary worldview, Russians were either true patriots or traitors, and Litvinenko's defection placed him in the latter camp. The president wanted revenge but the timing was a little awkward, because he was busy projecting himself as a moderate who wanted to shepherd his country towards political liberalism. The Russian leader appeared preoccupied with cementing his nation's pro-Western leanings that Yeltsin, his predecessor and the country's first post-Soviet president, had welcomed in the context of a foreign relations reset with the US and its allies.

That reset enabled Russia's admission into international organisations, including the World Trade Organisation and the G7, which became the G8 in 1997 to include Russia in the prestigious economic forum alongside the likes of the US and Britain. Putin carried forward Yeltsin's embrace of the West, and within a few weeks of being elected president in March 2000, he told the BBC that he wanted to maintain Russia's closeness with 'Europe and what we often call the civilised world'. He even declared that while he opposed the eastward expansion of NATO, he 'would not rule out' the possibility of Russia joining the military alliance if it were treated as an equal partner. 'It is hard for me to visualise NATO as an enemy,' he said.

Over the course of Putin's charm offensive, he even encouraged his intelligence services – the FSB, and Russia's external spy agency, the SVR – to start cooperating with their British and US counterparts. Soon enough the FSB's chief, Nikolai Patrushev, was sent to London in late 2000 to cultivate a working relationship between his organisation and MI5 in what seemed to be a new age free of Cold War hangovers. It was as though the historic distrust between Russian and Western spy agencies – fomented by traitors such as Kim Philby, or those who defected to the West, such as Oleg Lyalin – were rapidly dissipating.

Putin then stepped up his apparent warmth following Al Qaeda's terrorist targeting of the United States in September 2001, reportedly becoming the first foreign leader to call George W. Bush to express his condolences over the almost 3,000 lives lost in the attacks. He backed his words with actions the following month, helping to facilitate access to airspace and military bases in Central Asia, including Tajikistan, for the US invasion of Afghanistan, where Al Qaeda leader Osama bin Laden was hiding. Whether through genuine or strategic empathy, Putin identified with Washington's battle against Al Qaeda, because Moscow itself was embroiled in a similar confrontation with Islamist Chechen rebels.

The Russian president's love affair with the West appeared

even more convincing because he was not always in agreement with Western leaders. He strongly opposed the US-led invasion of Iraq in 2003, warning that it would be 'fraught with the gravest consequences' that could trigger far-reaching unrest in the Muslim world. But nonetheless, Putin maintained his reset outlook, and later that year embarked on a historic state visit to the United Kingdom that marked the first such visit by a Russian leader since Tsar Alexander II in 1874.

His cordial relations with the British prime minister Tony Blair saw Putin return to the UK two years later, a few months after home-grown terrorists had launched coordinated suicide attacks in London that killed fifty-two people and injured about 800. Putin and Blair agreed to improve ties between their countries across a range of areas, including 'joint efforts in counterterrorism'.

For his first six years in office, Putin appeared to be non-adversarial towards the West, despite blaming some of its intelligence agencies, such as the CIA, for inciting popular uprisings in former Soviet states – including Georgia in 2003, Ukraine the following year, and Kyrgyzstan in 2005 – which became known as the 'colour revolutions' and resulted in the removal of Kremlin-aligned, authoritarian regimes. But all along, he never lost sight of his mission to go after his enemies. He even revived Moscow's sabotage and assassinations operations that had existed within the KGB's Department V before Oleg Lyalin's defection to the UK three decades earlier.

By the time two FSB assassins landed in London in October 2006 to exact Putin's revenge on Litvinenko, the Russian dissident had changed his name to Edward Carter, was a paid consultant for MI6, and had recently become a British citizen. During an ostensible business meeting with Litvinenko, the assassins laced his tea with polonium-210, an invisible and virtually undetectable radioactive substance. He died about three weeks later.

While his assassins were not supposed to be caught, their botched mission pointed the finger of blame at the Kremlin. Putin denied Russia's involvement, but Britain's Scotland Yard uncovered insurmountable evidence that tracked the assassins back to Moscow. Eliza Manningham-Buller, MI5's director-general at the time Litvinenko was killed, told the author: 'To take the risk of carrying out such an attack in the UK suggested that they had trialled the method successfully elsewhere and were given approval to hit Litvinenko on that basis.'

A public inquiry in Britain would later find 'strong circum-stantial evidence of Russian state responsibility' and conclude that the dissident's murder had been 'probably approved by Mr Patrushev [the FSB's director] and also by President Putin'. Putin overreached with the killing of Litvinenko, and in so doing, forfeited the goodwill he had built during Moscow's post-Soviet reset. But instead of reversing course, he doubled down.

At the Munich Security Conference in February 2007, in what would become a chilling insight into Putin's resentment of Western diplomatic and military dominance in the post-Cold War world order, the Russian president declared that 'we have reached a turning point when we must seriously think about the entire architecture of global security.' His list of grievances included his long-held bugbear of NATO's eastward expansion, and he claimed the US's development of ballistic missile defences was provoking a nuclear arms race, saying Washington had 'overstepped its national boundaries, and in every area'.

The Russian leader, fast becoming a pariah in the West, scaled up his attacks on his enemies at home and abroad. In Russia, Putin's political opponents were imprisoned on trumped-up charges, anti-government groups and protesters were accused of being 'foreign agents' and subjected to police brutality or being made to 'disappear', and the Kremlin would eventually introduce a raft of repressive laws to restrict human rights, freedom of speech, and rights of minorities and religious groups.

Abroad, Putin's foreign policy objectives included violating international laws through the likes of cyber-hacking operations against the West, and deploying human spy networks, much like one in the US that would be exposed by the FBI's 'Ghost Stories' investigation several years later. Putin was on his way to surpassing Andropov's authoritarian legacy, but somewhat remarkably, still chose to observe Russia's constitutional ban on serving more than two consecutive presidential terms, leaving office in 2008 to serve as prime minister to President Dmitry Medvedev. It was a strategic move to help guarantee his return to office down the line, rather than a genuine cause of respite for the Western world.

The world was changing. In the US, George W. Bush had been succeeded in 2009 by an inspirational Democrat leader, Barack Obama, who had campaigned on the message of 'hope'. Obama considered Medvedev a moderate, and teased a fresh start with Moscow. Russia then agreed to vote for UN sanctions against Iran's nuclear programme, and Washington signed a new arms control treaty with Moscow and lifted some US sanctions against it, including those against its state arms export agency. Obama and Medvedev famously celebrated their 'resetting of relations', as the US president called it, by attending a fast food lunch at a restaurant in Washington and having a cheeseburger and a Coke.

It was a short-lived honeymoon, however, which fell apart soon after Putin returned as president in 2012 and embarked on a military campaign to annex Crimea in southern Ukraine two years later. Obama and Western allies sanctioned Putin and kicked him out of the G8 economic forum. But that did not stop the Russian leader from continuing to foment discord in the West, including through online hacking campaigns and electoral interference.

Bizarrely, it was electoral interference that helped realign Putin with the White House, when Donald Trump defeated Hillary Clinton in the 2016 presidential race.

Two weeks before Trump's inauguration, the US Office of the Director of National Intelligence (ODNI) published its assessment into Russia's alleged meddling in the presidential campaign. Its report, which drew on intelligence gathered by the FBI, CIA and NSA, stated with 'high confidence' that the Russian leader had 'ordered an influence campaign in 2016 aimed at the US presidential election' and that together with his government Putin 'aspired to help President-elect Trump's election chances when possible by discrediting Secretary Clinton and publicly contrasting her unfavourably to him'.

Moscow's goals were to 'undermine public faith in the US democratic process, denigrate Secretary Clinton, and harm her electability and potential presidency,' the report added. Trump dismissed the findings as a witch hunt by the 'deep state' to diminish his credibility and electoral victory. And in May 2017, as the FBI continued an investigation into Russian election meddling from the previous year, to establish whether there had been any collusion between the Kremlin and Trump's campaign, the president fired the organisation's director James Comey. It was widely seen as an act of retribution against the FBI investigation that Trump labelled a 'hoax'.

Putin must have watched the unfolding political circus with glee, because he could hardly have hoped for a better outcome in his drive to divide the US. In the summer of 2017, during his first face-to-face meeting with his American counterpart on the sidelines of an international economic summit in Hamburg, Germany, Putin even directly addressed Trump's questions about whether Moscow had played a part in his nation's election. 'As far as I could, I answered these questions, [Trump] noted them and he agreed,' Putin later told reporters. 'But you have to ask him how he really felt about it.'

The Russian leader then assured Trump again in other interactions later that year, including in a meeting on the sidelines of the Asia–Pacific summit in Vietnam in November. 'Every time he sees me, he says "I didn't do it",' Trump explained to journalists, when asked if he believed Putin's election meddling denials. 'And I believe, I really believe, that when he tells me that, he means it.' Trump's remarks suggested that he believed Putin despite the US intelligence community's own clear findings that Moscow was responsible.

So, to mitigate the backlash, Trump walked back his position. 'I believe that he feels that he and Russia did not meddle in the election,' Trump said during a press conference in Hanoi the following day. 'As to whether I believe it or not, I am with our agencies, especially as currently constituted with the leadership. I believe that our intel agencies, our intelligence agencies, I work with them very strongly . . . As currently led, by fine people, I believe very much in our intelligence agencies.'

Despite the clarification, Trump later made the point that he believed that 'a good relationship with Russia is a good thing, not a bad thing', essentially paving the way for what appeared to be yet another reset between Washington and Moscow. However, unlike Russia's first post-Soviet reset with the West, the US's allies, including its Five Eyes intelligence partners, remained very distrustful of Putin. And they were right to be, because as Putin cultivated a bromance with Trump, his assassins in 2018 planned to kill a man in Britain whom he deemed a traitor. It was the second known time in a little more than a decade that the Kremlin would plot to kill a British citizen in their own country.

Much like the timing of Alexander Litvinenko's murder, which came when the British were focused on the aftermath of the 2005 London bombings, in March 2018 MI5 and Scotland Yard were dealing with the tragic outcome of five terrorist attacks from the previous year, including the Manchester Arena suicide bombing, which had killed twenty-two people and injured more than a thousand. Perhaps the Kremlin calculated in its targeting assessments that its assassins could slip under the radar of overstretched British authorities; and in a worst-case scenario, seek refuge in subsequent denials regarding its actions, much like Putin appeared to have done successfully in denying to Trump Russia's role in election meddling.

What Moscow seemed to overlook, however, was the determination of US authorities to aid their British counterparts against Putin's regime, despite Trump's lack of appetite for a showdown with Russia.

\* \* \*

Most mornings, it was a routine part of Alan Kohler's role to obtain updates from his team members about their live counter-intelligence cases. The FBI's Eurasian section chief would arrive at head office, the Hoover Building on Pennsylvania Avenue in Washington D.C., make his way to the fifth floor from where he supervised the bureau's operations against Russian spying, and get on with his work day. Kohler's morning was a little different on 5 March 2018, however, most notably because a team member informed him about a new case in Britain, not the US, which by all accounts should have been more relevant to MI5 and MI6 than to the FBI.

The investigation across the pond related to a British citizen of Russian origin who had apparently been poisoned the previous day, likely by Kremlin agents, in a manner that somewhat echoed the attack against Alexander Litvinenko. At forty-seven, Kohler had spent more than twenty years specialising in hunting down Kremlin spies operating in the US, so he knew a thing or two about placing them under surveillance, disrupting their missions or turning them into double-agents. He was at the centre of efforts to develop methods to counter hostile operatives, including new ways of bugging their homes, phones and computers, filming them exhuming bundles of cash from dead drops, and monitoring their brush passes with Russian intelligence officers working under diplomatic cover.

Kohler was also immersed in the history of Moscow's aggression against the West, with an admirably geeky interest in the body of literature surrounding its targeting and killing of defectors. But just when he thought he had seen all there was to see in the espionage game, he was stunned by the Kremlin's new foray in Britain.

There was a lot for Kohler to process about the British poisoning case, particularly because he knew the victim, Sergei Skripal. He had met the former Russian military colonel on a CIA-chartered plane in 2010, during the biggest spy-swap between Washington and Moscow since the Cold War. Kohler was aboard the plane that July to help oversee the exchange of ten Kremlin 'illegals', whom his team had arrested in the US the previous month.

Using the evidence obtained by Kohler and his team through a decade-long investigation called Ghost Stories, Washington brokered a deal with Russia's post-Soviet foreign intelligence service, the SVR, which had been running the illegals. The operatives pleaded guilty to espionage offences and were then flown under guard from New York to Vienna to board a Russian aircraft awaiting them on the tarmac. By then four prisoners freed by Moscow had left the Russian jet to join Kohler on his plane. Skripal was among them. 'I sort of had a personal connection with him, because I was on the flight when we traded the illegals for the four Russians,' Kohler told the author.

Skripal's freedom was a win for the US but an even greater coup for British intelligence authorities, as he had been a British rather than an American asset. The fact that the Americans had negotiated for his release on behalf of their British colleagues underscored their deep intelligence ties and the Special Relationship between their countries dating back to the Second World War.

Skripal had been a rising star in the GRU, Russia's military intelligence agency, when he started spying for MI6 in the 1990s. For several years he provided the British agency with secrets, including the identities of Kremlin agents working in Europe, in return for money. Russian authorities caught him in 2004, put him on trial in a widely covered media spectacle intended to humiliate MI6, and sentenced him to thirteen years in prison for 'high treason in the form of espionage', according to the court proceedings.

At fifty-nine, all of that was supposed to have been behind him when he boarded the FBI flight in Vienna. Along with another former Russian prisoner, he disembarked in Dublin during a refuelling stop and was whisked by British authorities to the UK to begin a new life. 'They went to the UK and then we took the other two guys to the US,' said Kohler, convinced that Moscow would honour the pardons it had given them. 'In my mind everyone was operating on those espionage gentleman rules, where we've caught each other's spies, it's a spy trade, let's move on.'

Except Moscow had obviously not moved on, as Kohler discovered when he was informed that Skripal and his daughter, Yulia, had been poisoned on Sunday 4 March 2018 with what was later discovered to be Novichok, a military-grade nerve agent developed by Moscow during the Soviet era that attacks the nervous system and can paralyse or kill its victims.

Scotland Yard's deputy assistant commissioner Dean Haydon

was Britain's senior national coordinator for counter-terrorism policing, who oversaw the investigation into the Skripal poisoning. He had the most far-reaching job on the case at the time, comprising a range of activities from juggling top secret discussions with the likes of MI5 and MI6, to being able to call on as many as 8,000 counter-terrorism police officers from around the country. The Skripal investigation was the biggest investigation he had overseen in his three decades at Scotland Yard – and one of the biggest cases in the police force's 200-year history.

Haydon needed to stay on top of all discoveries made by his officers as they trawled through 4,000 hours of CCTV footage in pursuit of those who targeted Skripal. Haydon also quickly learned from government scientists and chemical weapons experts that unlike polonium-210, the radioactive poison used to murder Litvinenko that emits radiation detectable with a Geiger counter, Novichok is 'odourless, invisible and not radioactive', which made it far more difficult to investigate. 'One, it's really toxic, and two it's difficult to even find and trace from a forensic point of view,' Haydon told the author.

It would later transpire that two GRU assassins had been sent from Russia to target Skripal at his home in Salisbury, a town in south-west England, where his daughter had been staying with him while on holiday in Britain. The operatives smuggled the Novichok into the country in a perfume bottle and police would later find the highest traces of it on the front door handle of Skripal's home.

'The question is: is that why they used Novichok instead of polonium this time around, because it's easy to transport?' said Haydon. 'It's not radioactive, you can get it through borders and ports and aeroplanes and trains, what have you, without being detected. Yes, it's highly toxic, but it's only toxic when you open it, because it was sealed in a perfume bottle.'

Kohler, too, drew parallels between the Litvinenko and Skripal cases. He said while the first had exposed the Kremlin's shoddy tradecraft and indicated they may never do anything similar again, the second was even more shocking, because Moscow had given its word that Skripal was a free man.

'I think people viewed the Litvinenko thing as a one-off,' said Kohler, 'and that the FSB did it because they were really angry at that one guy and that it wasn't something that professional spies did. I never viewed it as a bellwether – like, "Hey, now the world has changed, this is suddenly a thing that spies are going to do." And then the attack on Skripal happens. Suddenly all of us thought this is a real thing: that's the second guy they've poisoned with a chemical weapon that only Russia would have. What does this mean? This was a game changer for all of us. It was one of those situations where we were thinking we've traded for this guy and he was pardoned by Putin. He's kind of untouchable; that was the way it was viewed.'

There were multiple considerations Kohler needed to take into account in regard to Skripal's case, including the potential threat against the other Russians freed in the spy swap, two of whom were still living in the US.

'So we were trying to figure out what we should do to protect them,' he said. 'This attack against Skripal [was] not just an attack on the UK. Skripal was brought out of Russia because of something the United States did and the United States has risk here, because his profile is exactly the same as people we have in the US – literally the same, released on the same day and everything. So we had to ask ourselves, "Are we going to let them do this to our best ally with whom we have a Special Relationship? How do we not respond and tell Russia that this is unacceptable?"'

In Britain discussions were ongoing within government about

using 'all kinds of available options' against Putin's regime, said Haydon, including sanctions and expulsions. Kohler and his team knew that there were plenty of officials at Russia's missions in the US, including its embassy, who were obvious targets for expulsion because the FBI had been monitoring them for some time. But there were numerous considerations at play, as going after them would naturally provoke a Kremlin retaliation against US officials in Moscow. And there was also the politics of it all.

On Tuesday 13 March, the day Theresa May had set as an ultimatum for Moscow to explain its attack, which the Kremlin was still denying, the British prime minister briefed Donald Trump about the latest developments in the poisoning case. He reflected on the call during a press conference shortly thereafter, saying that Russia could well be behind the Skripal attack 'based on all the evidence'. But he stopped short of blaming Moscow, and in the background during conversations with members of his National Security Council, the US president was questioning the benefits of taking any action at all. Kohler said, 'My understanding was that during the decision making, Trump was asking for justification about "Why should I do this?" and "Why do I care about this?"'

The day after May's phone call with Trump, as Skripal and his daughter continued fighting for their lives, the British prime minister made her move. She told Parliament that her government would expel twenty-three Russian 'diplomats who have been identified as undeclared intelligence officers' – and gave them a week to leave the country. It was Britain's biggest spy expulsion since 1971, when 105 Soviet spies were purged from the UK after Oleg Lyalin's defection.

But May wanted more. She wanted to galvanise a multilateral retaliation against Russia and had been appealing to allies, including those within the Five Eyes intelligence network and the European Union, to follow Britain's example.

'I suppose when you go into those things, you're never a hundred per cent confident that you are going to get the answer you want, but you have to persuade,' May told the author. 'And it's not just about the leader to leader call, it's about the work that is done by the intelligence services and that is where the sharing of intelligence is important.' May said the ability to share intelligence 'and to be public about what we had and why we believed it was Russia was very important in that whole process of others feeling that "Yes, we should do something about this". And because it was so egregious – the use of a chemical weapon.'

At FBI headquarters, there were multiple retaliatory options that Kohler needed to navigate with his team, including the expulsion of Russians from the US that UK authorities were pushing for. MI5 and MI6 had even sent officials to Washington to meet with their FBI and CIA counterparts to make the case for meaningfully confronting Putin's regime. 'I would say that the Brits put on a masterclass in diplomacy at all levels of government to get the United States government to do this,' said Kohler. While he and his team were able to collect the intelligence and make a robust argument for taking action against Russia, the final decision rested very much in the president's hands. 'There was a lot of preparation being done on our part, but there was still a question about whether any action would be approved,' Kohler said.

The question was compounded by Trump's apparent rapprochement with Putin over Russia's election meddling – a political landmine that the FBI had to step carefully around. The bureau's election interference investigation, which the US deputy attorney general tasked Special Counsel Robert Mueller to take over in 2017, had since charged thirteen Russians in addition to a former Trump campaign aide, George Papadopoulos, who had lied to the FBI about the timing of his discovery that the Russians had planned to release damaging material on Hillary Clinton.

It was Papadopoulos who was partly responsible for getting Trump into the whole interference mess, because he had told Australia's High Commissioner to the UK, Alexander Downer, over a drink in London in May 2016, that the Russian government was said to have obtained material on Clinton, and indicated that Moscow could release it anonymously to damage her campaign. Downer then tipped off the US Embassy and was debriefed by the CIA's London bureau chief, Gina Haspel, and her FBI counterpart, Brian Boetig.

Fast forward to mid-March 2018, Boetig, a seasoned FBI official with two decades of experience in national security operations under his belt, played a key role in both helping MI5 with its Skripal case and liaising with Kohler's team in Washington. Boetig would travel daily between his office at the US Embassy in central London to MI5's headquarters near the Houses of Parliament, where some of his FBI special agents were based.

'The battle rhythm of my meetings at MI5's head office increased substantially and the substance of those meetings was less about general updates and more focused on tactical updates and intelligence sharing and gathering,' Boetig told the author. 'My team was already over there working it with MI5 officers, but I was heavily involved because my conversations back to FBI headquarters meant my status as a senior executive gave me much faster access to colleagues at headquarters, including Alan Kohler, who I knew well because we had worked closely together a few years earlier when he was assigned to my office in London.'

Boetig said his team worked closely with MI5 officers to help the agency identify Kremlin networks in Britain, beyond those working in an official capacity. 'The expulsions were stage one and probably the most publicly facing and easy to do, because they were either accredited diplomats or known intelligence officers,' said Boetig. 'The second stage was really to disrupt the Kremlin's unofficial support networks and that included targeting oligarchs or Russian money stored in real estate or financial institutions. This is not just removing the icing of the cake, but getting into the deeper layers of the cake.'

Back in Washington D.C., Kohler's team had drawn up a hit list of Russian diplomats to target, but there was still no word from the president about the direction he wanted to take. The turning point came after the European Union announced on 23 March its intention to expel Russian spies from at least ten countries in the bloc. 'Here's how it got approved,' said Kohler of the FBI's argument to convince Trump that Washington should also trigger an expulsion. 'What swayed him was to say that Europe is going to be kicking out a lot of people and we don't want to be the only ones who don't do it. It really came down to something like that. That everyone else is doing it, America wants to be the best, so let's kick [them] out.'

The FBI's list of potential targets for expulsion was somewhere in the three digits. 'We did our own internal triage of the Russian intelligence presence in the US and we ended up with a list of several dozen potential expulsion candidates,' Kohler said. There was a classified process that the US intelligence community went through to determine the list of candidates to recommend to the president. People familiar with the list told the author that it had between ninety and one hundred Russian intelligence officers on it.

On 26 March 2018, Trump ordered the expulsion of sixty Russian officials and the closure of Moscow's consulate in Seattle. 'The president closed the consulate and kicked out sixty intelligence officers – those are never-before-done things,' Kohler said. 'It would not have happened without him approving it.'

As for the final number chosen for expulsion, that too was chosen by the president. 'Our list was presented to the president by other executives in the government, and the National Security Council through the process would have made a recommendation to the president about the final number of Russians to expel.' Overall, the US's purge made up for about 40 per cent of the total 153 Russians expelled from twenty-nine countries, with Five Eyes members such as Canada and Australia removing just four and two respectively

Martin Green, head of Canada's intelligence assessment staff at the time, was closely involved in identifying and targeting Russian espionage campaigns in his country and abroad. 'After these expulsions foreign interference seemed to drop off in Canada,' he told the author. 'It showed that they were really instrumental in espionage activities and the expulsion limited Moscow's capabilities in our country.'

He said the Skripal attacks exposed Putin's demonstrated willingness to ignore the rules-based international order, regardless of whether blame would be attributed to him. And he did so under the pretext of a warped inversion where he believed his actions were in response to Western hostilities. 'When doing assessments relating to Russia's extraterritorial killings, I used to say that Putin seems to have gone from plausible deniability to implausible deniability. He seemed to have evolved to that because he truly believes in his own victim narrative – a narrative that they have developed and they still use it.'

As expected, Putin retaliated with reciprocal expulsions against all the nations that sided with Britain. 'In our case, the Russians responded by kicking out sixty Americans,' Kohler said.

The attack against Skripal had far wider-reaching impacts on

Putin's relationship with the West than he could have calculated and would yet again dominate the news in the summer of 2018. Skripal and his daughter survived their ordeal before being taken into hiding. As did a poisoned detective who had been the first to enter Skripal's home during the early part of the police investigation. The attack claimed the life of its first victim in July, when the perfume bottle containing Novichok that had been used by the GRU operatives was randomly discovered by a British woman about eight miles from where it had initially been used to target Skripal's home. Dawn Sturgess, forty-four, died soon after she unwittingly applied the nerve agent to her skin thinking it was perfume.

The perfume bottle had 'enough poison to kill thousands of people', a public inquiry later found. The British investigation into the Skripal case, which became publicly known as the 'Salisbury poisonings', also identified a third GRU suspect linked to the nerve agent attack. Moscow denied their involvement and refused Britain's extradition requests for the three, who are also subjects of Interpol international arrest warrants.

Less than two years after the Kremlin's attack in Salisbury, Putin tried to make good on a public pledge to target another defector tangentially linked to Skripal – and who was based in the US. The Miami-based defector, Aleksandr Poteyev, was a former SVR intelligence officer whom the FBI recruited during his posting with the Russian mission to the United Nations in New York in the late 1990s. Putin believed that Poteyev informed the FBI about the ten-member espionage ring that became the subject of the 2010 spy swap in Vienna.

In December that year, during a televised event, Putin ominously warned that 'traitors . . . will drop dead' and went on to praise the Kremlin's intelligence operatives who were rolled up by the FBI. 'The traitor [Poteyev] exposed his friends – his comrades in arms whose lives were dedicated to serving their homeland,' said Putin, in remarks later transcribed and uploaded to the Russian government's official website. 'Just imagine what it means to speak a foreign language as a native tongue, to give up one's relatives and not even be able to attend their funerals. Think about it! A person spends his life serving the homeland, and then some bastard betrays him.'

Poteyev was exfiltrated by US authorities from Moscow and resettled in the US shortly before the FBI triggered its Ghost Stories investigation arrests in June 2010. He was given a new identity and eventually resettled in a secret location in Miami. Somehow, Putin's intelligence services found out where Poteyev lived and in February 2020 – within a month of Joe Biden succeeding Trump in the Oval Office – deployed a Mexican scientist to scout out his apartment block. The scientist was arrested and quickly admitted working under the instruction of the FSB.

The case was among retaliatory considerations made in April 2021, when the Biden Administration expelled ten Russian spies after an intelligence assessment concluded that Putin's regime had interfered in yet another US election: the one in 2020 that Trump lost. However, US spy agencies found the operatives failed to alter 'any technical aspect of the voting process, including voter registration, ballot casting, vote tabulation, or reporting results'.

Biden intensified his pressure on Putin in early 2022, when it became apparent that the gathering of Kremlin troops on the Ukrainian border for what Russia claimed was a defensive 'military exercise' was in fact the pretext for invading its neighbour. Washington's measures would play out in numerous ways, including a face-to-face confrontation that led the US intelligence community to place Putin's spymasters on notice.

It was Michael J. Driscoll's first visit to the Russian diplomatic mission on the Upper East Side of Manhattan when he showed up with an unannounced entourage. Driscoll's office had scheduled the visit saying the FBI's assistant director in New York, who oversaw the organisation's operations in the state, wanted to meet a senior Kremlin diplomat who doubled as an official representative to Russia's foreign spy agency, the SVR. While the FBI was vague about why the assistant director wanted the meeting, it did state that he would be attending with a colleague – not colleagues.

So when Driscoll appeared with four others at the 67th Street building from where Russia's representatives to the United Nations run their day-to-day affairs, the SVR officer was completely caught off guard. And as the Kremlin official would learn a few minutes later, Driscoll was there to warn him calmly that a Five Eyes intelligence campaign would be waged against Russia should it go through with its intended invasion of Ukraine.

In diplomatic terms, the Five Eyes tactic was the equivalent of appearing at a chess match brandishing baseball bats. When the United States wants to express an objection to the diplomatic mission of a country it is hosting, it usually does so through the State Department to its ambassador in Washington D.C., not through the FBI in New York to its resident spy chief.

Yet Driscoll was not there to observe diplomatic protocol, nor were his four colleagues, who had met him at his office earlier that morning in late February 2022 before heading in two cars to the Russian outpost just before midday. The four who accompanied Driscoll were the senior US-based representatives of their agencies – a woman from Australia's ASIO, and three men from Britain's MI6, the Canadian Security Intelligence Service, and the New Zealand Secret Intelligence Service respectively. It was the first time that intelligence representatives of all five nations had confronted an adversarial nation collectively, in person, and by targeting a spy chief at its diplomatic mission. 'To the best of my knowledge, I cannot think of any other time when that had been done before,' Driscoll told the author.

Alan Kohler, who two years earlier had been promoted to lead the FBI's counter-intelligence division, played a central role in coordinating the meeting with Driscoll and their Five Eyes colleagues, even though he did not attend it. 'Obviously by that point, Russia had seen the united response by the Five Eyes in regards to the Skripal case from a few years earlier,' Kohler told the author. 'However, we wanted to show them that we were not only responsive, but proactive in working together.'

After introducing themselves to the SVR officer, the Five Eyes officials explained their reasoning behind the unannounced visit. 'We explained that we were there to voice our concerns about the recent geopolitical activities,' Driscoll said. 'The SVR guy was obviously a little taken aback by our presence and made a comment that he was not expecting the group.'

The US official then produced a printed statement from his FBI-embossed portfolio case and read it aloud. 'The intelligence community of these nations stand firmly together because of further invasion by Russia of Ukraine,' the statement read. 'While the United States is prepared to engage in diplomacy in full coordination with our allies and partners, we are equally prepared for other scenarios.' The statement, however, was secondary to the 'symbolic mission' that the Five Eyes officials initiated in the week leading up to Russia's invasion of Ukraine on 24 February.

'We understood that the message was not going to have a direct impact,' Driscoll said. 'That they weren't suddenly going to hold back from the border to Ukraine, but we wanted to be clear that if they were to invade, there were going to be responses . . .

that all Five Eyes countries stood unified on the topic and that the intelligence communities of each would be investing resources to make sure that the Russians are held accountable.'

At the end of the brief meeting, which lasted between ten and twenty minutes, the SVR official explained that he would reflect their message to Moscow. 'He also said that he was surprised by it and – as we were leaving – he made a joke with a heavy Russian accent about us being the "five besties". That joke stayed with me not because any of us thought it was funny, but because it illustrated how important that unity is and how it is perceived and taken seriously by our adversaries.'

The world has changed a lot since Driscoll's retirement from the FBI in late 2023 to pursue a career in the commercial sector as a leading cyber expert. At the writing of this epilogue in the spring of 2025, longstanding security, military and economic alliances have come under repeated strain since Donald Trump's return to the Oval Office. Reflecting on the meeting at the Russian mission three years after he had led it, Driscoll said: 'I just hope that in times of great need that Five Eyes partners would take similar steps again to demonstrate that unity.'

The Five Eyes unity, once taken as an article of faith by its partners, appeared increasingly frail on the eve of the seventieth anniversary of the alliance's official formation. And that is largely because a seismic split had emerged between the US and its four partners on whether Putin's Russia could be trusted. Trump, much like he did during his first term in office, wanted a reset with his Russian counterpart – disregarding the fact that three post-Soviet resets between the West and Moscow went up in flames because of Putin's actions, including the assassinations and attempted assassinations of defectors and his invasion of Ukraine.

Within the first 100 days of his presidency, Trump labelled Ukrainian president Volodimir Zelensky as a dictator and accused him of 'gambling with World War Three' at a time when other Western leaders concentrated on the fact that Putin, rather than Zelensky, was the aggressor in the war. Trump then sided with Russia, among other authoritarian nations, by refusing to support a European-backed United Nations resolution that condemned Moscow and supported Ukraine. Trump also reportedly ordered an end to offensive cyber operations against Russia.

Trump's actions triggered an unease among his international allies, especially those within the Five Eyes, far greater than the reservations they had expressed about his cosiness to Putin during his first presidential term. Dean Haydon, who oversaw Britain's investigation into the Skripal case, warned that Putin had demonstrated time and again his willingness to disregard international laws in pursuit of his objectives and Haydon could not see why his behaviour would ever change.

'It seems that under Putin's leadership his intelligence agencies, including the GRU, seem intent to continue to operate with impunity in breach of those international laws,' said Haydon. 'There's been multiple resets in history, but Russia always comes back, doesn't it – and always comes back with a complete disregard for Western rules of law.'

Mike Burgess has been leading ASIO since September 2019, and immediately before that he ran Australia's signals intelligence agency for two years. He has been at ASIO's helm longer than any of his Five Eyes contemporary counterparts have been in their respective agencies. In an interview with the author in late March 2025, Burgess warned about the Kremlin's continued aggression.

'Russia continues to be a country that has very active foreign intelligence services and they are very aggressive, in terms of the range of what they do [which] is completely different to many people's, including assassinations and a whole lot of other sabotage activities,' he said. 'They've always been like that . . .

[and] we as a security service have a good hold on that.' He said he was equally confident that US intelligence agencies would continue to confront Russian hostility. 'I'm confident our US friends will continue to prosecute threats to their own national interests exceptionally well.'

But he warned that regardless of assurances given by Putin's Russia, he cannot foresee a change in Moscow's behaviour. 'I would never believe anyone saying we're not going to spy on you from nations like that,' he said. 'That's just silly. I get why our respective diplomats and government leaders have to have these conversations and reset the conversation. But in the end, it's the second oldest profession. Every country does it . . . It might pause for a while, but actually with the Russians, it never stops.'

# TIMELINE

1951: British officials Guy Burgess and Donald Maclean, who had been spying for Moscow since the 1930s, defect to the Soviet Union.

1952: Pyotr Popov, a GRU Lieutenant Colonel stationed in Vienna, approaches the CIA to offer Soviet military secrets. He becomes the US agency's first Soviet asset.

1954: Oleg Lyalin enrols at the Higher Marine School in Odessa, Ukraine, and at some point in the next two years becomes an informant for the KGB.

James Jesus Angleton becomes the CIA's director of counter-intelligence.

1956: Martin Furnival Jones is promoted to head of counter-espionage at MI5.

As Soviet ambassador in Budapest, Yuri Andropov plays a central role in advising the Red Army during the Hungarian Revolution.

1957: Lyalin visits the UK during a 'goodwill' tour of Western ports.

1958: Alexander Shelepin takes over the KGB and plans to step up its operations against Western nations, especially Britain and the United States.

1960: The Soviet Union executes Popov after discovering that he had been spying for Washington. The event heightens Angleton's suspicion that the CIA has been penetrated by the KGB.

1961: President John F. Kennedy threatens to break the CIA into a 'thousand pieces' after its failed Bay of Pigs operation in Cuba.

George Blake, a former MI6 officer, is convicted of spying for Moscow and handed a forty-two-year prison sentence.

KGB officer Anatoly Golitsyn approaches the CIA in Helsinki and defects to the United States. He eventually claims that the KGB has a mole at Langley and a programme to deploy false defectors to the US.

1962: Lyalin is posted by the KGB to Klaipeda after failing to qualify for the agency's 'illegals' programme.

Yuri Nosenko, a KGB captain, approaches the CIA in Geneva and offers secrets in return for money.

A thirteen-day confrontation between Washington and Moscow in what became known as the Cuban Missile Crisis.

1963: Kim Philby defects to the Soviet Union.

MI5 launches an investigation into its deputy director general, Graham Mitchell.

Martin Furnival Jones becomes the deputy director general of MI5.

Oleg Penkovsky, a GRU colonel who had been spying for MI6 and the CIA for about two years, is executed in the Soviet Union.

President Kennedy is assassinated.

1964: Anthony Blunt, a former MI5 officer, confesses to being a Soviet spy.

Nosenko defects to the US, amid fears that he is a 'sent agent'.

James Angleton alleges to MI5 that Harold Wilson, Britain's newly elected prime minister, is a Soviet spy.

HONETOL, a joint FBI–CIA investigation into Soviet moles is launched.

MI5 and MI6 create a joint investigative committee, codenamed FLUENCY, to identify Soviet spies within their agencies. The codename was changed in 1970 but remains classified.

1965: Furnival Jones succeeds Roger Hollis as MI5's director general.

Lyalin is promoted to senior lieutenant.

1966: George Blake flees a British prison for Moscow.

1967: Lyalin begins his Department V training.

Yuri Andropov becomes director of the KGB.

Human intelligence officials from the US, Britain, Australia, Canada and New Zealand meet in Melbourne for the inaugural CAZAB forum to discuss the Soviet threat.

1968: Lyalin prepares for a deployment to Czechoslovakia during the Prague Spring, but his mission to join 'illegals' there does not materialise. He then travels to Moscow to prepare for a posting to the United Kingdom.

1969: Lyalin arrives in the UK in to join the Soviet Trade Mission.

MI5 launches an investigation into Roger Hollis, its former chief, amid accusations that he had been a Soviet spy.

1970: Ted Heath is elected prime minister of Britain.

1971: Hollis is interrogated by MI5 in February.

Lyalin approaches MI5 in April to offer secrets.

Lyalin defects to the UK in early September, three weeks before Britain expels 105 Soviet spies.

1972: Furnival Jones retires from MI5; Andropov continues to reel from the KGB's defeat against the British agency; Angleton's credibility is irreparably damaged

1974: Angleton is forced out of the CIA.

# SOURCE NOTES

The 'Lyalin Files' cited below predominantly feature FBI intelligence documents relating to Oleg Lyalin's case, including material the US law enforcement agency obtained from MI5.

Documents contained in the Lyalin Files, which also include dated and undated newspaper cuttings, do not appear in chronological order – and in some cases contain no page numbers. For simplicity, I listed the page on which cited documents feature in the pdf file in correlation to the overall number of pages in the file, i.e., p. 32/174.

Other sources that I have relied on, including interviews, books, declassified intelligence reviews and journals, are cited accordingly.

## Prologue

*bit of a character*: interview by author with Susan Lewsey (née Woodthorpe), April 2024.

*He dialled 999 from a phone box in Highgate*: Christopher Andrew, *The Defence of the Realm: The Authorised History of MI5*, Penguin Group, 2009, p. 569.

## Chapter 1: The Walk-In

*Frank Friberg was preparing himself for a night out*: David Wise, *Molehunt: The Secret Search for Traitors That Shattered the CIA*, Random House, 1992, p. 3.

*On his promotion to CIA station chief in Helsinki*: Ibid, p. 4

*Klimov scribbled the four-letter word*: Ibid.

*Golitsyn made a name for himself*: JFK Assassinations Records, US National Archives, 2022; Release under the President John F. Kennedy Assassination Records Act of 1992, Document 104-10169-10125.pdf, p. 7/26.

*Stalin apparently expressed an admiration for his insights*: Barry Royden, *James J. Angleton, Anatoliy Golitsyn, and the 'Monster Plot': Their Impact on CIA Personnel and Operations*, Studies in Intelligence, Vol. 55, No. 4, December 2011, p. 44.

*Her parents were doctors*: Document 104-10169-10125.pdf, p. 23.

*a humiliating KGB honey trap*: David Wise, *Molehunt*, p. 47.

*trained and directed the invasion force*: Editorial pages, 'The Cuban Invasion', *New York Times,* 18 April 1962, p. 38.

*He vowed to break the agency into a thousand pieces*: Peter Kornbluh, 'End CIA Covert Operations', *New York Times*, 21 December 2014. nytimes.com.

*built-in inhibitions*: James Angleton interview, Thames TV, 1976, via https://www.youtube.com/watch?v=vTgneJQxCts.

*Shortly after Golitsyn arrived with his wife and daughter*: Document 104-10169-10125.pdf, p. 8/26.

*evil inherent in the KGB and the Soviet system*: Studies in Intelligence, Vol. 55, p. 44.

*interrogated on his biographic data*: Document 104-10169-10125.pdf, pp. 10–11/26.

*Golitsyn's disclosures about the KGB's targeting*: Studies in Intelligence, Vol. 55, p. 50.

*seen internal KGB documents identifying the mole*: Ibid, p. 45.

*The bug was buried inside a wooden carving*: Wise, p. 14.

*the CIA placed Karlow on administrative leave*: Ibid, p. 18.

*Popov was stationed in Vienna*: Historical Review Program of the Central Intelligence Agency, *Popov–short form*, pp. 1–5, and Wise, p. 20.

*It came five years into the US agency's existence*: Ibid.

*The KGB's attempt at a playback*: *Popov–short form*, pp. 1–5.

*Popov's then-unexplained* compromise: Ibid.

*even though Goleniewski had already been providing secrets*: John Hart, *The Monster Plot: Counterintelligence in the Case of Yuriy Ivanovich Nosenko*, Central Intelligence Agency, December 1976, p. 19/222.

*The CIA provided Goleniewski's disclosures to MI5*: Peter Wright and Paul Greengrass, *Spycatcher: The Candid Autobiography of a Senior Intelligence Officer*, William Heinemann Australia, 1988, p. 142.

*played a most prominent role*: Testimony and depositions discussing the HSCA memo hoax, May 1978, p. 32.

*Chekists discovered Okhrana's files*: R. Wraga, *The Trust: The History of a Soviet Provocation Operation*, via Central Intelligence Agency, January 1950, p. 8.

*the Cheka recruited former Tsarist officials*: Ibid, p. 7.

*Angleton saw the KGB as ten feet tall*: Studies in Intelligence, Vol. 55, p. 49.

*built the wartime agency in MI6's image*: Richard Kerbaj, *The Secret History of The Five Eyes: The Untold Story of the International Spy Network*, Bonnier Books, 2022, pp. 23–44.

*do not share intelligence, but exchange it*: Ibid, pp. 81–101.

*At the end of the war he was re-posted to MI5*: National Archives, 'Edward Martin Furnival Jones CBE', June 1965, CAB 301–231.

*Indeed I have not got an image*: 'Russian Intelligence tries to recruit MPs', *Daily Telegraph*, 30 September 1972, p. 7.

*Golitsyn could not identify the other three*: Wright and Greengrass, *Spycatcher*, pp. 163–5.

*Golitsyn was given a 'tax free' payment of $200,000*: Document 104-10169-10125. pdf, p. 7.

*Golitsyn was very demanding and very much a prima donna*: Studies in Intelligence, Vol. 55, p. 45.

*informed about a plan to kill the traitor*: US National Archives, *CI Information Report*, 24 July 1972, Document 104-10172-10192.pdf, p. 3

## Chapter 2: A Promising Recruit

*reading English newspapers*: Federal Bureau of Investigation, Oleg Lyalin Files (from here on 'Lyalin Files'), Series 1366648-0, File 1, Section 1, p. 32/174. Note: The files are based on communications between the FBI and MI5 in regards to Lyalin's case. According to the above file, Lyalin was born on 24 June 1938, but his birth was not registered until 28 August 1938. The KGB documents I obtained from the Lithuanian Special Archives, however, state that Lyalin was born on 28 August 1937 (not 1938). I have chosen to go with 1938 because it is more likely that a recording error was made by the KGB's Lithuanian branch, than Lyalin's debriefers at MI5, who appear to have been quite methodical in obtaining his biographical details.

*to portray non–Russians in language, culture and behavioural patterns*: Ibid.

*Local historians estimate that during the Stalinist era*: Michael J. Sulick, 'As the USSR Collapsed: A CIA officer in Lithuania', Studies in Intelligence, Vol. 50, No. 2, 2006, p. 15/19.

*expelled from the party for undeclared reasons in 1937*: Lyalin Files, p. 30/174

*working in close coordination*: Central Intelligence Agency, *Soviet Partisan Warfare Since 1941*, March 1949, p. 3.

*He separated from Lyalin's mother in 1950*: Lyalin Files, p. 30/174.

*After his father's death, there was very little money*: Ibid, pp. 31–2/174.

*population of about 125,000 in the early 1950s*: Central Intelligence Agency, *City of Pyatigorsk-Site, Structure, Functions, Installations, and Character of Population*, Information Report, May 1953, p. 2.

*she was cleared of the collaboration charge in 1956*: Lyalin Files, p. 30/174.

*a classmate working as a KGB informant told Lyalin*: Ibid, pp. 31–2/174.

*Western seamen and smugglers*: Ibid.

*goodwill tour of Western ports*: Ibid.

*running into a cyclone after leaving Colombo*: 'Telegram in Brief, Commonwealth', *The Times*, London, 29 August 1957, p. 6.

*Oleg Aleksandrovich Liabin*: Lyalin Files, p. 34/174.

*against some governments, political parties and public figures*: Ibid.

*Lyalin took his examination before the end of his course*: Ibid, p. 32/174.

*The Master Plan's success could only be gauged*: Studies in Intelligence, Vol. 55, p. 49; and Anatoly Golitsyn, *New Lies for Old: An ex-KGB officer warns how communist deception threatens survival of the West*, Dodd, Mead & Company, 1984, pp. 50–1.

*chilling symbol of the Iron Curtain*: The John F. Kennedy Presidential Library and Museum, *The Berlin Wall*, via jfklibrary.org.

*In reality, neither Washington, London nor Moscow were truly hopeful*: Ibid.

*routinely study the names of delegates*: Tennent H. Bagley, *Spy Wars: Moles, Mysteries, and Deadly Games*, Yale University, 2007, p. 5.

*a familiar pseudonym for Mikhail Tsymbal*: Ibid.

*He joined his parents at the soiree*: Hart, pp. 13–24/222.

*for reasons of health*: Ibid.

*Nosenko approached the American official*: Ibid.

*Bagley enlisted a young techie*: Bagley, p. 3.


## Chapter 3: This Man Has Come to Discredit Me

*Nosenko clicked his fingers three times*: Bagley, p. 8.

*frittered away an official travel advance*: Ibid, p. 6. Note: The sum of money that Nosenko claimed to have embezzled slightly differs in two accounts. Bagley reveals that it was 800 Swiss francs, while a CIA investigation states that it was 900. I have relied on Bagley's recollection because he was the first to debrief Nosenko.

*Nosenko was already through his second Scotch and soda*: Bagley, p. 7.

*Nosenko brought up the name of Pyotr Popov*: Ibid, p. 9.

*single-handedly supplied the most valuable intelligence*: Joan Bird and John Bird, *CIA Analysis of the Warsaw Pact Forces: The Importance of Clandestine Reporting*, Historical Collections, p. 11.

*Kisevalter was street-smart, dismissive of authority*: Wise, p. 21.

*he was not afraid of saying no to him*: Ibid.

*routine surveillance that had led to the GRU officer's downfall*: Bagley, p. 12.

*covered his mouth, pinned his arms and dragged him*: 'Foreign Relations: prefabricated agent', *Time* magazine, 26 October 1959, via content.time.com.

*forty-two microphones that honeycombed the US Embassy*: Wise, p. 72; and Hart, p. 171/222.

*envelopes were daubed with clear chemicals*: Ibid, p. 77.

*who worked as Smith's housemaid*: Ibid, p. 75.

*Subj conclusively proved bona fide*: Hart, p. 17/222.

*forced a British naval attaché in Moscow*: Ibid, p. 21/222.

*he ever seem glassy-eyed or off balance*: Bagley, p. 14.

*The CIA officers sent an urgent cable to Langley*: Wise, p. 68.

*scribbling on notepaper*: Bagley, pp. 22–3.

*the biggest fish of his life*: Hart, p. 17/222.

*replenish the account from which he embezzled the money*: Ibid.

*was of split motivation*: Ibid.

*10 to 15 volumes of files*: Ibid.

*the parallel insights Nosenko had provided seemed*: Bagley, p. 24.

*a disinformation operation possibly relating to his defection*: Hart, p. 19/222.

*sent to the Embassy by an alleged KGB person*: Ibid, p. 222/18.

*presented a situation because we didn't have a letter*: Ibid, p. 19/222.

*whatever the operation's main purpose might be*: Ibid.

*it was concluded that Nosenko had been allowed to expose him*: Ibid, p. 21/222.

*lamppost 35, had been designated by the CIA*: Wise, p. 117.

*their asset had unusually missed scheduled brush pasts*: Ibid.

*Davison spotted the chalk mark on the lamppost*: Ibid.

*promotion to lieutenant on 4 November 1962*: Lyalin's KGB record, via Lithuanian Special Archives.

*multiple meetings he had helped organise*: Studies in Intelligence, Vol. 55, No. 4, p. 44.

*his bid for a $10m fund*: Wise, p. 26.

*went on strike and refused to be debriefed*: Studies in Intelligence, Vol. 55, No. 4, p. 45.

*quarantine for his Alsatian dog*: Andrew, p. 504.

## Chapter 4: The Betrayal

*to bring Angleton up to speed in a courtesy call*: Ben Macintyre, *A Spy Among Friends: Kim Philby and the Great Betrayal,* Bloomsbury Publishing, 2014, pp. 268–9.

*frequent drinking sessions at Harvey's restaurant:* William R. Corson, Susan B. Trento, and Joseph J. Trento, *Widows: The explosive truth behind 25 years of Western intelligence disasters,* Crown Publisher Inc, *1989,* p. 97. Note: Angleton and Philby ate lunch together at the old Harvey's Restaurant almost every week.

*Philby had visited 113 times between 1949 and 1951*: Studies in Intelligence, Vol. 55, No. 4, p. 42.

*The one piece of evidence that does exist*: Ibid, p.43.

*He attended Malvern College*: Jefferson Morley, *The Ghost: The secret life of CIA spymaster James Jesus Angleton,* St Martin's Press, p. 5.

*briefed on MI5's Double Cross system*: David Robarge, *The James Angleton Phenomenon: 'Cunning Passages, Contrived Corridors': Wandering in the Angletonian Wilderness,* Studies in Intelligence, Vol. 53, No. 4, 2009, p. 3/21, via cia.gov.

*viewed himself more as chief of an operational entity*: JFK case extracts, *The Special Investigations Group of the CI Staff,* September 1998, p. 22.

*surrounded himself and his staff with an aura of mystery*: Robarge, p. 5/21.

*they must also be confident that we can give a full measure of protection*: Central Intelligence Agency, *Report to the Presidential Commission on CIA Activities Within the United States,* 1975, pp. 28–9.

*Hollis had sat hunched at his office desk*: Andrew, p. 506.

*During the Leconfield House meeting*: Ibid.

*reassuring Martin that he was taking the allegation very seriously*: Ibid.

*Golitsyn was even given the honour of selecting a codename*: Ibid, p. 507.

*right down to his tic of muttering to himself*: Ibid.

*briefed Harold Macmillan about it on three occasions*: Ibid.

*the prime minister authorised Hollis to travel to Washington D.C.*: Ibid, p. 509.

*Reportedly at the urging of Angleton*: Studies in Intelligence. Vol. 55, No. 4, p. 45.

*had incorrectly named the defector 'Dolitsyn'*: Tom Mangold, *Cold Warrior: James Jesus Angleton: The CIA's Master Spy Hunter*, Simon & Schuster, 1991, p. 80.

*welcome-home bonus of $200,000*: Ibid, p. 81.

*have more privacy and separation from the CIA*: Studies in Intelligence. Vol. 55, No. 4, p. 46.

*Nosenko arrived at a safe house in Swiss city*: Bagley, pp. 82–3.

*he unexpectedly wanted to defect to the United States*: Ibid.

*learn from him the details of his mission*: Hart, p. 23/222.

*He said the KGB had deemed Oswald mentally unstable*: Bagley, p. 85.

*solid career with a certain personal independence*: Hart, p. 23/222.

*the CIA flew him to the US on 12 February*: Ibid, p. 222/27.

*small-time con-man*: Ibid, p. 30/222.

*I would like now to make known my conclusions*: Ibid, p. 157/222.

*He also revealed another lie from that first debriefing*: CIA, *The Examination of the Bona Fides of a KGB Defector, Yuri I. Nosenko, 'Recall Telegram'*, February 1968, p. 325.

*insinuated that the Soviet agency may have been responsible for 'killing' Gaitskell*: Wright and Greengrass, pp. 362–3.

*poison rather than guns or explosives*: CIA, *Soviet Use of Assassination and Kidnapping*, February 1964, p. 13.

*General Nicolai Rodin, had served in London*: Wright and Greengrass, p. 363.

*The CIA mole-hunter eventually reported back with a clue*: Ibid.

*the British security service had taken an initial interest in Wilson* and *Norman John Worthington as MI5 codenamed him*: Andrew, pp. 414–16.

*If Russian intelligence can recruit a backbench Member of Parliament*: 'Russian Intelligence tries to recruit MPs', *Daily Telegraph*, 30 September 1972, p. 7.

*became known as the Wilson Doctrine*: Chapman Pincher, *Their Trade is Treachery*, Bantam Book, 1982, p. 248.

*insisted that he would only provide the evidence if MI5 assured him*: Mangold, p. 75. Note: Two decades later, a report in the *Observer* stated that the CIA had told MI5 that it would provide its evidence against Wilson but only if the British agency 'promised never to tell anyone in the Labour administration'. See 'Why MI5 suspected that Harold Wilson was a Soviet spy', *Observer*, 22 July 1984, p. 2.

*While Angleton's proclaimed evidence was a prerequisite*: Studies in Intelligence, Vol. 55, No. 4, p. 45,

*HONETOL was formed in November 1964 to work on Golitsyn's assertion*: Ibid, p. 50,

*Igor Orlov, a CIA contractor*: Ibid, p. 45; and Wise, pp. 162–3.

*victory in the great patriotic war:* Lyalin's KGB record, via Lithuanian Special Archives.

*His first marriage to Tamara Ivanovna Bondarenko had ended in divorce*: Ibid.

*Lyalin was made senior lieutenant on 17 December*: Ibid.

*He met the criteria, and in February 1967, Lyalin bade farewell*: Lyalin Files, p. 32/174.

*Department V which had been created in October 1966 to replace the KGB's 13th Department*: via Filip Kovacevic, University of San Francisco.

*Secrecy about the work of this department is maintained*: CIA, *Soviet Use of Assassinations and Kidnapping*, Studies in Intelligence, Vol. 19. No. 3, Fall 1975, pp. 1–5.

*Krivitsky was suspected to have been killed by the NKVD*: Kerbaj, p. 73.

*On Wednesday 1 March 1967, as Lyalin checked in*: Lyalin Files, p. 33/174.

## Chapter 5: The Export Agency

*The group would have to locate and identify the target* and *blew up a bridge*: Lyalin Files, p. 33/174.

*partisan warfare, including organising a small army*: Ibid.

*Andropov urged Soviet leader Leonid Brezhnev in early 1968 to approve a military invasion*: Christopher Andrew and Vasili Mitrokhin, *The Mitrokhin Archive: The KGB in Europe and the West*, Allen Lane, 1999, p. 328.

*On 2nd May 1968, Lyalin was sent to Moscow*: Lyalin Files, p. 34/174.

*instructions from the Foreign Trade [ministry] for his cover position*: Ibid.

*The identified intelligence personnel rose from 15 in 1950 to 120 in 1970*: Ibid, Section 2, p. 51/23.

*number of working wives as well as the numbers in other organisations*: Ibid.

*For example, the covert transfer of funds from Moscow*: CIA, *Communist Commercial Operations in Non-Communist Countries*, March 1983, p. 2.

*None of the five CIA officers who had been the primary subjects*: Studies in Intelligence, Vol. 55, No. 4, p. 50.

*Hoover's men pulled the pin altogether on HONETOL in February 1965*: Ibid.

*which would not be appropriate if CIA were forced*: Hart, p. 35/222.

*as an act of desperation following a decade of deception and disloyalty*: Ibid, p. 37/222.

*shown in the present sessions and over the past months that he is unable to support his legend*: Ibid, p. 57/222.

*virtual prisoner in a safe house in Clinton*: Ibid, p. 162; and CIA, *Family Jewels*, May 1973, Attachment A, p. 1.

*designed and staffed with the intention of engendering in Nosenko a feeling of hopelessness*: Hart, p. 63/222.

*voices emanating from various objects, such as his shoes and his spoon*: Ibid, p. 67/222. Note: Nosenko was forced to wake up each morning at 6.00 a.m., instructed to wash with 'cold water only', given sugarless 'weak tea' and porridge for breakfast, and 'watery soup, macaroni or porridge, bread, [and] weak tea' for dinner.

*On 4 February 1964, I told my CIA contact in Geneva*: CIA, *The Examination of the Bona Fides of a KGB Defector, Yuri I. Nosenko, 'Recall Telegram'*, February 1968, p. 325.

*On the morning of 14 March 1966, shortly after Angleton had landed*; and *Furnival Jones cleared his diary to meet with them*: Andrew, pp. 513–14.

*a joint investigation by MI5 and MI6, codenamed FLUENCY*: Ibid, p. 515.

*It was the first meeting of its kind that brought together*: Interview by author with Mike Burgess, director general of the Australian Security Intelligence Organisation, March 2025.

*This was a significant meeting that very few people knew about*: Ibid.

*Martin Furnival Jones authorised an investigation*: Andrew, p. 515.

*Oleg Adolfovich Lyalin . . . applied for a visa in February 1969*: National Archives, *CRIM 2/5681/1*, via Witness Statement, 25 October 1971, p. 34/13.

*And there were many behavioural rules uniquely relating to foreign postings*: Lyalin Files, Series 1366648-0, File 1, Section 6, p. 37/70.

*His father advised the government of Malaysia and was a distinguished lawyer*: National Archives, *DEFE 141/68*, p. 9/74.

*Abdoolcader was brought up in Penang*: Ibid, p. 24/74.

*British English bastards, English swine*: Ibid.

*It was a label distinguishing cars registered to the Royal Family, Metropolitan Police, and MI5*: Ibid, pp. 9–11.

*He explained those aspects of his job to Aleksander Savin*: Ibid.

## Chapter 6: Watching the Watchers

*Everything appeared to have gone to plan*: Lyalin Files, p. 34/174. Note: Department V officers stationed in residencies or overseas bureaus were known as 'Line F'. See Andrew, p. 955.

*the Soviet Trade Delegation official who was there to welcome him was in fact an undercover KGB officer*: Andrew, p. 569.

*ladder made of rope and knitting needles*: Clive Borrell, 'Sean Bourke raise £1,000 to free spy', *The Times*, London, 21 January 1969, p. 2.

*the 35-mile travel limit outside London that had been imposed*: Lyalin Files, Series 366648-0, File 1, Section 1A, p. 81/88.

*The KGB had given Costi this piece of craftsmanship*: Ibid, p. 2/88.

*Costi's bedroom at the home he co-owned with his parents*: CRIM 1/5681/2, p. 34/9.

*Costi would plug his headphones into a portable shortwave*: Lyalin Files, Series 366648-0, File 1, Section 1A, p. 2/88.

*In 1965, Costi, known as Ken to his close friends*: CRIM 1/5681/1, p. 3/56.

*holes in walls, dumps or containers such as packets or cans*: Lyalin Files, Series 366648-0, File 1, Section 1A, p. 2/88.

*to identify the voltage output of the Northfleet Power Station*: Staff reporter, 'Six and four years' jail for Cypriot spies in Soviet net', *The Times*, London, 8 December 1971, p. 3.

*Martianou was not given the exact reason for the KGB's interest*: Ibid.

*He was a natty dresser*: Staff reporter, 'The World: Spies: Foot Soldiers in an Endless War', *Time* magazine, 11 October 1971, via time.com.

*worth more than three times the average weekly earnings*: UK Parliament, *Hansard, Volume 792: debated on Friday 28 November 1969*, via https://hansard.parliament. uk/.

*Soviet businessmen from the Moscow Narodny Bank*: Staff reporter, 'Lyalin had a Cockney accent', *Daily Telegraph*, 2 October 1971, p. 28.

*The personal qualities responsible for his rise*: D.G.W. (Dick Goldsmith White), 'Sir Roger Hollis (Obituary)', *The Times*, London, 6 November 1973, p. 22.

*his leaks had been brought to the attention of the KGB by a senior British or American mole*: Mangold, p. 78.

*so secret that its whole existence was even withheld from the British prime minister*: Andrew, p. 516.

*His relationship with the Oval Office was conducted through*: Mangold, p. 282.

*became increasingly hostile to Kissinger's approach to Moscow*: Ibid.

*A clash between Kissinger and Angleton was on the cards*: Jefferson Morley, 'Nixon's Plan to Threaten the CIA on JFK's Assassination', *Politico*, 6 May 2022, via politico.com.

*textiles, leather, clothing and wearing attire*: Companies House, *Incorporation Document, Company Number 956055*, October 1969, p. 2. Razno is a Russian word which can also mean 'diverse' and 'assorted'.

*each staff member was sent home with a hamper*: Interview by author with Susan Lewsey (née Woodthorpe), April 2024.

*established to promote and develop trade between the UK and Soviet*: Lyalin Files, p. 124/174.

*Lyalin set up a deal for shipping tights worth £250,000*: Roger Todd and Ronald Rickets, 'Oleg: The man who was Russia's Mr Fixit', *Daily Mirror*, 2 October 1971, p. 5.

*sharp eye for a good business deal*: Lyalin Files, p. 108/174.

*Jones, Edward Martin Furnival, attached to the Ministry of Defence*: Staff reporter, 'The Saturday Evening Post Story', *Evening Standard*, 19 October 1967.

*with the problems of penetration of British intelligence*: Andrew, p. 947.

## Chapter 7: Spycatcher

*He became convinced that he was being spied on*: Andrew, p. 516. Golitsyn's visit to the UK had been at the invitation of MI5's director-general and the chief of MI6.

*when he accompanied Angleton to the CAZAB security conference*: Ibid, p. 514.

*dining at restaurants – especially ones near where he lived in New York*: Ibid, p. 511.

*transferred him to the home of an MI5 official*: Ibid, p. 516.

*On the basis of their past research the Security Service intend to provide*: Ibid, p. 947.

*complete waste of time*: Ibid, p. 516.

*Taking the general trend of all the polls together*: Ronald Butt, 'Mr Wilson's Style', *The Times*, London, 4 June 1970, p. 11.

*The British agency had first taken an interest in Wilson's interactions*: Andrew, p. 416.

*MI5 became increasingly interested in his trips*: Ibid.

*codenamed OLDING*: Ibid, p. 418. Note: Between 1974 and 1976, during Harold Wilson's second term in office, an alleged group of MI5 officials plotted to destabilise his government. As part of what would become known as the 'Wilson Plot', rogue MI5 officials allegedly burgled the home of some of the prime minister's staff members, spread falsehoods against Wilson in the press, and plotted to overthrow his government with the help of the army. Two inquiries into the allegations, including one ordered by Wilson's successor, James Callaghan, found no evidence to support the allegations. However, questions about MI5's alleged role in undermining Wilson remain to this day. MI5 insists that Wilson 'has never been the subject of a Security Service investigation or of any form of electronic or other surveillance by the Security Service'. See MI5.gov.uk.

*he was not personally popular among voters*: Staff Reports, *Politics Background*, BBC, 18 June 1970, via bbc.co.uk.

*Having dethroned 76 Labour MPs and gained a 30-seat parliamentary majority*: Ibid.

*forced to sack his shadow defence secretary Enoch Powell*: Ian Aitken, 'Enoch Powell dismissed for 'racialist' speech', *Guardian*, 22 April 1968, via theguardian.com.

*the inquiry's preliminary findings on 18 June 1970*: Andrew, p. 517.

*kidnapped by the Russians, carried on to a Soviet plane*: Kerbaj, p. 100.

*To this day it seems astounding that those investigating Hollis*: Andrew, p. 517. Note: In April 1964, after being granted immunity from prosecution, Anthony Blunt confessed to MI5 that he had been a Soviet spy. His case became public in 1979 and caused MI5 huge embarrassment.

*an agent in London codenamed JOHNSON*: Ibid.

*Heath had called that meeting with Furnival Jones and other security officials*: Edward Heath, *The Course of my Life: My Autobiography*, Hodder and Stoughton, 1998, p. 474.

*Heath's security staff walked them to a spring on a hill nearby*: Ibid, pp. 471–4.

*The informal lunch at Chequers on 3 October 1970*: Ibid. Queen Elizabeth II also attended the lunch.

*unacceptable for any appointment*: Lyalin Files, p. 146/174.

*In 1970 alone we have refused the visas*: Ibid.

*a call from Kentish Town Police Station*: Andrew, p. 571.

*There is of course a good deal of assorted sex*: Lyalin Files, Series 1366648-0, File 1, Section 6, p. 37/70.

*He would drop pencils, upset teacups and even trip over*: Alamy, 'The girl who called spy Oleg a "Charmer"', 10 October 1971, via alamy.com.

*public utilities, the railways, government and military communications*: Lyalin Files, p. 17/174.

*the arrival of American naval crews aboard*: BBC reporter, 'How US nuclear missiles found a base in Scotland', 2 March 2021, bbc.com.

*three KGB agents, including an American serviceman, were arrested and jailed*: Special correspondent, 'Seven years in gaol for a "ham-handed" spy', *The Times*, London, 24 June 1967, p. 2.

## Chapter 8: The KGB's Rulebook on Extramarital Affairs

*husky Russian voice*: Nick Davies and Mark Dowdney, 'Irina: the beautiful blonde who fell for a spy', *Daily Mirror*, 2 October 1971, p. 5.

*constant companion*: Ibid.

*I knew both Irina and Oleg quite well*: Ibid.

*Her own father, a former Soviet foreign service official*: Barton Whaley, *Notes for a History of the Structures of the Intelligence Services of the USSR*, Center for International Studies, Massachusetts Institute of Technology, Cambridge, Massachusetts, September 1969, p. 111.

*defences of Swedish naval bases*: 'Swedish Naval Aide Tells Court He Spied For the Soviet on Possible Invasion Routes', *New York Times*, 31 October 1951, p. 6

*She heard his story when she visited her parents*: National Archives, *Jaguar Report*, 20 March 1972, p. 3

*Oleg Lyalin used to come to the office*: Interview by author with Susan Lewsey, April 2024.

*various sums of money, the largest of which was about £100*: National Archives, DEFE 141/68.

*The MoD official had merely told him*: Ibid.

*Richardson's name had been flagged during her holiday*: Ibid.

*the suitcase in hand because he couldn't find the car*: Lyalin Files, Series 1366648-0, File 1, Section 1A, p. 2/88.

*in the streets, on buses and trains*: National Archives, CRIM 1/5681/1, 25 October 1971, pp. 46–53/56.

*This time he gave me more lessons in Morse code*: Ibid.

*He said now that I had been on holiday and was rested*: Ibid.

*appealed to Furnival Jones to inform Ted Heath*: Andrew, p. 518.

*It was indeed extraordinary that Heath had not been brought into the picture*: Ibid.

*his FLUENCY case was finally closed in August 1970*: Ibid, p. 516.

*Our countries have a Special Relationship which we often refer to*: The American Presidency Project, *Richard Nixon: White Remarks of Welcome to Prime Minister Edward Heath of Great Britain*, 17 December 1970, via presidency.ucsb.edu.

*Heath waited until the pair were in a private setting*: Heath, p. 472.

*feared that British membership would weaken the French voice*: Ibid.

*Heath said he preferred a natural relationship*: Ibid.

## Chapter 9: A Suspicious Walk-In

*he had sought them out on 21 April 1971*: Andrew, p. 569.

*nor had it even been aware that the KGB's Department V had officers*: Ibid, p. 955.

*He said he had called the 999 emergency hotline*: Ibid, p. 569.

*speaks good English, some German and a little bit of Spanish and French*: Lyalin Files, p. 34/174.

*He proposed furnishing information if the British would have him declared persona non grata*: Lyalin Files, pp. 7–8/174.

*In his intelligence role, Lyalin's task was to make contingency plans*: Ibid, p. 18.

*The KGB was also preparing for the infiltration of military sites, including RAF Fylingdales*: Ibid.

*Lyalin was in the process of selecting and reporting on sites*: Ibid.

*He funded Wilson's private office*: Andrew, pp. 569, 627.

*a bogus Ministry of Defence source, codenamed AFT*: Ibid, p. 570.

*designation within the Five Eyes*: Kerbaj, p. 255.

*From what Lyalin has said, there can be little doubt*: Lyalin Files, p. 17/174.

*not engaged in industrial sabotage in the UK in peacetime*: Ibid.

*Under that plan, Lyalin said, local agents would pose as delivery men*: Andrew and Mitrokhin, p. 499.

*Tamara stood in front of Lyalin's vehicle*: Andrew, p. 569.

*GOLDFINCH considered the matter and gave us his views on two cassettes of tape*: Lyalin Files, p. 37–8/77

*GOLDFINCH isolates the susceptibilities of intelligence officers*: Ibid.

*Lyalin would every now and then accept a small payment of between £10 and £20*: Andrew, p. 569.

*Furnival Jones had attended the interdepartmental meeting*: Permanent Under-Secretary's Department, Documents on British Policy Overseas, *Soviet Intelligence Activities in the United Kingdom*, Record of a meeting in the permanent under-secretary's office, Series III, Vol. I, No. 66, 25 May 1971, via Gill Bennett.

*hovering in the order of 1.2 per cent of total British exports*: Gill Bennett, *Six Moments of Crisis: Inside British Foreign Policy*, Oxford University Press, 2013, p. 137.

*the presence of 550 Soviet officials in London in 1971*: Lyalin Files, p. 144/174.

*The Quadripartite negotiations were expected to conclude*: Geraint Hughes, *Giving the Russians a Bloody Nose: Operation Foot and Soviet Espionage in the United Kingdom, 1964–71*, Cold War History, Vol. 6, No. 2, May 2006, p. 239.

*understood that the prime minister favoured a mass eviction*: Ibid, p. 237.

*had been detected in active intelligence operation*': David Bonavia, 'Soviet envoys expelled for spying', *The Times*, 23 June 1971, p. 1.

*By late July, British home secretary Reginald Maudling*: Hughes, p. 239.

*kill . . . as soon as they could find him*: US National Archives, *CI Information Report*, 24 July 1972, Document 104-10172-10192.pdf, p. 3.

*From the working of the telegram source*: Ibid.

## Chapter 10: No Way Back

*a Hillman saloon veered in and out*: BBC reporter, 'I arrested a KGB superspy', *On This Day* series, BBC, via bbc.com.

*It was about 1.30 a.m. and we were driving*: Ibid.

*Russian bailed over B-test*: News in Brief, 'Russian bailed over B-test', *Daily Express*, 31 August 1971, p. 5.

*was dissatisfied with his work in the KGB*: Lyalin Files, pp. 39–40/86.

*A personal note to him from a friend at the KGB Headquarters*: Ibid, pp. 35–6/174.

*One of the documents contained 13 pages and 54 photographs*: National Archives, Statement to be made to the House of Commons by Foreign and Commonwealth Secretary, PREM 15, September 1971, p. 3.

*Lyalin also snatched the keys to one of the trade mission's cars*: Lyalin Files, p. 24/88.

*So at 9.50 a.m. on Friday 3 September*: Andrew, p. 570.

*Lyalin then hung up and dialled the next number on the list*: Ibid.

*She did not want to go back to London*: Denis Blewett, 'Irena: the dossier of a defector', *Evening Standard*, 13 October 1971, p. 7.

*He informed them at 2.15 p.m. that he wanted to defect with a friend*: Andrew, p. 570.

*how the pair's defection would impact the October deadline*: Hughes, p. 239.

*Because on the same day that he and Teplyakova signed their asylum forms*: Bennett, p. 132.

*On Tuesday, 7 September, two days before their tenth wedding anniversary*: Blewett, p. 7.

*I knew Lyalin*: Ibid.

*KGB Headquarters [continued] the analysis of Lyalin's operational activities*: Lyalin Files, p. 28/174.

*Lyalin was the first Department V official to ever defect to the West*: Andrew, pp. 570–4.

*Facts relative to the defection were made known to the various Branch Chiefs*: Lyalin Files, p. 26/174.

*possible leads and cases*, Ibid, p. 3/174.

*Source learned that, concerning the reaction of KGB Headquarters regarding the defection*: Ibid, p. 28/174.

*Source stated that, as a result of Lyalin's defection*: Ibid, p. 78/174.

*The Soviet Union conducts espionage against Great Britain*: Ibid, p. 147/174.

*We are police officers – open up*: CRIM 1/5681/1, pp. 25–7/56.

*Everything you want is in my briefcase*: Ibid.

*Please speed up establishing friendship with Lucy customers*: Ibid, p. 45/56.

*I think it better I tell the truth*: Ibid, p. 28/56.

*After knowing Alex for about a year*: Ibid, p. 55/56.

*About two hours later, at 12.50 a.m. on 10 September*: Ibid, pp. 3–4/56.

*baby son born on the day of his arrest*: CRIM 1/5681/2, p. 8/34.

*Alex number three – Oleg Lyalin*: CRIM 1/5681/1, p. 13/56.

*The dirty rotten Russian swine blackmailed me into it*: DEFE 68/141, pp. 20–4/74.

*It would later transpire that Lyalin had rewarded Abdoolcader*: Ibid.

*Ted Heath was on the verge of approving a plan*: Bennett, pp. 130–1.

*He shared the prime minister's view*: PREM 15, September 1971, p. 4.

*We wanted to exhaust to the limit the possibilities of peaceful settlement*: Ibid, p. 6/9.

*Lyalin's name must also be held back*: Ibid, p. 3.

*Douglas-Home disagreed*: Ibid.

*exhibited a picture of Oleg Lyalin and the woman with whom he had defected*: Lyalin Files, p. 88/174.

## Chapter 11: Operation Foot

*Greenhill had informed London about the warning*: Denis Greenhill, *More by Accident*, Wilton 65, 1992, p. 158.

*Instead, it threw him out of the country in April 1949*: Department of State, Office of the Historian, *Foreign Relations of the United States, 1949, Eastern Europe; the Soviet Union, Volume V*, March 1949.

*Ippolitov arrived for the 3.15 p.m.*: Lyalin Files, File 2, Section 1, p. 50/86.

*forty-three of them will be diplomatic officials*: Ibid.

*betrayed no emotion of any kind whatsoever*: Greenhill, p. 158.

*would not be allowed to replace*: Lyalin Files, p. 50–2/86.

*An MI5 surveillance officer positioned near the Soviet mission's*: Andrew, p. 572.

*toasting the momentous occasion*: Ibid.

*KGB defector betrays London espionage ring: Britain Expels 105 Russians for Spying*: Robert Carvel, 'Britain Expels 105 Spies for Spying', *Evening Standard*, 24 September 1971, p.1.

*However, there is no evidence that the British agency took similar measures to appease the CIA*: Wright and Greengrass, p. 346.

'didn't want any interference': Tom Bower, *The Perfect English Spy*, William Heinemann Ltd, 1995, p. 364. Furnival Jones' message was to Cleveland Cram, the CIA's deputy station chief in London and his agency's liaison officer between MI5 and MI6. Although sceptical about Angleton's claims that the

KGB had penetrated MI5's top ranks, Cram had himself taken the controversial step in 1965 to aid a secret inquiry commissioned by President Johnson into the US-UK intelligence relationship, and especially the effectiveness of MI5. When two US officials, Gordon Gray and Gerald Coyne, were secretly dispatched to London to begin the inquiry, Cram introduced them to MI5 and MI6 officers as 'colleagues' rather than investigators. Gray and Coyne gained the full trust of the British intelligence community, and with it, unhampered access to its dirty laundry. On returning to Washington, the investigators produced a withering report of MI5's shortcomings, including the British agency's inadequate counter-espionage capabilities, poor management and Roger Hollis's uninspiring leadership. Although Angleton briefed Peter Wright on the report's findings in secret, the MI5 officer informed Hollis and Furnival Jones about it anyway. They were outraged by the betrayal, with Furnival Jones saying: 'Never trust the bloody Americans to play it by the rules'. Hollis and Furnival Jones raised their objection with the CIA and Cram was threatened with expulsion in the 'event of further transgressions'. (See Wright and Greengrass, pp: 273-5). Angleton was said to have used the inquiry's findings to try to gain more sway on MI5's counter-intelligence thinking.

*In a letter to National Security Advisor Henry Kissinger*: Richard J. Aldrich, *GCHQ: The uncensored story of Britain's most secret intelligence agency,* HarperPress, 2019, p. 269. Note: CIA director Richard Helms, whom Britain also did not inform ahead of its Soviet spy purge, was thrilled about the expulsions and sent MI5 a 'hearty congratulations', saying, 'It is not often we receive such good news.' See Andrew, p. 574.

*Mr Gromyko made a protest*: *Time* magazine, 11 October 1971, via time.com.

*The name of the Russian turncoat*: Staff reporter, 'Russians Still Silent on KGB Man', *Daily Telegraph*, 30 September 1971, p.1.

*Moments after 10.30 a.m. No.1 Court was opened*: BBC reporter, 'I arrested a KGB superspy', *On This Day* series, BBC, via bbc.com.

*Lyalin's absence had been authorised by the Attorney General, Sir Peter Rawlinson*: UK Parliament, *Hansard, Volume 823*, debated on 27 October 1971, via hansard. parliament.uk.

*large-scale . . . provocation*: Norman Leith and Frank Draper, 'Oleg Girl Defects', *Evening Standard*, 1 October 1971, p. 1.

*On each of these news organs*: Ibid.

*man about town*: David Floyd, 'KGB contacts face charges', *Daily Telegraph*, 2 October 1971, p. 1.

*Reports that he has been paid £25,000*: Guy Rans, 'Lyalin Misses Court Case', *Daily Telegraph*, 1 October 1971, p. 36.

*Beautiful blonde Russian seeks asylum*: Leith and Draper, p. 1.

*It must have been very difficult for her*: Ibid.

*couldn't imagine him doing anything sinister and underhand*: Floyd, p. 1.

*He always had money for a drink*: Ibid, p. 28.

*It was a way of telling agents through the pages of the press*: Ibid.

## Chapter 12: The Fallout

*They must have cleared out the Embassy's whole duty-free stock*: Lyalin Files, p. 42/88. Other Soviet officials left the UK for Moscow by plane.

*press cameras clicked away*: Ibid.

*The World War II troopship, Baltika, had been at the centre of another scandal*: Kennett Love, 'Defecting Baltika Sailor Defies Two Soviet Aides', *New York Times*, 12 October 1960, p. 1.

*It was past midday with a watery sun breaking*: Lyalin Files, File 1, Section 1A, p. 42/88.

*Boarding passes already issued to news men were declared invalid*: Ibid, p. 38/88.

*France's concern was shared by Nordic countries*: Hughes, p. 231.

*It really is a contemptible attitude*: Anthony Lewis, 'Wilson Accuses Heath in Spy Case', *New York Times*, 13 October 1971, p. 7.

*Eighteen British citizens were expelled from Moscow*: Lyalin Files, File 1, Section 1A, p. 33/88.

*Another ten former embassy officials were declared persona non grata*: Hughes, p. 240.

*And no amount of venting, political posturing*: Lyalin Files, File 1, Section 2, p. 41/51.

*We also succeeded in obtaining data on some modes of communication*: Committee of State Security of the Council of Ministers of the USSR, *The KGB's 1967 Annual Report*, 6 May 1968, via wilsoncenter.org.

*ideological delusions, religious fanaticism*: C.L. Sulzberger, 'Treating Andropov Disease', *New York Times*, 30 October 1977, p. 17.

*godfather of Russia's new era of deception operations*: Ion Mihai Pecepa, 'No Peter the Great', *National Review*, 20 September 2004, via nationalreview.com.

*diplomatic access and immunity make the United Nations a spy nest*: John Barrons, *KGB: The Secret Work of Soviet Secret Agents*, Hodder and Stoughton, 1974, p. 401.

*There are also hundreds each year who come in*: Benjamin Welles, 'Survey Indicates Increase in Espionage by the Soviet', *New York Times*, 3 October 1973, p. 1.

*Especially since at least seven of those who had been expelled from London*: Ibid.

*Since the defection of Oleg Lyalin*: Lyalin Files, File 1, Section 2, p. 40/51.

*The NY Residency has assumed a 'wait and see' attitude*: Lyalin Files, p. 84/174.

*Lyalin had very likely exposed the identities of Soviet saboteurs*: Barron, p. 401.

*MI5 also supplied the American law enforcement organisation*: Lyalin Files, File 1, Section 6, 45/70.

*It is therefore possible that with a review of the material*: Ibid, Section 4, p. 56/29.

*He also identified Nikolay Alekseyevich Kuznetsov*: Ibid, 70/174.

*It was thought . . . that Thoibev might have defected*: David Cross, 'Brussels report of another Soviet defector', *The Times*, London, 6 October 1971, p. 1.

*Lyalin has disgraced our organisation*: Oleg Kalugin, *Spymaster: My 32 years in intelligence and espionage against the West*, Smith Gryphon Ltd, 1994, p. 132.

*Andropov's intended redeployment of Philby's skills*: Ibid, p. 136.

*a monthly credit of 100 rubles to spend at a grocery store*: Ibid, p. 138.

*The Antipodean operative*: Ibid.

## Chapter 13: 'What Reports?'

*Angleton's attempt to discredit Lyalin*: Wright and Greengrass, p. 346.

*How do you like the British reports from their source Lyalin, Mr President?*: Ibid.

*The paper-and-records problem was high on the agenda*: JFK case extracts, *The Special Investigations Group of the CI Staff*, September 1998, p. 19.

*Neither could they think of any reason why it was appropriate*: Ibid, p. 13.

*Furnival Jones was so confident in his findings that he had flown to the US*: Mangold, p. 79.

*Unlike the Emperor and his imaginary clothes*: Hart, p. 211/222.

*whether the KGB had its arm on Kissinger*: Seymour M. Hersh, 'The Angleton', *New York Times*, 25 June 1978, via nytimes.com.

*Sino-Soviet split*: Studies in Intelligence, Vol. 55, No. 4, p. 46.

*somehow made up for Angleton's inability to speak Russian*: Hart, p. 8/222.

*the defector was mentally ill*: Morley, p. 107.

*Golitsyn's defection had been to gain status*, Mangold, p. 65.

*It was apparently felt that, if we could maintain his stability*: Hart, p. 9/222.

*one of the finest analytical minds*: US National Archives, *Assassination Records Review Board Final Determination Notification, Angleton Testimony*, 5 October 1978, pp. 60–1/176.

*On the face of it, it seems highly unlikely that Golitsyn'*: Studies in Intelligence Vol. 55, No. 4, p. 44.

*The CIA was for some time convinced that Igor Orlov*: Joseph Trento and Susan Trento, 'What Felix Bloch can learn from the case of Igor Orlov', *Washington Post*, 9 September 1989, via washingtonpost.com.

*Serge Peter 'Klibanski' Karlow, was cleared*: Studies in Intelligence, Vol. 55, No. 4, p. 45.

*the CIA's Sasha pursuit resulted in more than 40 senior CIA officers: Mangold*, p. 315; Wise states that more than 50 CIA employees were investigated; Phillip Knightley, 'When Kissinger Spied for Russia', *London Review of Books*, Vol. 13, No. 13, 11 July 1991.

*I have nothing more to say to you*: Walter Pincus, 'Yuri I. Nosenko, 81; KGB Agent Who Defected to the U.S.', *Washington Post*, 27 August 2008, via washingtonpost.com.

*It can be argued that Golitsyn had two interests*: Hart, pp. 157–8/222.

*Remarkably and tragically, all of Golitsyn's leads*: Studies in Intelligence. Vol. 55, No. 4, p. 50.

*As well as relying on historical myth, the monster plot conspiracy theories*: Christopher Andrew, *Moles, Defectors, and Deceptions: Keynote Address*, Wilson Centre, 2012, via wilsoncentre.org.

*By fixating on the Soviets, Angleton largely ignored the threat*: Robarge, p. 6/21.

*Golitsyn had convinced Angleton that any Soviet defector*: Milt Bearden and James Risen, *The Main Enemy: The inside story of the CIA's final showdown with the KGB*, Random House, 2003, p. 21.

*rejected at least 22 prospective Soviet defectors*: Knightley via lrb.co.uk.

*And though we may be tempted to look back*: Hart, p. 209/222.

*I find myself unable to avoid the conclusion that is and has been*: Cahal Milmo, 'How my grandfather duelled with Cambridge spy Kim Philby', *Independent*, 23 October 2015, via independent.co.uk.

*I am satisfied that neither of you falls into*: Staff reporter, 'Six and four years' jail for Cypriot spies in Soviet net', *The Times*, London, 8 December 1971, p. 3.

*I was threatened and blackmailed into this*: Staff reporter, 'Car numbers spy jailed for three years', *The Times*, London, 9 February 1972, p. 4.

*Lyalin was sentenced to death in absentia*: Felix Corley, *The KGB Wanted List 1979: Death Penalty for Defectors?*, 2021, via academia.edu.

*Lyalin's existence prior to his defection became known to only about ten senior MI5 officials*: Pincher, p. 103.

*And while Andropov succeeded in turning Lyalin into a hate figure*: Kalugin, p. 132.

*The expulsion of 105 Soviet intelligence officers*: Christopher Andrew, *The Later Cold War: Operation Foot and Michael Bettany*, via mi5.gov.uk.

*The counter-intelligence chief was also about to be embroiled*: William R. Corson, Susan B. Trento, and Joseph J. Trento, *Widows: The explosive truth behind 25 years of Western intelligence disasters*, Crown Publisher Inc, *1989*, pp. 96–7.

*keep his whereabouts to himself, not stay in one hotel for any length of time*: Hart, p. 173/222.

*Classified materials, in quantities that ultimately filled several packing boxes*: JFK case extracts, *The Special Investigations Group of the CI Staff*, September 1998, pp. 12–13/24.

*controlled his own interrogations*: Hart, p. 174/222.

*Petty's historical review left him convinced that both and Golitsyn were moles*: Corson, Trento, and Trento, pp. 98–9.

*I'm very unhappy to leave the agency*: James Angleton, 'James Angleton speaks out on resigning from the CIA', ABC News, 1975, via youtube.com.

*William E. Colby, the Director of Central Intelligence, had been pressing*: Hersh, via nytimes.com.

*The investigation ran for four months and resulted in an 80-page report*: Mangold, p. 310.

*Oleg Lyalin even told MI5 that Golitsyn's defection*: US National Archives, *CI Information Report*, 24 July 1972, Document 104-10172-10192.pdf, p. 3.

*All Russians who return to their country usually have their possessions packed*: Lyalin Files, Series 1366648-0, File 1, Section 6, p. 37/70. Note: perhaps unsurprisingly, there were multiple Russian press reports about what became of Lyalin and Teplyakova after their defection. Some reports claimed that the pair had a child together. Another alleged that Lyalin's son, Alexander, whom he had abandoned, tried to flee to Britain to reunite with his father in the 1980s, but was arrested and given a ten-year prison sentence. I was unable to substantiate the reports.

## Epilogue: Different Reset, Same Outcome

*And it was in that capacity, as Secretary of the Security Council of Russia*: Brian Whitmore, *Andropov's Ghost*, Radio Free Europe, 9 February 2009, via rferl.org.

*Such actions, if they ever occurred, certainly ended after Oleg Lyalin's defection to England in 1971*: US National Archives, *JFK Assassination Records, FBI Director, LHO, POST-RP, ASSOC, Defection to Russia*, 1983 (released 2017), p. 3.

*Europe and what we often call the civilised world*: Interview to *Breakfast with Frost*, BBC, 5 March 2000.

*joint efforts in counterterrorism*: Kerbaj, p. 274.

*To take the risk of carrying out such an attack*: Ibid, p. 275.

*we have reached a turning point when we must seriously think*: Thom Shanker and Mark Landler, 'Putin Says U.S. Is Undermining Global Stability', *New York Times*, 11 February 2007, via nytimes.com.

*Obama and Medvedev famously celebrated their resetting of relations*: Peter Baker and David E. Sanger, 'U.S. Makes Concessions to Russia for Iran Sanctions', *New York* Times, 21 May 2010, via nytimes.com.

*ordered an influence campaign in 2016 aimed at the US*: Intelligence Assessment, *Background to 'Assessing Russian Activities and Intentions in Recent US Elections': The Analytic Process and Cyber Incident Attribution,* Office of the Director of National Intelligence, 6 January 2017, via dni.gov.

*As far as I could, I answered these questions, [Trump] noted them and he agreed*: Chelsea Bailey, *Putin Says Trump Appeared to Agree Russia Did Not Interfere in 2016 Election,* 8 July 2017, via nbcnews.com.

*I sort of had a personal connection with him*: Interviews by author with Alan Kohler, February and April 2025.

*Skripal had been a rising star in the GRU*: Staff reporter, 'Sergei Skripal: Who is the former Russian intelligence officer?', 29 March 2018, via bbc.co.uk. Note: While the GRU (Main Directorate of the General Staff) had its name officially changed to GU (Main Intelligence Directorate) in 2010, its former acronym is still commonly used.

*to call on as many as 8,000 counter-terrorism police officers*: Interview by author with Dean Haydon, April 2025.

*ultimately trawled through 4,000 hours of CCTV*: Staff reporter, 'Russian spy: EU offers solidarity over Salisbury poisoning case', BBC, 19 March 2018, via bbc.co.uk.

*One it's really toxic, and second it's difficult to even find*: Interview with Haydon.

*I never viewed it as a bellwether*: Interview with Kohler.

*On Tuesday 13 March, the day Theresa May had set*: Oral statement to Parliament, *PM Commons Statement on Salisbury incident response,* 14 March 2018, via gov.uk.

*Trump was asking for justification about*: Interview with Kohler.

*I suppose when you go into those things you're never a hundred per cent confident*: Interview by author with Theresa May, June 2022,

*I would say that the Brits put on a masterclass in diplomacy*: Interview with Kohler.

*The battle rhythm of my meetings at MI5's head office*: Interview by author with Brian Boetig, April 2025.

*Here's how it got approved*: Interview with Kohler.

*After these expulsions foreign interference seemed to drop off*: Interview by author with Martin Green, April 2025.

*What Russia said was . . . We're [also] kicking sixty out*: Interview with Kohler.

*enough poison to kill thousands of people*: Pol Allingham, 'Novichok perfume bottle contained enough poison to kill thousands, inquiry told', *Independent*, 14 October 2024, via independent.co.uk.

*Just imagine what it means to speak a foreign language as a native tongue*: Rossiya and Rossiya 24, *A Conversation with Vladimir Putin, Continued*, Government of Russia Federation, 16 December 2010, via archive.government.ru.

*any technical aspect of the voting process*: Eric Tucker and Aamer Madhani, 'US expels Russian diplomats, imposes sanctions for hacking', Associated Press, 16 April 2021, via apnews.com.

*To the best of my knowledge, I cannot think of any other time when that had been done before*: Interview by author with Michael J. Driscoll.

*It seems that under Putin's leadership his intelligence agencies*: Interview with Haydon.

*Russia continues to be a country that has very active foreign intelligence services*: Interview with Burgess.

# ACKNOWLEDGEMENTS

I FIRST ENCOUNTERED OLEG Lyalin's case while researching *The Secret History of the Five Eyes* and was quickly fascinated by his sense of adventure, unpredictability and selfishness. He was a lousy husband and father, more interested in partying and boozing than in recruiting agents, and would only realise the full potential of his operational abilities by working against – rather than for – his Soviet employer. Lyalin felt more like a screenwriter's creation of a movie character than a real person. I was drawn to the colour and chaos in his life, and wanted to use that as a lens into a broader Cold War story about MI5's operational setbacks in the lead up to Lyalin's defection.

What I had not realised, however, was the extent to which a lot of MI5's insecurities and bad decisions had either been influenced, or completely imposed on it, by the CIA. That is not to obviate MI5 from its own responsibility for such failures, but to point out that there were two elements in the British agency's relationship with the CIA that I underestimated when I started my research. First was the pernicious sway the US agency had on British intelligence analysis during the period I was writing about; and the second was the extent to which MI5's decision to cut the CIA from its Lyalin case prior to his defection helped the British organisation triumph against the KGB.

Through Lyalin's story, I wanted to recreate the atmosphere of paranoia and intelligence misgivings that had prevailed at MI5 and the CIA – especially during the 1960s – and frame his personal and operational challenges against the backdrop of James Angleton's and Anatoly Golitsyn's bad judgement calls. And I hope the book goes some way to achieving that.

I sought some invaluable insights into the US's handling and mishandling of intelligence through declassified FBI, CIA, and JFK records. I also drew on Foreign Office records in Britain which provided a detailed picture of some of the decision making surrounding the expulsion of Soviet spies from the UK. Lyalin's KGB record, which I obtained through the Lithuanian Special Archives, presented a sense of his career trajectory and his personal life. But one of the most exciting parts of my research was finding Susan Lewsey (nee Woodthorpe) who had fond memories of Lyalin – and to whom I often turned for help to confirm matters relating to her old colleague. I am enormously grateful for Susan's time and for her willingness to be candid about Lyalin.

I am grateful to Mike Burgess for his thoughts on how Australia fared with the Kremlin threat during the Cold War and beyond; to Lord Evans for his invaluable wisdom and insights; and to Malcolm Turnbull who helped enrich my perspective on that Angletonian era.

I owe a huge thanks to Alan Kohler, Brian Boetig, Dean Haydon, Michael J. Driscoll, Martin Green, James Risen, and David Walmsley, who helped me contextualise the Kremlin's threat against contemporary Russian defectors.

I am also indebted to Peter Wilson with whom I frequently

discussed my findings. His sharp and unfiltered feedback about each chapter, and willingness to at times question and even successfully challenge my interpretation of historical facts, hugely improved the outcome of my work.

On the research front, I'm grateful to Tony Farag who played a considerable role in helping me access National Archives records and newspaper clippings, and often generated material outside the scope of my requests which proved to be very useful for humanising some of the characters who appear in the book. I'm also very thankful for the time and guidance provided to me by historians Gill Bennett, Gordon Corera, John Fox, Filip Kovacevic, Dan Lomas, and Robert Verkaik.

A special thanks also to Jack D'Arcy, JG Debray, Juliette Debray, Timothy Dowse, Kurt Pipal, Richard Sharp, Benjamin Sheehan, Mark Simkin, John Sipher, Jon Ungoed-Thomas, Richard Walton, Doug Wise and Anatoly Litvinenko.

There are many others who helped me but who wanted to remain anonymous. They know who they are and I am grateful for all their efforts – even though at times lawyers came in the way.

This book could not have been realised without Richard Pike, my literary agent, Toby Buchan, and Ciara Lloyd at Bonnier who championed the idea long before I had written the proposal for it. I'm also very grateful to Natasha Drewett, James Lilford, and Barry Johnston.

To Dominic Kennedy – you have finally chosen a car that I like . . . but please get out of third gear!

And finally, but most importantly, my thanks to Marine for her patience and wisdom – and to Leo and Nate who keep me young and injured.

# INDEX

———